Far From Unremarkable

A Wren Island Novel

Laura Joy Lloyd

Windy & Yaiyu Publishing

Published in the United States of America by Windy & Yaiyu Publishing.

First Edition May 2026

Cover by KUHN Design Group | kuhndesigngroup.com

Wren Island map by Tessa Burns | tessaburns.com

Author photo by Suzanne Rothmeyer | suzannerothmeyer.com

ISBN (paperback) 979-8-9988968-4-2

ISBN (e-book) 979-8-9988968-5-9

Library of Congress Control Number: 2026910144

For media inquiries and Wren Island updates, visit the author's website.

laurajoylloyd.com

Also by Laura Joy Lloyd

From the **Make It Home** series:
Interesting Enough: A Wren Island Novel

Praise

"*Interesting Enough* whisks readers away to the charming small-town atmosphere of Wren Island, where island life, meddling elderly aunts, and an unexpected romance prove that even the most stubborn heart can't resist love in bloom."
  -Lauraine Snelling, award-winning and best-selling author

"Laura Joy Lloyd writes in familiar yet wonderfully refreshing ways about pain, hope, and the loyalty of friends."
  -Bill Myers, best-selling author, award-winning filmmaker

"Wren Island is so endearing, I felt nostalgic for this enchanting place when I finished reading. The delightfully eccentric aunts and the quirky personalities of the characters brought the charming coastal community to vibrant life."
  -Holly Varni, award-winning author of the Moonberry series

"Laura Joy Lloyd's *Interesting Enough: A Wren Island Novel* is more than enough, from beginning to end. Lloyd's debut will hook readers, and her witty dialogue, beautiful setting, and intriguing storyline won't let go. You'll want to move in and stay awhile, just like her character's quirky family members."

-Robin W. Pearson, Christy Award–winning novelist

"Laura Joy Lloyd is a fabulous writer with a keen understanding of prose that cuts straight to the heart. I'm so glad she's gifted us with *Interesting Enough: A Wren Island Novel*. Within these pages, you'll find colorful characters and a setting you won't want to leave. Laura is definitely an author to watch."

-Brandy Vallance, award-winning author of *The Covered Deep* and *Within the Veil*

"This is the kind of story that gently restores something inside you. With humor, heart, and a cast of characters who feel like family, *Interesting Enough* invites you to believe—maybe for the first time in a long time—that you are already worthy of love, rest, and belonging."

-Tonya Kubo, community strategist, host of the *Find Your Freaks* podcast

"Readers will find *Far From Unremarkable* an oasis in our troubling times—a place of kindness, respect, love, and redemption. Like Jan Karon's Mitford, or Louise Penny's Three Pines, Laura Joy Lloyd's Wren Island is a place where one longs to live and share relationship with its inhabitants."

-Ginny L. Yttrup, Christy Award–winning novelist

"*Far From Unremarkable* is a touching exploration of grief, and a sweet story that integrates new and familiar characters we've come to feel are family. I was cheering for them all!"

-Linda Avellar, author of *Cassie Linden Finds Her Sweet Spot*

"*Far From Unremarkable* is gritty and realistic. Deals with disaster and loss frankly . . . The nuances of the storytelling are reminiscent of Francine Rivers' best-selling novels. And what a teaser of an ending!"

-Tim Riter, author, professor, jack-of-all-trades, and motorcycle enthusiast

Contents

WREN ISLAND
make it home

For every Wallace.
And for everyone who loves a Wallace.

I

Scuffle

He unfastens his seatbelt, not at all comfortable with the officers standing around, jawing under the front porch light like they've come for tea. They might as well ring the doorbell and ask if they can please make an arrest. He verifies the car door is unlocked if he needs to give chase, then eyeballs the distance between him and the house—his daughter Vanessa's house, about to be thoroughly searched thanks to a hard-earned warrant, not that Vanessa will know until later.

Shifting his position, he checks the modified ultrasonic sensor he pilfered from inventory before retiring from the force, after that supposedly botched investigation. Ryan Robinson, age thirty-seven, no priors, doggedly single while willing to leach from Vanessa, is still sitting on the blue plaid sofa in the room Vanessa optimistically refers to as the family room.

Shoot. Is that officer lighting a cigarette? Wallace Bernard worked in the background, off the record, for weeks, *months*, setting up this bust, and some nitwit getting a paycheck decides to advertise like it's the Super Bowl.

Wallace leans forward, wincing when he bumps the steering wheel with his bum knee—arthritis from too much sprinting on concrete, a doctor said once. He peers through the windshield, careful to not make any obvious movements.

What he really doesn't need now is a nosy neighborhood watchperson reporting a suspiciously parked car, old guy at the wheel, suffering a supposed medical emergency.

The cigarette is being passed around. Is there no limit to the incompetence? He's about to groan when the sensor shows Robinson moving from the sofa toward Vanessa's yellow-painted kitchen, decorated with roosters. She's always loved farm animals. *Finally*, the signal's given to go in.

As the scuffle plays out, in a typical pattern for this squad, Wallace keeps his eyes trained on each of the house's side yards, where Robinson will have to pass if getting away. Or where Robinson's no-good business associates might sneak in to help. Turns out, Wallace needn't have bothered. Out comes Robinson through the front door, handcuffed and being read his rights. No sketchy associates in sight. Wallace releases a sigh, so unrecognizably heavy that, for a second, he thinks someone else must be in the car with him.

Man alive, he's getting too old for this kind of thing. Even when he's not doing the heavy lifting or officially on the job. Maybe the length of this project wore him out. The seemingly endless surveillance. Weeks of gathering evidence, then making sure it'd be discovered in the right place at the right time. Maybe he's exhausted because this mission hit close to home. Too close to home.

At least it's over now. Robinson's in the back of a patrol car and out of their lives—assuming Vanessa has the sense not to cave when he begs her to take him back. Which he'll do. Because he's a jerk.

The patrol car's being driven by Roger Moore, no Double-O Seven, but chief of police in this neck of the woods. As Moore drives past Wallace's parked car, he lets off the accelerator. Just a shade, a signal he's seen Wallace. Thanking Wallace for helping bring in another crook. Or warning Wallace he's annoyed to find him at the scene.

Wallace checks his watch. In an hour or two, Robinson will be allowed his phone call. After that, Vanessa might call her dad right away. Or she might not call her dad at all.

He drives to the outskirts of town, finds a random bar he's never been seen in, and follows personal protocol for decompressing after a mission. A stool on the periphery, but not so near the shadows to seem like he's hiding. And a whiskey, which used to pack a lot of punch but isn't as effective anymore.

The grimy, wrinkled newspaper on the bar next to his elbow looks more than a day old. He unfolds it and pretends to read, listening to the inane conversations around him. When his drink arrives, he downs half before returning it to the counter. Celebrating a successful night for Wallace Bernard! If anyone is wondering. Which they aren't. Being entirely unnoticed is okay with him.

That's when he sees the spider—decent-sized with impressively thick legs—working its way toward him along the edge of the bar. A server with long blonde hair and an arm loaded with chunky bracelets is flinging a white towel, mopping up, creating a danger zone for any spider, even one as robust as this. When the server slaps several more newspapers onto the bar, the spider freezes, then reroutes into full view on the counter. Heading toward a plastic bowl of potato chips.

Wallace reaches for a chip and crunches. No mystery how this is going to go. Once the server spots Mighty Legs, she'll whack him with a newspaper or that biohazard towel. Mighty Legs will never see it coming. Never know what hit him. Worse, the server might trap him under a glass and invite everyone to peer in.

Sighing, Wallace goes to work. Positions a paper napkin so Mighty Legs can naturally crawl onto it. Tucks up the corners enough to contain but not constrict. Scans the premises.

A potted tropical palm in the corner is dream digs for any spider. Wallace wanders over to the plant, unfolds the napkin, and taps off his charge. Mighty Legs runs for dear life, as he should. Wallace ambles back to his seat at the bar, crunches more potato chips, downs another quarter of his drink. That's when the conversation happening nearby becomes less than inane. And more than a little unsettling.

Two guys, both young, both twerps. The one wearing a pink polo shirt, who might be one elementary grade smarter than the one wearing a green shirt, is bragging about his new girlfriend and how they're going to spend the night. It's the third date, and he won't be taking no for an answer. Pink Polo's got

Green Shirt covered, because the girlfriend's bringing a friend. At this, Green Shirt hoots like the idiot he is. Wallace tries to tune out the conversation's words, but just the tone of it is tightening his jaw. On the inside, he might be working up to a full boilover—a familiar feeling, one he'll need to do something about. Leaving the bar would be the sensible choice.

He asks the server for a glass of water with ice, then swirls it, focusing on how peaceful a mini whirlpool can be. Still he can't tune out the desperados. Polo says he chose his shirt because pink's the favorite color of the girlfriend's daughter, maybe twelve years old, never been kissed. Green Shirt's eyebrows go up, interested.

Wallace's jaw clenches. He wants to slam down his drink, but he sets it down quietly like nothing's amiss. A line's been crossed, and he can't unhear it, so he makes the decision he was already headed for.

2

Red letters

First, Wallace reaches into the inner left pocket of his jacket. Yep, just as he thought. Three cigars. He pulls them out and rolls them between his fingers, checking the labels.

Each cigar is circled by a paper ring with a company emblem—one that looks legit and high-end. On one cigar, the capital letter *S* in the brand name is blue. That's the cigar he'll smoke and the only one that's halfway legal. The other two cigars have a subtle difference—a subtle *visible* difference, that is. Instead of blue, the letter *S* leans toward red. The red-letter cigars are definitely black market, not just because they'd never be cleared by customs, but also because of what's been added to them. Not enough to wipe out a person, of course. He's not *that* bad of a character, toting around lethal cigars. These smokes have just enough toxicity to put a person out of commission for several hours. And thanks to lax rules about smoking in bars on tribal lands, patrons at this establishment are free to light up.

He returns the two red-letter cigars to his inner pocket and tucks the blue-letter cigar into the smaller section of the pocket meant for holding a ballpoint pen. Then he contemplates. "Strategizing" is what he called it in the old days.

He'll go with the "helpless old man" gag. Psychology says when one person asks another for help, the person helping views the person asking as nonthreatening. He didn't sit through all that federally mandated training and come out with nothing to show for it. So he'll drop something and pretend he can't bend over to pick it up.

What can he drop? Not keys. Wouldn't want to risk losing those. These bozos aren't going to help an old man out of the kindness of their withered hearts. They're only going to retrieve what he drops if they want it themselves.

He pulls a wad of paper money from a pocket and fingers through it. One twenty, four ones, two fives. But he can't drop money. Then his new friends will expect to be rewarded with cash instead of the humdinger gift he's got planned for them.

Dropping his money clip could work. Silver plate, magnetic, engraved with somebody else's initials. Though mostly worthless, it's flashy and looks like it could have sentimental value. He'll say it was a gift from the missus. Doesn't matter he hasn't had a missus in ages. And if he drops an empty money clip, it'll seem as if he spent his last cash on drinks. Make him more convincing as a drunk.

He leaves the two fives on the counter for his drink and stuffs the other bills into the back pocket of his pants. Watching the bozos for another minute or two confirms they haven't noticed him. So he stands, groans loudly enough to earn a glance, gazes as if confused, and slowly heads for the exit. Holding the money clip loosely, he adds a bit of a limp for the thrill. Wallace Bernard in action.

As he approaches the twerps, they carry on, guzzling beer. Good. The higher their blood alcohol, the harder this encounter will go for them.

When he's in line with them, he drops the money clip. It sticks the landing like he wanted, between the legs of their barstools. They don't notice, so he lets out another groan. They turn—bored, annoyed. *Look at the old geezer*. He gazes as if halfway gone. "Can't hardly hold on to anything." Motions to the floor.

Pink Polo glances down, spots the money clip, rolls his eyes, turns back to the bar. Green Shirt mimics him. These guys are more jaded than Wallace gave them credit for, letting a decrepit old man like him suffer. He'll have to increase the pressure. He stumbles into the back of Pink Polo's stool, bends forward incrementally, groans again, grabs his own back as if in pain. His head down, he can't see them, but he can tell they've turned and are watching him.

"Can't get down there like I used to." He shifts his half-focused stare from the money clip on the floor to gaze up at Pink Polo, who's clearly feeling superior now that he's positioned to reign above a weak old man. Resisting the urge to throttle the jerk, Wallace adds a pathetic tone to his voice. "Would you be so kind?"

Pink Polo rolls his eyes again but hops down to retrieve the money clip. He scrutinizes it, decides it's worthless, hands it back as Wallace slowly straightens.

"Ah. Thank you, young man. Thank you *very* much. The missus would kill me if I came home without that."

Their bored expressions say he's losing them, and he can't let them go now, not at this critical point. He smiles widely. "How can I repay you? Can I buy you a . . . ?" He pauses as if realizing an unforeseen option. "Hey! Want a smoke?"

He pulls the three cigars from his coat pocket and offers them, strategically positioning the two reds. Each twerp takes a red-letter cigar—Bingo!—and eyes it appreciatively. The old geezer holds up his own cigar—blue letter *S*, not that they've noticed—and grins. "Smokes are on me tonight."

They light up, the three of them, and Wallace puffs, beginning an internal countdown. With the way those two have been drinking, they'll start feeling the effects quickly. At most, he's got five minutes to clear the scene. After puffing more—golly, the blues are excellent—he taps his watch. "Is that the time?" Then he shakes his head. "The missus." Quiet scoffing from the twerps follows his exit.

Outside, he waits in the shadow of a dumpster, smoking his cigar like any dude. Green Shirt stumbles out first, retching before he's cleared the entry. Pink Polo staggers past and makes it to the dumpster before collapsing in his own vomit. Wallace steps deeper into the shadows. They haven't noticed him. No one has. Wallace Bernard has disappeared again.

He heaves a sigh. Tonight, three girls will be safe. But tomorrow night? With any luck, the girlfriend will wise up before then. He can't be expected to help the girls again tomorrow night, can he? Can't be responsible for *everything* that happens to them. He scans the scene around the retching bozos. No cigars. Wouldn't want those to fall into the wrong hands, even if they're not lethal.

Back inside the bar, he finds the cigars smoldering in an ashtray and snuffs them out, careful not to inhale. Passing the potted palm, he debates burying the evidence in the soil. But what if Mighty Legs got into the cigars?

He takes the long way back to his car, through the public park along the riverbank. At the edge of the water, he submerges the spent red-letter cigars until they're waterlogged and sinking. The ducks will leave them alone if they have any sense, which they probably don't. He returns to his car and heads home, for lack of a better word to describe the room where he's currently spending nights.

After showering, he lies on the bed, eyes closed, waiting for the phone to ring.

When it does, he's wide awake, but he puts a convincing amount of sleepiness into his voice. "Vanessa? Is everything okay?"

His daughter is crying, as he expected. The sound of shock is in those tears, but he thinks he hears relief too. "Honey? What's wrong?"

"Ryan's been arrested."

Wallace waits, his heart feeling all tied up and tight.

Vanessa goes on, whispering. "They found evidence, child pornography, on his computer."

That's not news to Wallace, but a million new rages surge through him. This is his *daughter* who's hurting. His *grandkids* nearly became victims. "I'm sorry, honey."

"You were right, Dad, when you advised me to never leave the kids alone with him. We're moving in with friends until I figure out a way to be on my own."

She'll brush him off, but he asks anyway. "Can I help?"

Her answer surprises him. "Haven't you helped enough already?"

It's not flippancy or annoyance in her voice. It's tenderness. Does she know? How could she possibly know? He steadies his voice. "What do you mean?"

She exhales. "I mean, isn't it odd the police came to the house on a rare evening when the kids and I were out with friends, who drove us home and were with us when we learned the news? Friends who can house us for a while?

Isn't it odd the evidence was within clear view, not hidden behind passwords? And the chief of police, a guy you've known for years, was here himself? And the fingerprint kit was lost in the confusion? And the . . ."

The speculations keep tumbling out, but he's not listening anymore because, good golly, she *has* figured it out. He's done something right, raising a daughter this smart.

". . . so really, Dad, I think you've helped plenty already." She pauses, catching her breath. "Thank you."

The tightness inside, all he's trying to keep contained, is going to bust out fountain-style if he doesn't rein it in. He clears his throat, goes for authoritative. "You keep in touch, you hear? Don't go haunted-housing on me."

"It's called ghosting, Dad. When someone suddenly ignores you."

"Whatever it's called, don't do it to me. Check in once in a while."

"I will if you will. And I mean more than sending me the GPS coordinates of wherever you're sleeping. We worry about you, Dad."

By *we*, she means her and her sister who wouldn't be caught dead asking her dad to check in. But it's nice of Vanessa to pretend both she and Melissa care. He pushes back on whatever tide is threatening to pull him under—this wash of emotion he'll have no idea what to do with and might never recover from—and reaches for what's left of the blue-letter cigar.

Finally, Vanessa says what he wants to and can't. "Goodnight. Love you."

3

Floating riffs

The next afternoon, Wallace drives to the Smiling O, where Sedric—the manager on duty, sole employee, and owner—hands over the usual. An apple fritter with three donut holes on the side. Wallace fills a paper cup with self-serve coffee, black, and heads for the corner table, where *Scott was here* is scratched into the surface. When the fritter's gone, he works on the holes, then drains the rest of his coffee, returns to the counter for an old-fashioned cake donut and a Boston cream, and pays the bill. At the car, he sets the donut bag on the passenger seat.

Before delivering the donuts, he swings past the jailhouse to assure himself a breakout isn't happening. Leave it to an inept young recruit to accidentally release the whole kit and caboodle. When Chief Moore strides around the corner, Wallace pulls his car up to the sidewalk, gets Moore's attention, and nods toward the jailhouse. "Thank you for that."

"Pleasure working with you again, Wallace. Even if unofficially." Moore shakes his hand. "We'll make sure Robinson doesn't go anywhere for a long, long while."

Moore's already turning to leave. In the old days, Moore would have hung around to see what other projected job Wallace might have for him. But Wallace is no longer associated with the force. And Moore's got a public image to maintain. He's several steps away when Wallace finally voices the truth they both already know. "Moore? We're even now."

He drives on and parks a few blocks away, near the post office, his aged car creaking even more than he does when he gets out. He sets the donut bag on the bench next to Simon, who nods and keeps picking at his guitar. Wallace sits, closes his eyes, listens to a musician who couldn't walk down a public street without being mobbed in the eighties. Now he's floating riffs around an indifferent intersection. Just another homeless guy.

Wallace sniffs. Melissa would correct him. Not "homeless" but unsheltered. Or unhoused. His daughter's the expert on whatever the approved terminology is these days. Tomorrow it will be called something different but still be the same thing. He sighs. Thanks his lucky stars he isn't that bad off, today at least.

Simon stops picking and hands over the guitar. Wallace strums and stops. Strums and stops. Working out the easy chord progressions in "Free Fallin'," though Tom Petty might not recognize his song. Simon eats the old-fashioned cake donut first, then the Boston cream. Always in the same order.

Wallace is just getting going on Petty's chorus, enough that a listener could recognize it, when a pedestrian slows and cocks his head, studying both Wallace and Simon with an expression of pity. Pity! For Wallace Bernard! The do-gooder drops cash into Simon's guitar case, and Wallace switches to another easy play, "Achy Breaky Heart," so roiled he's got to change *something*, even if all he can work with are basic chords and cheesy lyrics. He belts those lyrics out above Simon's guitar, which can produce a lot of volume when it needs to. "Achy Breaky" is supposed to end on a resolved chord—most songs do—but Wallace never ends a song that way. He'd rather leave it hanging. Waiting for closure. Just . . . like . . . so.

Melissa says it's his signature style to leave a song unfinished. She says it's the theme of her dad's life, to disappear and leave things unfinished. But it'd be difficult to prove he'd left anything *important* unfinished for a long time now.

He hands back the guitar. Simon won't be able to resist. Yep. First thing Simon does is strum the last chord. So the song got finished, eventually. What does it matter if Wallace was the one to make it happen or not?

Later, at the park, he scans the riverbank. The ducks he can see are all fine. One of them might have gotten to a cigar and drowned, but a dead duck would float, wouldn't it? These ducks are alive and kicking. So he's going with the theory that the cigars are at the bottom of the river, not causing any harm.

A fish might get to one. That thought makes Wallace pause. Innocent little fin swisher doing its thing, eating tasty stuff from the riverbed, nibbles on a discarded cigar, and suddenly its insides are burning up. Wallace steels his mind, shuts down thoughts of a fish without a name eating what it shouldn't—some people say fish don't feel pain—and focuses on a nearby patch of daffodils. Bright yellow blooms. Now those are happy flowers. Don't all the self-help gurus advise looking at life like a glass half full? Daytime's supposed to be easier that way. The daffodils know it, obviously. If fish don't know it, that's their problem. He scuffs his way along the riverwalk.

Lots of people are making the most of the spring day. Moms with kids, babies in strollers, an old couple together so long they look like each other. Wonder what that's like. To be with a person long enough to see another version of yourself.

He's standing near the edge of the riverbank, resting whatever parts need resting, when a skateboarder nearly splits him in half. The punk's gone before Wallace can holler, raise his fist, do anything. For Pete's sake! Little tykes are playing here! Another skateboarder shoots past, and this time Wallace is ready, shaking his fist. "Slow down!"

No one appears to care. Or notice an old man on his own. Wallace stuffs his hands in his coat pockets and kicks along, trying to think of new ideas for contributing to society, not that society's worth contributing to. He could revisit the bar from last night. Do a reconnaissance mission for Mighty Legs, see if the spider's enjoying its new home. Seems like a shot in the dark, though. Even if he finds a tough-looking spider living in the palm, how's he going to know if it's the same one?

Shoot. He knows what's wrong, why he feels restless. He's between projects. Last night he wrapped up a monthslong mission. Today he's got no purpose. Somebody need help, please. Somebody need a guy named Wallace Bernard.

4

Industrious buggers

Still standing around at the park—what else is he going to do on a sunny day with no obligations?—Wallace studies an anthill in the grass, careful not to stand in the path of the industrious buggers. Ants are exemplary when it comes to working hard. Ants can work *too* hard. If you accidentally step on an ant and smash it, the rest of the force comes along and eats the remains—which doesn't seem ideal for anyone, especially the one who got smashed.

When his cell phone rings, Wallace fumbles around in several pockets before finding it. Notices the unfamiliar number. "Who's this?"

"Wallace? Ralph Wesson."

"Holy—"

"Yep, been a long time."

The last person Wallace expected to hear from was his old cellmate from Rikers Island, late 1960s, early 1970s. Bonded with blood, the two of them are. Of course, once Ralph discovered Jesus, thanks to an overzealous prison minister, things got difficult. More difficult than they already were.

Wallace squints. "You still spewing Bible verses?"

"I've toned it down."

"Didn't know people could do that—ease up, once they'd started using religion as a way to criticize others."

"I've still got my faith, but I'm quieter about it."

Wallace steps back because the ants seem to be expanding their routes. When was the last time he spoke with Ralph? "You out?"

"I've been out for thirty-two years."

"Why are you calling me?"

"I need your help."

While those four words hang in the universe, a tide swells under Wallace, a rush of satisfaction. Someone *does* have a problem he can help with. Someone *does* think Wallace Bernard is worth having around. The news sends him dangerously near giddy, and if he doesn't rein in the feel-good stuff . . .

He snorts, casual, as if Ralph's got a lot of nerve asking for his help. As if Ralph Wesson doesn't know Wallace Bernard will do anything for him. *Anything*. "What kind of help?"

Ralph spells it out. Some punk blackmailed him, used him to get to a neighbor—rich guy, by the sound of it. Ralph's priors and tax evasion came to light, but he didn't get jail time thanks to his help when the FBI captured the crook.

Wallace frowns. "So what's the problem?"

"The punk also stole money from other people, including two brothers with a charter fishing business. I want to go help them get the business back up and running, but I've got responsibilities here on Wren Island."

"Wren Island? Never heard of it."

"In the Pacific Northwest, between Seattle and the Canadian border."

Wallace rubs his chin. The last time he was in British Columbia, he snuck out the back way after a misinterpretation of licensing. "Canada isn't exactly rolling out the welcome mat for me."

"I only haul cargo within U.S. waters."

"What kind of cargo?"

"Groceries and other staples for Wren's market. Farming equipment, automobiles. Livestock. You'd stay at my place and manage the freight business while

I'm away. And supervise the island-wide road improvements. We're getting paved roads, thanks to a donation by a private citizen."

Wallace snorts. "The same rich guy throwing his money around?"

"The pay will be decent, Wallace, and legal. Wren Island could be a soft place to land. If you're looking for something like that."

Wallace studies the ants. Hundreds of them, maybe a thousand. Are the same ants going in circles? Or are they adding to their numbers? If one ant wants to stop and rest, do the new recruits soldier on? Around or *over* the one who's resting?

Dodging another skateboarder, Wallace doesn't bother raising his fist or hollering. "What's so special about this Wren Island?"

"For one, it's the most enchanting place in the world." Ralph's voice takes on a dreamy tone Wallace remembers well. "Evergreen forests, sandy beaches, rocky cliffs. Tons of wildlife. Whales, seals, otters, salmon. I catch Dungeness crab right off my dock."

"No kidding? You always liked the idea of living by the water."

"Dungeness is the most flavorful crab you'll ever taste, Wallace. And I watch the sun rise and set every day. But it's more than that. I've got friends here, Wallace. People I want looked after."

Wallace feels his insides loosen, expand, fill with something that feels foreign yet slightly familiar. Hope, maybe.

Imagine a place where people might want him around. Might *need* him around. For a while, anyway. Until he makes a colossal mistake. "Send me the coordinates of this dreamscape. My daughter Vanessa will want to know where I am."

Ralph laughs. "Your girls are still trying to keep track of you? They could come with you."

A pure lightning bolt, that idea. Why didn't he think of it? Living on an island would be like living in a castle with a moat, wouldn't it? "Vanessa's got kids. One's a baby."

"She on her own?" Ralph's tone has turned wary. "Can't risk any deadbeats tagging along."

"She's on her own now. Except she's got me. If she wants."

Ralph is quiet for a few seconds. His way of acknowledging the hard truth Wallace has just admitted, that Wallace isn't sure he's wanted by his daughters. Either that or old age is stealing Ralph's ability to hear.

"You still there?"

"Yep. Heard everything you said." Ralph exhales. Probably gazing around at one of those evergreen forests or sandy beaches. Thinking about where to drop the next crab pot off his dock. "Thing is, Wallace, there's no better place than Wren for kids to grow up."

It's thrilling and terrifying, this feeling of being swept upward, as if he's on top of a geyser flooding the entire world. The glass half full has got *nothing* on this. Can he convince Vanessa to go with him to Wren Island? First Vanessa and the kids, then Melissa? The family together in one place. Is it too much to hope for?

Meanwhile, Ralph needs help. More particularly, Ralph Wesson needs *Wallace Bernard's* help.

"I'll be there by the end of the month."

5

Supposed best friend

That night, Wallace gets caught inside the same nightmare that's plagued him for years. He's going along thinking everything's fine. Someone's with him. He doesn't know who. Could be anyone. Then the person starts disappearing. Thinning into vapor. And suddenly Wallace realizes it's someone he wants with him, wants to not let go of. If he can just *say* something, *anything*, he can stop the disappearing. But all he has is silence, and the person's gone.

He wakes up panicking, sweating, his heart pounding. Then he curses, knowing who disappeared. He knows who he should have been able to help, who he should have been able to anchor in place, long ago.

Forty-nine years ago, to be exact.

John Smith is dead. The message behind those four words still pierces as deep as ever. Instead of sticking around, John missed out on everything that came after. Starting with the next day, which was—ironically, when Wallace imagines the darkness John must have experienced—the first day the sun reappeared after a string of gray, rainy days.

John missed seeing the Seahawks reach the Super Bowl. Never witnessed the introduction of DNA as evidence in criminal cases. Bypassed the changes from answering machine to pagers to voicemail to texting. Never got to drive an electric vehicle. Missed chewing Bubblicious bubble gum. Eating chicken McNuggets, blue-colored M&Ms, and microwave popcorn.

Sitting up, Wallace punches his pillow. Wish he'd known to say something. To John or someone who could help.

Others were shattered, too. John's fiancée, for one. John had talked about her like she was the real deal. Maybe she eventually became someone else's wife. A mother, grandmother. She probably lived life surrounded by people who loved her. She's probably glad Wallace didn't contact her at the time, glad he *never* contacted her, wouldn't have wanted him to, ever.

She might not even know Wallace existed. They never met in person, and John might not have mentioned Wallace to the woman he loved. That thought makes Wallace pause. If John never mentioned Wallace, what would that say about their friendship?

It would say what the silence said then and has been saying all these years. Wallace Bernard, supposed best friend, wasn't there to prevent John Smith from leaving. Wasn't there to stop his friend from dying alone.

Even if he wanted to find John's fiancée now and apologize, or whatever, he wouldn't be able to, because the skull-cracking years following John's death robbed Wallace from remembering her name. Amy, Emily, Annalise, Eleanor? Last name Thurman, Thornton, Thacker? If she married, she could go by any name.

His loss of her name, the identity she carried with her *then*, adds to his shame. He should have never let go of it. Because now there's no retrieving her name.

There's no retrieving a lot of things.

He lays back on the bed, studies the random patterns in the popcorn ceiling and the cobwebs in the corner, so dusty the spider who masterminded them must be long gone. Maybe smacked by a cleaning cloth or newspaper. Leaving behind the tangled evidence of having lived.

There'd be a benefit to getting whacked before you saw it coming. A goner all at once, snuffed out in one swoop.

Might be better than creeping along day after day, fearing someone would show up with the ability to see what you really were. Someone who could put you under a glass and magnify everything—scars, regrets, hideousness—then pull you apart, piece by ugly piece. While you pray to the gods, especially the prison minister's god, that whoever's looking at you sees something worth saving. And has half an inkling about how to put you back together again.

6

Aloha

Amelia Theodore rotated the carousel of postcards and leaned closer. The swimming sea turtle would be nice to send her sister Macy, holding down the fort at home on Wren Island. Other images easily fit her friends. Palm trees by water for peace-loving Judy, a red-crested cardinal for birdwatcher Virgil, and the paniolo, Hawaiian cowboys, for Jax, Virgil's adventurous son.

How much would all these cost? And were the pictures local? Amelia pulled the cards off the carousel and squinted at print too small to read without her magnifying glass. She dug through her shoulder bag, sewn special by Macy for this vacation, white fabric with green palm leaves and pink plumeria blossoms.

The cards all mentioned the island of Kauai, and they all cost the normal amount of postage. Just right for sending aloha to family and friends on Wren Island.

Not until next in line for the cashier did Amelia remember Ed Piper. He'd feel left out if he didn't get a postcard. She returned to the carousel. Which image to send Ed?

A sunset on the beach might suggest romance, definitely not what she wanted to suggest to Ed. Hula dancers and bikini-clad women were also a no-go. Too risqué. The postcard with surfers was cool. Maybe too cool to send Ed.

She rotated the carousel to an outrigger canoe, checked the price and postage requirements, and got back in line.

Two reasons supported being certain each postcard differed from the others. For one, Wren Island was a small place. So remote it didn't have regular ferry service. Residents knew each other, and people might compare their postcards or tack them on the grocery market's bulletin board.

Throat-clearing from behind Amelia broke into her thoughts, and she stepped forward to pay for her purchases. The friendly cashier waited while Amelia searched for the credit card her niece had given her for times like this, when it would take embarrassingly long to count change through tired eyes while a line of people waited. Amelia did verify the total dollar amount before she signed. That only took a few seconds, no magnifying glass necessary. She tucked her purchases into her bag and headed outside to wait on the bench where her niece had promised to meet her.

The second reason for making certain Wren Islanders received unique post-cards was that it might fend off sympathy. Ever since people had learned about Amelia's age-related macular degeneration, they'd been making special allowances. If she sent the exact same postcard to everyone, people might assume she'd been limited by circumstances. Maybe the lighting was too dim. Or she couldn't see other options across the room. Or no one was around to help. *Poor Amelia Theodore. She tries so hard.*

People had been taking care of her all her life. Her parents. Her older sisters. Helping Amelia Theodore, who never married or created a family of her own. Now she lived with her sister Anne's daughter, Allison. Also still Theodore. By following Anne's example and keeping her maiden name when she married, Allison ended up with one less detail to sort out when her marriage ended. So Wren Island was home to two Theodores. In addition to everyone else, curious as they were.

Honestly, Amelia had nearly reached her limit of being looked after. People offering concessions she didn't ask for. Hovering, worrying, doubting. Ed Piper was the worst of the bunch, constantly assuming she needed help. Not asking if she *wanted* help, but if she *needed* help. One word made a difference and was probably the key reason Ed wasn't getting the postcard with cool surfer dudes on it. A postcard like that ought to go to someone noteworthy. Which simply wasn't how Amelia felt about Ed.

She smiled at that conclusion. See? Sitting by yourself, thinking through whatever popped into your mind, set up opportunities to resolve matters you didn't know you weren't clear on yet. In comes an unexpected revelation. A new line item on your list of nice things that happened unexpectedly.

Just then, a mother hen clucked near, three chicks peeping along behind. Amelia pulled out her phone. A video of this might go over well on her YouTube channel. She hit record and spoke in her narrator's voice. "Hello, everyone! Remember I mentioned how chickens are everywhere on Kauai? They're as prolific as pigeons in a city. Here in the historic town of Koloa, a sweet mother hen and her chicks are rambling past." Amelia stood and wobbled a bit before walking slowly behind, continuing to record. Just another few seconds of video and then she'd—

She was falling before she could do anything about it. Fortunately, the chicken family scattered.

7

Yellow, of course

While Amelia caught her breath and thought about trying to stand, a wor-ried-looking teenager appeared at her side. About the age of Jax back on Wren.

"Are you okay?" The boy helped her back to the bench.

She shuddered onto it. "I'll be all right. Uh-oh. Look at my bloody knees."

He handed her a tissue or napkin. She did what she could with it. Then she realized he was gone at about the same time she realized he'd returned, when he handed her damp towels and antibacterial ointment, and set a box of bandages on the bench.

Allison appeared in the doorway of a surf shop across the street and waved. "Stay where you are, Aunt Amelia!" From that distance, it must look like Amelia was chatting on the bench with a new friend—no skinned knees, no problem-o.

Traffic stopped, as it always did when Allison stepped into the road, whether or not she was in a crosswalk. That was mostly because of Allison's outward beauty. Tall and thin, energetic and strong-looking. She usually dressed in average clothing, masking her status as a millionaire many times over. Today she wore a secondhand tank top and short skirt. Actually a skort—a skirt with shorts inside—but no one could know just by looking.

Allison was a songwriter! And the most benevolent person ever, maybe. But the underlying reason Allison caught people's attention was her magnetism. People like Allison attracted attention whether or not they wanted or noticed it. They might live their entire lives in the spotlight and never realize it.

Other people never seemed to leave the periphery, even when they *wanted* to be seen. If sixty-eight-year-old Amelia Theodore stepped into the road, traffic would not automatically stop. Even back when eighteen-year-old Amelia Theodore stepped into the road, traffic might not have stopped. Certainly no one tooted their car horn and whooped, like that man in the silver Jeep was doing. By the time she was forty-six, Allison's age, Amelia had all but disappeared. Most of the time, she was nearly invisible. Unless someone happened to be searching for a bumbling old lady. Then, Amelia Theodore became exceptionally visible.

Right away, Allison figured out what had happened. Not rocket science, unfortunately, because tripping and falling wasn't all that uncommon for Amelia. Her niece bent to help her clean up.

While Allison chatted with Keoni, the nice young man who'd helped, Amelia realized Allison wasn't carrying any bags. "Where are the groceries?"

"I didn't get them yet. I'll come back later for the groceries and my new surfboard." Allison's smile revealed her perfectly straight white teeth.

"I can get your groceries." Keoni glanced toward the market. "Pick up your surfboard too. Where are you staying?"

Allison waved him off. "You don't need to do that. You've already helped us a lot."

Keoni deflated a bit. Amelia took in his worn clothing and rickety bicycle. His bare feet. The kid could probably use a few extra bucks, and wonderful Allison was in the unofficial business of being benevolent. Amelia turned to her. "Actually, Allison, I was hoping you and I could hang out at the house together this afternoon."

Allison reached for the paper tablet Amelia handed her, jotted a note, then ripped off a sheet and handed it to Keoni. "Our address. It's not far. And here's the grocery list and cash for it. My surfboard's paid for and will be ready in an hour."

Amelia squinted. "Groceries, sure. But how is he going to deliver a surfboard on a bike?"

Keoni demonstrated his bike's handy side rack.

Helping Amelia to her feet, Allison beamed at Keoni. "When you arrive at the house, we'll discuss the delivery fee. Thank you!"

Amelia waved at the smiling boy. "Mahalo!" Adding her own thanks in Hawaiian made expressing gratitude feel more poignant.

She and Allison headed for the parking lot. Amelia had a sneaking suspicion her niece had chosen their rental house because it included use of a convertible in Allison's favorite color, bright yellow. The house's other appealing features included beach access right out the back gate. Their own swimming pool and garden, landscaped for privacy. A chef's kitchen—not that either of them exerted the culinary energy Macy did back on Wren. And plenty of space for Shasta and Ralph when they weren't knocking around elsewhere on the island.

That was the reason Amelia and Allison were vacationing on Kauai. To be near Amelia's sister Shasta and her boyfriend, who was helping a family get a charter fishing business up and running. Allison's mom would have gotten a kick out of her millionaire daughter funding the entire project—the boat repairs, airfare between Wren and Kauai, the rental house on the beach. All thanks to five miniature paintings Anne picked up for fifty cents each at a yard sale.

It was still hard to believe the second youngest Theodore sister was the first to go. They'd been four—Macy, the oldest; Shasta, the free spirit; sensible Anne; and Amelia, the baby. Now they were three. Amelia sighed.

With Allison at the convertible's wheel, they reached the rental house faster than Amelia would have liked. But pretty much the entire world was going faster than felt comfortable these days.

As Allison punched in the numbers at the security gate and sped up to the house, her cell phone rang. Allison flushed as she listened to her boyfriend talk. Virgil had a real way of making people feel cared about, one reason he and

Allison made such a super couple. If Amelia were narrating a YouTube video about them, she'd say *supercouple* like it was all one word. That was how it was supposed to be, right? Two people becoming much more breathtaking together. *Folks, meet Allison and Virgil, supercouple.*

While Allison chatted with Virgil, Amelia headed to her room to clean up and change into a swimsuit. A one-piece, for sure. With a built-in skirt. To spare the lovely island of Kauai from yet another tourist flaunting pale, flabby skin.

In a lounge chair by the pool, Amelia closed her eyes. Cooing zebra doves. A chattering mynah and another answering from far off. Virgil had taught her how to identify the birds on Wren Island by listening to their songs. On Kauai, she was teaching herself.

What kind made that twisting, whistling sound? She reached for her phone, opened an app, hit record when the song burst forth again, and waited for possibilities to come up. A warbling white-eye. The wonderful world of technology.

She recorded a quick video for her YouTube channel, being careful to film herself only from the neck up so the online world wouldn't see her in a swimsuit. Once she'd voice-overed the bird's identity and song, she tucked away her phone.

Allison joined her, wearing a sarong over a swimsuit with tiny shoulder straps. "Virgil says hi. He hopes the fellas in Hawaii aren't getting forward ideas about his favorite YouTube star. If any bother you, I'm supposed to wallop them."

Pleased with every aspect of that message, Amelia laughed. *Allison is perfectly capable of taking care of Allison.* That's what Virgil liked to say. He made it sound like the highest of compliments. Amelia watched her niece drop the sarong and sit on the edge of the pool. She just leaned forward and slid in. Not long ago, Allison couldn't walk after shattering her hip in an accident. Now, no stairs or handrail needed.

As Allison was drying off, Keoni buzzed at the gate. He helped them unload the groceries to the refrigerator and pantry. After Allison paid him in cash, they all wandered back outside to admire Allison's new surfboard.

"Yellow, of course." Amelia nodded. "It'll look cute in the backseat of the convertible."

Keoni hung around longer than Amelia would have expected for a boy who might have additional paying jobs lined up. Eventually, he cocked his head toward the convertible. "It's not a Jeep."

Allison laughed. "No off-roading in it."

"You like off-roading?"

"I do."

"My brother's got a Jeep for sale. Maybe you're interested?"

Right away, Amelia knew how this was going to go. Since day one of their travels, Allison had been purchasing things, then giving them away. Before they'd collected their luggage, Allison bought handmade beaded necklaces from a vendor in the concourse, then gifted them to four women waiting for a hotel shuttle. Their first morning on Kauai, Allison bought a dozen fresh juices being sold by local kids and handed the drinks out to surfers. Yesterday, Allison purchased traditional dresses from a local seamstress, then mailed them off to friends on the mainland. Add in Allison helping a fishing business stay afloat. Talk about something not being rocket science.

Allison had already perked up. "Yeah, I might be interested in a Jeep."

8

Showstopping moments

The next morning, after a brief call to her sister Macy back on Wren Island, Amelia prepared breakfast for herself and Allison. Granola made by a local family. Fresh fruit from the farmers' market. A side of poi, which neither of them liked but both had been eating because it was supposed to be healthy. Generous slices of chocolate haupia pie—they were on vacation, after all—and a pot of 100% Kona coffee.

Sliding open the doors to the lanai, Amelia brought her breakfast outside. She listened to mynahs and chickens. Watched a gecko watch her. Relished the scent of plumeria. No wonder people referred to Hawaii as a paradise.

Allison joined her, sipping from a mug of coffee and refilling Amelia's. "Thanks for making breakfast. I talked with Virgil earlier. He says Ralph's friend Wallace is really coming through. The road improvements are ahead of schedule. Wallace is also handling all the deliveries between Wren and the mainland."

"Sounds like Wallace is helpful to have around." Amelia stood, hugged her niece, and sat down again. "That hug is special delivery from Macy. She says to tell you she misses you."

"Aww." Allison added fresh mango to her granola. "I wish Aunt Macy would have come with us. She's going to love the floral bark cloth we're sending her."

Amelia pushed bits of granola around in her bowl. "Macy's fabric will get home before we do." She set down her spoon. What was this unexpected feeling? Homesickness? She glanced at her niece. Did Allison also seem a fraction conflicted? Their days were blissful here on Kauai! Yet not, without all of them present to enjoy it together.

Allison sipped coffee. "Virgil's going to be surprised when his fancy surfboard arrives. Hope he doesn't try to use it."

"That would not turn out well—for the surfboard or for Virgil." Carved by hand from koa wood, the board was meant to be a decoration at Virgil's market. "We're doing okay on gifts, aren't we? I sent a kimono to Judy at the commune. Handmade because they prefer those kinds of things there."

"Nice! Are you also sending a gift to Ed at the commune?"

Shrugging, Amelia finished her granola.

Allison chewed a bite of granola, thoughtful, and swallowed. "We could send Ed one of those hats woven from palm leaves. From both of us."

"Okay."

"The dogs are getting matching Hawaiian shirts. No need to buy anything for Shasta and Ralph, since they're here with us. That just leaves Jax." At the last part, Allison's tense tone backed up Amelia's suspicions. Allison worried about building a solid relationship with Virgil's fourteen-year-old son. She and Jax were both amiable people, though, and seemed to get along swell, without much effort.

Amelia took a bite of haupia pie and chewed, savoring the cookie crust, chocolate mousse, and coconut cream.

Allison finished her granola and set down her spoon. "I'm sure we'll think of a gift for Jax."

Amelia grinned at her. "What are you going to do with the Jeep you buy this afternoon?"

"Give it to someone here who needs it, I guess. Imagine the expense of shipping a vehicle from here to Wren Island."

"You can afford it."

Allison reached for the haupia pie. "True."

Later that afternoon, the Jeep rusting in the shade of a banyan tree was going nowhere fast. Allison and Wai, Keoni's brother, settled on a price far higher than the vehicle was worth, after Allison made a convincing argument about the value of the original parts. Then Allison pretended to suddenly realize she didn't want the hassle of selling parts. She asked Wai to take care of parts sales, and they lowered the purchase price a fraction to reflect the adjustment. Wai ended up with a bundle of cash *and* a Jeep he could still sell in parts.

Despite or maybe because of Wai's delight, Amelia started feeling sad about the whole thing. A windfall of a few thousand dollars wouldn't last long for this family. Allison didn't look discouraged at all. She was homing in on a second Jeep peeking out from under a tarp in the carport. "Is that one for sale?"

Wai pulled off the cover to reveal a four-door in a custom yellow. Which probably sealed the deal before it began. As Amelia peered inside at the dashboard, shiny and fingerprint-free, Allison's voice broke in. "And is that one for sale, too?"

In the corner of the carport, a smaller, dusty Jeep. Two-door, open-top, camouflage paint. The vintage-looking ride may as well have had the name of almost-old-enough-to-drive Jax written all over it. The Jeeps went for an astronomical price, because Allison was finding everything she'd been looking for all in one place and said assigning a price to convenience was impossible.

Amelia had just enough time to finish the pineapple lemonade Wai's wife offered. Then they were off to arrange the shipping of the yellow and camouflage Jeeps to a mainland port on the West Coast. From there, Ralph's friend Wallace could bring the two Jeeps to Wren Island.

That evening, Amelia sipped orange juice with rum by the pool, then set aside her drink. It wasn't much fun indulging in an alcohol-laced drink her sister, celebrating two years of sobriety, wouldn't be comfortable with, even when Macy was half a world away. Had Macy been present earlier that afternoon, she would have been impressed by Allison's Jeep negotiations.

Amelia turned to her niece. "That was a whopper of a deal you made today."

From her lounge chair, Allison smiled. "Virgil's going to be thrilled with Jax's gift."

Amelia studied the pool's pristine water. Sure, Virgil might be delighted. Or he might *not* be. Buying his only son his first car seemed like a project a man might want to do himself. But what did Amelia know?

"Aunt Amelia?" Allison's voice sounded dreamy. "Were you ever in love?"

All at once, the feeling flooded over Amelia again. The breathtaking beauty of being in love. The extraordinary splendidness. Its showstopping moments, when time both sped up and slowed down. The soaring feeling of nothing but the two of you.

Until there was only one of you. The other one leaving too soon. Too quickly, too unfairly, too unexplainably. "I was engaged once. His name was John."

"I didn't know! You've been keeping secrets."

Her sisters knew, of course. Her parents had known. The fact that Allison didn't know meant Anne must have never mentioned it. A flood of gratitude swept over Amelia for her family's willingness to let this be Amelia's story to tell, even after all this time.

Allison stirred her own rum-laced orange juice. "So what'd you do? Wise up before the big day? Tell him to get lost? So long. See you later, buddy."

Picking up on a halfway-serious tone behind Allison's teasing words, Amelia looked up. Did Allison *still* resist the idea of marriage? Even to a man as wonderful as Virgil? Think of everything Allison would miss out on!

Amelia shook her head. "I would have liked to keep John around."

"Hmm." Allison set aside her drink. "What happened?"

Amelia took a breath. "He died."

Allison gasped. "I'm sorry, Aunt Amelia."

"It was sudden. Unexpected."

"Oh, gee. An accident? You poor thing."

There it was again. *Poor Amelia Theodore.* Left by her fiancé in the most unnatural, unwanted way. In the most difficult way to talk about. The most unexplainable. Amelia braced herself to tell the truth, unwilling to let Allison continue *not* knowing how much Amelia had missed out on. How much Virgil was offering Allison at this very moment in a loving, committed marriage, if Allison would accept it.

"It wasn't an accident, Allison. It was a decision. He . . . took his own life . . . before we . . ."

"Oh, Aunt *Amelia*." Allison was at her side, wrapping her into a hug. "I'm *so* sorry."

Tears were flowing. Soaking, wet tears. Not the usual tears that chafed out so parched they must have flowed around the world a million times, drying up before finally aching their way out. These tears were new, yet also old. Nearly fifty years later, and still Amelia found herself upended in a churning wake of sorrow, with no horizon in sight. She wiped her eyes with the tissue Allison handed her.

"We were making plans. We were going to be married when John finished his time in the Peace Corps." Amelia blew her nose. "I don't know why he did it. He'd been acting different. Back then, we only had letters and rare phone calls, so a lot of time would go by between correspondence. Then I got a notice telling me what happened, and that was the end."

Allison handed her another tissue. "I'm so, *so* sorry. I never knew."

"It's not the kind of thing you tell people. Unless it somehow comes up. And even then, you don't talk about it unless you're feeling strong enough."

Allison put her arm around Amelia's shoulders. "Do you want to keep talking about it tonight?"

Now that she had given attention to the old wound, it throbbed more. Measured doses of examination were how she'd gotten along so far. She patted her niece's knee. "Not tonight. Some other time, yes. Maybe when we're home again, with everyone we love."

They sat. Quiet. Watched a flock of ring-necked parakeets screech overhead and flutter into palm trees to roost.

"Almost sunset." Amelia turned to Allison. "Want to go watch the turtles?"

Every evening, Hawaiian green sea turtles crawled out of the surf to spend the night on the sandy beach, where vigilant volunteers guarded their safety. Agile in the water, the endangered creatures were extremely at risk on land.

Amelia held her breath as turtles washed close in the lapping waves, then maneuvered onto the sand. The largest turtles might be older than her. Had traveled around the world in the timeless pattern of their ancestors. Yet here they were making their way up to the sand at the end of a day. Exposed, vulnerable. Resting in a place that perhaps felt like home, surrounded by others watching out for them.

Next to Amelia, Allison pulled a tissue from her pocket and wiped her eyes. "Virgil once said sea turtles cry."

"Turtles feel sadness?" Amelia watched one labor to shift its position in the sand.

"Shedding tears removes excess salt from their bodies." Allison drew a breath. "But who knows? Maybe they also feel sad."

When the sun had gathered its last light and stars dotted the deepening sky, Amelia reached for her niece's hand. "I know we said we'd stay in Hawaii a while, and I'm happy to if you want. But I'm also ready to go back to Wren. Anytime you are."

She couldn't see her niece's response, not in the darkness, but she felt it. A slight nod of her head, a squeeze of her hand, complete agreement. Allison was ready to go home and be surrounded by people she loved, too.

9

Cavity

Feeling discouraged wasn't unusual for Frank Winkler Jr. Another evening alone, same miserable city. A convenience store like every other, flickering with fluorescent lights and anti-shoplifting measures. Earlier in the day, another job interview gone swimmingly for sixty seconds, until he opened his mouth to speak. The interviewer spied the wicked teeth of a potential drug addict—employers could never be too cautious about such things—and the conversation wrapped up with predictable efficiency. *Don't call us. We'll call you.* None of that was unusual.

The part that was unexpectedly discouraging tonight was the realization he could meander down a seemingly harmless aisle, spy a tube of topical pain killer, and instantly fantasize about how agreeable it had felt to smoke pot. Back when he was still mucking around on the fringes of addiction, before marijuana wasn't enough. Before Xanax, cocaine, and meth weren't enough either.

Early in Frank's recovery—a lifetime effort, as any former addict knew, no degrees in higher education required—people suggested he'd been trying to fill the emptiness inside. As if every person was a big cavern. Needing to be filled to the brim with quality content, all the time.

Frank figured all he'd been trying to fill was one tiny, aching cavity. The hollow that would overflow if his dad acknowledged Frank's existence. Gave the slightest indication Frank deserved a place in the world. Maybe even a seat at the family dinner table. Fantasizing about any of that happening razzed the cavity into a raging abscess. And without feasible means of filling that particular hole, Frank might throw himself off a bridge—sober, drunk, high, or any combination of the above. So mostly he didn't think about it.

Lots of people lived with cavities.

Standing in the pharmacy aisle, Frank considered the over-the-counter options for bleaching teeth, the fix he'd come in for. He chose a box of strips that promised instant results, turned the box over in his hands, read the back label. Probably safe. Tamper-proof packaging, highly recommended by dental professionals.

He made his way to a rack of bathroom accessories and peered into a hand mirror. Pulled his lips back, ran his fingers around what was left after drugs and prison.

A few customers wandered around. None near enough to see or hear when Frank plastered on his best society smile, made eye contact with his buoyed reflection, and practiced what he'd say, given a chance.

"Thank you very much, sir. I'm pleased to accept the position, and I promise I won't let you down."

Nah, that wouldn't fly. His new boss might be a sir, ma'am, or other. Best not to assume. He rephrased his acceptance speech.

"Thank you. I really appreciate your faith in me. I promise I won't let you down."

A crooked row of brown nubs mocked him from the mirror. Even if whiter, they'd look less than trustworthy.

Deflating, Frank replaced the mirror and the box of highly recommended product.

"That stuff'll make them whiter." The nearby voice sounded informed yet relaxed. "But to get where you want to go, you'll need professional help. Crowns on the six top front teeth could be a promising start."

Back when Frank never knew which end was up, an unfamiliar person initiating a conversation, seeming to offer help, might have precipitated havoc. But this balding dude, carrying a shopping basket with sunscreen and earplugs, seemed harmless.

Crowns, though? His dad wouldn't bat an eye at spending thousands of dollars on dental work. But only for a member of the family.

Shrugging, Frank looked away. "I don't have money for crowns."

"How long have you been clean?"

Frank cringed. Would it always be this obvious to people who'd just met him? Would he always be instantly pegged as a former drug addict? Possibly current, because a model citizen would be smart to not assume otherwise.

Facing the man again, Frank made eye contact. He wasn't proud of his past, but he sure as standing here was proud of his current track record. "One year, four months, five days."

The man set down his basket. Pulled a business card from his front pocket—it got stuck on two pens also lodged there—and reached to shake Frank's hand. "Stephen Tangent, DMD. What are you doing tomorrow?"

Frank took an automatic step backward before deciding to not resist Stephen Tangent's friendliness. After their handshake, businesslike and reassuring, Frank accepted the card and shrugged again. "Tomorrow? Probably nothing."

"Come by my office in the morning and we'll get going on those crowns. Might finish all six at once if you're able to give up an entire day."

Frank scrutinized the business card, then looked up. "You're a dentist?"

"Guilty as charged, but only for two more weeks. I'm closing the practice and taking my wife to Portugal. Got a box of crowns that can either be your new smile or add to my inventory losses."

Dr. Tangent strode down the aisle with his basket, then linked arms with a middle-aged woman who looked like the other half of a couple anticipating the next chapter. He glanced over his shoulder.

"Tomorrow morning at 9:00 a.m. The front desk will be expecting you."

10

Getting crowns

The next morning, Frank's housemates hadn't returned from wherever they'd been all night. Probably sleeping around. Frank felt nauseous thinking about all that coming and going with no permanency to the relationships.

Stale city air was more tolerable than stuffy bus air during the monotonous trek between Frank's apartment and Dr. Tangent's office. There'd be no vehicle driver's license for Frank Winkler Jr. anytime soon. Or legal access to a car.

Acquiring six crowns on his upper front teeth did take all day, including breaks to use the bathroom, work his way to level 17 of the latest video game craze (no math-based challenge could defeat him), and chat with the receptionist. About Frank's age, she was as ditzy as she was cute.

Back in the dental chair at the end of the day, surveying himself in a handheld mirror not unlike the one he'd stared into at the convenience store the previous night, Frank was astonished at the transformation.

"They look like real teeth!" He tweaked his lips to effectively display the glittering top row and hide the depressing bottom row, so all anyone would see was dazzle. "They're much whiter than my real teeth ever were."

Blindingly white, actually. Frank angled his face away from the operatory lights. Practiced the shape of his new smile again, watching the mirror.

Could this be the same Frank Winkler Jr.? Instantly transformed to look less ragged, more reliable?

Dr. Tangent patted Frank's shoulder. "The shade's whiter than ideal. Had to use inventory already on hand. I hope those crowns serve you well, son."

The idea of the crowns serving Frank, actually working for him, was promising. But the word *son* tucked in there zapped him. How could a man who'd been a stranger twenty-four hours ago be so accepting? While another man, knowing Frank from the moment he'd been born, wouldn't acknowledge Frank's existence?

Shifting his gaze from the mirror, Frank peered at Dr. Tangent. "Last night, at the store, why'd you bother talking to me?"

"There's a lot I'd like to do and can't. So when I see an opportunity within my reach, I go for it. You happened to be in the right place at the right time."

Frank hitched a grin. "How soon can I eat?"

"Whenever you're hungry. But chew carefully until you get a feel for how your new teeth work. They're secure, but might feel awkward at first."

Peering back into the mirror, Frank polished up his smile. "Maybe I can get a decent job now."

"Maybe you can." Straightening, Dr. Tangent nodded. "Maybe you can do a lot of things now."

About to exit the office, Frank experienced a moment of panic. What if this was a trick? What if he now had to pay for crowns glued in place? Yanking them out of his mouth would cause serious hurt.

But the cute receptionist shrugged. "No charge. I'd say we'll see you next time, but there will be no next time. We're closing up shop."

Frank practiced his new smile.

"Ooh! Eye candy!"

"Well, thanks. Thanks a lot."

The stroll back to his apartment conveniently went near one of the Salvation Army's soup kitchens at dinnertime. Free bowl of soup to anyone, even if they were suddenly wearing a million-dollar smile.

Inside, Frank spotted Michael Grant, prison chaplain during Frank's time at Monroe, and made a beeline. Michael was one cool dude, not much older than Frank and sailing around the Pacific Northwest, doing chaplain-type stuff wherever needed. Frank was a little jealous—of the euphoric lifestyle, not the heavy-duty ministry responsibilities. Michael was familiar enough with Frank's messy history to appreciate the new look.

Opening wide, Frank showed off the eye candy. "Look what happened!"

"Wow! That's a lot of smile." Michael pretended to squint at blinding brightness, then whacked Frank on the shoulder. "Good to see you, Frank. Been too long. Though considering the circumstances of where we've met before, not seeing you for a while might be a good thing."

They each got a bowl of soup, plenty easy for six new crowns. Then they found a quiet corner for a sit.

After praying aloud, giving thanks for their food and their paths crossing again—outside of prison—Michael glanced at Frank. "So, what have you been up to?"

"Trying to rise above." Frank slurped a bit of chicken noodle, better flavor than the last time he'd eaten at this particular kitchen. "Rooming with a couple of losers. Haven't been able to get a job. Still can't get my dad to talk to me."

Michael just nodded. Might be part of chaplain training, learning to not jump in and talk. Let the needy person set the conversation's pace.

"I'm hoping these crowns will help me land a decent job. Help me look less like a junkie."

Michael finished a bite of soup and set down his spoon. "Didn't you once tell me you went to college and studied mathematics?"

"Yeppers. Before drugs and prison."

"How are you on the water?"

"Huh?"

"Do you get seasick?"

"Don't know. Never been on a boat." Not that Frank wouldn't like to be. At one with the wind and waves. No illicit drugs in sight for fathoms. Or would it be nautical miles? Either option would be fine.

Michael pushed his empty bowl away, wiped his mouth, returned his napkin to the table. Solid, civilized manners. Probably had a mother somewhere checking in on him. Or Michael was checking in on her. Yeah, that was how it would go in Michael's world.

"I know a guy hiring crew for his trawler. Based off Reclamation Island, north of here, near the Canadian border. He might let you live on board. Bilbo Churchill is a fair, conscientious man. Keeps a small but devoted crew."

Frank scratched his forehead. Living and working in close quarters with people he didn't know? He'd done that before, and a boat wasn't a prison. Even if he had other options, which he didn't, Michael's recommendation was credible enough.

Maybe his new boss would see Frank's fixed-up smile and feel assured Frank Winkler Jr. was trustworthy—which he very much was, if only an employer would take a chance on him. He might not be much of anything else, but he was definitely trustworthy. Or trying to be.

Michael got Frank's attention again. "If you're seasick, you'll be no help. I'm heading back to Reclamation tomorrow. You could come with me and get your sea legs. Might find a landlubber job on Reclamation if the deckhand job doesn't work out."

Frank spooned the last bit of soup around the bowl. What did he have to lose? With enough cash on hand to pay what remained on the month's rent for his room, he could leave without owing anyone anything.

He made arrangements to meet Michael the following morning at the assigned Seattle slip.

"Don't be late, Frank. *Henceforth* will sail at first light."

"Hear ye, hear ye!" Pretending to wield a royal scepter, Frank spoke in a dramatic tone. "Let it be known throughout the kingdom that henceforth we shall sail and be merry!"

Laughing, Michael elbowed him. "*Henceforth* is the name of my boat. Look for a Nordic Tug."

"How will I recognize a Nordic Tug?"

Collecting the dishes—his own and Frank's—Michael headed for the exit. "Just follow the directions to the assigned slip, Frank. Sturdy-looking vessel with a green hull. *Henceforth* printed on the bow. You'll know her when you see her."

II

Craving substance

That night, alone because his housemates were still MIA, Frank packed up his few belongings. Limited space on a boat? No problem. Frank Winkler Jr. wouldn't bring much with him.

He didn't call home until 9:00 p.m., when *Jeopardy* and *Wheel of Fortune* ended. His mom always said those television shows were her favorite part of the evening. Except when her son telephoned. Then talking to him became the highlight.

Hoping his dad might unwittingly answer, Frank called the landline. But his mom answered on the first ring.

"I'm starting a new job, Mom. Up north, on an island, working for a guy with a boat. You'll be able to reach me on my cell."

"That sounds wonderful, Frankie. You've always loved the water."

Frank scrunched his face. "I have?"

"Don't you remember all those family reunions when you begged to spend the entire time on the pontoon?"

An achy sorrow washed over him. Followed by anger at himself, for surrendering to a substance that erased happy memories years after they happened.

"Yeah, I guess I do remember." He sometimes lied to spare his mom more heartache. "This will be deep-sea fishing though, not floating around on a lake."

"You'll be fine. You got your love of the water from my side of the family. Generations of Finnish fishermen prepared you for this."

His mom's gentle voice conveyed confident pride that her son would thrive on the sea, same as her ancestors. Frank squinted away any tears that might spill over. Then braced himself to voice the question he might have to ask for the rest of his life.

"Does Dad want to talk?"

"I'll ask."

Waiting, Frank heard a muffled conversation. His dad's voice, slightly raised. Would he come to the phone? Getting yelled at would be better than not being acknowledged.

"I'm sorry, Frankie." His mom sounded sad and worn. "Your dad's about to start an important conference call."

"At this time of night?" As soon as he asked, Frank regretted the question—and the desperate tone. His mom already felt dismal enough about the rift between her son and husband. "Never mind, Mom. Love you."

The next morning, with his single bag of belongings strung over one shoulder, Frank counted out his remaining rent money. He'd just placed it on the kitchen counter when his housemates returned. First time Frank had seen them in three, four days. They were so hungover they didn't notice his new teeth.

Frank added his key to the cash. "Guess I won't need to leave this under the mat."

Edging past his housemates, Frank held his breath. They both stank to high heaven of alcohol, smoke, and vomit. As relieved as he was to part ways with those two losers, he waited to sigh until he'd left the apartment and was inhaling sidewalk air, best quality to be hoped for within the city.

Later, leaning out over the bow as *Henceforth* cut through the sapphire blue of the Salish Sea, Frank breathed deep. Filled his lungs, again and again, with the substance he must have been craving all his life but hadn't identified until now.

Ocean air. Wild, free, cleansing.

It threw salt spray on him, then danced around him with a confident intimacy, purging a former drug addict and convict's record of wreckage. Promising, with every pulsing thrum, a clean start.

Maybe there was truth in his mom's belief he would take to the water like his Finnish ancestors. Maybe Frank had been born to live on the sea and had taken the roundabout way finding out. All he knew was that before his encounter with untamed ocean air, his insides had been perpetually caving in. Now, being relentlessly pursued, he was overcoming in an inexplicable way.

A few nautical miles south of Reclamation Island, Michael slowed *Henceforth*'s speed, dropped the engine into idle, and pointed to a pod of three orcas traveling west. The sleek creatures with distinctive markings of black and white emerged rhythmically to breathe, always in sync with each other.

"Whoo-ee! Those are powerful-looking males." Michael offered binoculars to Frank, who studied the majestic whales.

"Are they from the same family?"

"Could be brothers. Or, if unrelated, they might have banded together for this part of the journey." Michael exhaled a low whistle. "Seeing one of these guys would be magnificent. But three together? We're making memories, Frank."

When the orcas moved on, Frank handed back the binoculars and Michael got *Henceforth* going again.

Then Frank took one breath, another, more. One expanding inhalation after another. Craving and being satisfied by the one substance he could now never be without. Whether alone or accompanied by people he banded with along the way, if he just kept breathing this ocean air, inhaling more and more of it, he might somehow get somewhere worth being.

12

Reclamation

Frank's new boss, Bilbo Churchill, was exactly how Michael described him. Hardworking. Fair. Honest. Didn't probe into his employees' personal lives or invite questions about his own. Bilbo's crew seemed content with each other, their work, and the pay.

On Bilbo's trawler, *Jeannette*, Frank found his sea legs right away. Slept well in a tiny assigned bunk. Most days, he worked on deck. Whenever the boat got a limit, the crew hauled back to Reclamation, where Bilbo sold the catch to local grocers and restaurateurs.

After a couple of weeks, Frank finally earned a day off. He intended to spend the afternoon exploring neighboring islands in a mini cabin cruiser borrowed from Michael, who motored off in *Henceforth* a few days earlier but said Frank knew enough about boating now to be trusted with Michael's backup vessel, *Sweet By and By*. Plus Frank had acquired a boating license, and legally.

First though, Frank wanted to explore the only area of Reclamation trying to be a town, the few blocks of businesses built on a rise above the public marina and the Washington State Ferry terminal. A single four-way stop—signaled by signs, not lights—marked the busiest intersection.

Crewmates had designated Reclamation's landmark pub, The Turkey &
Hambone, as a hub for interisland travelers as well as locals. Award-winning fish
and chips—thanks, in part, to catch supplied by *Jeannette*. Legendary burgers,
Seahawk Sunday specials, and not-to-be-missed ice cream flavors. A secret carafe
of one-dollar coffee stowed behind the sign suggesting *Relax—You're on Island
Time Now.*

Frank ventured in.

"Welcome to The Turkey & Hambone! You're Frank, right? Working for
Bilbo Churchill?"

Frank took an instinctive step back from the oldish guy immediately making
a big deal about them meeting.

"Eli Orsini, co-owner of this pub with my friend Zane Goodnight." Eli
motioned toward another oldish dude working an espresso machine. "The tea
shop next door is my wife's project."

Peering through French doors to the space adjacent the pub, Frank blinked
at the brightly lit shop lined with shelves of colorful yarn. Girls gabbed at a
counter topped with silvery, sparkly stuff like Frank's mom set out for holidays
and special occasions. What could so completely absorb the attention of girls,
maybe same age as him, that they'd ignore the tantalizing burgers and ice cream
next door? He hauled his attention back to the pub.

"What will it be for you, Frank?" Eli tapped a pencil on a small paper tablet.
Old school.

"A burger, I guess."

"Bacon and goat cheese with microgreens is a current local favorite."

Frank glanced around at the pub's sophisticated but welcoming decor. He
could ask for a burger with typical toppings. But when in Rome . . .

"I'll try that. And a strawberry shake." Glancing past the bar and down a hallway, Frank spotted tables and chairs soaking in sunshine. "Can I eat outside?"

"One burger coming up. The shake whenever you're ready. Find a spot on
the deck and make it home."

He sat at a small round table for two, not unlike ones he'd seen in movies
set in Italy. The pub's deck offered an expansive view of the marina. Pleasure

craft, commercial and charter fishing vessels, and tour boats sporting banners advertising whale watching came and went through the channel marked by red and green buoys.

Propping his feet on the empty chair across from him, Frank soaked in the odd sensation of having nowhere to be and nothing to do, yet not craving anything. Simply resting, satisfied, on a well-earned day off.

Sure, it'd be nicer if a cute girl was perched on the chair across from him. He could tell her about working on a fishing vessel. Or she could tell him about her day. Bits about that fancy tea shop maybe.

When his meal arrived, he understood why the pub's piled-high burgers had been dubbed legendary. Top-of-the-line food, surroundings worth observing, wide-open sky, fresh air. He could definitely live this way every day.

Only thing to figure now was which island to explore first.

Not one serviced by the Washington State Ferry system, like Reclamation, which was already starting to feel crowded. He'd visit an island accessed only by private boat or floatplane. It'd probably be much quieter in a place you could only get to under your own power. A place people went to lose themselves.

Was that what he wanted? To lose himself?

Nah, just to lose the old part of himself. The one that still sometimes felt tempted. Incomplete. He ran his tongue around six crowns, flawlessly handling a legendary burger.

His dad's disavowal could partly be explained by a priority of keeping up appearances. The senior Frank had worked hard to build a business empire and an impeccable image. Married a pedigreed woman with family resources and her own talents. Raised a robust son and an attractive daughter, each of them intelligent enough to succeed at Ivy League schools, yet kind enough to not use their wit to lord it over the masses. In record time, Frank Winkler Sr. watched his daughter move up the ranks to become CEO of a major corporation.

Then he watched his only son, his namesake, hang with a disreputable crowd, experiment with the wrong substances, and spiral downward, well past the lowest dredges the senior Frank could be expected to tolerate. Never one to show emotion, he'd responded in the only way he could. By cutting off all association with the source of the pain.

Did Frank Winkler Sr. *ever* cry? When alone, did he let himself lose control?

Frank sat with that image. Picturing his dad in tears, with no one to witness or to offer comfort. Then Frank turned off that line of thinking, because it was taking him somewhere physically he didn't want to go, fueling a familiar craving inside.

He breathed deep. Filled his lungs with cleansing marine air.

The shadow suddenly falling across the table belonged to Eli, bill in hand. "I can put this on a tab, if you like. A friend of Michael Grant's has credit with me."

Under his breath, Frank chuckled. He'd mentioned working for Bilbo but hadn't mentioned knowing Michael. News seemed to travel exceptionally fast in this one-stop town. Especially among the tight-knit folk who belonged here.

"Can I pay you next time I'm in?"

"Sign here." Eli handed over the bill.

Frank checked the amount, signed on the line, handed the bill back. When Eli moved to serve another table, Frank released a careful exhale.

Did Frank Winkler Sr. ever sign his name and think of Frank Winkler Jr.?

Frank thought of his dad. Every time.

13

As good a place as any

Sunshine, light wind, no clouds in sight. Ideal weather for an afternoon off in a borrowed boat. After carefully working through the predeparture list Michael had posted near the helm, Frank maneuvered *Sweet By and By* out of Reclamation's marina and no wake zone. Then he picked up speed, just to find out what a mini cabin cruiser could do.

Satisfied with a few wheelies, or whatever the equivalent nautical term was, he dropped the boat's speed into a lazy cruise and checked his navigational maps. A little island called Wren was as good a place as any to start exploring, especially since a quick internet search recommended a complimentary tie-up yards from a south-facing beach. Provided visitors registered at the island's only grocery market on arrival.

Approaching Wren from the south, he spotted two docks at either end of a sandy beach. The west end was clearly off-limits, no signage needed. Against a picturesque backdrop of forest, boulders, and cliffs, the fancy boathouse and bright yellow sport boat spelled money, money, money.

The other dock, an everydayish option, extended from where the beach ended and a thick evergreen forest began. He tied up there behind a spiffy SAFE boat sporting three outboard motors, its all-black substrate in better condition than any he had seen around Reclamation.

West end of Wren? Glamour and desirability. East end? Functionality and pride.

The grocery market within walking distance up the hill boasted a covered porch. Reaching it, Frank paused and took in the vibe. Cushioned benches, rocking chairs. Rustic tables with unfinished games of checkers and dominoes. In one corner, a basket of dog toys. A person could while away an entire day here. He'd been right to begin his island tour on Wren. He might even end his island tour on Wren.

Something cold and wet nudged his hand. The nose of a big brown dog, looking up at him, wagging its tail.

"Hi."

The tail wagging increased in speed, creating its own weather system. The dog followed Frank into the market and all around as Frank selected his purchases. Premade sandwich (whole wheat bread, turkey, cheddar, mustard, mayo), freshly baked snickerdoodle cookie, bunch of grapes, bottled Dr. Pepper, box of crackers, can of squirt cheese. He brought his purchases to the checkout counter, manned by an affable-looking dude with an enviable head of hair.

"Hi there. Where're you visiting from?"

At first Frank felt annoyed. Why would this guy presume Frank didn't belong on Wren? Then Frank realized he was no longer in the city. Wasn't on news-travels-fast Reclamation. He was on a tiny island in the Pacific Northwest with no regular ferry service. This clerk scanning and bagging Frank's groceries knew everyone who belonged on Wren Island. And, therefore, when someone didn't.

"I'm working for a guy on Reclamation Island."

The clerk's eyebrows went up. "Name?"

Frank hitched a smile. "My name or my boss's?"

Chuckling, the clerk stashed another of Frank's purchases into a paper bag. "Whatever you want to share, I guess."

"Frank Winkler Jr. Been working for Bilbo Churchill for a couple of weeks now."

"Virgil Tagaloa, market owner. Note your vessel arrival time on that bulletin board over there. Welcome to Wren!"

Just like that, Frank was approved. If only it were that easy everywhere. And with everyone.

Sweet By and By's approximate arrival time added to the clipboard, Frank, the dog still following, wandered out to the porch again. Chose a wood-planked chair to sit on, pulled a lightweight table close, brought out his sandwich and Dr. Pepper. While he ate, he took in the view. Across the water from Wren, more islands blanketed in evergreen forests rose from the depths. A section of Wren's beach, opposite where the road ended, had been graded smooth. Maybe so a cargo hauler could unload supplies. Life on an island without regular ferry service.

Finished eating his sandwich, Frank tossed the wrapping into the trash bin three-pointer-style, as if he were still the star of his high school basketball team. He pulled out the box of crackers and can of cheese, decided he wasn't hungry enough for crackers, and returned them to the bag.

Popping the can lid, he aimed the nozzle and shot a decent amount of cheese directly into his mouth. The big dog lying nearby looked up. Got to its feet while Frank worked a second cheese blob around six crowns.

"You like cheese?"

The wagging tail created another weather system.

Frank held the nozzle close enough for the dog to sniff, then lick. "Now open wide." Frank pressed the tip gently at first to help the dog get the hang of it. Nothing to it. They took turns until they weren't getting any more out of the can.

Standing, Frank tossed his trash, bagged up the rest of his snacks, and made his way down to the beach. An old guy was inspecting an epic pile of ropes at the private dock on the west end, home of the yellow sport boat. Nearby, an annoyed woman stood with her hands on her hips.

Frank chuckled as he watched the two old-timers face off. For a while, it looked like the man was holding his ground, winning. Then his body language softened. Conceded. The woman relaxed too.

Not wanting to intrude, Frank stopped walking. The big brown dog continued, padded out to the end of the dock, nosed around, clearly familiar with the man, the woman, and a little white dog the woman tugged at the end of a leash. Everybody getting along, island peace restored.

Waves lapped at the sand near Frank's feet.

Restoration. That's what he wanted with his dad. Like what he'd just watched play out. One person gave a little, then the other gave a little something back. Next thing you know, everyone's so relaxed two dogs are nosing around happily.

Two hours from now, Frank was due to check back in with Bilbo and help prepare *Jeannette* for tomorrow's run. Untying his borrowed boat from the dock, he spotted Virgil Tagaloa standing on the market porch. Frank waved. Virgil waved.

Pulling away from Wren, Frank didn't look back. He could picture what was happening. Virgil was heading inside to the bulletin board, marking the vessel's departure time. Another visitor, someone who didn't belong on Wren, come and gone.

14

Making demands

When the woman repeats herself, insisting he do what she says—it's definitely a demand, not a request—Wallace sets aside the nylon rope he just coiled, squares off, and barks a response. "Why in tarnation can't I drink here?"

"This is a dry property, Mr. Bernard."

She knows who he is, though he doesn't know her from Eve. She motions toward most of Wren Island's south side—the boathouse and dock, beach, forest, massive English Tudor house beyond the dunes. She's fixed on him a look so stern it would make anyone squirm. Maybe she's a lawyer. That thought makes him pause. Would it be a benefit to have this woman fighting on his side? Or a liability?

"*Dry*, Mr. Bernard. If you're drinking alcohol, go elsewhere."

Shaking his head, he pulls another rope from the pile and coils it, inspecting as he goes. He's tending a rich neighbor's fancy boathouse, at the same time practicing his next plea for Vanessa to join him on Wren, and what happens? He's accosted by a banshee.

He sets aside the inspected—and approved—rope and reaches for another. Runs it through his hands, slowly. The tremor in her voice gave her away. He's seen it before, a recovering alcoholic facing the nemesis. He'd bet a blue-letter cigar this woman attends at least two AA meetings a week. He glances at the open can on the dock, not his first beer this afternoon, though so far his work doesn't seem to have been affected. The theme of the day is Irish red ale, John's drink, because tonight's another new moon. That same phenomenon marked the last day of John's life. And the first day of his death.

"As I said, Mr. Bernard, please pour it out. Or take it elsewhere."

On the inside, she's probably feeling terrified. Wondering if this will be a battle she wins or loses. He watches, fascinated, as her back goes ramrod straight and she holds his gaze. Employing a classic life strategy. Pretend to have courage, and you might become brave.

Shoot. This kind of determination coming from a woman always does him in.

He sets aside the inspected line. Picks up the beer can and empties it into the ocean, a rolling, swelling marvel so immense it can absorb anything, even decades of unfinished business. If John were here, he'd give Wallace an approving look.

After crushing the can under his boot, Wallace picks it up, raises it like a white flag. Some battles are worth surrendering.

The woman lets out a shaky sigh. Wallace feels so contrite he almost apologizes. Almost.

"Let's begin again." She holds out her hand. "Macy Johansson."

He shakes the hand being offered to him, feeling unnerved, like when he got summoned as a third grader to the school principal's office. Admonished for zip-tying a bully's backpack closed. Sent back to class with a warning and a new seat assignment. "Wallace Bernard. Apparently, my identity preceded me."

Macy eyes him. Maybe she's not a lawyer but a school principal. "Ralph Wesson said you have expertise in many areas."

Good ol' Ralph. Talking up Wallace before he arrived. Wallace drawls his answer, not surprised by the hint of pride in his voice. "It's been said before."

She motions toward the massive house beyond the dunes. "We are overrun with mice. Does rodent control fall within your areas of expertise?"

Glancing at the pile of lines yet to check—he's made progress, but there's still so many—he shifts his attention back to Macy Johansson and shakes his head. She probably saw one mouse and overreacted. "Why not let the buggers be? They're not hurting anyone."

"They are in my kitchen, laundry, and garage. The dogs don't bother giving chase anymore. Yesterday I found a mouse drowned in a freshly made dish of chocolate pudding on my kitchen counter."

He's shuddered before he can help it. Feeling the awfulness. Although dying in a bowl of sweet treats wouldn't be a bad way to go, for a mouse. "The situation does sound like it's gotten out of control."

"And the thing is, I'm on a timeline now. I need the mice taken care of before my sisters get home."

"There are *more* of you? Holy—"

"Please watch your language, Mr. Bernard. We sometimes have children around. And we always have dogs around. No need for the little ones to hear words they shouldn't."

Gaping, he stares at Macy, then drops his attention to the dogs. The small white one's on a leash, head up, sniffing the air, happy in its own doggie world. The bigger one, just trotted up to them, looks like it could take a yahoo down if need be. Always handy to have a dog like that around. When Wallace blinks, the big dog blinks back.

"Mr. Bernard? Can I count on you to take care of the mice before my sisters and niece return?"

Good golly, there's a niece too. The Henhouse population is multiplying by the minute. No wonder Ralph asked him to take care of things around here. A bunch of women living under one roof can create any number of problems. And whenever you see one mouse, there's usually a hundred more you don't see. Put the wrong person in charge of this mission, and it could end in mass destruction. "I'll take care of it, but I'm not going to kill them."

"I don't care what you do with them, as long as they're gone by next Friday. Deal?"

He shakes her hand again. Squints at the surprising strength of her grip. Wonders if he should try to match that strength, but she's released his hand before he can decide. When he sort of dips his head instead, his glance lands on the dogs, and it feels like he's sending them a wordless apology—but for what, he doesn't know. Nearly using offensive language around their sensitive ears? Not being able to stomach the idea of a mouse drowning in pudding? Imbibing in a way that earned him a warning?

The small white dog is still sniffing the air, tail wagging. That's when Wallace realizes the dog is missing both eyes. Closed slits mark where eyeballs used to be. The half-pint seems happy as a bug in a rug, though, with the big dog hovering. Not to mention Macy Johansson at the other end of the leash.

She seems to expect Wallace to move along. Well, if she's okay with leaving the boathouse work unfinished, he is. A cup of coffee would be a benefit before he tackles another task. Wandering off, he sticks his hands in his pockets and uses all his willpower to keep facing forward and not look back. If he let a woman like that know she'd bested him, he'd never, ever hear the end of it.

He's all business when he begins rodent reconnaissance at the Henhouse that afternoon. One after another of alcoves, turrets, chimneys, and stairwells require hours to survey, but he locates most, if not all, favorite hangouts. Then he heads to the market and stacks cheese, peanut butter, and cookies on the counter by the cash register. Also, four wire crates with latching doors.

Virgil Tagaloa, the market owner, laughs. "I've been trying to off-load those crates for more than a year. Ordered them when a commune member got the idea to rehabilitate injured squirrels."

"Commune, huh? Been wondering about that disheveled property. Anything else squirrely going on there?"

"Probably not. It's basically a retirement village with sustainable ideals. How about I take twenty percent off the price since the crates are lightly used?"

Wallace shrugs. "Okay, but they're quality enough for capturing mice at the Royal Henhouse."

Handing over items to scan, Wallace notes that Virgil doesn't ask for an explanation. *What Royal Henhouse?* Nope. Virgil can identify the location referred to. Probably wishes he'd come up with the apropos nickname himself.

Virgil is one capable-looking dude. In his youth, he might have been one of those kids from a Pacific island recruited to play college football. Strong facial features, dark eyes, defined jawline. A mass of dark hair flopping around, practically rolling in waves down his back.

Wallace squints. "Ever tie back your hair? Keep it out of your eyes."

"Now there's an idea."

Wallace puffs up a bit. Another solution he's thought of before Virgil. Age and experience winning out over strength and good looks, yet again. Then he catches Virgil's expression—amused, but trying not to show it. Saving an old man's pride.

Yep, Virgil Tagaloa is a first-round draft pick. Strong, smart, kind, handsome. The guy can probably handle anything. Might be kinda nutty, though. Choosing to make his home and run a business on this island.

Stuffing the groceries in a paper bag, Virgil looks up. "I'm supposed to be taking care of the mice, but I've been busy. Are things that bad?"

"The most recent casualty drowned in chocolate pudding on the kitchen counter."

Virgil says something under his breath—swearing maybe, unless he's already been persuaded against using offensive language on Wren—then adds the last item to the bag. "Allison's not going to be happy if she comes home to that."

Wallace frowns. "Which one is Allison?"

"The niece." Virgil straightens, beaming. "And the woman I hope to marry."

Ah. Probably one first-rate cheerleader running around with this all-star. "Here's to keeping women happy." Wallace thumps Virgil on the back, careful to not get his hand caught in hair. Then he collects the supplies and heads back to the Henhouse.

15

Retaining wall

Mice will eat anything, especially if the options rotate so they're not counting on any one type of food being available. Like fellas snagging dessert first at a buffet in case it isn't there next time they go through the line. The crates will hold about two dozen mice at a time, each mouse with room to roam. Wallace isn't willing to pile mice on top of each other—that wouldn't be comfortable at all—so once he gets Operation Relocate in motion, he checks the crates every few hours.

Sure, there are easier and faster ways to "remove" mice. But who wants that on his conscience? Not to mention turning up in his nightmares.

Every time a crate fills up, Wallace loads it onto Ralph's mostly reliable but unornamented seventy-three-foot rig, aptly named *Lucy Jo*. Wallace met Ralph's cantankerous aunt Lucy Jo once. Long gone now, the original Lucy Jo would throw a fit if she knew she'd been memorialized with a patched-up, flat-fronted cargo hauler.

With the mice on board, Wallace's interisland deliveries include a stop at nearby Seal Rock, an uninhabited island where someone built and has been maintaining a sturdy dock. Virgil recommended the island for Operation Relocate, said something about Allison having a motorbike incident there a while back. Seal Rock is home to a pair of ospreys, at least two good-sized garter snakes, and a red fox. The mouse population will stay under control naturally, best option for a rodent in this mixed-up world.

The fun part is letting the mice go. Watching their whiskers twitch when the crate is opened and they sense freedom. Seeing their tiny legs pick up speed as they scamper off. What the mice do from there Wallace can't be held responsible for.

On Thursday, the day before he's supposed to pick up Virgil's golden girl and her sidekick on the mainland and bring them home to Wren, he relocates a handful of remaining mice. A few renegades will inevitably turn up. He'll continue to monitor the situation.

At the Henhouse, he knocks on the service door and waits. Voices drift out from an upper-level window. Sounds like bossy Macy. At least it's not him under fire this time.

He cups his hands and aims. "Hey! Got a minute?"

Macy's head appears. "I'm in an online meeting, Mr. Bernard. Is it terribly important?"

"I want to confirm the specs about picking up your niece and sister."

She disappears. He scuffs around in the grass. Lime would green things up, plus coffee grounds for nitrogen and phosphorous, and those are all ingredients mostly safe to use around dogs. He studies a retaining wall. If the edge isn't shored up, they'll have grass growing in the rhododendron beds.

The door opens. Macy strides out and hands him a piece of paper. "Their flight info. They'll be waiting outside the baggage claim. Bring them home safely, please."

"Will do."

Macy's heading back inside when he realizes more info would be helpful. "What are their names?"

"Allison and Amelia Theodore. Allison is the younger one. She's our niece. Amelia is my sister."

"Niece, Allison. Sister, Amelia. Theodore." A sort of fissure runs through him, feels almost like something's opened inside him.

He glances around. Maybe a shift in barometric pressure. The wind has picked up, a breeze seeming to come out of nowhere. The island is full of microclimates. He figured that out right away. It has something to do with the position of the island between the mainland and the Olympic Mountains. The topography lends itself to—

"Remember, Mr. Bernard, you're being paid to bring them *safely* back to Wren. No shenanigans, please."

"Yes, ma'am. Wallace Bernard is accepting responsibility for safe transport of Allison and Amelia Theodore."

Again, a disorienting sense of pressure that makes him reel. As if a whirling breeze out of nowhere, one that doesn't move tree branches or seem to affect anything outside him, has found its way inside. Cracked open a rift and left him wide open to uncertainty. With one hand, he steadies himself on the retaining wall. Squints until the plants come into focus.

"Are you still drinking, Mr. Bernard? I thought I made it clear this property is—"

"Save your coffee grounds."

"Excuse me?"

"I'll work your used coffee grounds into the soil around these plants. They'll green up right away." He kicks at the retaining wall, then turns to go.

"You haven't answered my question."

He strides back to within inches of her. Talks breathy to corroborate his words. "Do I smell like I've been drinking?"

"N-no. I can't say that you do. And I admit you look . . . alert."

"Good enough?"

"Good enough, Mr. Bernard."

He spins to walk off, muttering. Fires his main complaint back in her direction. "Only people I'm in trouble with call me Mr. Bernard."

Her schoolmarm voice reaches him across the lawn. "Say again, Mr. Bernard?"

He tosses back what she wants to hear. "I said with me in charge of transport, they'll make it home all right."

Walking away, he thinks through the implications of what he's committed to. Definitely no more drinking today. He practically promised a recovering alcoholic he'd lighten up, and there's probably a sacred law about that. Before heading to the airport, he ought to shower. When was the last time he trimmed up his beard? Checked his nose and ear hairs? Wouldn't be appropriate for Wren Island's official chauffeur to look like someone's charity project.

Back at Ralph's place, Wallace packs a bag for tomorrow's day of travel. Beef jerky, sour gummy worms, breath-freshening gum. Spearmint-flavored because it doesn't bite as much as peppermint but he thinks it still does the job. Though few people have been close enough to indicate if his breath smelled acceptable—not counting Macy Johansson just now.

Since the pandemic, was it rude to breathe in another person's face? Some people hold lingering fears about germs. Others assign conspiracy to nearly everything. All he knows is there's all kinds of idiots out there. He might be one himself and not know it.

While the info's still fresh in his mind, he picks up a pencil to add the passengers' names to the paper Macy gave him. Wouldn't do to lose that pertinent info. Once someone's name has been known, it ought to be remembered. A mantra he would have benefited from recalling himself over the years.

The pencil is a nub. Not enough left to sharpen. He presses hard.

Niece - Allison Theodore

Sister - Amelia Theodore

What's left of the pencil lead breaks away from its wooden casing. And there's that feeling again, the pressure of an internal windstorm rushing through him. Does he have gas and not know it? He sniffs. No, it's some other built-up feeling that's staying inside, not coming out at all. High blood pressure? Or would low blood pressure feel this way?

Any of those ailments could be bad for transporting precious cargo. Just in case, he adds cans of tonic water and Ralph's bottle of Beano to his travel bag, drops the bag off on *Lucy Jo*, then heads to the cottage where Wren's new full-time on-call clinician keeps part-time office hours. Wallace, the island's only mouse mover, can appreciate the liabilities of holding specialized skills on a small island.

16

Picking up women

When Wallace draws near, Jacob Yoon is pulling scallions from a garden patch. Crouching rather than sitting or kneeling. Probably will effortlessly stand up whenever he needs to, all in one motion, no creaking or instability.

Ever since learning of Yoon's background in physical therapy, Wallace has hoped he never needs that particular remedy. Though amicable, Yoon seems like he'd be hard-pressed to show mercy when a person's health is at stake. A trait that's handy when a seventy-year-old man needs answers.

"Sometimes I feel a pressure inside. Wonder if I have gas and don't know it."

Yoon tosses a clump of scallions into a basket and stands—yep, all in one motion, no support needed. Wallace was once capable of that, back in the day.

"Flatulence can be normal. Is it bothering you?"

"Only because I don't know if it's happening. I'm picking up women in Seattle tomorrow." *Picking up women.* Wallace grins at how that sounds.

"I see. We wouldn't want you to be anything less than fit for your first impression on Allison and Amelia." Yoon throws a knowing—or warning?—look toward Wallace, wipes his hands on his jeans, and motions to the cottage. "Come inside."

Yoon pokes around and figures out it's not gas. Blood pressure is okay. Heart and lungs sound normal. He's suggesting bloodwork, to be on the cautious side, when Wallace waves him off.

"Just wanted to be certain I'm fit to drive a boat and the van with passengers. I got this far without a major illness. I'll probably die with a clean bill of health."

Yoon cocks his head. "Your reasoning is full of irony. To die, something must go wrong."

"Nope. To die, you just quit. Ever see a bumblebee take a sick day? They keep working right up to the day they don't. Bumblebee system ought to work for Wallace Bernard."

He tries to pay Yoon for the visit, but the clinician taps notes into an electronic tablet and says they'll figure it out later. Explains Wren's new medical facility, grand total of one employee, is being subsidized by Allison Theodore. Same rich girl Wallace is picking up at the Seattle airport tomorrow.

Shrugging, Yoon sets aside the tablet. "I don't know yet if I'm supposed to charge for this kind of visit."

"This kind of visit, as in, you didn't find anything wrong with me?"

"As in, an older gentleman wants assurance he'll be able to work tomorrow same as he did today."

Walking away from that conversation, Wallace isn't sure whether to feel complimented or criticized. But the pressure inside is gone, so he's going to call it a success.

Next morning, he's driving *Lucy Jo* away from Wren and toward Seattle like a teenager in a sports car, almost, if *Lucy Jo* had more horsepower and maneuverability. In calm water, he lets go of the wheel, backs away from the helm, gets into a crouch, and tests his ability to stand up again, no hands.

He can't, and not because he's been anywhere near a beer. Because he's getting old. As consolation after finally creaking into a standing position using both hands for balance, he chomps on a few sour gummy worms. Chases them down with tonic water and Beano just in case.

A few miles outside of Seattle, he registers *Lucy Jo* in a temporary slip. Lowers the ramp and drives Ralph's scrubby-looking but well-maintained van off the cargo deck and onto the dock. Closes up *Lucy Jo*, bringing his bag of snacks with him. Drives the remaining distance to the Seattle airport.

The airline app alerts him the ladies' flight landed. Macy follows up with the same info in a text. After he pulls up to the Arrivals curb, he snaps back he's been tracking the flight himself. But a millionaire and her aunt are nowhere in sight, so he has to circle around again.

The second time he drives up to Arrivals, a gorgeously tall girl and her placid aunt are waving his direction, both wearing clothes better suited to a Hawaiian beach than a Pacific Northwestern airport. At first he thinks their big smiles are for him. They're glad to see good ol' Wallace Bernard. It's unexpectedly intoxicating to be greeted like that by women like this.

Then he realizes they're waving at Ralph's familiar van and their ride home. Any driver will do.

He parks the van, gets out, introduces himself, confirms he's got the right Allison and Amelia. Then he gripes about all the luggage. Any rational person would. How many bags do two people need anyway? Especially coming from Hawaii, where people don't wear much clothing. Unruffled, Amelia goes on about how pleased she is to be home.

When the last luggage is stowed in the van, she hands him a giant box of chocolate-covered macadamia nuts. "This is for you."

He stares at it, the industrial-size box dwarfing his two hands, which are fairly large themselves. "That's a lot of chocolate."

"Don't you eat chocolate?" Amelia's expression is going from surprised to disappointed.

He's already made a mistake, causing a happy-go-lucky lady concern when there's no problem in sight. Welcome to the world of being around Wallace Bernard.

He looks up. "I like chocolate. Just wasn't expecting it."

Suddenly, Allison Theodore, millionaire, spectacular girlfriend of the admirable Virgil Tagaloa, puts a hand on Wallace's arm and leans close. Right then and there, at the curb of an international airport, she plants a kiss on his cheek.

A man she's just met! Hasn't anyone taught this girl anything about protecting herself? Good thing he's Wallace Bernard, not a scheming hoodlum.

Unnerved about Allison's lack of caution and maybe about how his heart is flip-flopping—good golly, look at the lashes framing those pretty brown eyes—he nearly drops the chocolates.

Allison steps back, smiles almost like she's proud of him. "Thank you for picking us up, Wallace." Her warm voice zings right into him.

He mumbles a response. Fiddles with stowing the box of chocolates. What-ever he expected Allison and Amelia to be, it wasn't this. A hoity-toity attitude would have been typical. Extravagant clothing and gifts, not surprising. Tanned skin and freckled shoulders, sure.

But warmth, welcome, trust? Camaraderie right from the get-go? Like they're already old friends?

Now he understands what Ralph meant when he asked for Wallace's help.

I've got friends here, Wallace. People I want looked after.

Well, here he is. Looking after. Welcome to Wren Island with Wallace around. Except they're in Seattle. And it's his responsibility to fix that.

When an airport security guard screeches a whistle and motions the van's time at the curb is up, Wallace corrals his charges, confirms they've fastened their seatbelts, and eases into traffic. Sticks a piece of spearmint gum in his mouth and passes the pack around the van.

17

Mile markers

Sitting in the backseat of Ralph's van, seatbelt fastened, chewing gum in her mouth, Hawaii-tanned hands folded in her lap, Amelia listened to the conversation happening in the front seats, where Allison and Wallace chattered about everything and nothing.

During the first moments of the drive, Wallace had been quiet. But by finding common and comfortable ground, Allison encouraged Wallace to open up.

"I had a bedroom full of Pound Puppies and My Little Ponies too."

Wallace nodded. "They were all the rage when my girls were young. You must be about the same age."

"Forty-seven on my next birthday." Allison sounded pleased, as if she'd passed a significant mile marker. Amelia smiled. Considering that some people never made it to that point, a forty-seventh birthday did seem like a monumental accomplishment.

"My girls are a bit younger than you." Checking the rearview mirror, Wallace's glance fell on Amelia. Right when she was trying to blow a bubble and not succeeding! She started to smile around the chewing gum, but Wallace looked away before she could manage to do more than unstick the gum from her lips.

He clicked on a blinker and moved the van into a faster lane to pass a recreational vehicle. The blinker clicked off, then back on, the van returning to the slow lane, Wallace's eyes settling on the road ahead.

"My oldest, Vanessa, has two kids. Boy and a girl. Vanessa's always wanted to live on a farm. My younger daughter, Melissa, would be useless around animals. Too intent on keeping her clothes clean. But if you're planning any sort of shindig, you want Melissa's help. She could convince a sloth to get up and dance. Real motivator, that girl."

Wallace also talked about his arthritic knee, which a doctor said was from too much sprinting on concrete. But as Wallace said he secretly knew then and was only now admitting to anyone else, the bum knee came from getting whacked with a crowbar years before.

"Happened shortly after I got out of the Peace Corps." Wallace snorted. "Maybe I should have stayed in."

Perking up, Amelia tucked her chewing gum into one cheek. "You served in the Peace Corps? When?"

"Seventy-four to seventy-eight."

Amelia's breath caught. John had been in the Peace Corps during those years. She didn't mention the connection though. Allison was already asking about potential long-term effects from bone injuries, and there was no sense airing dirty laundry to a new acquaintance.

Amelia basically stopped listening then. Immersed herself in memories of what life with John had been like. Sitting on a bench feeding ducks by the lake, sharing a bottle of French white. Starlit nights dreaming of the future, bundled under one blanket. Tucked in the quiet corner of a café, enjoying a single-malt chocolate shake.

What would John have been like if he were here today? Would he look like this grizzled man at the wheel of Ralph's van? The image instantly seemed unlikely, and she deflated. All these years later—mile marker sixty-eight!—and she was still picturing the man she loved as a twenty-year-old. Trim and fit, a face without lines or hair, smooth voice.

No possible way of knowing what John would look like now. Oh, sure, she could upload a photo into an app and ask AI—which Jax said was short for *artificial intelligence*—to produce an image of an aged man with John's physical traits. But AI couldn't reveal what'd happened underneath, like a knee arthritic from being whacked with a crowbar. And who could ever be certain the projection was accurate?

Plus, AI-created photos tended to creep her out. Something always seemed oddly not right, although she could rarely put her finger on specifics. A photo generated by AI seemed to exist without a soul. Such a confusing conclusion that even though she was already seated and belted in, she felt it would be helpful to sit down to think about it.

She studied Wallace's face framed in the reflection of the rearview mirror. A picture with a soul. Jaw set with determination, yet yielding to an occasional twitch. A casual glance swinging to intense scrutiny, then relaxing again. Hands firm on the steering wheel except when minutely and unpredictably flexing.

One of these days, she'd ask Wallace about his time in the Peace Corps. To imagine what John might have experienced. To wonder, again, who John might have become.

18

Setting aside inventory

In the stockroom of the grocery market on Wren Island, Virgil Tagaloa slid a box cutter through packaging tape, then pulled out a bag of new dog treats. Bone-shaped cornstarch chews, giant-sized for Louise, tiny for Lokita. The clicking of approaching toenails indicated both dogs had smelled the treats from the other room, where they'd been supervising café business. Virgil handed each an appropriately sized chew.

Louise took off with hers, probably to the top step of the market's covered porch. Blind Lokita laid down near Virgil's feet, gnawing and trusting despite not being able to see the big wide world around her. The scent of wet, smoky cheese filled the air.

"Mind if I take that back for a minute?" Virgil gently took the treat from Lokita and examined it. Smelly, sticky, and already crumbling apart in places. He returned the treat. "These will have to be enjoyed here at the store. Your mom will never allow this kind of mess at her house."

It felt like an eternity since Allison left. Maybe she meant it when she said staying in Hawaii for weeks didn't have anything to do with feeling scared about where their relationship was going. But Allison might always be tempted to run off. Lured by those bewitching friends Independence and Self-Reliance, promising a life free from entanglements. Especially from the kind of mess brought on by a fifty-two-year-old guy with a teenage son and an ex-wife who let drugs destroy her life.

Opening another shipment, he tallied boxes of facial tissue. Twenty-four total. Twelve in tones of blue and green, five red, five yellow, two pink. He set aside the yellow and pink boxes for Allison and her aunt Amelia. A perk of being the store's owner was setting aside inventory for special customers in their favorite colors. He added the remaining tissue boxes to a nearby shelf.

Moving to a remote island in the Pacific Northwest was the best decision he ever made. Surrounded by friendly neighbors and a peaceful environment, he and Jax had everything they needed. Or so Virgil thought until Allison Theodore arrived and the world suddenly became more colorful, more brilliant. Nowhere near complete without her. He'd always loved Allison, somehow, even before he knew her. There'd never been a beginning to his love, and there wouldn't be an end. His heart had chosen *her*. Forever.

Virgil snorted. Took him a long time to convince Allison of that. Then, just when he thought she was settled, she ran off to Hawaii. One-way ticket, no return date in mind. Whenever the thinnest veil of uncertainty crept into Allison's voice or body language, it didn't seem unreasonable to ask himself if Allison was as convinced of his love as she claimed.

Lokita stood and stretched, finished with her chew. Her uncertain steps indicated she'd been so absorbed in chewing she'd lost track of where she was. Virgil gave the little dog a few reassuring pats before he stashed the treat box high on a shelf, out of reach from Louise even if the big dog got motivated and stood on her hind legs.

"Let's restock the *Made on Wren Island* shelf. What do you want to bet Amelia will check it right away?"

Lokita followed the sound of his footsteps to the front of the store, bumped against the stainless-steel water bowl and took a drink, then snuggled into her bed near the cash register.

After adding more of Amelia's shell wreaths and Macy's fabric bags to the shelf of local products, Virgil meandered over to the market's bulletin board.

Checked the clipboard where visitors noted vessel tie-up times at the market's private but hospitable dock. No new arrivals.

The same old handwritten notices advertised the usual farm equipment for sale. A new note offered a free tabletop aquarium and accessories, fish not included. Allison's aunt Shasta posted her request for spare yarn so long ago the ink was starting to run. Several postcards from Hawaii overlapped the board's edges, recipients wanting to be known for having heard from Wren's world travelers.

Virgil checked his watch. The only reason he didn't pick up Allison and Amelia at the airport himself was market business had been so steady, leaving Jax in charge alone would have been asking a lot of a teenager. Not that Jax couldn't handle it. He was a diligent worker. So conscientious that when business slowed today, it'd been nice to let Jax go fishing with a friend.

With no one around, Virgil headed to his office, punched the code to the safe, and pulled out a small velvet box. The engagement ring had set him back some—to adorn the emerald-cut diamond, itself one and one-half carats, with the smaller diamonds on either side, plus the antique filigree and carvings. But just looking at the wedding band with matching filigree sent his heart thumping into overdrive. Allison had helped him choose the rings' design, though she might not realize it. During a conversation with Allison and her aunts about Allison's great-grandmother's wedding rings, Virgil had taken mental notes. Then he'd worked with a jeweler on Reclamation Island to re-create the heirloom rings, paying partly with cash, partly with bartered groceries. One more cash transfer and the deal would be complete.

After checking his bank account's balance, Virgil sent the final payment to the jeweler, Thomas Barnes, who immediately followed up with a text wishing Virgil good luck with the proposal.

Reaching into the safe again, Virgil pulled out his notes about the prenuptial agreement in the works at his lawyer's office. Once he and Allison were married, they'd not be separated by anything but death. But he wanted Allison to be assured her money and assets were entirely hers, would never be desired or needed by her husband and adopted teenage son.

The Tagaloa men had gotten along fine all these years. Never rich, but always having enough, thanks to creativity, bartering, and carefully conserving resources. He wasn't above admitting resourcefulness as a point of pride.

Still, large expenses had to be planned. Now that the rings were paid for, the next significant purchase, barring unexpected medical bills, would be a car for Jax. Not happening until the boy turned sixteen more than a year from now, giving Virgil time to work out a bartering deal with the repo man on Reclamation. And get comfortable with the idea of his little boy being that much more grown up.

19

One little postcard

After returning the rings and the notes about the prenup to the safe and closing it up, Virgil wandered back out to the main grocery area—still no customers—and checked his watch. Plenty of time to tweak a favorite muffin recipe by replacing peaches with canned pineapple in honor of travelers returning from Hawaii.

Following Jax's recipe notes about cutting the sugar in half, Virgil combined the ingredients and slid the filled muffin tins into the café's oven. Drummed his fingers on the counter. Studied a framed photo of Jax, Allison, and himself on a fishing expedition, all of them shiny and smiley.

Jax had been on board with the idea of Allison officially being part of their family—excited about it!—until the day that blasted postcard arrived.

For nearly ten years, no word at all. Then, just when Virgil was about to pop the big question to the woman he loves truly, loves more than himself, the darkest shadow from his past crept into the picture.

Given that he had been a diligent gatekeeper—his ex-wife legally forbidden from direct contact with their son—it was immensely annoying to find the postcard addressed to Jax. Plus, it had been sent to Reclamation Island first, which meant anyone and everyone there could have read it before it finally reached the Tagaloas' mailbox.

In handwriting known to Virgil but completely unfamiliar to Jax, the short message had packed a solid punch.

Thinking of you, the son I've always loved.

No return address. Stamped Bellingham, Washington. Uncomfortably close.

At first, Jax seemed uncaring about the postcard. But its condition when Virgil restocked Jax's desk with pencils a few weeks ago indicated a different scenario. The card's corners were worn from being cradled in soft hands, the blue ink of the handwriting smudged by teardrops in multiple places.

Plus, a worn plush bear had been brought down from the attic and was snugged up to Jax's pillow. Mama Bear had come home from the hospital with newborn Jax. *A gift from your mom because she was sad she couldn't be with you,* Virgil always said.

The night after making those discoveries, he had put together a pizza with Jax's favorite toppings (pepperoni and olives), mixed up a batch of Jax's favorite apple streusel muffins, flipped the market's sign to *Closed* earlier than usual, and declared a movie night.

Over dinner, Virgil had tiptoed into uncharted territory. "Jax, do you want to talk more about the postcard you received from your mom?"

"No."

"You can tell me anything."

"I know."

"We've always been best buddies. Able to talk about anything."

Anything but this, apparently.

That night and later, Jax bottled up more and Virgil pressed harder—panicking as insecurities he thought he'd squashed rose to the forefront. Outrageous ideas crossed his mind. Maybe he was a horrible, rotten, incapable husband, dad, man. Maybe relocating to Wren had been less about protecting Jax from an unstable mother, more about giving up.

Crystal recovered enough to send a postcard, didn't she? Had Virgil robbed his son of time spent with his mother?

The son I've always loved.

If Virgil had stayed with his ex-wife longer, even one more day, could she have turned her life around? Kicked drugs, come home, wanted her son? Returned her husband's love?

Now, after weeks of hoping Jax would talk about the postcard, Virgil was still reeling from the unknowns. Squeezing his eyes shut, he took a deep breath and inhaled the comforting scent of freshly baked goods. When the oven timer beeped, he pulled out the tins of pineapple almond muffins and set them on a rack to cool.

To pass the still seemingly endless hours until Allison returned, he poured himself into physical work. Hauling cartons of fresh produce to the appropriate bins. Refreshing the salt and pepper shakers on the café's tables. Scrubbing counters and cabinets, trusting that his conflicting thoughts would settle into place. And they did.

He didn't want to be loved by Crystal. Not anymore. It'd been a lifetime since he'd loved her, or had thought he did. He felt compassion for her—God knows what all she'd been through. He felt gratitude because she'd given him the gift of Jax. And if she had turned her life around, he would feel sincere admiration.

But none of that could unanchor him from the life he treasured here and now. The life he'd built on Wren with and for his son. Surrounded by friends who cared. Choosing to love a woman his heart would never let go of, couldn't let go of, because she brilliantly lit up everything inside him and the world around them too.

Tackling the floor with the broom, he swept the island's mix of sand, dirt, and spruce needles out to the covered porch. Pushed the dusty cloud around the big dog sprawling on the top step. Sent the debris floating into the flower beds. Headed back inside.

Therapy had been helpful to both him and Jax. From the beginning, Jax had been aware the woman who birthed him had given up all rights to be near him. *Because she loved you,* Virgil always said.

Ten years later, the kid gets a note from the mother who'd always loved him. How could the boy *not* let the tiniest bit of hope flicker into longing? How could Jax *not* dream of being wanted, being *known*, by his mother?

Sighing, Virgil stowed the broom on the wall rack Allison had installed and labeled *Cleaning equipment*, one of her unending efforts to organize the market. If only tidying issues of the heart were so easy. He and Jax might be in for a rocky ride before resolving whatever this potential situation with Jax's mother was.

Virgil would do what he'd always done. Be there. Ask questions. Keep his mouth closed when it was less helpful to offer solutions, more helpful to listen. Allison had taught him that, teasing him for asking too many questions in an effort to solve a problem. Sometimes the other person just needed to be heard.

And held. Wrapped in arms unwilling to let go. He spent a few moments imagining how satisfying it was going to feel to welcome Allison home.

She'd probably have helpful insight about the situation with his ex. Allison was not only gorgeous, she was intelligent. Clear-thinking. Predictably reasonable. And she dearly loved Jax. Wanted the boy to thrive.

But was telling her about it the wisest approach? Virgil refilled the dogs' water bowl. He didn't need a repeat of his first conversation with Allison about his ex. When he mentioned he'd been the one to leave the marriage, not the other way around, Allison bolted. Literally ran off.

With one seemingly innocuous comment, he'd landed back at square one in the formidable task of earning Allison Theodore's trust. Like when he and Jax played the board game *Chutes and Ladders* and a flick of the dice sent Virgil sliding back to start.

He wanted to believe he and Allison had gotten through that iffy stage of their relationship. That Allison knew, *really* knew, he loved her and was devoted to her for the long haul. But what if she came home from Hawaii with a remnant of her fears remaining about trusting Virgil Tagaloa? One little postcard could cause her unnecessary angst.

Sighing, Virgil leaned over and patted Lokita's warm, soft head. "That's why we'll not say anything about the postcard to your mom, Lokita. If she happens to hear about it through the island grapevine, we'll talk about it then." He smiled at the little dog snuggling into his hand. "You'd be a welcome addition to the conversation. Bring your calming vibe."

No need working up Allison over one random postcard. The only legitimate concern at the moment was helping Jax process and move on from this one-sided encounter. If history repeated itself, another ten years might pass before the Tagaloas again heard from Crystal.

20

Hyperawareness

Just as Virgil was about to check if he'd missed any messages from Allison, his phone buzzed one of his special settings—short-long, Morse code for the letter *A*. He opened Allison's text.

Arrived in Seattle and on our way back to Wren. Don't worry. Wallace is a good driver.

Virgil replied with a smile emoji and tucked away his phone, mostly reassured. Lately, he found himself unexpectedly and perhaps justifiably concerned for Allison's safety. Even if Allison didn't flash her money around, her millions sometimes brought unwanted attention. Like the debacle not long ago that included a scammer landing the only punch on Virgil that had ever knocked him out.

Shaking his head, Virgil looked around the market with Allison's eyes. Wouldn't want her to think he'd neglected orderliness just because she wasn't around to comment on it. She'd wipe the smudges off the glass muffin case, though few customers would notice. He grabbed a clean towel and made the case shine.

To his credit, he hadn't been expecting that jerk's punch, thanks to Allison keeping a colossal secret, which she promised never to do again. With a twinge,

Virgil thought of the postcard he was keeping secret. Anyway, since that night, which was also when Allison finally began to trust him, he'd basically launched into hyperawareness about potential threats to her well-being.

He scrutinized the muffin case from all angles. Not bad. The jerk who punched Virgil had been brought to Wren by Ralph Wesson, like Wallace Bernard. Ralph hadn't realized the threat though. And anyone could see the difference in the men. The other guy hadn't stopped swaggering from the moment he landed on Wren's beach to when he was hauled off again, handcuffed and flanked by federal agents.

Wallace appeared a broken but earnest old man. May have seen a few too many hurts. Probably hoping for a new start. What word had Ralph used to describe Wallace? Unremarkable. Nothing wrong with that. Solid and predictable could be admirable traits.

That didn't mean Wallace had necessary driving skills for city traffic. Let alone an interstate highway. He might be distracted by cataracts, slowing reflexes, an aching back or hip . . .

Virgil tossed the used towel into the laundry and punched a text to Allison.

Can't wait to see you, hold you. How much longer?

Allison's reply came a minute later.

Easy, tiger. Wallace says seventy is progress worth celebrating, in birthdays or miles per hour.

Virgil was still chuckling when Allison's next text buzzed in.

Aunt Amelia giggles every time Wallace points to a 70 mph sign.

After Allison's brief text about boarding *Lucy Jo*, Virgil's phone fell understandably silent. Twiddling his thumbs, Virgil rechecked the weather and tides. Closed his vessel tracking app when the blip representing *Lucy Jo* made such frustratingly slow progress he nearly pulled out his hair. Returned scattered dog toys to the low basket on the market's porch. Took a run on the beach, eyeing the horizon for *Lucy Jo*, then showered.

Finally, Ralph's cargo hauler chugged past on its way to Wren's south-facing beach. Virgil covered the porch steps in one leap and was fidgeting on the beach when Wallace finally powered flat-fronted *Lucy Jo* onto the sand.

Unwilling to wait for Allison to climb off, Virgil reached up and lifted her into his arms. Held her close. Every part of him instantly alive, electrified.

"Ah, I've missed you." He inhaled the sweet scent of her hair, her skin, all that was her, and wrapped her tighter. "Please don't ever go away again."

She snuggled close. "This feels good, Virgil. Being home. I forgot how strong your arms are! But you can put me down. I've got my own feet."

For half a heartbeat, he ached with a vision of her Hawaii-tanned legs running away from him as soon as they hit the sand. She stayed close though, leaning into him. He reached for her left hand, brought it to his lips, and kissed the finger that, if he had his way, would soon hold a ring with unequivocable meaning. He moved in for a real kiss, which she returned. Warm, willing, leaving him blissfully content yet craving more.

A throat clearing came from *Lucy Jo*'s deck. Wallace, waving Virgil's attention toward a beaming Amelia and a pile of luggage. Virgil helped Amelia disembark and returned her enthusiastic hug. He pulled a bright yellow, heavy suitcase from *Lucy Jo*'s deck and hauled it toward Allison's house.

Every few steps, he stole another glance at Allison. When she returned his smile with a knowing wink, he thrilled all over inside. She'd come home, hadn't she? Was ready to say yes when he proposed. He could feel it in every pulse of her warm hand in his, her arm linked through his, her shoulder leaning into his.

Time to think up a romantic way to pop the big question. If he waited too long to ask, the slightest moment of distrust might send her off and running again.

He pulled away from her, just a fraction. Adjusted his hold on the suitcase and slowed his steps. Watched Allison walk on ahead and not turn to look back at him.

His heart clenched. He didn't doubt his love for Allison. Not hers for him either. He'd been ready to marry her from the beginning. But hadn't he always said Allison was perfectly capable of taking care of herself? She would never need him—though she might want him and seemed to be sending those signals. What if there came a time when she didn't want him either?

The uneasiness inside him swirled into understanding of his current predicament. He'd completely failed as a husband the first time around, even after offering everything within his power. What made him think he could possibly measure up if Allison ever truly needed him?

21

Delicate treasures

One morning a few days after returning home from Hawaii, Amelia walked along the line of debris zigzagging the beach after high tide. Not finding any treasures, she made her way through the brush to the road, Louise nosing around at her side. Unlike the main roads now being paved, the dirt path, running parallel with the beach all the way to Virgil's grocery market, was just wide enough to accommodate the commune's all-terrain vehicle Ed often puttered around the island.

Near Miss Fox's Rock, Amelia stepped more quietly. Only once had she seen the fox, and she'd gone with *Miss* because it felt right. No offense to all the Mister Foxes in the world, of course.

Circling the boulder, Amelia visited the hollow basin on its back side. Oh! Someone must have discovered her stacks while she was away. More smooth stones had been balanced. Like playing a game with a mystery partner! Probably it was Wallace. Before, Amelia had been the only one stacking rocks. Now Wallace was on Wren, now more rocks were stacked.

Amelia searched the side of the road. The trick was finding a rock shaped and sized correctly for the next move. She found one and balanced it into place. "Your turn, Wallace."

Too bad people couldn't make money from piling rocks into random towers. If people could do that, Amelia Theodore would be golden.

She meandered through the rolling swaths of dune grasses between the house and beach, plucking yellow blooms of arrowleaf balsamroot for drying and attaching to shell wreaths. The blooms went into the new fabric bag slung over her shoulder, a gift from Macy, white sea stars on navy, with an extra pocket sewn in for delicate treasures.

Once, Macy had told Amelia that recovering alcoholics often redirected to other compulsory behaviors. Cigarettes, coffee, sweets, slot machines, exercise, shopping. How agreeable to have a sister whirring out endless creations on a sewing machine.

When Amelia reached the beach, she tossed a stick for Louise, who galloped after it, splashing in the surf. Pulling out her phone, Amelia recorded Louise's antics. Videos of Allison's dogs usually went over well on the YouTube channel. People liked watching goofy Louise. And everyone had a soft spot for little blind Lokita. Amelia sighed. Lack of perfect eyesight wasn't perceived as quite so endearing in a bumbling old lady. She switched the camera to photo mode and snapped a photo of Louise to send her sister Shasta, still in Hawaii with Ralph.

Sitting on a driftwood log (a toothpick tossed aside by a giant?), Amelia opened the transcription app on her phone and speech-to-texted a list of necessary craft supplies. When she finished, she almost said *thank you*. Even if not a real person, AI sure was helpful.

Near her feet, a bright red piece of plastic caught her eye. Five days in a row, she'd picked up garbage, each piece a different shape and size, with edges softened by waves and sand. The trash might have come from Wren, washed up from a nearby island, or arrived from a distance. A commune member, maybe Ed, once said mounds of toxic garbage floated in the ocean, posing a danger to fish and other marine animals. Some days, it really did feel like the world was going to pot.

That was a phrase Macy used. *Going to pot*. Amelia had been testing out the phrase, but only inside her head, because she wasn't certain *pot* still meant what she thought it did. These days, certain words seemed to change meaning every time she thought to use them.

She picked up the red plastic and several pieces in other colors, tucked them into her fabric bag (but not in the special pocket for delicate treasures), then wandered farther down the beach. Could she repurpose the plastic? Sell crafts made by recycling garbage, in addition to her shell wreaths? Thanks to Virgil displaying the wreaths in his market, Amelia sold a few a month to tourists wanting to take home a piece of Wren Island.

With the money she made selling crafts, plus the money added to her account by Allison, Amelia was richer than she'd ever been. But double of not much was still not much.

Here she was, sixty-eight years old and never lived on her own. Always taken care of by parents or a sister. Maybe that was acceptable back in the Dark Ages, but this was the twenty-first century. Women could be completely independent if they wanted! Why didn't anyone think of Amelia Theodore that way?

When Louise came barreling back from the surf, Amelia tossed her another stick. Then she added several smaller driftwood sticks to her bag. They could be hot-glued to a twig wreath with bone-shaped biscuits. Add a frame to hold a photo of the family dog.

The problem was, she had lots of ideas but not always enough know-how. Especially when it came to using the technology that always seemed to be advancing way ahead of her. For instance, besides her YouTube channel, how could she spread the word about wonderful Wren Island? If only she had a team! If only she could wave a magic wand. *Hey, you over there! Here's what I want. Make it happen, please.*

It would be like talking to AI, only much, much better. A real live person on the receiving end of an idea might smile at you and say *Great idea, Amelia!* Might give you a warm hug or squeeze your hand—gently, because they knew your arthritic fingers ached. They might tell you they believed in your idea, they believed in *you*, before they sprang into action and made your dream happen right before your very eyes.

22

Perception

Back at the house, Amelia found Macy in a dither, pointing the business end of a broom at the refrigerator. "A mouse ran behind the fridge."

Amelia glanced at Allison. So far, her niece had shown surprisingly minimal annoyance at finding mice in the house. Maybe Allison's deepening relationship with cool-as-a-cucumber Virgil came with an unexpected benefit. Allison Theodore slightly less type A. Calmly reaching for Louise, Allison buttoned her into a pink-flowered Hawaiian shirt to match Lokita's.

Taking a cue from her niece, Amelia shrugged. "Wallace told us stragglers would turn up."

The hammering on the service door sounded like Ralph's knock, but with Ralph in Hawaii could only mean Wallace. Amelia opened the door and motioned him in. "Heads up. You're probably in trouble again." She led the way to the kitchen, sat at the table, and reached for a brownie with a thick layer of coffee-flavored frosting.

Hands on her hips, Macy scowled. "Mr. Bernard. I thought you had taken care of our rodent situation. Why am I still seeing mice?"

"Good afternoon to you, too. Thought I'd stop by and see if you'd like anything brought over from the mainland." Wallace took his time petting Louise's big head, then Lokita's tiny head. "Two dogs in matching Hawaiian shirts, freshly ironed. Now there's a sight not seen every day."

When Amelia giggled, Wallace flashed her a whiskery smile. And winked! Amelia sucked in her breath, then took another bite of brownie to mask her fluster.

Wallace turned his attention to Macy. "Need any supplies?"

"What I need is to be free of mice."

"I'll rebait the traps and keep an eye out."

Allison pulled a box of dog biscuits from the pantry. "Any updates about when the Jeeps will arrive?"

"Next week, maybe."

Spic-and-span Allison placed one dog biscuit at a time into a ceramic canister. Less risk of crumbs than dumping all the biscuits in at once. "You haven't said anything to Virgil about one of those Jeeps being for Jax, right?"

"You asked me not to."

While Allison chattered about surprising Jax with his own vehicle, Amelia studied Wallace. His weathered face remained expressionless, except his lips tightened a bit. Indicating worry? Disapproval? Was Wallace thinking the same thing she had been thinking all along? That Virgil might prefer to buy his only son his first car? *Stay tuned, folks, while the ongoing romance between Allison and Virgil unfolds.* That's what Amelia would say if she were narrating a YouTube video about it.

She reached for her water cup—plastic was all Macy allowed her since returning from Hawaii, as if she were a child—but her vision blurred at the wrong second and the cup went spinning off the table and across the floor. Darn this age-related macular degeneration. Throwing her into the unwanted spotlight again.

Allison patted her arm. "It's all right, Aunt Amelia. I spill stuff all the time."

Amelia couldn't remember the last time her niece had to clean up a mess she'd made herself, but it was nice of Allison to be gracious.

Wallace appeared with a clear glass (breakable!) and a pitcher of water. "Refill?"

Amelia nodded and waited for him to pour. But Wallace set the glass and pitcher on the table within her reach, then turned his attention to the dogs. Delivery of the glass and pitcher, check. From there, though . . .

She poured her own refill. Shakily. But successfully!

So many things always seemed to be working against her. She wanted to earn her own income but was too old to start a new career. Had a vision of independence but sometimes couldn't see ten feet ahead. She'd started a life once—a carefree life promising romance and babies, birthday cakes crowded with one more candle, Christmas Eves tiptoeing around the house. Then, for way more time than she'd felt the promise, she'd carried the grief of having lost it. Of missing the person who might have made it all happen.

Sighing, she eyed the shelf holding crystal stemware sent from a friend of Allison's who didn't know there'd never be alcohol in the house. "If this house wasn't dry, I would definitely go for a drink right now. A French white, maybe."

"Aunt Amelia!" Allison glanced at Macy and back at Amelia. "That doesn't sound like you."

"Maybe I could say a lot of things that don't sound like me."

A look of concern crossed Allison's face. Macy pulled a chair close, sat, and patted Amelia's arm. "Poor Melia."

Entirely annoyed now, Amelia spun to face her sister. "Always Melia, not my *real* name. And why don't you let me do things? Pour my own hot coffee. Into a *ceramic* mug. Walk on the beach without having to report back by a certain time. Pour detergent into the clothes washer myself. Order my own shoes." Tears edged into her voice. "Why can't I spill water without it being evidence of my eyesight worsening?"

No one had ever said each new blunder indicated more interference from her age-related macular degeneration. But that's what was happening, wasn't it? Every time she stumbled, fell, bumped into a wall, her world became more confining. Even if she didn't want help from her sisters and everyone else, she needed it. Would continue needing it, more so, in the future. She leaned into the arms Macy wrapped around her.

Wallace shifted into view. He was still around? Another detail she'd lost sight of. Add it to the list of everything she was missing out on. His gravelly voice was kind, but firm. "News flash, missy. When you stop feeling sorry for yourself, the rest of the world will too."

Mopping up the spill on the table, Allison rolled her eyes. "Gee, Wallace. Thanks but no thanks for the shrink stuff."

He left, shaking his head and slamming the door behind him, an audible punctuation mark hammering home truth. If all Amelia did was mope around, how could she expect anyone to think of her as independent? How could she expect to accomplish anything on her own if she waited for support every time she got a new idea?

Wallace Bernard, courier of Wren Island essentials and incognito rock stacker, had just delivered exceptionally perceptive news.

23

Expanding edginess

When he's gathered the last of the renegade mice, Wallace stows the cage on the floor of *Lucy Jo*'s wheelhouse and pats it—lightly, to avoid scaring the buggers. It'll take forty-five minutes to get to Seal Rock, another ten or so to unload. "Fifty-five minutes to freedom, guys."

He maneuvers *Lucy Jo* to give the submerged rocky ledge at the western point of Wren Island a wide berth. Navigating into the widening strait, he feels an expanding edginess. You'd think, in a gazillion generations, mice would have taught each other not to run across the path of Wren's tightest-wound queen of Sheba. Especially when she's holding a broom as if its main function is sweeping mice, not floors.

Did the real queen of Sheba ever sweep floors? Somebody somewhere probably figured that out. Excavated an archaeological site, found a new hieroglyphic, filled out the right government forms until—presto—they had evidence the queen of Sheba never swept floors.

When the engine starts running rough, Wallace lets off the throttle to rest whatever parts need resting. Later, back on Wren, he'll look under the hood, so to speak.

He checks his phone, just in case Vanessa has texted, which she hasn't. Both his daughters are intelligent. So how come Vanessa's incapable of recognizing a twerp? If he hears she's hooked up with one more supposedly crypto-rich desperado, he'll likely do damage. A fist punched through drywall for starters.

Maybe he's feeling edgy from being around so many women. Foremost Macy Johansson, with her raised eyebrows and pinpoint glare daring you to take a different tack than she wants you to. It's all a smokescreen, though. You've got to admire a woman who can appear that managerial while shaking like a leaf inside.

The other sister, the one taking turns stacking rocks, is the one keeping him on his toes. How many times has he seen her stumble on a trail, wander into high surf, or venture too near a cliff edge? Twice, she got lost in the woods on her way to that derelict commune up the hill—whatever the draw was for her there. She circled three times before those sturdy legs of hers finally got going in the right direction. Ralph wasn't kidding when he said people on Wren needed someone keeping an eye out for them.

Amelia, that's her name. Or Melia, as Macy calls her, unless his hearing's fading. Wasn't *Amelia* the name of that spectacular clipper that went down with no warning a few years ago? Right off the coast of Cornwall. Maybe hit an underwater boulder like the ones off Wren. Not to mention adventurous Amelia Earhart crash-landing an airplane. No wonder the name *Amelia* leaves him feeling unnerved.

And the niece, Allison. Sweet girl, good-looking all around. Got the finest legs he's ever seen. And enough composure to keep a tsunami wave at bay. If he were twenty years younger, even ten years younger . . .

That Virgil is an exceptional guy. But he's an idiot for not putting a ring on that woman's finger.

Approaching Seal Rock, Wallace slows *Lucy Jo*. The cove entrance is tricky to find, hidden unless you're searching from just the right angle. Once *Lucy Jo*'s in, she's invisible to passing traffic. Wallace ties up to the dock there with a bit of a thrill. Nothing around now but Wallace Bernard and the natural world. Twice, he's seen whales in the cove. None today. So far.

He collects the cage of mice and walks them off the dock. At the top of the beach, where grass grows ahead of the forest, he sets down the cage and props open the door.

Some people would tip and dump. Faster that way. But freedom ought to be embraced in its own time. Maybe the mice have gotten comfortable in the cage. Maybe they're napping or enjoying the warm sun on their shoulders. Once, he waited seventy-eight minutes for the last mouse to poke out its whiskers and scamper off.

See? Operation Relocate is evidence he doesn't leave important things unfinished. If only Melissa could see her dad in action now.

Seal Rock is remote and uninhabited, but it has cell service. He pulls out his phone and calls Vanessa, because he can't think of a plausible excuse for calling Melissa. His younger daughter wouldn't answer anyway, unless he used a pay phone and she didn't realize it was her dad calling. A pay phone—ha! A relic from the past, getting more and more outdated, not unlike him.

Vanessa's not answering her phone. Wallace clicks off without leaving a message. Young people don't listen to voicemail. They see you called and reply by text. They maybe call back if they need something. Sometimes they say they forgot you called, but that's unlikely. They might like to forget a detail their dad mentioned, but how could they completely forget their dad called?

The next time Vanessa texts or calls him, he'll be ready with a whopper of a temptation for getting her to Wren. A local outfit on a neighboring island is stocking Virgil's market with handcrafted kettle corn, not available on the mainland. Vanessa's never been able to turn down an opportunity to try an obscure brand of popcorn.

Wallace stands, stretches. The last mice have left the cage and are nibbling on clover. The Wren Henhouse provided a steady diet of pudding and peanut butter. Nice for short-term snacking, but largely sickening over the long term. "Enjoy the first day of the rest of your lives, guys."

It's a happy-go-lucky day. There's no reason to rush back to Wren. Just like for the mice, this is the first day of the rest of everyone else's lives, including

Wallace Bernard's. Following a wide trail from the beach, he snaps a photo of sunlight on cedar tree trunks and texts it to his daughters. Both of them.

When the trail forks, he chooses the path heading west. Twenty yards farther, he stops short at what he sees. Not the very last thing he'd want to find on Seal Rock, but definitely in the last one hundred.

24

Disturbance

A pile of garbage. Dumped behind the brush, right off the trail.

Wallace squints. Why cart garbage to Seal Rock?

He steps closer and pokes around. Not trash. More of a junk pile. Loose metal. Car parts. Bicycles. A red scooter. Inside a large, battered cooler, several cell phones and laptops. Under the right circumstances—or wrong circumstances, depending on perspective—everything could be resold.

He pulls the scooter free. Must have been a cute ride at one point. Now it's missing the engine, battery, other parts. The VIN's been rubbed out. No way to identify who the scooter belongs to.

Retracing his steps, he connects back to the main trail. Several hundred yards farther, the brush has been torn up. Branches broken, roots exposed. The disturbance must have happened a while ago, because young growth is crowding in. Pushing his way through, Wallace finds himself at the edge of a deep ravine. More junk at the bottom.

He steps back. Tries to wrap his head around the discoveries.

The stuff he found earlier on the side of the trail could be easily retrieved. But no one would come back for anything in this ravine. Whatever's down there is on its way to disappearing.

He peers over the ravine edge again. Looks like a scooter, similar to the one he found earlier. This one's yellow, though the color's dulling with time and neglect. Didn't Virgil mention Allison had a motorbike incident on Seal Rock? Same Allison who drives a bright yellow boat.

When Virgil answers Wallace's call on the second ring, Wallace starts talking. "You mentioned Allison had a motorbike incident on Seal Rock a while ago. I think I'm looking at the spot."

Virgil exhales. "We've been meaning to go back there. She has the well-intended but unreasonable notion she'd like to haul out the bike. It was borrowed."

"Yellow bike?"

"Yep."

"Well, there's no retrieving it. Not without bringing in a crane and tearing up the hillside." Wallace eyes the near-straight sides of the ravine, where a few trees are hanging on for dear life until a gust of wind will make them also disappear below. "Did Allison end up in the ravine? I don't see a way out."

"She landed partway down."

Wallace scans the terrain. Finds a hint of a scrambled edge. Steps back and waits for his head to stop spinning. Good golly, Allison survived that accident?

He exhales. "Funny thing, Virgil. Someone's been storing junk here on Seal Rock. Metal parts, mostly."

"Interesting." Virgil's tone indicates he's intrigued. Deep thinker, Virgil is.

"Interesting enough to investigate further?"

"Maybe."

Wallace lets Virgil roll with his thoughts until he's ready to speak again.

"Allison ran into a couple of people while she was there. A young girl who helped her. And a guy named Lester Locum, not at all helpful. Lives on Reclamation Island."

"What kind of not at all helpful?"

"At best, he didn't help Allison when he could have. At worst, he had other designs."

Wallace frowns. Not helping a woman in need, signature sign of being a twerp. "Was the girl with him old enough to look out for herself?"

"Hard to say."

Wallace swears. Someone's been maintaining the dock in an out-of-the-way cove. Someone's been dumping junk for resale, maybe hiding stolen goods. Someone's toting around a girl, maybe taking advantage. Are they the same person? Are more yahoos coming and going from Seal Rock?

He rubs his chin. "Think I'll head over to Reclamation. See if I run into this Locum fella."

Once *Lucy Jo* clears Seal Rock, Wallace angles the boat north until a beat-up shrimping vessel appears around the island's southeast point. Two guys on board, unless there's more out of sight. The shrimper edges into the cove and disappears from view.

Temporarily abandoning his plan to go to Reclamation, Wallace cuts *Lucy Jo*'s engine and listens. After a few moments, the shrimper's engine is cut, the crew likely tying up at the dock. Wallace lights a cigar—blue-letter—and strategizes.

The shrimper was riding low with cargo, but there's no reason to deliver fresh seafood to an uninhabited island. Which means the cargo might be something else. For instance, more stolen goods. He can't enter the cove unnoticed. For now, he'll move far enough off Seal Rock to appear unconcerned, but close enough to see when the shrimper leaves. He'll need a convincing reason for being dead in the water. One that's clear from a distance.

A couple of giant saltwater fishing rods will do it. He props them and a big landing net along the gunwale. If anybody wonders, he's a less-than-ambitious geezer. Supposed to be making deliveries, but dropped a couple of lines because he heard the fish were biting.

Once the shrimper's underway, he'll follow and see what he can learn. A timeless strategy that usually works. And always guarantees a thrill.

25

Not complaining

That afternoon, inside the rehab aviary at the commune, Amelia dropped vitamin water into the open beak of a baby robin, then moved to the next cage to do the same for an injured starling. When all the rehabilitating birds were fed and watered, she tidied their cages, one at a time. Caring for sick, injured, or orphaned wildlife required focused effort. Not that she was complaining. From here on out, Amelia Theodore was no longer a complainer.

Ed or Judy or someone else from the commune usually helped with aviary chores. Today, Amelia was on her own. She glanced up at the flapping canvas roof, which had needed repairs for weeks. Through the tent's mesh sides, Amelia could see the goats up the hill chewing on their fence, needing a new toy or other distraction. Bored goats were destined to cause mischief.

Lately, it felt *too* quiet around the commune. One day last week, Amelia had spotted orcas off the western point of Wren, right where their songs would be picked up by the hydrophone, a tool scientists used to understand whales, especially the endangered Southern Resident orcas. But ever since Amelia had returned from Hawaii, no one seemed to be monitoring the underwater microphone, so no one hit the monastery-style bronze disk as a friendly way of alerting neighbors.

If Amelia could wave a magic wand, she'd prioritize monitoring the hydrophone. That's the way it used to be here at the commune. Right away when the gong sounded, everyone on Wren knew to open the app on their phones and listen to real whales singing in real time. Way better than a pre-recorded YouTube video.

If Amelia could wave that magic wand, she also wouldn't let dirty dishes pile up in the aviary sink. What did people expect to see happen around here? A fairy swishing in to make everything sparkle? Oh, there she went again, complaining about what could be. When she'd finished scrubbing, the stacks of bowls, cups, and reusable water bottles looked so tidy she almost snapped a photo for spic-and-span Allison.

With the aviary in order, Amelia removed her apron, smoothed her pink linen dress, and wandered up to the main building. Twenty-three short posts, rope strung between, marked her progress. She had a sneaking suspicion one reason for installing the posts and ropes all over Wren was to prevent poor Amelia Theodore from getting lost. More special allowances she hadn't asked for. And there she went again, sort of complaining.

She hadn't always been hangdog. Most people agreed Amelia Theodore was quite chirpy. Why did it feel like not just her vision but everything about her outlook was dimming now?

When she neared the courtyard, she heard arguing. One voice belonged to Ed, who hadn't gotten a postcard with cool surfer dudes on it, not that he would ever know. The other voice belonged to Judy, who'd been as companionable a friend as any, introducing Amelia to shampoo in bar form, no plastic packaging required. And inspiring Amelia to simplify her wardrobe and repurpose stuff.

Ed and Judy quieted when they saw Amelia. Fiddling with the handles of a gardening basket, Judy looked embarrassed, possibly apologetic.

"Here's our aviary assistant now!" Ed, turning on the charm. "Need help?"

Overall, Ed was a nice guy. A while back, he'd been johnny-on-the-spot when a wave knocked Amelia off her feet. Then Ed had helped hide Amelia's mishap from Macy, who would have put the kibosh on Amelia visiting the beach alone.

He saved Amelia's cell phone from becoming waterlogged. He'd taught her lots about whales and marine life too. For all that, she was grateful.

What drove her nuts, what really drove her entirely nuts, was Ed constantly asking if she needed help. Was that a full-on, bona fide complaint? Yes indeed. But the new Amelia Theodore didn't wallow around feeling sorry for herself.

"Thank you very much, Ed, but I didn't *need* any help in the aviary today. By the way, where is everyone? Away for summer?"

"Away forever." Judy sat on the low retaining wall of the courtyard's herb garden.

"Huh?"

Ed shrugged. "We've recently lost a few members. But we're rebuilding. That's one reason we're hoping you'll decide to join us."

Amelia pulled lightweight shears and a piece of hemp string from her apron pocket, leaned over the garden, and snipped a few sprigs of rosemary. She'd been considering the idea of joining the commune. While not whiz-bang, her skills were more in demand here than at Allison's house. She tied the string around the sprigs and added the bundle to Judy's basket. Living here would give her more independence, out from under Macy's watchful eyes. The only problem was it cost money to join. A *lot* of money, last time she'd checked.

Allison would pay the fees if Amelia asked. Wouldn't that be more of the same, though? Amelia Theodore depending on others instead of herself.

Still, if she wasn't around, who would care for the rehabilitating birds? Who would make sure the goats didn't chew their way out? Who would collect eggs from the chickens? Or listen for whales on the hydrophone?

She was already doing tons of work around the commune. The two differences between her and the other members were she didn't pay fees and she lived off-site.

"So what do you think?" Ed's voice held an urgent edge.

"Take your time deciding, Amelia." Judy smiled. "Make the best decision for you."

"I'll look over the contract you sent me a while back."

Ed tossed a bundle of scraggly dill into the basket. "Contract's changed. Just a few minor wording updates. I'll email you the new version."

You couldn't go through life thinking everyone was out to get you. But Amelia Theodore—yesterday's version, today's, and hopefully tomorrow's—knew enough to recognize a red flag.

26

Looking into it

The good news was Allison was super on board with the idea of Amelia being more independent and taking on additional responsibilities. The bad news was Allison *wasn't* super on board with the commune's membership fees and budget. She pointed to a line item. "Surely it doesn't cost this much to feed chickens?"

Amelia shrugged. "All the livestock and crops are raised organically. More expense, probably."

Shaking her head, Allison scrolled through the document. "It still doesn't add up. And I don't like how this contract makes it difficult to leave if you change your mind. What all do they do up there?"

Amelia ticked off the projects she knew. "Organic fruits, vegetables, and herbs. Free-range chickens for organic eggs. Goats for milk for making bar soap and shampoo. Rehabilitating injured or sick birds. Monitoring the hydrophone."

"I can see why you enjoy spending time there. Will you let me look more into the situation?"

"Sure." Pulling on a cardigan, Amelia sagged her way outside. Halfway to anywhere she was trying to go—that's where she always seemed to be. Making

YouTube videos and shell wreaths might be her life from here on out. Not a complaint, just an observation.

Less than an hour later, Allison jogged down the beach toward Amelia. "You'll never guess what I learned. I poked around on the internet and asked my financial adviser to investigate. The entire property is in arrears, Aunt Amelia. They haven't been paying their mortgage and other bills, and they're about to fold."

"What will happen to the birds? And the goats?"

Allison peered at her. "Aren't you at all concerned that these people nearly snagged you into a complicated financial situation?"

"I'm more concerned that Muffin Top, the quail with the broken wing, won't survive if someone doesn't feed her."

Reaching for Amelia's hand, Allison got Amelia's full attention. "I have an idea. I could make an offer to buy the property. Then we'd own it and you could take care of things however you want to."

Amelia blinked. Had the sand just shifted under her? "We could *own* the commune?"

"It would be a big responsibility. In addition to the projects you know about, the property is equipped to be a retreat center. If I buy it, the first thing I'll do is hire you to manage it. Depending on how many of the current commune members stay after the sale, we might need to hire help. And this is all *if* the current owners are willing to sell before going to foreclosure."

"Would purchasing the commune be a wise investment for *you*?"

"Part of the property borders mine, so the purchase makes sense. The owners' financial situation probably predisposes them to be agreeable to any offer, but I'd ask my agent to make a fair one. And I'd buy the place under a trust. It won't be a complete secret I'm the buyer, but it won't be obvious."

Nodding, Amelia squinted at Allison. "That's to avoid the possibility of them increasing the purchase price."

"Aunt Amelia, you're a natural businesswoman."

She studied the surf, always pushing, always in perpetual movement. Never sitting around expecting someone else to tell it what to do.

If Allison bought the commune, would Ed stay on? How would he feel about Amelia being his boss? Would Judy stay? Could Amelia manage a team, when she'd always been the one being managed?

She eyed her niece. Beautiful, strong, intelligent Allison, perfectly capable of taking care of everyone and everything. "Would you help me?" Her voice came out sounding as scared as she felt.

One arm around Amelia's shoulders, Allison nodded. "Of course I'll help you. Whenever you want. Even better, I'll *not* help you whenever you want. You've got this, Aunt Amelia. This could really be your thing."

27

Defensive moves

Virgil propped his feet on the stone edge surrounding the firepit at Allison's house, draped one arm around the shoulder of the woman he loved, and listened as Allison spun one idea after another for pouring her nearly unlimited resources into her latest project, the commune's transformation. Her enthusiasm for assisting others never stopped surprising him. Yesterday he'd thought she couldn't be more beautiful. Yet here she was today, glowing brighter.

"And buying the commune will be a smart investment because the property borders mine. It's got earning potential as an event venue or retreat center. We'll have to work to get it up and running, but Aunt Amelia can definitely manage it. I told her we'd be happy to help whenever she asked."

"We?" Tugging her closer, Virgil smiled, eyebrows waggling.

"Yes, *we*. Her entire family." Allison sent him a pointed look.

"Hmm." Pretending nonchalance, Virgil studied the firepit. Marriage would make him and Jax officially part of that family. But rather than pounce on that subject like Allison probably expected, he could stick with her topic. "Do you think it will stay a secret you're the one purchasing the property?"

Gazing into the forest, Allison sighed. "I won't be directly involved in any of the conversations. My financial advisor's office will communicate with the real estate agent. We'll offer a fair price, maybe more than fair. If the sellers get curious, they'll be able to find out who's buying. But they're eager to sell, and money is money. Keeping my identity quiet is just a precaution. Probably—hopefully—unnecessary."

Virgil rubbed one hand up the back of Allison's neck, repeating the motion, soothing tension—hers and his. Lately, Allison had become more willing to trust others. Look how she welcomed Wallace right away. Inherent wariness that had previously served as her armor was disintegrating. No wonder Virgil felt more need to beef up protection. Tackle any threats approaching from her blind side.

Allison is perfectly capable of taking care of Allison. He'd said it many times, to Allison and to others. He admired her for her independence. Longed to be part of her inner circle. Also longed to *be* her inner circle. The man she relied on. Her hero.

Maybe that was a problem. Not the fact Allison didn't need him. But the way he needed her to need him. To become less of herself so he could feel more powerful.

The idea that one person must lose for another to win was zero-sum thinking, a concept he'd learned during therapy. Crucial to athletic team rankings, but problematic in relationships. In the long run, one person becoming less for another to become more produced an unhealthy disequilibrium.

His hand stilled at the back of her neck, his every mental resource poured into analysis. Was zero-sum thinking why he'd held off on proposing? Was asking her to marry him asking her to relinquish the independence she treasured? Just so he could get what he wanted, keep her close, feel satisfied about being in a position to protect her.

Thinking of Allison fading into anything less than all she already was caused a horrific ache inside. As if life itself was being squeezed out of him.

Taking a breath, he shifted on the bench. Moved his hand again, running his fingers through the curls at the back of her neck.

"Where are you at, Virgil?"

Turning at the sound of her soft voice, he found her gazing at him. Everything in him resisted diving into the honest but complicated answer. "Tiny island in the Pacific Northwest. On a bench by a firepit. My arm around the woman I love."

"I mean where are you at with *us*."

Her brilliant brown eyes held his, demanding an honest answer. One without secrets behind it. What true answer could he say, given that he'd live with the consequences?

She inched away, the thinnest of veils clouding her eyes. "Is it the money? Am I too rich for you?"

If only that were the problem! Chuckling, he pulled her close again and kissed her forehead. "You're definitely too rich for me."

"I could give it all away."

"Absolutely not." Virgil cringed. Spoken like a man who expected his woman to do as he said, no questions asked.

He tugged at a curl and clarified. "I mean, sure, give it away if you want. But not on my account, because it doesn't matter one way or the other to me. I've got a prenup in the works."

She gasped. He'd been waiting to spring that particular detail on her at just the right moment, and the effect was every bit as satisfying as he'd hoped.

When she tucked in, he pulled her closer. Breathed her lemon-scented hair, silky and golden. "I don't have a lot to offer, Allison."

"You're already everything, and offering everything."

"Let me finish."

"Okay, boss."

Exactly the kind of comment he did *not* want his future wife saying. Huffing, he plowed on. "I'm a middle-aged man—"

"We were born less than six years apart, and I certainly don't feel middle-aged."

He kissed the top of her head. "Because you're timeless. Somehow more gorgeous today than you were yesterday. Tomorrow I'll wake up and find you've transformed to be even more stunning, though I can't imagine how you could be more breathtaking than you are at this moment."

"Wow. You really know how to make a girl swoon."

"So I've been told. Many times, many places."

The teasing comment earned him a whack on the arm. Pulling her close again, he continued.

"I've got a few bucks in the bank. A business that stays out of the red most of the time." Thinking of his measly bank account and the inherent woes of owning a small business, he closed his eyes. No, he wasn't marrying Allison for her money. But might other islanders wonder if he was?

"I could help financially with the market, if you want."

He knew her offer came only from the truest benevolence, not pity or oblig-ation. But the Tagaloa men had gotten along fine so far, and he intended to keep his business independently financed. "I appreciate that, but I'd rather you didn't."

"You know where to find me if you ever change your mind."

An in-house bank called Allison Theodore. Small wonder if islanders viewed their relationship with raised eyebrows. He shuffled through more of his assets, so to speak.

"I've also got a teenage son working through the effects of abandonment by his mother."

"I'm sorry for that. I want to help, if I can."

"That's support I welcome." A vision of Crystal's postcard, softened by Jax's hands and tears, flashed through Virgil's mind. Just as quickly, he squashed the image. Not the time to bring up the card.

Catching his gaze, Allison threw him a flirty smile and fluttered her eyelashes. "You've also got a nifty boat. Any girl would be impressed by *Incremental*. Especially with you behind the wheel."

The way Allison was looking at him made him think he ought to shift into high gear and propose right now, sitting at the firepit with his arm around the woman he loved. *Hello, wedding. Hello, honeymoon.* All delivered at top speed.

"And you stock my favorite brands at the store. Check on my aunts." She ticked off on her fingers assets he hadn't thought of yet. "Play with the dogs. Fix things around my house. Hold me whenever I need to be strong enough again. You know how to make me feel like I'm worth a million."

He tapped her on the shoulder. "You are worth a million. And then some."

"Ha! You've also got a sense of humor. Brains. Brawn. Courage. You're the whole package, Virgil Tagaloa."

He breathed deep, letting her love settle over, around, and through him.

"But you don't want to propose, for some reason." The edge to her tone signaled he'd missed a key piece of subtext.

"What?"

Pulling away, she looked at him, disappointment drawn across her face. "For whatever reason, you're having trouble with the actual proposal part. I thought you were waiting for me to be ready. Turns out it's you who's not ready."

"That's not true!"

How could she think he wasn't ready to marry her? He'd wanted to from the beginning! Well, *this* discrepancy was easily settled. "Allison Theodore, will you marry me?"

She rolled her eyes—not the response he'd imagined. Not at all.

Then she nodded, serious. "Yes, I will marry you."

The words were the answer he'd been hoping to hear, but the conditional tone wasn't. He tried to backtrack to the point where their conversation had gone off the rails. To blazes with subtext! He needed her to spell things out. "I don't understand. What's going on with us?"

Standing, she pulled him to his feet. "I've been ready to say yes for a while now. But for whatever reason, you're holding back. I love you, Virgil. I want us to share a life together. You said my secrets would be safe with you. The flip side of that is your secrets, whatever they are, should be safe with me too."

"I'm not keeping secrets."

She shook her head. "I trust you're not keeping secrets intentionally. Maybe something's happening inside that you haven't figured out yet. Until we both understand what's going on in that marvelous mind of yours, marriage doesn't seem a smart idea."

"I don't want you running off again."

Blundering idiot! He'd really messed things up by blurting that comment. Didn't require a marvelous mind to figure out she was heading from annoyed to angry and at a frightening clip.

Hands on her hips, she leveled a gaze at him. "Do I look like I'm running off?"

He took in her firm stance and glinting eyes. "For someone your size, you look surprisingly like a defensive tackle preparing to rush the quarterback."

"I don't want to *tackle* you. But if I go inside the house now, will you think I'm running off?"

"I guess not."

"All right then. See you tomorrow?"

Say goodnight with still so much unsaid between them?

He reached for her. Drew her close, closer, until she softened. Helping Allison Theodore be strong enough again.

Finding her ear, he whispered. "See you today, tomorrow, and the day after."

"And the day after that?" Her voice was muffled in his neck.

He dipped his head, breathing in everything that was the woman he loved.

"Yes, darling. The day after that too."

She tucked in, just the way he loved because it let him wrap his arms around her more firmly.

Her next words came out in the sweetest of tones. "Do you want to watch a movie tonight? That remake of *Pride and Prejudice* I've been telling you about?"

Smiling into her hair, he nodded. Of course she'd ask when he was willing to do anything for her. Even watch a drawn-out romantic saga cluttered with historical references to a piece of literature he'd never understood.

"Sure, let's watch that movie tonight." When he felt her smile against his chest, he held her closer.

28

Partly an act

The sun is working its way toward the horizon when the sound of the shrimper's engine disturbs the peace. A few moments later, the vessel emerges from the cove. Riding higher, with less or lighter cargo, she moves into the strait, heading north. Wallace stows the fishing rods and, after a couple of false starts with *Lucy Jo*'s engine, follows at a distance.

Ending up at Reclamation Island's marina is no surprise. The shrimper moors at an assigned slip, and Wallace selects a temporary slip nearby. He writes the shrimper's ID and name, *Pinch Hitter*, in a spiral notebook Ralph keeps at the helm. Mental notes aren't as easily recalled as they used to be.

The two dudes tying up the shrimper have seen Wallace but haven't acknowledged him. They might recognize *Lucy Jo*, be familiar with Ralph, wonder about Wallace. So he'll be the mostly clueless friend helping out. Which is only partly an act.

"Hiya!" He waves like a harmless geezer, also only partly an act. "Nice day, huh?"

They maybe nod, maybe don't. One of them stays on board while the other hoofs it up the dock. Wallace takes his time tying up. This part is unexpected, the two dudes going separate ways. Should he keep watching the guy babysitting the boat or follow the one who left? Which one's more likely to be Lester Locum?

Wallace kicks around the dock. Acts casual and curious about banal stuff like how tightly the cleats are screwed in and how much kelp is hanging off the pilings. Appearing to be a half-witted old guy can tempt a young dude to puff up and tell stuff he knows, just for the sake of appearing superior. Wallace is kicking tires that act as bumpers when Runaway Dude returns and sets *Pinch Hitter* chugging out of the marina again. They didn't even stay long enough to eat a meal!

Following them now will blow his cover. He drew too much attention by arriving the same time they did. Sensible option is to hang around Reclamation Island and wait for them to return.

On Main Street, a pub called The Turkey & Hambone reminds him of his bowling days. Three consecutive strikes, a turkey. Four consecutive strikes, a hambone.

Inside, he chooses a stool at the bar with a view of marina traffic. Orders a turkey pot pie with a side of ham because the ingredients are front of mind. Enjoys an Irish red ale because tonight's a new moon. *Cheers, John!*

Outside, a multilevel vehicle ferry arrives, unloads, reloads, leaves again. Will Wren Island ever be serviced by a public ferry? Bring in more riffraff for Macy Johansson to boss around.

Wallace keeps to himself, not looking for conversation, but has to give credit to the friendly folks of Reclamation Island when one after another says hi. Doesn't seem like the kind of place to tolerate hooligans, but there's no accounting for what people will put up with.

Anyway, he doesn't have anything solid on Lester Locum—or anyone else around here. Yet.

29

Reverse sunset

Waiting for his meal at the pub, Frank drummed his fingers on the bar. Twisted his stool in circles a couple of times. Said hi to folks he recognized and one or two he didn't. Watched a reverse sunset light the islands east of Reclamation with a brilliant orange hue.

When his burger arrived, he tore into it. Nothing like The Turkey & Hambone's bacon and goat cheese burger, topped with microgreens, sandwiched into buttery brioche, followed by a strawberry shake. He was celebrating. Clean one year, six months, twenty-three days. Best string of days since before he got addicted to drugs.

He might not have his job for long though. Lately, Bilbo had been hinting about cutting bait. Commercial fishing was tough enough for a young man, let alone an old guy finding it harder to leave the warmth of home. The last few outings with *Jeannette*, the crew worked their tails off and didn't get their limit.

Speaking of old guys, Frank's ears perked up when the one parked at the other end of the bar, another down-and-out fisherman maybe, placed his order with Eli. "Turkey pot pie, side of ham, Irish red." Frank nodded to himself. Irish red had always been his go-to also. Sometimes more than it should have been.

The old guy looked familiar, but Frank couldn't place where he'd seen him. Probably just around the island. Caught looking at him, Frank nodded hello before returning his attention to his fries, adding plenty of ketchup. Reclamation was a real friendly island. People talked to each other, even when they didn't know each other.

That's how Frank had gotten to know more about pub co-owner Eli Orsini and his wife, Gemma Campana. Learned she used to be a superstar cellist, even recorded Hollywood movie soundtracks. No commercial fisherman worth his salt would do more than glance in the direction of her frilly tea shop next door. Though it was universally acknowledged Gemma herself was worth sneaking a lingering glance.

The shop always seemed bubbling over with gabbing girls, some close to Frank's age. What did girls do in a tea shop? And how would anyone ever use up all that stashed yarn? Every so often, the door between the pub and Gemma's place would stand open long enough to allow classical music to mingle with the pub's pop music. And let a sweet scent waft past. Freshly-baked cookies, maybe.

Without looking toward the marina, Frank knew when the ferry arrived. A load of tourists burst into the pub, fresh-faced and ready for dinner on the first night of their much-anticipated vacation. Head down, Frank finished his fries.

After the guy at the other end of the bar announced the weather was hot and raised his voice over the tourist ruckus in the booths to order another Irish red, Frank waved at Eli and ordered a Dr. Pepper. The strawberry shake was gone, and it'd be hard to occupy the bar along with another Irish red without a drink of his own.

A couple of girls entered the pub, grabbed a booth by a window like they owned the place, and opened up bags to pull out . . . Yarn! Frank threw a glance in the direction of Gemma's tea shop. Seriously, was every girl on Reclamation preoccupied with yarn? One girl at the table was wearing a wedding ring. The other wasn't but was glammed up as if expecting to shop on Fifth Avenue, not duck into a pub in a town with a single four-way stop.

Between sips of Dr. Pepper, Frank studied her. She probably wouldn't last long on Reclamation. She'd hightail it home, wherever that was, the first morning she woke up to smelly seaweed exposed by a super low tide.

Plus, a sadness about her made her seem like she'd recently been through a wringer, so she probably wasn't receptive to being picked up by a guy. Even a guy with six staggeringly white crowns.

Frank sighed. Lonely was something he could handle. Been there, done that, still surviving.

Just when Frank was thinking of packing it in for the night, Bilbo strode in and leaned on the bar. "We're heading out. Big run happening to the southeast."

Frank squinted at the deepening blue sky. "It'll be dark soon."

"If we get a limit, I'll add a percentage of the catch to your pay."

Plopping cash on the counter, Frank downed the last of his Dr. Pepper and nodded to Eli as he followed Bilbo out the door. A chorus of good-natured cheers followed them. On the boardwalk, Frank glanced through the windows back into the pub at the slaphappy tourists—and the old dude at the bar still hunched over his Irish red.

Striding down to the dock with Bilbo, Frank felt optimistic. Already, stars were twinkling in the sky. On a calm night like this, with minimal wind and waves, and strategic use of spotlights, fish might rise to the surface asking to be caught. When he called his mom tomorrow to tell her about it, she'd get a proud tone in her voice.

30

Fragility

When the next Irish red arrives in a glass covered with condensation, Wallace mops it with a napkin, then swipes the cool, damp cloth across his eyes. To make certain anyone watching knows *why* he's mopping his face, he calls it straight out. "Sure is hot today." The young guy at the other end of the bar nods. *Yep, real hot today.*

Wallace has finished his meal, best he's had in a long time, and is eking out the last of his ale when he notices two women in their thirties sitting across from each other in a booth, finagling yarn into a craft. They're chatting, but cautious. As if they want to know each other but are scared to reveal too much. Push and shove. Give and take. A friendship unfolding right before his eyes. He watches, head down and pointed in the opposite direction, in classic surveillance mode.

When one of the women stands and heads for the restroom, Wallace averts his eyes and focuses on his drink. Then he glances back at the woman still at the table, dressed for a corporate business deal, not for relaxing on island time. She sees him looking, holds his gaze, and a jolt slams into his chest. In this stranger's eyes, he recognizes a familiar fragility. She's recently come back from the abyss that others don't come back from. Made the choice to climb up, go on, keep breathing. She's here. And in this moment, that's the only thing that should matter to anyone.

He offers a small smile. She smiles back, a genuine it's-good-to-be-alive smile, even when you're a fish out of water—or in this case, a city girl in a small-town pub. When she looks away, he looks away too, because now everything inside him is in turmoil again.

Here's someone right here, right now, boldly facing the day because she somehow crawled across to the other side instead of giving up. Wish John would have made it. Wish John would have come back to offer a tentative smile.

A brief ruckus erupts when a fisherman strides in and reports a supposed run to the southeast. Several guys leave the pub. Later, the carefree tourists eventually fade out too.

After a few more ales—long live the mighty Irish—Wallace has forgotten what he was trying to stuff down. Maybe has a better grip on whatever he was losing control of.

It's fully dark when he swaggers down to the marina. Been a long time since he's felt this way. Footloose and encumbered, all at once.

The shrimper he followed to Reclamation, *Pinch Hitter*, is tied up again. So much for Wallace Bernard's surveillance skills. A couple of commercial fishing vessels are exiting the marina, testing spotlights across the channel as they go. Or is it one vessel testing one spotlight? He might be seeing double, thanks to commemorating another moonless night.

He unties *Lucy Jo* and casts off—clumsily, but not too bad considering the circumstances. He grins when *Lucy Jo* starts up right away, no hiccup. Then he heads home.

Home?

Wren Island is what he meant.

31

Drifting

Problem is, just before entering the strait, *Lucy Jo* runs rough, then gives up. Wallace cranks the engine. Tinkers around, sort of, with fuel filters and other stuff that's a strain to focus on with bleary eyesight, but he can't get the engine going again. Throwing down an anchor would be useless in this depth. Radioing for help would be the responsible choice.

He'll drift instead and hope he doesn't end up on the rocks—figuratively and literally. Maybe the downtime will help *Lucy Jo* make up her own mind about running again. Ralph prepared for a situation like this by keeping aboard a near-full bottle of whiskey and a battery-powered boom box loaded with Roger Whittaker. Wallace sings along. "New world in the morning takes so long."

When his cell phone rings, Wallace nearly drops it overboard fumbling to answer through the floatable, waterproof case. Any boater with half a brain knows not to risk losing their phone. Good golly, do cell phone buttons get smaller with each update? He clears his throat and swipes to answer Vanessa's call.

"Dad? I think I need your help."

He snaps to awareness.

"Ryan got out of jail this afternoon. On a technicality."

Wallace only just stops himself from swearing. Keeps it inside, instead of what he wants to do, rage at the increasingly black surroundings. Years of feigning fearlessness are worth something, though, and his voice comes out sounding stable and authoritative.

"Vanessa, pack up the kids. Get yourselves to the airport. I'll email you tickets to Seattle. Don't tell anyone where you're going."

"I thought I'd—"

"We'll talk about it once you're here." Should he tell her how serious the situation is? If Ryan Robinson heads straight back to Vanessa, his so-called business associates on his tail . . . No, better to not give her any reason to panic. Go for lighthearted instead. "Hey kiddo, if you're not with me by tomorrow, check the news. Your dad will have made headlines going AWOL because he's worried about you."

She laughs. An encouraging sign. He exhales, and the other bit she mentioned resurfaces. "What kind of technicality?"

"Ryan's attorney, Carl Grimwald, says there's proof Ryan was set up."

Wallace freezes, on the outside and on the inside. If the attorney knows, who else knows? With all the precautions Wallace took, what did he miss? What did he overlook? Worse, has he been ratted out? He switches his cell phone to speaker mode and opens a rideshare app. "I'm arranging for a car to pick you up in . . . eight minutes."

"I need to pack."

"No time. Please, *please* trust me on this, Vanessa. Do not tell *anyone* where you're going."

"I want Melissa to know."

"Okay. But neither of you can say anything to anyone else. Do you under-stand?" He describes the rideshare vehicle and identifying license, ends the call, purchases the airline tickets, emails them to Vanessa.

Then he calls Virgil. "I need a big favor."

"Just a sec." Virgil's voice sounds muffled. Wallace waits intolerable seconds while other sounds indicate Virgil's phone is being moved around. Allison's voice filters through. Then Virgil's back on, clearing his throat. "Can it wait until tomorrow? I'm watching a movie with Allison."

"It can't wait until tomorrow, Romeo." Hearing his sharp tone, and imagining Virgil's surprised and possibly hurt expression, Wallace winces but plows on. "My daughter and her kids are in danger. Bad guy might be after them. Long story, too long to tell right now. I've booked them a flight to Seattle that arrives after midnight. Can you pick them up and bring them to Wren? *Lucy Jo*'s engine has gone wonky and I'm stranded. I know it's a lot to ask of you, to pick up my family at the airport, last-minute notice, middle of the night. You and I don't know each other well, and I can understand why you wouldn't—"

"No problem, Wallace. I'm getting ready to go right now. Text me the flight info and your daughter's name. How old are the kids?"

"Nathan's three, Natalie's one."

"Hang on, Allison's trying to tell me something."

Wallace inches toward optimism. Johnny-on-the-spot Virgil is preparing to help! Virgil's clear-eyed girl is part of the conversation too! Solid intel that eases the burden a fraction.

Virgil comes back on, sounding decisive and capable. "On my way. Taking *Buttercup*. Allison's right about the bunks being nicer for sleepy kids to nap in."

"You'll need to show ID to my daughter and use a code word."

"A code word?"

"My daughters and I use a code word that means *Trust me*. Vanessa will expect you to show ID and use the word *persimmon* within the first few sentences of talking with her."

"Could say I was thinking of stocking them at the market?"

"That'll work."

"Okay. Hope *Lucy Jo* gets going again soon. See you on Wren."

Once Virgil's zipping toward the Seattle airport in *Buttercup*, thoughtfully chosen for the comfort of weary travelers, Wallace heaves a sigh. Thanks the gods—especially the prison minister's god—that a guy named Virgil Tagaloa on Wren Island cared enough to answer the phone when Wallace called.

After tinkering around in *Lucy Jo*'s engine room with a weakening flashlight, Wallace has to admit the worst. In the wheelhouse, he pulls out Ralph's insurance paperwork and calls a marine towing company. Learns rigs equipped to help a vessel of *Lucy Jo*'s size are either out on other calls or in the maintenance yard. Shaking his head, Wallace agrees to be put near the top of the priority dispatch list.

Then he downs the remaining coffee in the cooling pot. If he's going to hand over Ralph's insurance information, he'll need to be straight-up sober. Another round through the engine room yields nothing helpful. He heads back up on deck. Remembers—better late than never—to switch on the appropriate lights indicating *Lucy Jo* is not making way.

Then he's got nothing. Just a drifting boat that isn't his. A mental checklist of details he might have overlooked, loose ends he might not have wrapped up. A clawing fear that a bad guy wants to hurt people Wallace would be willing to die to protect.

Add to that, he's got a lifetime of not doing enough. Not being around when someone needed him. Not saying what needed to be said. Not saying anything at all when he should have known to say *something*.

There are words he needs to say to Vanessa. Words he's needed to say for her entire life, and if ever she ought to know, it's now. He reaches for his phone again. Three words. *I love you*. The call goes through, rings a few times. Vanessa's probably digging through her purse in the rideshare backseat, the sleepy tykes next to her wearing their jammies.

"Dad?"

"Vanessa, listen. I just want you to know . . ."

But if he says it now, when he's never said it before, what will Vanessa think? She must know, by how he reacted earlier, that her physical safety is in danger. If he says the other words, those three important words, will Vanessa panic? For the next few hours, his daughter needs to be levelheaded.

He clears his throat. "I just want you to know I ordered in-flight meals so you and the kids don't have to take time to eat before boarding. You're on your way to the airport?"

"Five minutes away. Thanks for doing all this, Dad."

In the background, one of the kids jabbers, and Wallace is certain he hears the word *grampy*. His favorite word in the entire world, especially when it comes from a tiny voice under the brim of a pint-size cowboy hat.

"A guy named Virgil Tagaloa will pick you up at the airport. He'll show you ID and use the code word right away."

Vanessa laughs. "Melissa and I loved using the code word when we played spy as kids. We're pulling up to the airport now. Bye, Dad. Love you."

He almost says *Love you* back. Then she's gone, and for a long while, there are only are few sounds. Rhythmic waves hitting the side of the boat. A ferry's foghorn—so far off it doesn't matter. And Roger Whittaker making sense of the world.

Later, he's drifted into an area without cell service, and *Lucy Jo* hasn't given up any secrets to her recovery. Vanessa and the kids are at cruising altitude, eating cheeseburgers, chicken nuggets, carrot sticks, and oatmeal raisin cookies. Virgil's within an hour of the airport. It's reasonable to expect this dark night to end like every other has by turning into a new day.

Now, though, the expanding blackness can't be ignored. The massive emptiness crowds closer. There's no reason, none at all, to pretend Wallace Bernard has more than a perilously slipping grip on anything within his reach. No reason to not let himself fall deep into the rising lament.

He whispers for help first because he doesn't know where to start. When did tears last flow like this from his tired eyes? Raising his voice feels better than whispering. He gets louder, much louder, and with every wail, he sends another bit of his fractured life into an ocean so vast it can absorb anything.

No one's around to hear. Or care. Except maybe the prison minister's god, who, from what everybody says, ought to be able to handle it.

32

The need to shield

Navigating *Buttercup* south toward Seattle, Virgil kept a wary eye out for floating debris. Loose logs or pilings, lost fishing gear, anything that might cause a scratch—or worse. Tomorrow morning, Allison would casually but very intentionally inspect her returned boat.

He did the same whenever Allison borrowed *Incremental*. Concerned about whether Allison had been safe on the water. Also concerned about the way she tended to allow less than ideal time between gear switches, especially when she felt nervous bringing *Incremental* up to a crowded dock. He'd like to avoid an expensive transmission repair.

One thing he never had to worry about when Allison returned his boat was crumbs or spills. Reaching for his travel mug, he confirmed the coffee wasn't leaving drips in the cup holder.

During their phone conversation earlier, Wallace had sounded calm and authoritative—but also as if he were keeping frantic fear under wraps. In Virgil's experience, the need to shield another person from the full extent of fear usually indicated the worst kind of threat. Hearing a bad guy might be after Wallace's daughter and kids, any self-respecting person would hup two and steam down to Seattle.

Persimmon. That's the word Wallace said Virgil could use so Vanessa Barone would know to trust him.

Virgil frowned. What kind of trouble was this girl in? Should he be concerned about anyone following her? Would bringing Vanessa to Wren attract someone undesirable to the island?

If there was one thing Virgil had learned over the years, it was to be vigilant about potential threats to those he loved. He tried—and failed—to keep his ex-wife safe. He'd been more successful at protecting Jax, though there'd been mishaps over the years. Now that Jax was a teenager, it was probably time to make adjustments, but Virgil would never be able to entirely back off of looking out for his son. With Allison in the mix now, and with the way she got herself into unexpected pickles . . . Sometimes he felt like a full-time bodyguard. He didn't mind. It'd always been a sort of passion of his to protect those he loved.

Had he told Allison he loved her today? Maybe he did, back at the firepit when they were arguing about, of all things, whether he was ready to propose. They ended up snuggling under a blanket in Allison's television room. Sort of watching the dreaded *Pride and Prejudice*, which turned out to be more appealing than he'd expected. By some small miracle, their first interruption was Wallace's phone call. The aunts were getting better at knowing when to give them privacy.

Feeling a chill in the air, Virgil rechecked the weather reports. Clear skies, minimal wind, mostly smooth seas, but temperature dropping. Good thing Allison had opted to remain snug at home rather than make the trek to Seattle. He bumped up the heat in the wheelhouse.

After checking his gauges and scanning the area, he refocused his gaze on the water ahead and moved into the shipping lane. He'd be at the Seattle port in less than an hour, get a rideshare to the airport, meet Wallace's family, bring them back to *Buttercup*, cruise home.

Using his phone's hands-free option, he called Allison and didn't waste a second when she answered. "Have I told you I love you today?"

"Does that romantic, carefully thought-out marriage proposal by the firepit count?"

"You think that was romantic? Wait until you see what I've planned for improving the woodpile. Stacking cords by texture and color, just for you."

She laughed. "How's *Buttercup* behaving for you? You're a hero, you know. Taking off in the dead of night to pick up a stranger at an airport in a city you'd rather avoid. Wallace chose the right person to call for help. I miss you already."

Grinning, Virgil checked the time. If the airport pickup went as scheduled, he'd soon be back on Wren. Within touching distance of the woman he loved. The woman who said she missed him right at this moment. Same woman who could laugh at a botched marriage proposal.

After glancing around again at his surroundings, Virgil resumed looking ahead and sighed. "Can't wait to be back home with you."

"You've hardly been gone any time at all!"

"But didn't you just say you miss me? Reason enough to turn around, speed back to Wren, sweep you off your feet and confirm you were right to miss me."

"Oh Virgil." Her tone indicated she thought him ridiculously silly. He also heard the contented smile behind her words.

He pictured her putzing around her luxurious house, safe and warm. "You wearing your fancy peacock bathrobe?"

"Is that where this conversation is going? You saw me in that bathrobe *one time*, when a hotel fire required emergency evacuation. We won't have any sirens tonight, Virgil."

No sirens calling him except alluring Allison Theodore. Smiling, he drummed his fingers on *Buttercup*'s wheel.

"I've been tracking *Lucy Jo*." Of course she was. "Very little movement. And no signals from nearby vessels on their way to help. Wouldn't Wallace have called for a tow by now? He probably wants to get back to Wren as soon as possible, with his daughter on her way."

"And possibly in trouble."

"How so?"

Virgil repeated what Wallace had told him, details Virgil hadn't had time to relay before he left. "The situation's so shifty I'm supposed to show ID and use a code word when I meet Vanessa. *Persimmon*. It means 'trustworthy' in their family. I'm going to say I'm thinking of stocking persimmons at the market."

"Seriously?"

"I'm not actually considering it. Unless you'd like me to?"

"Like you to what?"

"Stock persimmons. It sounded like you might be pleased with the idea."

"I was exclaiming over using a code word when you meet Vanessa. I don't care whether you stock persimmons. It's your market."

He reined in the snort laugh that almost burst out of him and relaxed into the comfortable silence between them. *His* market? On paper, yes. But even without Allison's financial assistance, the market was undergoing a major overhaul. Her most recent improvements were to straighten and label everything in and around the cash register. Small bags, large bags, shopping baskets. The money drawer itself. Seasonal impulse items.

More and more, the market felt predictable but also fresh and new. His entire life was being gloriously influenced by the woman he'd chosen to love. Watching Allison Theodore be her brilliant self was one of the most fascinating things he'd ever witnessed.

Through the phone, he listened to her draw a deep breath and let it out slowly, the way she did when attempting to ground her thoughts. "With the code word and all, this situation with Vanessa and the kids rushing to Wren sounds incredibly high-stakes. I doubt Wallace will want to sit around waiting for *Lucy Jo*'s mechanical problems to be fixed. Maybe I should go get him."

Shoot. He should've known Allison wouldn't be able to stay put in an emergency. "Oh, I don't think—"

"When the tow arrives, I'll zip him back to Wren. We'll get home around the same time you arrive with his family."

He gritted his teeth at her determination, which he both feared and admired. Even if *Buttercup* hadn't already been on her way to Seattle, her pristine high sides, nice for cutting arcs through the water, would have made it harder for Allison to pull close enough to *Lucy Jo* for Wallace to hop over. "Take *Incremental*. She's designed for bumping against another vessel for passenger transfer."

"I'll ask Aunt Macy to go with me. She can boss the tides and currents into doing what we want them to."

Conflicted, Virgil both chuckled and shook his head. Allison should have someone with her. If necessary, no-nonsense Macy would hold her ground as well as anyone might with Allison. But during Macy's most recent driving lesson with *Incremental*, she'd nearly caused irreparable damage by assuming low-grade fuel would fix a "funny sound" that ended up being the door of the galley refrigerator flapping open.

"*Incremental* respectfully requests Allison drive, not Macy." At the sound of the woman he loved laughing lightly, he smiled.

"All right, it's decided. I'll go get Wallace in *Incremental*." That was his girl, going out of her way to help a neighbor. Pleased to, even when she'd rather stay home.

"Keep me posted how it's going. Be careful, hon. And I mean be careful with *you*, more than *Incremental*. Love you."

"Love you too. That's twice today you've said you love me. Three times if you count your bang-up marriage proposal."

They were both still chuckling when she ended the call. It took every ounce of his strength to not turn around and go back to her right then and there. Why all this leaving all the time? Why couldn't two people in love stay with each other every moment, every day, forever?

For now, he could only indulge in imagining Allison in his arms, which he did, happily, until his phone erupted with "Forever Young," Jax's ringtone. "What's up, kiddo?"

"Dad, something awful's happened."

The most recent "awful" news had been two new zits emerging on Jax's still distressingly hairless chin. Virgil glanced out the wheelhouse's windows, then settled in the captain's chair. "Go on."

"Are you driving anywhere you need to pay full attention? You might want to slow down."

"Out with it, Jax." But his son's voice was shaky enough Virgil eased off the throttle.

"Wallace's daughter just called the store. Said there's been an accident. Her sister's plane crashed."

Jax's words only halfway registered. A plane crash? Virgil must have missed key information. Or Jax confused the report. Virgil squinted at the inky water ahead. "Wallace has two daughters? Which one called the store?"

"Melissa."

"Melissa? Not Vanessa?"

"How could Vanessa call? She was on the plane that crashed. With her kids."

The horrifying reality sank in. Moving out of the shipping lane, Virgil slowed *Buttercup*'s speed more and switched the vessel to autopilot. A quick news search on his phone revealed a plane bound for Seattle had crashed in a Nebraska cornfield.

Gripping his phone, as if doing so could bring his son closer, Virgil steadied his voice. "Jax, how certain are we Vanessa was on that flight?"

"From all the crying Melissa was doing, pretty sure, I guess. She's at the Seattle airport. Can you pick her up?" Jax's voice cracked. "Instead of her sister?"

"I don't understand. Why is Melissa at the Seattle airport?"

"She was going to come from there to Wren with Vanessa and surprise Wallace."

"Does Wallace know that now? Did he tell her to call the market?"

"No. She can't get him on his cell phone and said she called the store hoping to find someone who could reach him."

"So Wallace might not know yet. About the crash."

Except for the low rumble of *Buttercup*'s engine, a solemn silence engulfed Virgil and Jax.

An hour or two ago, Wallace had been able to call Virgil from *Lucy Jo*. Why wasn't Wallace answering calls now?

Muffled sounds indicated Jax had set aside the phone to speak with someone. Allison! Preparing to leave with *Incremental*.

"Jax, hand the phone to Allison."

More muffled sounds.

"Jax?"

33

Beyond fast enough

"Dad?"

Finally! "Jax, hand the phone to Allison."

"Too late. She's already leaving."

Virgil didn't stop himself from swearing.

"Sorry, Dad." Jax's heavy tone deflated Virgil's sense of urgency.

"I'm not upset with you. You're doing fine, kiddo."

"You're upset with *Allison*?" The incredulity in Jax's voice would have been comical if the overall circumstances had been lighter. Had Jax never seen Virgil show annoyance toward Allison? The question was worth considering. Later.

"I'm upset about the situation, Jax. Not at a particular person."

A familiar engine roar reached through the phone. All three of *Incremental*'s motors powering Allison away from Wren, sounded like around thirty-five knots, well beyond fast enough to make Virgil feel uneasy. Soon the woman he loved would become a blip on the frigid ocean, approach a midsize vessel in distress, encounter a distraught skipper.

Virgil swallowed against his fear of the unknowns. "Is Allison aware Wallace's daughter was in a plane crash?"

"Yes, and she said—"

"Does she have anyone with her?"

"Macy. And Allison said it was important to tell you something right away."

Jax's lull and teenage concept of time were baffling. "And that is?"

"She likes persimmons."

Trust me.

Switching off autopilot, Virgil scanned the water in all directions and ticked up *Buttercup*'s speed. The woman he loved was undertaking her mission. His was to bring Wallace's family to Wren.

He talked through a few instructions with Jax, routine stuff that didn't need to be said but felt comforting to voice. "Most important, kiddo, remember you're the best thing that ever happened to me."

In the silence that followed, he could picture the teenager rolling his eyes. *Same old lovey-dovey stuff from Dad.* While Jax decided how to respond, Virgil checked his gauges.

"Dad?"

"Yep, still here."

"I might be the best thing that ever happened to you. But lately I've been wishing that best thing could be me *and* my mom."

Virgil's heart seemed to stop. That wish hadn't occurred to him. But of course Jax would desire it. Virgil cast about for an answer, though none could be entirely comforting, until Jax cleared his throat.

"I know that's not possible."

"I'm sorry, son."

"But the thing is, sometimes I feel like Allison's the best thing that ever happened to both of us."

Virgil smiled through the tears springing to his eyes. He'd tried to protect his son from life's worst agonies. Also tried to raise a young man with the habit of looking for the good. Unafraid of expressing gratitude. Undaunted by the prospect of going deep.

"So are we stocking persimmons now? At the market?" Jax's move of the conversation back to ordinary showed his typical resiliency, though his quick, nervous laugh indicated he was still shaken.

More than talk of code words, normalcy could be settling. "If I can find a supplier."

"You'd better get on that, Dad, because it sounds important to Allison." A resigned sigh emerged from his son. "I guess I'll make another label for the produce bins. Helvetica font, size regular. Allison will want it to match the others."

After ending the call, Virgil opened the throttle. The sooner he got to Seattle, the sooner he could turn around and go home. Be with his family again. Hold them close.

Waves of sadness washed over him as he imagined the horror of a young woman and her children dying in a fiery plane crash. The other passengers and crew too. The loneliness of an old man coming to Wren for a new start, then losing what must feel like his entire world.

Renewed grief from Virgil's own past emerged. Excruciating moments he wondered if he'd ever see his wife again. Nights a newborn screamed his need for a mother who'd passed out on the sofa. Conferences between a single parent and multiple teachers, full of questions and reprimands. Fumbling answers to challenging questions asked by a toddler, child, adolescent, young man.

Crystal's addiction had brought grief upon grief. Virgil had found saying goodbye to his ex-wife painful, but methodical—their parting of ways anticipated, prepared for.

Wallace hadn't been given such mercy, his daughter and grandchildren wrenched from him in a literal flash. Virgil couldn't believe losing Jax like that wouldn't kill him. Same for losing Allison.

Sometimes I feel like Allison's the best thing that ever happened to both of us.

Of course Jax would also experience grief upon grief. Mourn the loss of his biological mother, Crystal's postcard resurrecting the old, familiar sorrow of abandonment, just when Jax was learning to love a woman who represented all he had missed. A woman offering to be whatever Jax needed her to be. Doing her best to fit into their family, seamlessly.

Virgil straightened. Wished he'd thought to ask Jax whether Allison or Macy was behind the wheel when *Incremental* blasted off from the dock. Felt a pang of guilt for caring about trivialities at a moment like this. But if Macy wasn't careful how she drove . . .

He called Allison. "Jax told me about the plane crash. Everything okay on your end?"

"Aunt Macy's with me. Stuffing snacks into the fridge, although I can't imagine anyone's going to feel like eating. She keeps slamming the door closed in a most annoying way."

Virgil winced. But at least Macy wasn't behind the wheel. More important concerns needed his attention. Allison sounded breathless, upset. Had she instantly cried about Wallace's loss? Or was she holding back her tears? He pictured her being brave for the benefit of others, her silhouette lit by *Incremental*'s control dash adjusted to a dim setting for nighttime driving.

"I can't talk more, Virgil. I'm on the radio with nearby vessels requesting a tow."

"I understand. I'll monitor your channel. Is there anything else I can do?" He cringed at the stupid question. What help could he offer from this distance?

She didn't reply right away. Distracted? Needing a moment to pull herself together? "What I'd really love is for you to be there when I get home." *And hold me*, he heard, though she didn't say it.

"Count on it. Love you."

"Love you too." She clicked off the call.

He switched *Buttercup*'s radio channel to pick up chatter between *Incremental*, *Lucy Jo*, and any nearby vessels.

Buttercup could reach thirty knots in ideal conditions, though Allison preferred not to go over the recommended top speed of twenty-five. But what did Macy often say? *What Allison doesn't know won't hurt her.* Keeping *Buttercup* solidly in the southbound shipping lane, Virgil kept his eyes alert for debris in the water and his ears attuned to any warning from the engine, and pushed the speedometer as much as he dared—incrementally, of course.

When the lights of Seattle came into view, he slowed. Pulled near the assigned slip, eased into it. Then, exhaling, he nearly broke into a sob from the force of an overwhelming longing. For his family to be kept safe. For Allison to be protected from any threat to her extraordinary, sensitive heart. For Jax to grow into everything he was meant to be, always, forever.

Virgil wasn't too proud to beg. He'd done it before, many times. Would do it again, as often as needed. Tying up at the assigned slip, he breathed a familiar prayer.

Please, God, keep my family safe.

34

On the bridge

Frank decided fishing on a clear, windless night felt almost like a vacation. A million stars overhead. Sea air in the lungs. Fewer pleasure craft to work around. Not that the evening wasn't spent working hard.

"Good haul, guys." Bilbo beamed when the catch was determined a limit. Before angling *Jeannette* toward Reclamation, he provided celebratory drinks on the bridge—though with the jaunt back to Reclamation still ahead and with three mates avoiding alcohol, tame options were the name of the game. Frank chose a Dr. Pepper.

Bilbo toasted his crew, his boat, and God above for blessing them up to the limit. The crew toasted Bilbo, who held his stainless steel mug aloft until everyone fell silent, all eyes focused on him.

"After a run like that is as right a time as any to tell you I'm done." The mates exchanged questioning looks and shifted foot to foot while Bilbo drained his mug. "If any of you are of a mind to buy the boat, we'll draw up a deal. I'm getting too old for this."

Meeting Frank's eyes, Bilbo held them, then glanced at the rest of the crew. Frank wished he could afford the commercial fishing outfit. His mom, descended from all those Finnish fishing families she liked to mention, would say he was destined to make a living on the ocean.

But Frank's crewmate Matt spoke up first. "I'll buy if you'll accept payments. You boys can stay on." Matt grinned at them as if making a concession.

Frank stole another look at Bilbo, whose fidgeting confirmed Frank's judgment that Matt—lackadaisical about equipment maintenance, unconcerned by regulations, often scheming up a prank—would be a liability as a boss.

If Matt's plans to purchase the boat fell through, maybe Frank could work out a deal with Bilbo. Otherwise, maybe Frank ought to cut bait and move on. It'd be easier to think clearly about the options if his dad's voice wasn't running through his head. *What happened, Frank? Lose another job?*

The crackle of the marine radio interrupted them. A woman's voice reported her own vessel's identity and position, then requested an emergency tow for a different vessel, a seventy-three-foot cargo hauler with apparent engine and power failure, no established radio contact.

After confirming *Jeannette*'s coordinates, Bilbo reached for the radio handpiece and responded with an offer to help. They waited while skippers of other vessels responded they were less equipped and not as close.

Bilbo spoke into the radio again. "Captain Bilbo Churchill confirming *Jeannette* is en route to meet *Lucy Jo*." He clicked the handpiece back into place. "Look alive, boys."

The radio crackled to life again. Same woman, Allison Theodore. "If I meet you there and evacuate the skipper, will you tow *Lucy Jo* to Reclamation's shipyard?"

Bilbo affirmed the plan as *Jeannette* angled west. With a rush of adrenaline, Frank joined the other crew on deck, checking equipment and preparing towlines. Later, he'd tell his mom the story of whatever was about to happen. It'd be nice if his dad wanted to listen too.

35

Saying it

When Wallace has emptied lingering laments into the absorbing ocean, he is absolutely *finished*. With *everything*. Pretending to be a tough guy every stinking minute. Feigning fearlessness. What's wrong with being *real*, as Melissa says?

Everything will remain unfinished, though, until he says three words that need to be heard. He'll do that the moment he's got cell service again. Then get on the horn and insist on an emergency tow. His daughter and grandchildren are on their way to Wren! He's needed there.

During her flight, Vanessa may or may not have cell service. If she doesn't answer, he'll leave her a voicemail. She can listen or not. First thing when he sees his precious daughter, one of two gorgeous daughters he's loved forever and ever, he's saying three words that are more true than any others. He's wrapping his daughter and grandkids in a big hug. Maybe never letting go.

It's revitalizing, being this new version of Wallace Bernard.

He pulls out his phone—back in service!—and sees a number alerting him to five missed messages, more than he's had in years, even more than when Macy was pestering him about mice, though Macy didn't usually call in the middle of the night. He'll check the messages after making the most important call. He waits for Vanessa's voicemail to kick in.

"It's your dad. I just want to tell you I love you, honey. In case I never said it before. I love you. A lot. Well, bye. See you and the kids soon."

Then he calls Melissa. Why not? The new Wallace Bernard is on a roll with restructured priorities. When Melissa answers, he almost falls backward in surprise. "Melissa! I didn't think I'd get—"

"Dad? Where *are* you?"

He glances around, delighted the daughter who rarely speaks to him is showing interest. "I'm on a boat. Stranded north of—"

"You didn't get my messages?"

"No, my phone—"

"Dad, listen. Vanessa and the kids—"

"On their way here. She called you, right?"

"*Listen* to me! They won't . . . They won't get there."

The way his daughter is gulping for breath tightens his gut. Something is terribly wrong. "What are you saying?"

"Their plane. Crashed." She gulps again. "All gone."

All gone, all gone, all gone. His mind is replaying the singsong voices of the girls when they were little. Playing a game with him. He shows them his hands. *You see this, right? But look now! There's nothing in my hands. All gone.*

"Dad? Did you hear what I said?"

"I'm not sure."

"Their plane—"

"No! Don't say that. It can't be true. Where'd you get the information?"

"I don't want to say it. But it *is* true, and I *have* to say it." There's no uncertainty in her voice.

While she cries on the other end of the phone, he brings up the latest online news. Searching for any indication that what's happened hasn't happened. Every report is horrifically verified.

"Maybe they didn't get on the flight, Melissa! Lots of reasons they might have missed it. Maybe Vanessa dropped and broke her cell phone and couldn't show the tickets. Maybe security took longer than expected. Natalie might have needed a last-minute diaper change, or Nathan a snack. And Vanessa hasn't called to let me know because . . ."

All those missed messages! Scrolling through them, he finds calls and texts from Melissa, Virgil, Allison, Melissa again—and again.

Nothing from Vanessa.

Through tears, Melissa hammers home the truth. "I was contacted as next of kin. Vanessa, Nathan, and Natalie Barone boarded at 10:32 p.m. and sat in their assigned seats. The plane went down at 11:42 p.m. God in heaven, please have mercy. I can't bear to think the babies are gone too." Melissa wails, openly.

Slowly, Wallace opens his phone's list of time-stamped outgoing calls. *I just want to tell you I love you, honey. In case I never said it before.* He said those words to Vanessa at 12:52 a.m.

She was already gone.

36

Rescue

As *Jeannette* steamed toward *Lucy Jo*'s coordinates, Frank's adrenaline ran high—in a healthy way. So often before, he'd been the one needing to be rescued. A new job, a cash loan, a free meal. Another supplier, the next hit. An alcove protected from the wind. Emergency medical care. Even his front teeth were a handout.

Playing a role in rescuing someone else was new. When was the last time Frank Winkler Jr. had been anyone's best available option?

Jeannette approached *Lucy Jo* an inch at a time, spotlights on, Frank and a crewmate leaning over the gunwale to throw out fenders. From the wheelhouse, Bilbo's voice came through the megaphone, *Lucy Jo*'s radio still not being responded to, apparently.

"This is Captain Bilbo Churchill of the trawler *Jeannette*, hailing *Lucy Jo*. Permission for my crew to come aboard?"

No answer. Bilbo repeated the request. Gave the signal for Frank and Matt to transfer when able. With no help coming from *Lucy Jo*'s deck, tying up before transferring wasn't an option. Frank latched *Jeannette*'s transom open. Gave his life jacket a quick tug and watched Matt check his own. All secure.

Matt went first. A leap that would make a safety course instructor cringe. But *Jeannette*'s deck wasn't much higher than *Lucy Jo*'s, and the water was relatively calm, and Bilbo had maintained steady position. Frank and Matt both landed on their hands and knees, not their feet, but they weren't injured. No harm done.

As Matt headed for the wheelhouse, Frank stood and saw *Lucy Jo*'s would-be skipper, sitting with his knees up, back huddled against the gunwale. The only light came from *Jeannette*'s spotlights as Bilbo moved the trawler a safe distance away.

The approaching roar of a small but high-powered vessel indicated more help had arrived. A familiar-looking SAFE boat bumped up to *Lucy Jo*'s port side, no fenders needed. The woman at the helm called to Frank.

"Can you take responsibility for *Lucy Jo* and send the skipper over?"

Frank glanced at the man huddled on the deck. "I don't know if he's aware yet of what's happening."

"Give me a minute to get Aunt Macy set up here." The SAFE boat skipper spoke a few instructions to an older woman, who responded with a firm nod and waved the younger woman away.

While Matt made his way from the wheelhouse toward *Lucy Jo*'s bow, checking bollards and cleats, Frank lowered the emergency ladder over the gunwale. Steadied it while the SAFE boat's skipper climbed up and onto the deck.

"I'm Allison Theodore."

He shook her hand. "Frank Winkler Jr. Welcome aboard." *Welcome aboard?* As if he was hosting a sunny afternoon cruise.

Allison nodded toward the huddled skipper. "That man over there, Wallace Bernard. He . . ."

When Allison Theodore's voice faded, Frank's head swiveled. Was she about to faint? No, just gathering her breath. Or courage. To say whatever was coming next.

"He's just lost his daughter in a plane crash."

Something released inside Frank, soundless and empty. Grief maybe. It had spilled out of him. Or it had spilled out of Allison and flowed into him.

She rapped one hand on the gunwale. "If you can take responsibility for *Lucy Jo*, I'll evacuate Wallace. And if you're into praying, ask God to help Aunt Macy remember everything Virgil taught her about keeping his boat alongside another."

"Virgil Tagaloa, the grocery market guy on Wren?" That's where Frank had seen the SAFE boat.

"One and the same. He's on his way to Seattle to pick up Wallace's other daughter."

Frank nodded. "We'll wait to set towlines until after you've disembarked. One less vessel to coordinate with the others." He signaled Bilbo, observing from *Jeannette*'s wheelhouse, to keep a distance.

As Allison approached the crumpled man at the other end of the deck, Frank did pray. Not with words at first. Just by acknowledging an ache as he watched a full-grown man, probably one fully under control every other time, sobbing at the loss of his child.

God, this guy needs your help.

He didn't have to think to find those words, and twitched at a connection his mind made. Is that what watching Frank's battle with drugs had felt like to his dad? Losing his child?

Frank Winkler Jr. made his plea heavenward again, applying it not only to the crumpled old man on deck but also to himself and his father.

This guy, this guy, and this guy need your help.

Chaplain Michael Grant always said when your heart ached for something you knew was right but had no idea how to get, that was the time to fling your remaining hope at God with all you've got. To throw it hard. Let the Savior know you're hurting, aching, powerless.

So Frank let it fly.

But silently. And without any physical indication he was doing so. No hint of showing emotion.

Because as much as Frank Winkler Jr. didn't want to admit it, he was a lot like his toughened father. Might be getting more so with each new aching day.

37

Strong enough

Under the spotlights the approaching vessel aims at *Lucy Jo*'s deck, Wallace's first impulse is to run. Some habits are hard to break. But he's got nowhere to run anymore.

When someone he thinks could be Vanessa appears on *Lucy Jo*'s deck and comes toward him, he stands. For half a moment, all he wants to do is throw Allison Theodore overboard, because she isn't Vanessa and never will be. With Melissa still crying, he hands his phone to Allison. Mostly because he doesn't know what else to do.

Allison talks to Melissa, then reaches her hand toward Wallace, who suddenly needs more comfort than a light touch on one arm. He collapses into her, sobbing on her shoulder. In the back of his mind, he's surprised a girl like Allison is strong enough to prop up a dude like him.

Voices rise above the din, calling out instructions to prepare equipment. The harsh noise frays Wallace's last nerves. "Tell them to stop shouting!"

A whisper in his ear, Allison's voice, tells him the rescue team must shout to hear each other. That's when he notices the sound drowning all other voices. His own wailing. When he stops, a dark quiet presses in, comforts. The only sounds now are low, competent voices and gentle waves hitting *Lucy Jo*, the nearby trawler, and a smaller vessel at *Lucy Jo*'s side.

Allison straps Wallace into a life jacket, like Vanessa would tug the baby into a coat, then helps him up and over *Lucy Jo*'s gunwale. From there he'll be on his own, descending the ladder until he's close enough to let go and land on the vessel waiting below—if he aims right. The SAFE boat, bobbing like a toy in a bathtub, doesn't leave much room for error. Even in daylight, the transfer would be a dicey operation. From a few hundred yards off, the trawler's spotlight pierces the dark and lights the ladder, following his progress.

Halfway down, he pauses. It'd be so simple. Unclick the life jacket, fling himself into the frigid water, then kick with all his strength downward. Deep enough they won't find him in time.

But he can't do that to Melissa. Leave her with all the questions. She'd point to it as proof her dad left things unfinished.

"Two more rungs to go, Mr. Bernard." Macy Johansson, bossing as usual, is at the helm of the small craft below, which he now sees is Virgil's *Incremental*. "Mr. Bernard? That's it. Two, one."

Once his feet reach *Incremental*'s substrate, he skedaddles to the stern deck and looks up. *Lucy Jo*'s a midsize vessel but massive viewed from water level. Feeling numb, he just observes as Allison checks her own life jacket is secure, climbs over the gunwale, and begins descending the ladder. Is Allison moving painstakingly slowly? Or has grief muddied his perception?

"Come on, Allison." Macy's muttered bossing won't reach the girl.

That's when a wave pushes *Incremental* well out of reach from *Lucy Jo*'s side. The trawler's spotlight immediately shifts to illuminate not just Allison but the water below, the light operator preparing for the unthinkable to happen.

For a long minute, while Allison clings to the ladder and waits for Macy to maneuver *Incremental* into position again, Wallace squeezes his hands into fists and shuts down visions of how this night could get worse. Figures that, even if he felt up to it, suggesting Macy let him take the helm at this crucial moment would only heighten the danger. Finds himself wishing, not for the first time, he had a right to pray.

When Allison finally descends the remaining rungs and gets solid footing on *Incremental*'s deck, she doubles over. Is she seasick? In physical pain? She straightens. Wallace follows her into the cabin, where she gives Macy a one-armed hug. Takes the helm, hits the throttle. And they're clear of *Lucy Jo* and the trawler.

Wallace moves to Allison's side. "Thank you."

Her nod says enough.

Macy sits him down on a padded seat and wraps a blanket around him. The cabin is dimly lit from the dashboard. Time passes, hard to say how quickly. His mind runs through the crash reports he saw on his phone. He dwells on the worst images. Exhales into fresh emptiness. Glances at Macy. "There are no survivors. They're certain about that."

"I'm so sorry, Mr. Bernard."

He groans. "Only people I'm in trouble with call me Mr. Bernard."

"Wallace, then." A hint of a smile appears on Macy's face. "Your daughter Melissa is on her way to Wren Island."

A flare of hope lights his insides. "Did she say that?"

"She'll get there before we do."

When Wren Island comes into view, the rising sun's still below the horizon but casting its first light across the sky. The woman waiting on the dock is Melissa. No matter how many new tattoos she's gotten, he'll always recognize his daughter. The last hundred yards to reach her is the longest distance he's ever traveled.

Finally, he's wrapping Melissa in his arms.

Holding on. Tight.

Saying it. Again and again. "I love you, honey. I love you so much."

And, somehow, it becomes a new day.

38

Ursa Minor

Squinting in the late afternoon sun, Amelia dangled her legs over the edge of the grocery market's dock and checked the vessel tracker on her phone. Virgil's *Incremental*, finished weaving through islands, was approaching from around Wren's southwestern peninsula and would pull up to the dock soon. Amelia would be able to reach for her sister Shasta and cling to her. Maybe never let go of either of her sisters ever again.

When the news of Wallace's loss reached Shasta and Ralph, they'd dropped their work in Hawaii and caught the next available flight home. Virgil trekked to the Seattle airport for a second time in twelve hours. Now here they were, zipping close, Shasta leaning through *Incremental*'s open wheelhouse window and waving.

Standing, Amelia waited while Shasta hopped onto the dock. When Shasta enveloped her in a bear hug and a cloud of perfume, Amelia held on, answering Ralph's questioning look. "He's at your place."

Ralph headed into the forest, toward his property.

"Can we help with anything, Virgil?" Amelia peered at him as he checked the boat's fuel and oil.

Virgil shook his head. "See you at the house later."

Amelia held Shasta's hand as they walked off the dock, up to the road, down the driveway to Allison's house. Shasta's fuchsia-colored lipstick and shirt matched, as usual. "You look real put together, Shasta. How was the flight?"

"I knitted five hats in six hours. You know me, quantity over quality." Shasta stopped walking and pulled the hats out of the bag hung over her shoulder.

Amelia lifted a soft beanie loosely made from chunky yarn. "Yellow for Allison?"

"Maroon for Macy. Rainbow for me. The two lavender hats are for you and Melissa. If she wants one."

With the hats tucked away again, Amelia accepted the arm Shasta offered as they made their way.

Inside, they collected Macy, and the three sisters headed upstairs to the suite they'd stayed in when they first arrived at Allison's. At a time like this, why sleep in separate rooms? Why be any farther apart than necessary? Like Melissa, each of them knew how it felt to lose a sister. But each of them still had two sisters to hold on to.

Shasta hopped onto her old bed, sat cross-legged, and pulled a basket of yarn close. Although Shasta and Macy were older than Amelia, they both seemed to have more energy. Today especially, Amelia felt older than time. She sank into an upholstered chair and pulled a cozy wool blanket across her legs.

"So what's the plan?" Shasta checked and approved her bright fingernails. "How are we going to take care of Wallace and poor Melissa? Where is she, by the way?"

Amelia smoothed the blanket over her lap. "Right now, she's with her dad at Ralph's place. But she'll sleep at the house with us. In the wing off the sunroom."

"Good idea. With just one bedroom plus a foldout cot, there isn't enough room for her *and* Wallace at Ralph's." Shasta glared at a tangled skein. "You guys still haven't learned how to wind a ball of yarn?"

Watching her sister work through the tangles, Amelia thought of all the nights Shasta had spent at Ralph's. And the nights Ralph spent with Shasta here at Allison's house. No discussion about room then. But all that mattered now was offering Wallace and Melissa comfort—and as much space as they wanted.

Straightening, Macy cleared her throat. "Shasta, you should know a tidbit about Melissa before you meet her."

Shasta flipped the yarn skein back into the basket. "She's a girl who's just lost her sister. What else do I need to know?"

When Macy fidgeted, Shasta narrowed her eyes. "Spill the beans, sis."

Bringing the blanket with her, Amelia joined Shasta on the bed. Sitting next to them, Macy described Melissa. Her poised way of carrying herself. Her petite frame. Her tattoos. "Hardly leaving a blank section of skin! As far as one can see, anyway."

Amelia clarified. "The tattoos aren't scary-looking. Most are related to stars and the universe and stuff like that. Melissa says she likes to be reminded she's small compared to everything else. She's got Ursa Minor filled in like a bear cub on the top of her head, the North Star on her forehead. On the back of her head is the winding dragon of the Draco constellation."

Shasta frowned. "How can the top and back of her head be tattooed?"

Inching closer, Amelia caught her breath. Finally, they were getting to the most unusual part. "She doesn't have any hair. No eyebrows, no eyelashes. It's called alopecia, and she's got it all over."

Macy sighed. "Tattoos *everywhere*."

Shasta's eyes were lighting up more and more. "She sounds *fabulous*!"

"Try not to stare when you first meet her. Like Melia did."

"I did not! I was taken by surprise, that's all."

Amelia stuffed down the injustice she'd felt all day. After having slept through the hullabaloo last night, she woke up and traipsed into the kitchen for breakfast, unaware the world had been altered. Hadn't anyone thought to wake Amelia Theodore? She could have helped, maybe.

If she stared when she first saw Melissa, it was because she'd just discovered a new person chatting with Miss Kitty and Marshal Matt Dillon, her pet Australian zebra finches no one else gave much attention. If Amelia had stared, it didn't have anything to do with how Melissa looked! At least, Amelia hoped it didn't.

Shasta reached for another skein. "I adore this Melissa character already. But I still don't understand how she got to Wren so quickly."

Standing, Macy began fluffing the bed pillows. "Before boarding the plane to Seattle with her kids, Vanessa gave Melissa their flight info and said from Seattle she'd go to Wren to visit their dad. Melissa had just finished attending a work conference in San Francisco and decided to meet Vanessa in Seattle and visit Wren too."

Shasta stopped winding yarn. "What kind of work does Melissa do?"

Neither Amelia nor Macy knew. Winding the yarn again, Shasta motioned for Macy to continue.

"Arriving in Seattle, Melissa noticed all departing flights had been grounded. Then she heard another passenger say a plane bound for Seattle had crashed."

"Poor girl." Shasta exhaled. "She learned about her sister's flight from a stranger?"

"Then searched online. Then got a phone call and, later, an email confirming the passenger list."

Amelia's eyes filled with tears again. Losing your sister was nearly unbearable. Learning about it first from a stranger and a generic news source, unthinkable. She passed a box of tissues among her sisters.

Macy blew her nose, then continued. "Unable to reach her dad, Melissa looked up businesses on Wren and called the grocery market. Jax answered the phone, thank goodness. He called Virgil, who was already on his way to pick up Vanessa and the kids."

"I see." Shasta dabbed a tissue under her mascaraed eyelashes, then smoothed a perfectly wound skein between her hands. "So instead of getting Vanessa and the kids at the airport, Virgil got Melissa."

Macy nodded. "Jax also told Allison about the crash, and Melissa finally got Wallace on the phone and told him. Allison and I went to get Wallace, who was stranded on *Lucy Jo*. It took a while to arrange the tow and for Wallace to disembark."

Wiggling, Amelia interrupted, eager to share this part of the story. "And it took a while for Allison to disembark because Wallace had wrenched her shoulder out of its socket."

"What?"

Amelia lifted both her hands in Wallace's defense. "He didn't mean to. He still doesn't know he did. Allison said it's just one of those things that can happen when someone's hit with grief. They're not always aware of what's going on."

Shasta set aside the yarn basket. "*Lucy Jo* can't be easily disembarked in open water. Don't tell me Allison used the emergency ladder with a dislocated shoulder."

Amelia and Macy nodded.

"Is there *nothing* our Allison can't do?"

Nodding, Amelia smiled. "Like Virgil always says, Allison is perfectly capable of taking care of Allison."

"And perfectly capable of taking care of everyone else, apparently. You said Melissa was unable to reach Wallace for a while. Why didn't he answer her first phone calls?"

"He hasn't said." Macy began refluffing the pillows.

Amelia shrugged. "But for sure he had a good reason."

39

Each new wave

Waves, so many unending waves. Sitting on a driftwood log, Wallace watches them roll gently across the stones exposed by low tide at Ralph's property. Picturesque beach, this niche belonging to his host, who returned from Hawaii to be with a grieving friend.

Wallace snorts. *A grieving friend.* All his life, he's been grieving. Didn't think life could hold much more grieving. Then, whammo, an airplane supposed to be at altitude drops into smithereens, wrenching away people he loves.

If only he hadn't followed the shrimper. Hadn't fooled around in the pub at Reclamation, drinking. If he'd returned to Wren sooner, he might have been there when Vanessa first called, been able to think more clearly about protecting her and the kids. He might have found them a safe place near their home, so they'd have no reason to board an airplane destined for a Nebraska cornfield. He could have packed up and gone to be with them.

Why had he held to a pie-in-the-sky dream about the entire family being together? As if Wren Island could save a family from demolition by the ultimate wrecking ball, Wallace Bernard.

"Dad?"

He startles at the sound of Melissa's voice, so like her sister's. On the phone, he sometimes couldn't tell his daughters apart. Now there will be no wondering which is which. Now there is only Melissa.

How lonely she must be now, being only Melissa.

Inside, part of him shrinks more. A horrid feeling that comes as easily as each new wave rolling onto the beach. How can one daughter suddenly not be part of his family? Vanessa's still his daughter. She still *is*, isn't she? She's just not here now. The kids too. Nathan, Natalie. Never see them again? He winces in pain. The thought is too much to bear. Too, too much.

"Dad?"

Again her voice. His only daughter Melissa. She comes into view. Sits next to him on the driftwood log.

He reaches for her smooth hand. Runs a thumb across the elaborate half-moon inked there. Studies it. Did she bring it with her through this loss? There hasn't been time for a new tattoo, has there? Did the world end last night or a lifetime ago?

All those rolling waves. Hard to tell how much time has passed when moments keep crashing into him. Instead of receding so he could return to one moment, make one slight adjustment, and forever alter course.

"Will you please eat this?"

Melissa, his only daughter, offers a bowl of steaming soup. Golden broth, chunky noodles, chicken pieces. She's thinner since the last time he saw her, though he's not sure when he last saw her. An hour ago? A year ago? Her flat expression and red-rimmed eyes, trademark signs of drug use, send an ingrained flash of alarm through him. The condition of her teeth will tell him more.

"How about giving your dad a smile?" His voice comes out sounding hoarse.

"You're speaking again." Her genuine but pained smile reveals whitish teeth, mostly straight, no rot or staining. It is grief, not drugs, that has changed his daughter, the daughter with him here on the beach. What a heartache, knowing Melissa grieves this viscerally.

There will be no more need to worry about Vanessa. No need to thwart her latest destructive romantic liaison. No future need to keep tabs on Nathan and

Natalie's teenage friends. Now there is only Melissa to be concerned about. He sighs at the bittersweet realization.

"I'm worried about you."

Did he say the words? His focus finds his daughter again. She said the words, not him. He wants to reach for her hand. Oh, he's already holding it.

"No need to worry about me, sweetheart. Your old dad will keep on ticking, I suppose." Rubbing the half-moon tattoo again, he wonders. "Is this new? I mean, since . . ."

"Vanessa and I each got one at the same time, remember? When you took us to Vegas."

The turbulent past flattens into distinct memories. Not long after the girls' mother died, Melissa turned eighteen and the girls asked to go to Vegas. He'd said no, of course. Learned the skylarkers were going anyway. So he tagged along and footed the bill, which wasn't as hefty as he'd feared. Thwarted a few attempts by twerps to pick up his daughters. Wished his wife were there as backup—keeping track of his daughters by himself was exhausting. They celebrated their last night in Sin City with fresh ink. "I remember. Dimly lit shop with a sketchy hostess. Turned out okay, though, didn't it? Looks nice, even though . . ."

His insides cave more, pained at the image of his daughters linking their hands, comparing matching tattoos.

"Even though the other half isn't here?" So much sadness in his only daughter's voice.

"Your half looks okay on its own. Not complete, but . . ."

Wonder what Vanessa's tattoo looks like now.

A curtain of tears spills across Melissa's face, blurring it. Or are his own tears engulfing her? He rushes to say something, anything, that might save her. Save both of them.

"You're doing a good job, sweetheart, of being the only one."

She leans into him, tears flowing. "I don't want to be the only one."

"None of us do."

"Please come back to me, Dad."

He looks around, confused. Where has he been, if not here?

Melissa's voice is soft against his shoulder. "I know I haven't been a good daughter. But please don't shut me out. Don't go wherever it is you wander off to, in your mind, ever since . . ." Tears flow again. "I need you here with me."

A racket arises down the beach. Two oystercatchers chittering to each other, black feathers gleaming, bright orange beaks punctuating.

Has he ever seen an oystercatcher on Wren? Seems like he'd remember if he had, though they tend to blend in. Until they've got something to say.

How can Melissa think she hasn't been everything he ever hoped for in a daughter? Sure, their relationship has been rocky. Does any of that matter now?

"You've always been a good daughter, honey. I'm sorry if I never said so."

She nods, wipes her tears.

He points to the birds. "Not sure I've seen an oystercatcher on Wren. Wonder if they're here only part of the year. Might be migrators. Might . . . fly away."

He accepts the bowl of soup she offers. When he's finished eating, she speaks, raising her voice to be heard above the chittering oystercatchers.

"Do migrators come back to the same places they've been before?"

"Don't know the answer to that, honey. But I do know why they fly south."

"Because it's warmer?"

"Because it's too far to walk."

"Oh Dad."

His only daughter giggles. When the giggling turns into gulping sobs, he shuts his eyes against the piercing pain. Holds her while she catches her breath enough to speak. "I didn't think I'd ever laugh again."

He tightens one arm around her shoulders, the other arm achingly unoccupied.

40

A grieving island

In the days following the crash, Amelia often wondered about Vanessa Barone and her children, three-year-old Nathan and one-year-old Natalie. She pictured them collecting shells on the beach. Listening to singing birds. Which ones would intrigue Nathan? Which ones would Natalie point to?

Under a giant umbrella one rainy afternoon, Amelia imagined Vanessa walking to the market with her and choosing a muffin—pumpkin chocolate chip, rhubarb bran, or cinnamon pecan. They might have shared the muffin while rain cascaded over the porch awning.

This odd angle of grief was not unfamiliar to Amelia. Missing events that had never happened. Missing memories that would never be made.

Even the weather seemed to express grief. In a swirl of dead leaves and gray skies, the diminishing warmth of summer disappeared with the migrating kingfishers and oystercatchers. On the first morning chilly enough, Amelia pulled on one of the lavender hats Shasta had thrown together and tucked the matching hat into her shoulder bag. She found Melissa helping her dad remove moss from Allison's boathouse and dock. "Shasta knitted this for you."

Melissa frowned. Amelia pointed to her own matching hat and clarified. "You're not getting a hat because of your alopecia. You're getting a hat because

Shasta knits like a maniac and thought you might not have packed clothes for colder weather. Hope you don't mind yours matches mine."

Softening, Melissa pulled the hat over her smooth, constellation-covered head.

Glancing up, Wallace laughed. "You two look like twins."

Right away, Amelia decided to tuck that moment away and think about it more later. For one thing, it was nice of Wallace to sort of say she looked young enough to be Melissa's sister. For another, it felt like an honor to be considered a stand-in sister for someone who'd just lost their real one. And for yet another thing, this was the first time she'd heard Wallace laugh since the accident.

The moment was all worth going over again later to enjoy and add to her list of nice things that happened unexpectedly. For now, she said a casual goodbye and breezed, as much as her sturdy sandals and failing eyesight would allow, back up the beach, navigating driftwood, clumps of seaweed, and rocks.

When she'd traveled out of hearing distance, she pulled out her cell phone and opened her new favorite app. Hit one button and it would record her voice! She could also ask the app to transcribe her words and save them as a document. Like keeping a hands-free journal. Not at all like her public YouTube channel. Just a private documentary of her life in real time. She hit the big red record button.

"Today I heard Wallace laugh. It's going on my list of nice things that happened unexpectedly. Also worth noting, now that Wallace and Melissa have teamed up, a lot is getting done around Wren. I've never seen Allison's boathouse so shipshape! Of course, there's no predicting when Wallace might withdraw again. That's okay. That's how grief goes."

Weeks later, the plane crash was confirmed an accident due to technical failure. Melissa sagged to her room in the wing off Allison's sunroom. Four days later, Amelia, Allison, Shasta, and Macy compared notes and realized none of them had seen Melissa. They scurried down the hallway to Melissa's room.

While Amelia and her sisters hovered, Allison knocked on the door. "Melissa? Are you okay? We haven't seen you for a while."

"I'll be all right."

"She'll *be* all right." Whispering, Macy shook her head. "Not she *is* all right."

Allison motioned Macy quiet and called again. "Can I bring you lunch?"

"I ate an apple earlier."

"*Earlier* could mean anything." Macy's whisper gained strength. "Today, yesterday—"

Shasta huffed. "Shush, Mace. Let Allison do her thing."

"We care, Melissa." Allison's soft voice was tinged with tears. Did Melissa know Allison well enough yet to recognize the sound? "Please let us know if you need anything."

When they'd returned to the kitchen, Shasta erupted. "Mace, you can't force a person to eat if they don't want to."

"One apple? Eaten who knows how long ago? She'll wither away under our noses if we aren't better caretakers."

While her sisters bickered about how much food there'd been in the pantry earlier in the week and how much everyone in the household might have consumed in the last four days, Amelia made her way outside. Walking along the narrow road running parallel to the beach, she came around a bend and spotted Wallace ahead. Slowed her steps. Watched Wallace pause by their stacked rocks, the fun game they'd played *before*, then continue past without bothering to add a rock.

Amelia's heart deflated. After Wallace disappeared into the forest, she pulled out her phone, opened the app, and recorded her voice.

"Wallace has become a shell of his usual self. He mostly just scuffs around. Stops every so often and stares at nothing. Seems to want to be left alone. Which is ironic, isn't it? Since he probably already feels lonely. I think I understand, though. Grief is odd. Hits you any which way, no rhyme or reason."

Sometimes, if Melissa was near, Wallace would reach for her hand or kiss her head, bald or covered. He'd say *I love you, honey. I'm glad you're here.* But after the words were spoken, his face would reveal an expression so haunted Amelia would look away.

That kind of grief was meant to be private. She didn't even comment on it in her audio journal.

Two weeks later, an event worth comment occurred. Amelia opened the app and hit record.

"Funny story! First the background, because I'm not sure if I've mentioned it before. When Ralph returned from Hawaii, he resumed responsibility for the jobs he'd brought Wallace to Wren to manage. Like the interisland deliveries. And the road improvements—which everyone has been saying are slowing more and more the nearer they come to completion."

Amelia glanced around, catching her breath. This next part was the most entertaining.

"So this morning, Wallace came to the rescue! He stormed to a construction site, read the so-called supervisor the riot act, and didn't leave room for mis-interpretation. That's exactly how Ralph described what happened." Amelia giggled. "Three cheers for Wallace!"

Within days, the long-awaited improvements to Wren Island's roads were completed. The workers packed up as one, glad to get out of Dodge. Ralph crowded them and their equipment onto *Lucy Jo* for a minimal number of crossings back to the mainland.

A few times since, when Ralph landed *Lucy Jo* on the beach on weekends with clear weather forecasts, a car or two clunked off before whizzing merrily past the market and up the hill, escorting people who were laughing, singing, carousing. But that was the way the world always went. Continuing to roll after tragedy. No one could expect a visitor, anyone from anywhere else, to understand the need to be gentle. To understand Wren was a grieving island.

One evening at dinner, Amelia and her sisters invited Melissa to consider Wren Island her home. "No matter what your dad decides to do, you could stay with us."

Melissa nodded. "I appreciate that. But I'm only here for Dad."

Amelia looked up from her plate of lasagna. "So if Wallace stayed on Wren, you'd stay?"

"Yes, because I've spent too many years wishing things between us were different. Finally, we seem to have found a way to connect. Vanessa would want me to keep an eye on Dad—not that he'll admit he needs looking after." Melissa passed the salad bowl. "Besides, I don't have anywhere to be."

Shasta leaned close. "What about your work?"

"I'm on leave. I don't think I want to go back."

"And your work is . . . ?"

"A thing of the past." Sighing, Melissa passed the basket of steaming bread slices. "What I want most is just to be with Dad. We'll never have a perfect relationship. But we'll have each other. Wherever he goes, I'll go. Whether he wants me around or not."

Macy passed the salad dressing. "Does Wallace know you feel this way?"

"We've talked about it. I've told him I'll be tagging along with him now. The problem is, he doesn't know where he wants to be. I don't think he's ever known."

Macy tsked. "The man is completely unmoored. Understandably."

The next day, Amelia discovered the pile of rocks she and Wallace were stacking had been demolished, the stones appearing kicked, thrown, shattered against each other. All that intentional construction, all that wondering when the other would take a turn, and now their special place was in worse shape than if they'd never tried to start something new. Pulling out her phone, Amelia spoke into her voice-recorded journal.

"I feel ridiculous crying about it. But of course I'm not crying about rocks. I'm crying about what they represented. Friendship. Optimism. A light, summery day, so distant now it seems to have occurred in another lifetime."

She had questions, but they felt too private to record in her audio journal. Should she start a new pile of stacked rocks? Would Wallace be offended if she resumed the game? Must they also relinquish stacked rocks to the past?

Amelia imagined what Wren must look like from above. Her family and Wallace going about their business in much the same way for days, weeks, months. Then, in one pivotal night, everything changed. They wept in unexpected places. Stopped to stare blankly at nothing. Reached for each other more often. Kicked a stack of rocks they'd labored over for months. If Martians were looking down from above, they'd wonder what was going on. But there wasn't any such thing as Martians, probably.

She hit the button to record her voice. "Ralph and Allison are helping Melissa make decisions about a memorial on Wren. Wallace is too distant, mentally, to help. It will be months before the remains of the victims are returned to their families, and Melissa wants a special place *now* for remembering Vanessa, Nathan, and Natalie. Melissa says that because Wren Island was where Vanessa had been going, she would have liked knowing a corner of it belonged to her and the kids."

Glancing up at the gray sky, Amelia noted the glint of a commercial airplane. She stopped recording and sighed. The memorial also had to be on Wren because none of them had the courage just yet to leave. If they *had* to go anywhere anytime soon, they'd travel by boat.

Not seaplane. Not chartered flight.

Even the sight of a distant airplane, piercing the sky thousands of feet above, brought a new, yet familiar, ache.

41

For later contemplation

Amelia wasn't eavesdropping when she overheard Ralph ask his friend Michael Grant to lead the memorial service. Ralph phoned Michael in front of her and Allison. After Ralph ended the call, Allison gave him a wary look. "Do you know Michael Grant well?"

A fair question. Ralph's track record of bringing people to Wren wasn't unblemished.

"Michael volunteers as a prison chaplain. I met him through mutual friends." According to Ralph, after Michael attended seminary, he decided against becoming pastor of just one church. Instead, Michael lived on his boat, a Nordic Tug hailing from Reclamation Island, ministering wherever needed.

On the day of the memorial service, Amelia dressed in a solid blue jumper with a matching cardigan and headed for the beach. Anchored just offshore, Michael Grant's sturdy-looking tug gleamed in the early sunlight. Several other visitors' boats were anchored or tied up at the market's dock, with overflow vessels tying up at Allison's dock.

Sitting on a driftwood log at the high-tide line, Melissa motioned for Amelia to join her. "Come sit with me."

They compared notes as people arrived. Amelia recognized islanders who knew or knew about Wallace. Melissa recognized mainland colleagues who'd worked with Wallace. She guessed a man and woman carrying guitar cases were the married couple from Ohio who led worship at the church Vanessa had been attending.

"Vanessa went to church?" Amelia squinted.

Melissa bumped her shoulder against Amelia's. "Isn't that the neatest thing about memorial services? We get another opportunity to learn about the person we loved."

Amelia tucked that idea away for later contemplation. She would have liked to open her audio journal and explore more thoughts about it right then, but it didn't seem considerate to do so with Melissa next to her.

"Uh-oh." Melissa pointed to a man disembarking a visiting boat. "Dad's not going to be happy about him being here."

"Who is he?"

"A former colleague. The officer who signed off on letting out of prison a guy who might have retaliated on Vanessa. It's the reason Dad put Vanessa and the kids on an airplane that night. To get them to safety."

Before Amelia could process this new bit of stinging news, a storming Wallace crossed the beach, hauled up to the colleague, and swung a punch. The man didn't budge. Just waited, inviting a second hit.

Instead of obliging, Wallace crumpled, then turned and walked toward the opposite end of the beach. The colleague followed. Quarreling voices were raised, lowered, raised again. Amelia and Melissa listened in uncomfortable silence until the dispute finally faded.

"Well, it's about time to start the service, I guess." Melissa stood and offered a hand to Amelia. Which just went to show how remarkable Wallace's daughter was and what a loss it would be to never meet his other daughter. Amelia should have been offering Melissa a helping hand, not the other way around. So, again, grief was hitting from unexpected angles.

They all assembled in a grassy area at the east end of Allison's beach. The colleague Wallace had punched stood near Wallace, the two of them having reached solidarity.

Shasta introduced herself to the colleague, Roger Moore, and giggled about Double-O Seven being much more hunky in 3D. Knowing Shasta could flirt on this day, of all days, was oddly comforting—assuming Ralph didn't mind. Amelia glanced at him. He too had stationed himself near Wallace, arms folded across his chest. Even-keeled as usual.

Amelia glanced around at the others who had gathered. A few lookie-loos. People with random connections to Wren. Like the kid Allison pointed out earlier, who'd rigged towlines for *Lucy Jo* the night of the accident. Wearing sneakers and a drab jacket, Frank Winkler Jr. peered at everything and everyone through his thick eyeglasses as if on a much-anticipated field trip.

During the memorial service, Michael Grant said all anyone had to do was trust Jesus and they'd be welcomed into heaven. Was that all there was to it? How could anyone be certain? But it was nice to imagine Vanessa and the kids in a better place—somewhere even better than Wren.

The married couple from church stepped forward with their guitars. "Vanessa knew where she was going. The kids will always be with her. God has already given everything to bring his children home. Let's sing a favorite song of Vanessa's, 'All My Tears.'"

A few people who knew the words joined in. Wallace reached for his remaining daughter. He might have toppled over without Melissa and Double-O Seven propping him up.

Later, a newly installed swing set and boat-shaped playhouse was dedicated as Nathan and Natalie's Playground. A meadow was dedicated as Vanessa's Butterfly Garden.

Much later, after most people had gone home, those remaining built a bonfire on the beach. They roasted hot dogs and toasted marshmallows for s'mores because Vanessa had looked forward to doing that. They passed Goldfish crackers and peeled apple slices—snacks her kids would have been eating.

After Macy had turned in for the night, Wallace dug through a cooler and offered Irish red ales. Amelia nearly accepted one. John had been inclined to enjoy a timely Irish red.

The clear, moonless sky brightened with stars. The sea and fire died down under a blanket of crisp, clean air. As if a long, difficult chapter was ending. They might turn the page tomorrow morning and find the story changing. Improving. The past over, the present and future promising enough, especially for someone surrounded by love, as were Wallace and Melissa.

Flickering in the dim light of the fire, Wallace stood. "Thank you all for coming. Thank you for all you've done for me and my daughter Melissa. Thank you for helping us remember Vanessa, Nathan, and Natalie."

Amelia joined in the murmurs of agreement and sympathy working their way around the bonfire. When Wallace cleared his throat and waited for everyone's attention, she felt a tightening inside, intuition all was not right.

"I'll be leaving tomorrow morning. Helping Michael for a few weeks. I appreciate you islanders continuing to look out for Melissa while I'm gone."

Wallace was leaving? Without Melissa? She swiveled to gauge Melissa's response. In the darkness, she couldn't read Melissa's expression. Or maybe, like her dad, Melissa was an expert at appearing indifferent. She appeared that way the rest of the evening.

When family and friends gathered on Allison's dock the next morning, Wallace hugged Melissa. He pushed up the lavender hat and kissed the North Star on her forehead. Amelia lifted one hand to touch her own matching hat. What would it feel like to have Wallace kiss *her* forehead? An unexpected wondering. Wallace glanced at her and the rest of them, his own way of saying goodbye, then climbed aboard with Michael.

When the boat had put significant distance between itself and the shore, Melissa sighed. "I wonder if he'll ever come back."

Her heart aching, Amelia reached for Melissa's hand. "Of course he'll come back. You're here."

Overhearing, Ralph stepped in. "Michael will get him home."

Melissa turned to Ralph. "Michael will get him back to Wren Island, hopefully."

"Michael will get him *home*. Where he belongs."

Melissa gazed at the disappearing boat. "But where does Wallace Bernard belong?"

For a long while, they stood there on the dock. Wondering. Trying to come up with an answer.

42

Taking chances

On the morning of the memorial service for Wallace Bernard's daughter and grandchildren, Frank traveled with Michael from Reclamation to Wren. He helped drop anchor so *Henceforth* could wait offshore instead of taking up Wren's limited dock space. Then he buzzed the dinghy toward the dock at Wren's east end, veering to port when Michael indicated a tie-up at the west end's fancy-schmancy dock.

Michael hopped out, notebook in hand, and headed toward the crowd gathering on the beach. He would deliver a top-notch message worth hearing—always did, wherever and whenever he spoke.

Frank took his time tying up the dinghy, admiring the charismatic sport boat bobbing nearby, going by the name of *Buttercup*. Custom paint, loading gates on both sides, teak accents in the galley. The snazzy boathouse and dock had set someone back a pretty penny too. Composite decking, mechanized roll-up door. All of it squeaky clean and well-maintained. Whoever owned this stuff employed plenty of help.

A heavy sigh escaped Frank. Constantly starting over might be the death of him. Once again, he no longer had a paying job. Bilbo Churchill's trawler had been sold to Matt. In the transfer, Frank's position was confusingly eliminated, then reestablished and offered to Matt's cousin. The long hours of every day-after-day-after-day were now entirely Frank's to fill, and he was going to lose his mind if he didn't find a way to be productive. Preferably a job that earned him money.

That might have been one reason Michael asked if Frank would like to tag along to the memorial service. To stave off Frank going stir-crazy for one more day. Michael said he'd put out a few feelers for job opportunities for Frank, no guarantees.

After securing Michael's dinghy, Frank walked the length of the dock, joined a few other people on the beach, and discovered an even more compelling reason to be on Wren. Melissa Bernard, sister and aunt of the deceased, was hands down the most striking-looking girl Frank had ever laid eyes on. It was worth sticking around to find out if love at first sight was a real thing.

He stayed on the periphery most of the day, awed by islanders' unreserved support of Wallace and Melissa. He tried not to be too obvious about observing Melissa. Or catch flies in his gaping mouth when old guy Wallace smacked another old guy, then voluntarily caved in surrender. Frank would have been happy to talk with the friendly folks of Wren Island, but other than Allison Theodore and Virgil Tagaloa, who went out of their way to welcome him, hardly anyone noticed Frank was around. That was okay. It was right for people to focus on supporting the bereaved, not a down-on-his-luck former fisherman.

In the evening, snug in a sleeping bag on *Henceforth*'s deck and watching stars appear, he listened to snippets of conversation happening around a beach bonfire. It all sounded natural and relaxed until Wallace made an announcement, which was followed by a silence that felt awkward even from across the water.

Soon after, everyone disbanded. The bonfire died down. Frank drifted off.

Early the next morning, before full light, Michael nudged him awake.

"I'm heading south to the Columbia River, taking Wallace Bernard with me. Want us to drop you off on Reclamation?"

"The dad is leaving?" Frank rubbed his eyes. Everything inside still felt foggy with sleep.

"For a time. He needs to get away."

"He needs to get away?"

Frank knew he sounded like a dork, repeating Michael's words. But it didn't make sense. Hours before, strongman Wallace had powered through a memorial service. Now the man was abandoning his one remaining daughter?

"Frank, you know people grieve in different ways. When Wallace is ready for the next season of his grief, I'll bring him back."

Reaching for his eyeglasses, Frank huffed into full wakefulness. If any people ever cared about Frank Winkler Jr. like Wren Islanders cared about Wallace Bernard, Frank would never, ever leave them. Wouldn't put one iota of space between him and them. That kind of devotion was nearly impossible to come by.

"So, do you want dropped on Reclamation?"

"Nah. I'll take my chances on Wren."

Less than an hour later, Frank watched from the beach as off Michael and Wallace went. Michael at the helm. Wallace offering a stoic goodbye, then disappearing belowdecks.

An odd combination of emotions rose up in Frank. Annoyance at the man deserting a daughter who loved him, probably needed him. Confidence that if anyone could bring Wallace back around, Michael Grant could. Awe at the early morning sunlight reflecting off Melissa Bernard's smooth skin when she pulled off her knitted hat briefly to reposition it.

Eventually, all those feelings gelled into paralyzing fear. His connection to Reclamation had just disappeared. He had no job. No roof over his head, and wind from the north was picking up this very moment. Wren was more remote than Reclamation. How many work opportunities could possibly be here?

He shifted his single bag of belongings on his shoulder and wrapped his arms around the warm sleeping bag Michael had offered him. If nothing else, he could sleep on the dry ground under a dense evergreen tree. Maybe stand under a neighbor's garden hose to shower. Grow a beard, stop combing his hair and using deodorant, survive on berries and nuts and the occasional rusting can of beans. It'd be all fun and games until years from now, when an unfortunate kid poking through the forest unearthed the skeleton of a relatively healthy male, twenty-six years old, dental records conclusive.

A chilly wind stirred falling leaves around him. His mom would say his adventurous spirit was a tribute to his Finnish fishing ancestors. In a poetic way, she might be right.

His dad would say Frank was living like a bum. And would definitely be right.

43

A better guy

Frank walked to the grocery market with his head mostly down, his coat collar up against the wind.

Now would not be the time to pursue Melissa Bernard. She'd just lost her sister, nephew, and niece in a horrible accident. Then her dad deserted her.

He would admire Melissa from a distance for a while. Test the waters, so to speak. Find out if she was halfway interested in a guy with a past that included drugs, prison, and a lot of failed attempts at other stuff. A guy who didn't have a job at the moment, although that could change. And while he was looking on the bright side, he couldn't forget the six pieces of eye candy flashing out front.

A girl like Melissa could inspire him to pull his life together. If nothing worked out with her, he'd be more ready for the right relationship. Hanging around Melissa could help him become a better guy, maybe the best option going for him now.

Arriving at the market, Frank found Virgil pulling dozens of clean dishes from an industrial washer and stacking them on shelves. No doubt the memorial service was the biggest event Wren would host for another long while.

"Hi, Virgil."

"Hey there, Frank."

Frank scuffed the toe of one worn shoe across wooden planks that seemed to be the building's original floor. And looked like they'd just been scrubbed. So no need to hire help for that job.

He took a breath. "Wondering if there's any work on Wren for me?"

Virgil stacked more plates on a shelf. "You sticking around?"

"If I can find a job."

"What about the gig with Bilbo Churchill?"

"He sold the business."

Virgil stacked the last of the clean dishes, closed the dishwasher, and leaned against the counter. "Ralph Wesson's got his hands full these days. He takes care of interisland deliveries and Wren's road maintenance. He might have a job for you."

"Okay, I'll talk to him. I don't mind working hard. Prefer it."

"Hello!" Just like that, Allison Theodore was at Frank's side. How had he not noticed she'd entered the market?

Virgil made a beeline to her. Wrapped an arm around her waist, kissed her cheek as she melded into him.

Watching the two of them, nearly perfect halves making a more satisfying whole, Frank felt a pang similar to an electrical current, head to toe. He might revisit the feeling later and see if he could figure out where it came from.

One arm circling her, Virgil spoke to Allison. "Frank's looking for work. Wants to stay on Wren for a while."

Scrunching her face, Allison turned to Frank. "What happened with Bilbo Churchill's outfit?"

Frank repeated how the business transfer had gone down, leaving out the part where Matt's cousin got the job Frank used to have. No need to spread nasty reports about others, even if true.

Allison turned to Virgil. "The night *Lucy Jo* was stranded, when Bilbo's crew helped, Frank's the one who helped me over the gunwale with my tweaked shoulder."

"Thank you for that." Virgil addressed Frank, then turned to Allison. "A dislocation is more than a tweak."

She patted his arm. "Wallace didn't mean to. And it mostly feels like a tweak now."

Virgil pulled her closer. Dipped his head. Murmured a few words. She responded, quietly.

Frank had become invisible.

When he cleared his throat, they blinked back at him, remembering he was present. "So, if you hear of anyone hiring help, Michael Grant can vouch for me. I haven't always made the best decisions, but my track record for the past several months is respectable."

Focused on Frank now, Allison tilted her head, thoughtful. "I need help around my property. Gardening tasks, a new coat of stain on the boathouse. There's always tons of maintenance for *Buttercup*."

"That shiny get-up belongs to you?"

"And Aunt Amelia's got loads of work up at the commune." Allison named an hourly rate that was so high it nearly blew Frank backward. Virgil didn't bat an eye.

Glancing from one of them to the other, Frank shook his head. He looked Allison square on, something he'd learned to do early in recovery. Take ownership. Take pride in what you do or say.

"That's too much. How about paying me half that for a couple of weeks, then reevaluate whether you still think I'm worth it."

A slow smile spread across Allison's face. She was pretty, for a forty-something-year-old. Virgil got an admiring look about him while watching her. Frank probably had a silly grin on his face too. Six crowns on full display.

Speaking to Virgil, Allison nodded toward Frank. "I like this kid. Wherever he came from, I bet they're missing him."

The pang shot through him again, this time barreling through with a tectonic zap in the gut. He knew exactly what the feeling was. Longing. To belong to and with someone. Be wanted. Missed when he wasn't around.

No need to sit with the feeling. This kind of pain could bring him to tears. Blinking, he drew up his shoulders.

Allison moved to the produce section and started inspecting bananas. "Come by my house this afternoon, Frank. We'll get you started on those jobs."

Virgil walked Frank to the door. "Ask Ralph about work too. You have a place to sleep?"

Frank shrugged. "I'll figure something out."

"The market porch is open to you, provided you're up before the first customers arrive. I can leave on the overhead heaters to warm the porch on chilly evenings."

"Thanks. Don't worry, I won't loaf around making customers uncomfortable."

"You can use the outdoor shower around the side of the building."

"Oh. That too?"

"Frank?" Virgil got his attention. "You going to be okay?"

Exhaling, Frank let himself hope. "Yeah. I think maybe I will be."

44

Voice from the past

After Frank shuffled off, Virgil headed back inside the market and straight for Allison. Alone, finally! With the memorial service wrapped up, things were settling down, everyone inching forward with the rest of their lives. He pulled her close.

"You used to be so cautious about trusting people. Now you're quicker to give the benefit of the doubt. Like offering that kid a job before you know much about him."

"I'm trying to be more trusting." She snuggled closer, sending Virgil's heart thumping nearly out of his chest. "My past misjudgments sometimes haunt me."

The tiny edge of fear in her voice broke his heart. Did part of her wonder if marrying Virgil Tagaloa would prove to be a misjudgment? What was it she'd said about marriage when they first talked about it? Far too entangling.

He kissed the top of her head. Helping her be strong again. "I love you."

In his arms, looking up at him, she captured his eyes. "And I love you. When are you going to ask me to marry you for real, so you can be done worrying about whether I'll say yes?"

His heart flip-flopped. But he played it cool, grinning. "Oh, I see how it is. A new level in our relationship. Proposals on demand now."

"We already know you're good at asking questions." She kissed his jaw. "You've definitely proved that point, time and again."

Holding her face in his hands, he watched expressions cross it—hopefulness, contentedness, courage, optimism. And the vulnerability she was having increased difficulty hiding as she opened more of her heart to him.

He reached for her hands again, brought her to his chest, held her close. Breathed in her scent.

The real proposal ought to be special and memorable. With a sense of permanency to it. How to ask in a way that would forever sear the moment into their memory?

He had lots of questions. Not as many answers. But at the moment, he did have momentum. He plowed ahead with a heart-racing move.

Dipping his head, he whispered. "Allison Theodore, if I were to ask you to marry me, would you say yes?"

She whispered her answer. "Of course I'll say yes, when the time is right. When we're both ready for our lives to get completely tangled together."

He kissed her.

Eventually, wiggling free, she wagged one finger at him. "But plan a proper proposal. One that's more romantic than blurting the question at the firepit or asking me in the produce section after I've prompted you."

He burst out laughing. This brilliant woman would get her romantic proposal all right. Once he came up with a fancy idea for going about it.

"And I want you to propose without spending any money."

"What?"

"I'm sick of money conversations being part of nearly everything we do. When you ask me to marry you, Virgil Tagaloa, I don't want to feel like you threw money at the affair to make it sparkle."

He frowned. Not spend any money at all? What about the wedding rings he'd purchased? "What if I've already spent a few bucks preparing for this long-awaited proposal?"

"Oh! You're already planning! I guess whatever you've already spent is okay. But not a penny more. I want to feel absolutely assured you're committed to sharing everything—insecurities, secrets, celebrations, heartaches, weaknesses, strengths, the whole convoluted mess." She was making her way toward the door.

"Please don't go yet." He reached for her.

"I promised I'd help Aunt Amelia with projects at the commune. She's got all kinds of dreams for that place. I'm going to make sure they come true."

"I've got all kinds of dreams too. All wrapped up in you."

Eventually, he let her go. After crossing the road, she headed down her driveway, turned to wave at him. Then kept walking. It was all he could do not to race after her, sweep her into his arms, and—

His ringing phone interrupted his high-voltage thoughts. He pulled it from his back pocket. An unfamiliar number, not unusual for the personal phone of the only market owner on Wren.

He swiped open the call. "Hello?"

"Guess who?"

Virgil's heart, thumping wildly seconds ago, decelerated to an abrupt stop.

Her voice sounded more gravelly than before. He wouldn't voice her name. Not yet.

"It's me. Crystal."

He'd anticipated the possibility of this moment, but still needed more time to decide how to respond. He wanted to give his ex-wife the benefit of the doubt—take a cue from Allison, the woman he loved. But he also needed to be on guard. To protect his son, his soon-to-be-wife, their life here on Wren.

"Virgil? Are you there?"

"Yep." *Like always*, he thought but didn't say. "Where are you?"

"You'll never guess."

A sinking feeling told him his ex-wife was much closer than he'd like.

"I'm on a Washington State Ferry!" With a calculated tone of triumph. "Headed to Reclamation Island. Will you meet me at the ferry terminal?"

Studying the water separating Wren from Reclamation, he shook his head. "Why now? And why would you think I'd come meet you?"

"Still asking questions! We'll get all caught up soon."

No way. He was squashing whatever this was before it got started. Before Crystal could work a new angle to disrupt their lives. But he needed to buy time. "It will take a while for me to get over there."

"Oh, right. When I sent Jax's postcard, I thought you lived on Reclamation."

So she'd already found out they didn't. He could make up a fake island, but she'd find out the truth with little effort.

"We live on Wren."

"Yeah, like the *bird*. You'll bring Jax with you, right?"

"Wrong." No second thought. He was not taking Jax to meet the woman who'd abandoned him. Not without first establishing more protection. "Jax and I have created a life for ourselves on Wren. One that doesn't include you." He cringed at not only the words but his callous tone. Also applauded himself for keeping boundaries.

"Whatever. I understand. I just wanna see you. And Jax. I won't tell anyone we're related."

"We're not related."

"We *were*, and I'm certainly related to Jax. I'm his mother. I have rights."

"You gave up those rights."

"Things have changed. More might be changing." A familiar, wheedling tone had crept into her voice.

What could have changed enough for Crystal to be allowed access to Jax without Virgil first being aware? He massaged his forehead.

"I hear you've got a millionaire girlfriend. That might change things."

Virgil winced. Hearing his ex refer to Allison made him feel all scrunched up inside. He really wanted to punch something. A nearby carton of facial tissue seemed a promising target. He took a deep breath. Tried to remember how Allison taught him to release pressure through focused breathing.

"I'll head to Reclamation later this afternoon. Near the ferry terminal is a pub. Lots of visibility, always people around. You can meet me there if you want. Can you please keep quiet about being Jax's mother? For his sake?"

"You know me. *Hush-hush* is my middle name."

Sure it was. Until Crystal was drinking, using, or just feeling spiteful.

After ending the call, he thought about the clichéd timing of her arrival. She'd turned up *now*? Just when he was planning to marry Allison? Legally, he wasn't required to give Crystal access to Jax. And nothing she'd said indicated she'd given up her manipulative ways. But on the off chance she was in a healthy mental state, he wanted to give Jax an opportunity for a restored relationship. He rubbed his forehead again. The situation could get complicated.

He ought to talk about it with Allison. Part of him wanted to. Another part resisted. Allison might suspect an unresolved issue with his ex meant Virgil wasn't ready to get married again.

Blast it all! He needed Allison's help, even if it meant bringing her into a tenuous situation. He pulled out his phone and called her. "Hey, do you have a minute?"

"I always have time for a handsome man, last name Tagaloa."

"Okay, can we—"

"Oh no! Aunt Amelia just spilled a huge bag of rice. Virgil, I'm sorry. Can I call you back in a few?"

"Sure."

By the time he was untying *Incremental* from the dock, Allison still hadn't called. He sent her a text.

Something's come up. I'm headed to Reclamation. Can we talk over dinner tonight?

Her reply came right away. *Anything I can help with?*

He punched back a response. *Keep being beautiful you. See you tonight.*

Once *Incremental* was underway, Virgil phoned Reclamation's pub. Asked to speak to co-owner Zane Goodnight.

When the retired lawyer and trusted friend picked up, Virgil rehashed the recent developments. "And Crystal seems to be on the next ferry bound for Reclamation."

Zane exhaled in a low whistle. "How long has it been? Eight years? Nine?"

"More than ten. Jax doesn't know she's in the area. I've arranged to meet her at the pub this afternoon. Would you . . . ?" What exactly did Virgil need from his friend?

Zane chuckled. "Want me to keep an eye out for the unusual? Run interference if necessary? Provide an alibi if questions get asked? Post bail if letting you out is an option?"

Gritting his teeth, Virgil ticked *Incremental*'s speed up a bit. "Let's hope it doesn't come to all that."

45

Tranquility Hill

Amelia Theodore was now managing director of Tranquility Hill, an up-and-coming retreat center located on pastoral Wren Island. (Look out, world!) Her first official act had been to hire Melissa Bernard as assistant director. Next, Amelia delegated responsibilities to all full-time residents, including Judy and Ed, and posted a daily checklist in the library of the main building. Willing volunteers monitored the hydrophone at all times. Amelia noted the progress on her clipboard, then made her way down the hill.

Inside the rehab aviary, Amelia listed a full page of ideas for improvements, including better lighting and improved safety precautions. To be done someday, not right away. With elbow grease and careful attention, the aviary could become a shining feature of Tranquility Hill. Maybe visitors would want to help with aviary tasks!

Not visitors, *guests*, Amelia corrected herself. Melissa was helping Amelia learn to be more PC—short, Melissa said, for *politically correct*—so the Tranquility Hill experience felt less like being in backwater boondocks.

After walking back up the hill and down a path toward the garden, Amelia found Judy labeling plant starts. Snapped a photo of the two of them holding up clearly marked popsicle sticks. Property owner Allison loved seeing projects carried out in an organized way.

Following the open wood fencing, inspecting it as she went, Amelia noted posts to be shored up. Arriving at the weathered barn, she switched on her phone camera and recorded a video for her YouTube channel.

"Look at the new sign for our goat barn, hand-carved by Ed, a full-time resident here at Tranquility Hill. Guess what? We're planning to add *more* goats to the herd! Here comes our assistant director right now. Want to say hi to our YouTube friends, Melissa?"

Melissa stepped into the view frame and waved. "We're looking forward to hosting you here at Tranquility Hill."

For a few seconds after that, Amelia and Melissa stood still, smiling at the camera. Then Amelia switched off the recording. Now another video was ready to upload with minimal time spent editing. Amelia tucked her phone away and accepted the colorful flyer Melissa handed her.

"I just finished these drafts of promotional materials. What do you think? We can change anything you want."

Amelia pulled the magnifier from her bag and took her time going over the flyer. It mentioned the option of hosting overnight events, the availability of accessible lodging. The quiet setting, opportunities for beachcombing and wildlife viewing, soapmaking classes. There were QR codes for listening to whales through the hydrophone and watching the YouTube channel.

She handed the flyer back. "Looks great to me. Are you happy with it?"

"I'll tweak a few things. If I change anything significant, I'll ask for your opinion again."

Watching Melissa step lightly back to the main building, Amelia hoped the young woman's sometimes full-on perfectionistic traits, often playing out in endless fixes to already adequate material, wouldn't delay Tranquility Hill's opening. Collecting her clipboard and bag, Amelia continued checking the grounds, taking the shorter but steeper path to the main building.

Actually, Melissa's perfectionist traits came in handy. Whenever bumbling Amelia overlooked details, in swooped Melissa, making everything shipshape.

Melissa knew about online resources too. Like a co-op for swapping digital books and audiobooks, an informal library among friends. Imagine living in a world with that kind of technology! Melissa relayed the news to Amelia as if anyone halfway smart would make use of it, not just a floundering old lady with dimming eyesight.

Melissa championed the underdog. No one got away with less than kindness when she was around. No bullying of people, goats, chickens, or roly-poly bugs. She was a lot like her father.

Though when Amelia once said so, Melissa about bit Amelia's head off. Said her dad had always been detached, morose, and rarely willing to stick around, while Melissa herself would never ever leave something unfinished. Even if that sad lineup of traits was mostly accurate for Wallace, Amelia figured Melissa's estimation of herself was a stretch. Didn't every person leave *something* unfinished in their lifetime?

Amelia shifted her bag on her shoulder. The other area they disagreed on was Melissa's music choices. Rock and roll made Amelia's ears hurt! Melissa consented to enjoying her favorites through noise-canceling headphones Frank Winkler Jr. helped her buy. Frank had worked in electronics at one time, unofficially, and knew a guy who could snag unheard-of deals.

Huffing her way up the hill, Amelia laughed quietly to herself, remembering when Melissa asked Virgil to add rock music to the Wren Island playlist. *No way and no how*, Virgil had said, thumping down a bag of dog food so heavily the counter shook.

Maybe the request had come at an inopportune time. Lately, Virgil seemed a tad edgy. And since he listened to the playlist all day every day in the grocery market, it was fair for him to take a stand on it. He made a nice gesture, though, as a nod to Melissa's tastes. The next time Amelia was in the market, she noticed OneRepublic's "Counting Stars" had been added to the playlist. Amelia didn't mention it, in case Virgil was still in a bit of a mood.

Holding the handrail as she ascended the final stone steps to the courtyard of the main building, Amelia reflected on her biggest disappointment regarding Melissa. She was determined to avoid getting her hands, shoes, or clothes dirty.

Corralling the goats was out. Cleaning cages in the rehab aviary was out. Feeding the chickens depended on a windless day, dry ground, and Melissa wearing clothing she didn't care much about.

It takes all kinds to make the world go round. That's what Amelia's father used to say, way back in the day. And there were so many admirable traits about Melissa, it hardly mattered if she didn't want to participate in jobs that might ruin her clothes.

With or without her help with the messy animals, and despite a mercurial relationship with her dad, Melissa had become a reliable powerhouse Tranquility Hill would be mostly bereft without. Melissa was so uniquely inspiring, you started looking at the world differently just from being around her.

46

Asking for peace

Traveling with Michael Grant leaves limited time for Wallace to think. Every few days, they move *Henceforth* to a different area of the Columbia River, where Michael boards a cargo ship, in port or anchored off shore, and does his ministry thing. While Michael's saving the world, Wallace maintains the tug and hires out for small boat repairs. Sometimes Wallace scuffs through whatever town they're in. Sees a lot he's seen before, and sometimes stuff he hasn't.

That's what he's doing the afternoon he wanders into a creaky old marine supply store and leaves with a cast-iron gizmo similar to one he lost years ago, after John figured out a fella could exhale hot air on an antique sail iron and press a shirt collar.

Back in his cabin on *Henceforth*, Wallace digs out the one collared shirt he packed, huffs on his new purchase, and tests its mettle. Yep, still effective. Though if Wallace shows up wearing a pressed shirt tomorrow instead of his usual sagging getup, the typically unperturbed Michael might fall overboard in surprise.

Michael doesn't push his religion on Wallace. Their agreement is that Michael won't if Wallace lets Michael pray aloud the mornings they're both on board. It's a tolerable arrangement. Better than wandering around Wren Island with the Henhouse women clucking at him.

That evening, a temporary slip welcomes *Henceforth*. When Wallace can't put it off anymore, he heads to his cabin for the night, always the worst part of his days since the plane crash. He lies awake, staring at the vinyl ceiling, thinking. Kicking himself for panicking when he heard Robinson had gotten out of jail. Maybe the reason for the release had nothing to do with Wallace. He'd made a gut decision, while mostly drunk, about protecting his family, and rushed Vanessa and the kids into a death trap.

And speaking of stupid decisions, he's an idiot for not saying what he should have sooner, before it was too late. What kind of failure father never tells his daughter he loves her? If he'd said it when he first thought of it, that night when the world began reeling out of control, would it have altered their destinies? Instead, there's a voicemail floating around the universe that will never be heard by the person it was meant for.

Heaving a sigh, he rolls to one side, punches his pillow. Early on, he got himself worked up over the plane crash being a sinister plot to get back at him, for setting up Robinson or for some other past miscue. He's worked with a lot of thugs. But none would stoop that low. Besides, Roger Moore put that theory to rest the day of the memorial. Showed Wallace behind-the-scenes evidence that hadn't been released to the public. Moore also confirmed Robinson was back in jail—and that his incarceration had been fixed, as it can be, so future release would be highly unlikely.

That part feels confusing. Wallace doesn't wish imprisonment on anyone. But if Robinson ever got out, how many more people might get hurt?

On this night, like every other, random stuff floats through his mind. Did Vanessa enjoy the cheeseburger he ordered for her in-flight meal? Did the kids eat the carrot sticks or just gnaw on them? Did raisins get dropped on the cabin floor?

Thinking of his daughter spending her last moments tidying sticky crumbs could send him into a downward spiral, so he switches gears and imagines her and the kids cuddled together under a blanket, snoozing. Until, in those final moments, they weren't.

He rolls to lie flat on his back again. Exhales their names. "Vanessa. Nathan. Natalie."

Virgil once said some cultures believe death never comes if a person's name continues to be spoken. Right now, that's as close as Wallace can get to a pleasant thought. It'd be nicer, though, to say his daughter's name and not have it return empty. To poke Natalie's round tummy and be given a gummy smile. To tap Nathan's cowboy hat and hear the word *grampy* come out from under it.

Will anyone ever call him grampy again? That's another bit of life he's lost. Maybe that will be the grief that ends up being too many. The one that topples the stack.

Staring at the ceiling, he cringes over another decision, not giving Melissa a heads-up he'd be leaving. He should have told her in private before announcing it at the bonfire. But isn't it better for a young woman to blaze her own trail? Melissa might get completely messed up if she hangs around a sad sack like him.

The morning he left, he promised to come back. She rolled her eyes. Said she was getting a job working for Amelia. That part confused him too. What kind of work does Amelia Theodore do? Does the job require they wear those matching hats? They look so alike, the two of them, both wearing the same purple-colored hat.

Later, he thinks he's still staring at the ceiling but ends up in the old nightmare. Someone's disappearing before his eyes. He needs to say something but can't. Hues of violet, lavender, and purple cascade down, blurring out the person. Is it Melissa?

He wakes up panicking. Yelling. Loud enough Michael must have heard. In the thrumming silence, he imagines Michael in his own cabin, reading his Bible and praying for poor lost Wallace.

It's too late to help Vanessa. He's told Melissa he loves her. Many, many times now. What else is there to say?

Was it Melissa in the dream? If not Melissa, who?

The next morning, Michael's got his Bible out and is praying aloud. Since it's part of their agreement and since breakfast is on the table, Wallace listens in. Michael's requests become extra peculiar when Michael asks his god for peace for Melissa. Peace isn't a trait Wallace would associate with go-getter Melissa. But then again, she does have all those tattoos of star systems to remind her the galaxy she lives in is mysteriously immeasurable. Does feeling small help someone feel peaceful?

Michael's asking for peace for Wallace, too. Probably so Wallace won't feel left out. Obviously, a man with Wallace's background will never experience peace.

When he's finally finished praying, Michael closes the Bible and pushes it across the table to within Wallace's reach.

Wallace shakes his head. "I don't need anything from your Bible."

Michael sips his coffee as if he has all the time in the world. "What if someone in the Bible needs you?"

That part is unexpected. That someone in there might need Wallace Bernard. With everyone else dead two thousand years ago, there's only one possible option. "You trying to tell me your god needs me?"

Michael stands, finishes his coffee, and sets his mug in the sink. "It's your move, Wallace."

Annoyed with the cryptic talk, Wallace throws his own dishes into the sink. But after Michael heads out on deck, Wallace sits back down. What if someone in there does need him?

He opens the Bible and flips through from the beginning, sort of. Mostly finds wars, laws, plagues, famines. Long lists of patriarchs who begat other patriarchs. Generations and generations of offspring, still being talked about eons later. The Bernard family is barely surviving the current calendar year.

Then he ends up in the book of Ruth. Reads about Naomi, who changes her name to Mara because it matches how she feels, bitter. Mara's got two girls. One's named Orpah. Wallace double-checks the spelling on that. It's close but different from the celebrity Oprah's name. The other girl is Ruth, probably the hero of the story, since her name's in the title. After all their husbands die, Orpah and Ruth beg Mara to let them stay with her. Bitterness is their best option.

Mara sends them away. One girl cuts her losses and leaves. The other, Ruth, gets clingy. Says she's not leaving Mara, ever. *Wherever you go, I'll go.* That's when it hits him. He's Mara. Bitter. And Melissa is Ruth. Without Mara, Ruth might not have survived to become the hero of a story with her name on it.

When Wallace charges on deck and discovers Michael's still around, he doesn't hide his eagerness. "How soon can we get back to Wren?"

Michael tucks a pencil behind one ear and a small book of crossword puzzles into a back pocket. "If we leave now, we'll be there by late afternoon."

Several ships in port are home to international crews Michael's talked about ministering to. Michael doesn't seem like a guy to leave things unfinished. Doesn't seem like Wallace, in other words. "Don't you need to wrap up stuff here?"

Michael's already checking hatches and securing loose items. "The work here will wait for my return. Let's get you where you need to be."

By noon, they've left the Columbia River and are motoring north along the Washington coast. Headed toward Wren Island. Heading home.

47

Back in place

Wallace spends the travel day anticipating everything he's missed. When Melissa sees *Henceforth* returning, she might shriek and run to greet him—unless she's still annoyed at the way he left. Macy will boss a celebratory dinner into place. Amelia and Allison might be on the beach with the dogs. He's even missed being flirted with by Ralph's girlfriend.

When they approach Wren's south-facing beach, no one's watching for them. Tying up at Allison's dock, no one notices. Except a kid on the beach, who hurries over to help. The kid tucks earbuds into his gray hoodie's front pocket. Closer, Wallace recognizes him from the day of the memorial, when he hung back on the periphery, out of notice. Shy, or hiding? Wallace frowns. "Who are you?"

"Frank Winkler Jr., sir."

Wallace narrows his eyes. The kid doesn't seem old enough to have been in the military and doesn't have a southern accent, so the *sir* bit seems fishy. Like he's trying to impress. "Well, Frank Winkler Jr. Sir, can you tell me where everyone is?"

Clunky eyeglasses get pushed up his nose. "By *everyone*, do you mean everyone other than me?"

Before Wallace can sling back a response—it's been a while since he had to put together a witty comeback this quickly—Michael disembarks and claps the kid on the shoulder. "Good to see you, Frank!"

Wallace heads for Allison's house, a solid start for finding his daughter. If Melissa's at the commune, he'll traipse up there after he—

"If you're looking for Melissa, she's at Allison's house."

Wallace stops short. How does this punk know so much about his daughter's whereabouts? He does a one-eighty, as fast as his seventy years allow. Strides back to within inches of Winkler's nose. "What else do you know about my daughter?"

Winkler doesn't flinch. A promising sign, assuming it's because Winkler's confident enough to stand his ground. Or a dangerous sign. Of a complete lack of fear.

"I know she's at the house. And I know she'll be glad to see you."

Wallace studies the boy. His teeth are a conundrum. Obnoxiously white crowns across the top, rot and breakage below. Fine lines crease his eyes and mouth, so he must be older than Wallace first thought. Mid-twenties, maybe more. Old enough to have a history. "Where'd you come from?"

"By *where'd you come from*, do you mean where was I born, or where was I before this?"

Wallace whirls to Michael. "Does this punk ever give a straight answer?"

Laughing, Michael nods assurance. "Frank's a friend of mine. Allison phoned to tell me she's hired him to work at her place."

Wallace isn't convinced. He can picture Michael Grant, a minister to scoundrels, hanging with a punk like this. Allison Theodore, not so much. He pins Winkler with a steely gaze. "How do you know Allison?"

At this, Winkler fidgets. Uncomfortable with the question? Or the answer? Now they're getting somewhere. "I met Allison the night you lost your family in the plane crash. I'm sorry for your loss, sir."

The worn phrase hangs in the air. *I'm sorry for your loss.* When will those words stop hurting so much?

Winkler keeps talking. "I was part of the rescue crew for *Lucy Jo*."

In a flash, it all comes back. The dark night, the blinding spotlights, the emergency descent down the ladder. How he wept on Allison's shoulder, actually pulled it out of the socket, which she didn't tell him until much later because everything about that horrific night had been about taking care of Wallace Bernard. He swallows. "Thank you for your help."

Frank Winkler Jr. nods.

Wallace squints at him. "How come you're not still working that job? How come you're hanging around here now?"

"I want to live on Wren."

"Why Wren? Why's it so important to be here?" Behind Wallace, Michael shifts his weight from one foot to another. Michael knows, or thinks he knows, how Winkler will answer. "Well?"

Winkler tightens his jaw and braces himself, a posture Wallace recognizes as expectation he'll get walloped for whatever he's about to say. But Winkler answers while looking Wallace square in the eyes. "I never saw a man cry like you did. I'd like to . . . be allowed around."

A shudder runs through Wallace. The kid wants to be in close quarters with all-encompassing grief? For half a moment, Wallace wants to push the punk off the dock and hold him under the water—just long enough to screw his head on straight.

But while Winkler waits for an answer, Wallace doesn't see judgment or scorn or haughtiness. He sees . . . Respect?

Will the world ever start making sense?

Deflating, Wallace sends Michael a look, letting the minister know Wallace will think about the upstart's request. Then he strides off with as much swagger as he can put together, heading toward Allison's house, where Frank Winkler Jr. says Melissa is.

As Wallace walks, he pictures the activity behind him. Winkler's probably giving Michael an uncertain look, wondering if it's okay to stay. Shoot. Wallace owes this kid. And Winkler was honest when pressed. Willing to say something difficult.

Keeping his stride, Wallace yells over his shoulder. "If Winkler wants to be helpful, he can bring my bags to Ralph's place."

A few strides later, he glances back. Winkler's springing in and out of *Henceforth* like he's won the lottery.

On the narrow road running parallel to the beach, Wallace stops at the site where he and Amelia Theodore stacked rocks a lifetime ago. Surveys the destruction he left last time he was here.

He kicks a few rocks out of the way. Searches for a foundational rock to form a new pile. Finds one, positions it, stacks several more on top.

Now John's monument is back in place, with room to grow, though Amelia has no idea she's contributing to a remembrance of Wallace's old friend. Wallace starts a second tower for Vanessa. A third and fourth for Nathan and Natalie. Stepping back, he takes a deep breath.

"Your move, Amelia. Thanks for waiting."

48

Head honcho

At Allison's house, Wallace hears voices coming from the kitchen. Chirpy, chatty women. Hoping his appearance doesn't spoil the lightheartedness, he lets himself in and pokes his head through the door frame. "Do I get a welcome home?"

"Dad!"

Melissa's voice holds only delight. His daughter who would have given him little more than a wave in the past hugs him, hanging on for longer than he hoped. He blinks stinging eyes, his own fault since he invited a welcome. He's got better control of his emotions by the time Allison, Amelia, and Macy greet him.

Accepting the mug of coffee Macy hands him, he leans against the counter. "What have I missed?"

"We own the commune now!" Amelia's practically bouncing with excitement. "Melissa's the new assistant director!"

"Assistant director? Who's the head honcho?"

"Me!"

Holy smokes, Amelia Theodore is pretty when she's excited. Why didn't any fella ever marry that woman? Somebody missed out, for sure. "Shouldn't you be stacking rocks, missy?"

"Oh! Are we doing that again?"

Wallace nods, grins, nods more. Amelia's so *bright* when she's happy. Lights up the entire room. He tears his attention away and turns to Allison, pretty bright herself. "How's your shoulder?"

"Good as new."

"I met Frank Winkler Jr. What do you girls know about him?"

"He's all right." At Melissa's bland response, Wallace raises his eyebrows.

Allison measures coffee grounds for another brew. "He's helpful."

"What do you know about his background?"

When Allison shrugs, Wallace sighs. This is exactly how a bunch of women living under one roof can end up with any number of problems. "Allison, you shouldn't hire someone you don't know anything about."

"I hired you."

That's another thing eating at him. His paycheck comes from a woman. If he'd known, he would have never . . . Oh, who's he kidding? He'd help Ralph at any cost, even to his pride.

"Michael Grant knows Frank." Amelia pipes up.

"Michael knows a lot of hoodlums. Scares them up from everywhere and nowhere."

When Allison pins a teasing look on him, arching one immaculate eyebrow, Wallace realizes the implication against him in what he's said. Reaching for his coffee cup, he focuses on it. "A background check's easy to do here in Washington state. Let me do some digging. Verify your new employee's on the up and up."

"Whatever you say, Wallace. We put ourselves in your capable hands."

They're giggling. Allison, Amelia, Macy, his own daughter. Let them.

He spots a platter of brownies on the counter and chooses one loaded with frosting. Takes a bite. Swallows a jolt of rich cocoa and sugar.

Chewing, he sneaks a glance at Amelia. She's sipping from a mug printed with *Not before coffee*. Also watching to see if he likes the brownie. He takes another bite, makes a show of enjoying it.

Amelia Theodore. Now there's a name that ought not be forgotten. She was under the radar at first. Not a girl you'd instantly notice or pay attention to, because she's not flashy. Looks ordinary at first, then blooms as you get to know her.

He hams it up about enjoying the brownie, with the goal of hearing Amelia giggle again. He ought to tone it down. Especially because Amelia's close enough to his age for them to possibly . . . He turns his attention to Allison, too young for him. And taken. By good ol' Virgil. "You get your Jeeps yet?"

"They're in waterfront storage in Seattle. Ralph says bringing them to Wren is a two-person job."

"Virgil can't help? Or your new friend Winkler?"

"Virgil's extra busy right now with special orders for a customer on Reclamation Island. Goes over there a couple of times a week. Plus he—"

"Virgil's delivering cargo? In *Lucy Jo*?"

"No, some kind of specialized goods in *Incremental*."

Wallace frowns. What could pull Virgil away from his market so often? Did he need money? Fast money? As in, contraband? Narrowing his eyes, Wallace glances from Allison to Amelia to Macy to Melissa, none of whom seem to be concerned about the obviously suspicious activity happening under their noses. Women on their own! What a headache.

He spells out the obvious. "Reclamation's got its own suppliers. Much more inventory than we have. Just what kind of specialized goods is Virgil delivering?"

Allison sips her coffee. "I don't know. But he's busy. Plus he doesn't know the Jeeps are coming. Jax has been told his birthday gift will arrive late, though he doesn't know what the gift is. I don't know why Ralph doesn't want Frank's help."

"Probably because Ralph's savvy enough to recognize Winkler's fishy. And it seems to me Virgil's also acting—"

A strange sound filters into the kitchen. A gonging. Amelia hops up from the table, faster than Wallace would expect for a stout girl like her. He glances around. "What's that? An outdated fire alarm?"

"Whales! The gong means we can hear them through the hydrophone." Amelia pulls out her cell phone and taps the screen. The sound of singing whales fills the kitchen. "It's one of the lapsed activities we've reinstated at Tranquility Hill."

He's propelled by the elbows outside, through the dune grass, to a ridge with panoramic views of the water off Wren's south side. Melissa hands him binoculars. "Over there. Orcas!"

Beyond Allison's dock, several orcas are traveling east, rhythmically emerging in sync. Breathing at the same time. Diving at the same time. Separate creatures, yet unified. From Amelia's cell phone, chirps, chatters, and an occasional forlorn note fill the air.

Melissa taps his arm. "Bet you didn't realize we have a hydrophone and an app for listening to whales. Bet you'd like Wren Island more and more if you stuck around."

He gazes at his gorgeous daughter, one of two precious girls he's loved forever and ever. "Honey, Wren Island's best treasure is you."

Melissa rolls her eyes. "There you go again. Annoyingly charming." But her smile of contentment could light a solar system.

He puts an arm around her shoulders and kisses the North Star on her forehead. "No hat today?"

She shakes her head.

"I love you, honey. I always have."

Standing on tiptoe, his daughter plants a warm kiss on his cheek.

He gives her shoulders another squeeze—gently. From Allison, he's learned women's shoulders can seem stronger than they are. He salutes the rest of the whale watchers, then strides toward Ralph's place—changing direction when he sees *Incremental* approaching Virgil's dock.

Amelia's voice reaches him. "Wallace? It's nice to have you around again."

He pauses. Wanting to be certain first. Then he turns. Amelia, Melissa, Allison, and Macy are waiting for his response. They're standing there looking hopeful. About *him*.

He clears his throat. He's walked far enough away, the words will need to rise above sand, travel across dunes, bounce off surf. And these words need to be heard.

"It's nice to be around!"

49

Disclosure

Approaching Wren Island, Virgil noticed a pod of orcas traveling directly across his route. Following local regulations, he slowed *Incremental*'s speed. Put the motor in idle and the engine in neutral. Turned off the depth finder to minimize interference with the orcas' biological sonar. Offering space. Similar to car traffic waiting for deer to cross a suburban road.

Watching the elegant whales, their crisp markings of black and white shining in the sunshine, Virgil repositioned his ball cap, stretched the tension from his arms, and shook off another fruitless trip to Reclamation.

Maybe it was time to give up this whole circus of trying to learn more about his ex-wife's situation. He could tell Jax everything he knew so far. Offer for Jax to join him on Reclamation next time. Bring a picnic lunch, drop fishing lines, invite Allison to come along and enjoy a family outing.

To do all that, he'd first need to tell Jax—and Allison—what had been going on. But the longer Virgil hadn't said anything to either of them, the harder it was becoming to broach the subject.

When the orcas had moved safely out of the area, Virgil drove *Incremental* to his dock and tied up next to Jax's fishing pontoon. He was securing the last line when he saw Wallace—home from cruising with Michael!—barreling toward him.

Allison's dog Louise tagged close behind. She greeted Virgil with a wagging tail. Wallace greeted Virgil with a scowl.

"Tell me about these specialized goods going to Reclamation."

"Welcome home to you too." Virgil busied himself with dock cleats that didn't need checking. There were no specialized goods going to Reclamation. Just a deepening sense of regret that he'd lied to Jax and Allison.

"You'd better not be delivering drugs. Or any other contraband."

Contraband? Virgil burst out laughing. "If you think I could do that, you don't know me at all."

Shaking his head, Wallace set his jaw. "You'd better have a watertight excuse for running off to Reclamation Island when there's a jewel of a woman here who loves you and needs your help."

Said the man who sailed away when his daughter needed him! But Virgil let the comparison slide. Too distracted by the other news Wallace had hinted at.

"Allison needs help? What's wrong?"

"Oh, Allison herself is fine, just fine. What's wrong is the way you're acting. The market on Wren is great, but it doesn't offer much people can't get on Reclamation. I want to know why you're making so-called specialized deliveries to an undisclosed customer. Virgil, I swear in the name of everything that's decent, if you're seeing another woman, you're about to get walloped—to within an inch of your life, maybe less. Then you'll get thrown off the dock. With no remorse on my part."

Virgil took in Wallace's set jaw, tightening muscles, furrowed brow. A quick glance at Louise, wary from the raised voices and stern tones, told Virgil he couldn't be sure whose side the dog would take.

Not that Virgil planned to fight. Wallace was right to be upset. In fact, it was comforting to find out Wallace cared so much. And a seventy-something-year-old trying to beat up on a fifty-something-year-old wouldn't end well for either of them.

He raised his hands in surrender. "I'll tell you everything. Honestly, it would be a relief to unload to a friend. But please listen to the end before throwing punches."

"Start talking."

"Several years ago, I divorced my wife when she couldn't get unsnagged from a drug addiction we'd tried everything to overcome. Jax and I moved here to Wren. Eventually, I lost contact with Crystal, and as the years went by I assumed the worst. A few weeks ago, she called me. From a ferry bound for Reclamation."

Wallace let out a string of swear words, then glanced at the dog by his side. "Please excuse my French, Louise." A wide grin and slow tail wag answered him.

"Jax doesn't know his mother is in the area, although he got a postcard earlier this year from Bellingham. I've tried to tell Allison, but I always get interrupted or wimp out. She's been hurt by people leaving her. It's taken a lot of time and effort to build her trust."

"The you-know-what's going to hit the fan when she finds out the real reason you're going back and forth to Reclamation." Wallace shook his head. "Why all the trips there? Why do you need to see your ex?"

"I haven't even seen Crystal! She never shows up at the agreed time. I haven't said anything to Jax yet because I don't want him to be hurt if the situation falls apart."

"A father protecting his son is an admirable line of reasoning. But it doesn't hold up for not telling Allison."

Virgil kicked at another dock cleat unnecessarily. "It sort of holds up, if you figure Allison might be hurt knowing my ex is around."

"Come off it, Virgil. Allison can handle having your ex around. What she'll be hurt by is you not trusting her with an important part of your life."

Wallace was right. Virgil should tell Allison all about the situation ASAP. As in, he should have told her weeks ago. The moment that blasted postcard arrived. He was an idiot, a complete, entire idiot.

He swallowed, nodding. "While on Reclamation, I scout around. Try to learn if Crystal's living an upstanding life or if this is a ploy to take advantage. She's drained my finances before, not that I ever had much to take."

"You'll have a lot for her to take once you marry Allison."

Virgil shook his head. "Allison's money will stay hers."

"That so?"

At the surprised tone in Wallace's voice, Virgil restrained a groan. Did everyone think he was marrying Allison for her money? Worse, was their relationship risking harm to Allison, and possibly Jax, if others thought they could get to Allison's money through her soon-to-be family? First Crystal using Jax, then what? He ought to put a sandwich board outside the market. *Still independently funded. Tips welcome.*

Wallace rubbed his chin. "Your ex might have sobered up enough to realize what she's lost. She might genuinely desire to make amends and reconnect with Jax. Or she might see an opportunity for funding her habit, especially if she's heard about Allison's benevolence. Might figure Allison will do anything for her adopted son, at any cost."

Virgil's insides felt all scrunched up again. He was supposed to be protecting his family, not opening them up to potential harm. Helping his family be strong, not running around telling lies.

Wallace cocked his head. "Why do you have to go to Reclamation to ask around? Why not do your sleuthing from here?"

"The island grapevine's always worked reliably before. A couple of friends on Reclamation are keeping their eyes open, and it's easier to talk in person rather than risk messages showing up on my phone, which both Jax and Allison use all the time. I thought about digging around online. But could an average guy like me turn up helpful info?"

"An average guy, no. But lucky for you, Wallace Bernard hasn't been average for a long time." Punching Virgil in the arm, Wallace beamed. "Been years since I had legal access, but I've still got ways of getting around the system. I was going to run a check on Frank Winkler Jr. anyway. Can't let a kid like that hang around the Royal Henhouse without knowing his history."

Virgil braced himself. "Still want to throw me off the dock? I deserve it."

"Can't argue with that, Romeo. But you're getting a pass this time. Once your golden girl finds out what's been going on, you'll have trouble enough."

50

Skeletons

As it turns out, Virgil's ex-wife has the record they knew about and then some. But her last five years are a blank slate. No employment, home address, licensing, or voting records. Reporting the findings to Virgil, Wallace promises to ask a buddy to dig deeper.

The background check on Frank Winkler Jr. turns up a twenty-six-year-old former high school basketball star, son of a prominent businessman, brother of a glass-ceiling-crashing female CEO. The kid has a college education four courses short of a degree in mathematics—a bit of a surprise. And a fair share of skeletons in the closet—not a surprise. When Wallace asks about the blots on the record, Winkler is straightforward.

"Yes, sir. I did time at Monroe for selling and manufacturing."

"How long have you been clean?"

"One year, nine months, seventeen days."

"What have you been doing since getting clean?"

"Staying alive, mostly."

Wallace narrows his eyes. "You still in contact with anyone from before?"

"No, sir."

Wallace steps closer, nose to nose. As usual, Winkler holds his ground. The kid's not easy to scare, that's for sure. "If you ever bring *anything* of that life to Wren Island, I will make you regret it."

"Understood . . . sir."

The slight flinch and pause are exactly what Wallace wanted to see. An indication that Frank Winkler Jr. is taking Wallace Bernard seriously.

Wallace claps him on the back. "All right. Let's go get those Jeeps."

Together with Ralph, they chug *Lucy Jo* away from Wren, head into the strait and south to Puget Sound. In Seattle, they tie up at the designated loading dock. Winkler says he's always wanted to drive a Jeep. Came close to doing it once, but the cops arrived before he could jimmy the ignition. So there's no call for drawing straws. Winkler is unanimously voted to be the one to rev the Jeeps out of storage and spin them, one at a time, onto *Lucy Jo*'s deck.

While they're tightening the last tie-downs, Ralph's phone rings. Michael Grant's in the city with four tickets to the afternoon football game. The Seattle Seahawks are hosting the Dallas Cowboys, one of the teams Ralph, a Green Bay Packers fan, enjoys cheering against the most.

The four of them meet outside the stadium. Michael's tickets include gift cards, and before they get to their seats, they've collectively eaten fried shrimp, poke nachos, bang-bang chicken tenders, burgers, pizza, clam chowder, garlic fries, crab rolls, and turkey legs. It's turning into a fantastic day.

And the Seahawks win! After the game, Michael heads home to Reclamation Island, where, best-case scenario, the girl he's interested in will want to see him. The rest of them check into hotel rooms. The night is still young, so they wander until they find a sports bar.

Wallace is sitting there drinking a ginger ale—slowly, because he's already eaten so much he might explode—when a creepy feeling crawls up the back of his head. He's felt it enough times before to know he's being watched.

He scans the premises, casually, one zone at a time. A guy at a table of suits might be familiar, but Wallace can't be sure.

Winkler is yakking about missed field goals when he fizzles and lowers his voice. "I know that guy. Worse, he knows me."

Wallace stiffens. "Which one?"

"Scraggly guy wearing a black hoodie. Sitting alone at a round table, my eleven o'clock."

Ralph looks first. Wallace needed a few seconds to sort out the relative clock. If Winkler had said Wallace's eleven o'clock, Wallace would have known right away where to look. Finally, Wallace takes his turn glancing in the right direction. Yep. The scrapper in a black hoodie is pretending he's not interested in them.

"How do you know him?" Ralph's tone is hard.

"Used to sell to him. Before he figured out I was ripping him off."

Wallace swears. They definitely don't need a run-in with one of Winkler's old cronies. At least he can write off the guy in the suit as the problem. He glances over once more, and the suit meets his gaze. Wallace *does* know him. Carl Grimwald, Ryan Robinson's lawyer. The man responsible for Robinson being released from jail, for Vanessa needing to run, for her hasty boarding of a plane that blasted a hole in a Nebraska cornfield.

Carl Grimwald. Right here in a Seattle sports bar. What are the odds?

Wallace stands abruptly, bumping the table, spilling the drinks. "He's going to pay."

"Whoa, Wallace." Winkler has stood, too. "This is my fight, sir."

For half a second, Wallace wonders why walloping Robinson's lawyer would be Winkler's fight. Then he sees the black hoodie making its way to their table. He claps Winkler on the back. "You fight yours. I'll fight mine."

In four steps, he's towering over Grimwald and throwing a humdinger of a punch, which lands where he hoped it would and, despite having cracked his knuckles in a corroding way, feels great. Then he doesn't feel great at all. He feels entirely unnerved. Like he's started something he can't finish—even if he wants to, which he's not sure about anymore. He could grab a nearby chair. And then what? Slamming a chair across Grimwald's back doesn't seem like a step in the right direction.

"Wallace." Ralph's low voice reaches him.

Turning, he registers Ralph's concerned look and sees thugs mobbing across the room. Black Hoodie's friends must have been in the wings. Winkler's voice rises from the center of the mob.

Wallace turns back to an awake and focusing Grimwald and pats him on the shoulder. "You'll be all right. Won'tcha, buddy?"

The suits with Grimwald gape. Two are holding up their phones, recording.

Ralph's heading for the thugs. Wallace follows close—but on a different route, in case it will be helpful for the two of them to have spread out, although what two geezers might do hasn't been strategized. When the city police storm in, all movement comes to a halt.

Hands in the air, Winkler slowly steps away from the thugs. Ralph and Wallace raise their hands along with everyone else. Even Carl Grimwald is surrendering.

The deflating feeling inside is only partly due to having been outmaneuvered. Taking a careful whiff, Wallace grimaces. Wish he'd thought to pop a couple of Beano tablets before indulging in all that stadium food.

51

Here on Wren

On the day before Wallace, Ralph, and Frank were due to bring Allison's Jeeps to Wren Island, Amelia collected eggs from Tranquility Hill's hens while Melissa stood a clean distance beyond the coop. Out of the blue, Melissa proved how unique she was.

"I'm thinking about adopting a kid."

Amelia set down the basket of eggs.

"I've looked into it. People don't need to be married or in a partnership to adopt a child. Vanessa was eager to get her kids here on Wren, thought it would be a place kids could thrive."

Leave it to Melissa to think in a nontraditional way. "You'd be okay raising a kid on your own?"

Melissa pulled off her lavender knit hat, ran one hand over her smooth head, and tugged the hat back into place. "I'm not on my own here. Am I?"

Amelia retrieved the egg basket, let herself out of the coop, and fastened the door latch. "You've got us, for sure. What would Vanessa say about you adopting?"

"She'd be thrilled. She'd also think I was off my rocker, which I probably am."

A sister who loved and supported you, even when she thought you were nuts. Same experience as Amelia's. "What about your mom? Could she help?"

"I wish. She died about fifteen years ago. After living with a debilitating illness for some time."

"I'm sorry, Melissa."

"She died right before my eighteenth birthday. Dad took us to Las Vegas to try to forget."

"Forget your mom?" Amelia gaped only until she realized doing so was rude.

"To forget the anguish at the end. They met in Vegas. Dad was trying to hold on to a more sentimental time, I think. It's hard to see people we love suffer. And it's hard to lose them."

"I would have liked to meet your mom. And Vanessa, Nathan, and Natalie." Amelia would have reached to hug Melissa, if it weren't for her chicken coop hands and clothing.

Melissa just nodded.

Sighing, Amelia tucked a lightweight towel around the eggs. "I lost my parents. And my sister. Years ago, my fiancé took his own life before we could get married."

"Oh, Amelia, that's awful. I'm so sorry." Melissa stamped dust off her boots. "My dad had a friend, John, who took his own life."

A swirling feeling swept through Amelia's insides. Another John lost to those who'd loved him. Would the world ever stop hurting? Walking toward the main building with Melissa, Amelia carried the egg basket with both hands.

Melissa turned to her. "You know how Dad doesn't talk much? Once in a long while, he'll open up about stuff that matters. Years ago, he told me and Vanessa about losing his friend. Sometimes I think Dad's still running from the moment he learned John was gone. Or running back in time toward it, trying to prevent it from happening. He still remembers John with an Irish red ale on the new moon of every month."

Amelia slowed her steps, the swirling inside turning into a prickly feeling. His name was John. Irish red ale held significance. "This friend of your dad's . . ."

"They were in the Peace Corps together. Before I was born. Back in the seventies."

"Oh my gosh."

When Amelia stumbled, Melissa reached to steady her—and the swinging egg basket. "Are you okay?"

Straightening, Amelia handed over the basket. Caught her breath as her heart thumped faster. "Fine. Thanks for helping me find my balance."

Later, alone, Amelia stood in front of her open clothes closet. Pulled out the shoebox that had once held wedges the color of spring grass, espadrilles from Sears. Blew dust off the box's lid. Untied the faded lavender ribbon holding the lid on. Fingered through the dry, crinkly envelopes inside the box.

Early on, she reread John's letters all the time. She hadn't attended the funeral because she didn't want to remember John that way. His printed block lettering brought more comfort than an afternoon with strangers would have.

When had she stopped rereading John's letters? Probably when she finally accepted there would never be anything new in them. Now, all these years later, might letters she'd read countless times reveal more to the story?

She pulled out one envelope at a time. Read the familiar words. Ran her hands over paper more fragile than it ever had been. Traced handwriting she recognized as if it were her own.

And found it. A funny story John shared about his best friend. Wallace Bernard.

52

Jittery

As Virgil followed the curving forest trail past a rocky outcropping, he tried to settle his racing heart by breathing deeply. Even so, his jittery nerves muscled him to the designated meeting place in record time. Allison was already sitting on the usual log at their favorite overlook. Enjoying the expansive view of shimmering ocean, distant islands, billowy white clouds.

He sat next to her. "Thanks for meeting me here."

She bumped his shoulder with her own. "Always happy to meet you in our special place. So many fond memories here."

He tensed, about to blow that treasure trove sky high. Maybe wreck this comfortable place forever. Possibly set back their relationship immeasurably. How had he let the situation with his ex progress so far without bringing Allison into it?

In the surrounding forest, sparrows chirped. A junco rustled among dry leaves on the ground. Probably the barred owl Virgil had often seen was snoozing. Or keeping one eye on the man about to ruin the harmony.

He stood. No way was he having this conversation here. "Let's walk." He motioned toward the trail, helped her stand. She gave him a concerned look but said nothing.

A few strides down the trail, she turned to him. "Virgil, you're worrying me. You haven't asked a single question yet. What's wrong?"

He stopped walking. Braced himself to tell the truth. "Something significant is wrong."

"Between us?" Her wounded expression showed her foremost fear. She thought *she* was what was wrong. He reached for her hand—both her hands—and held them in his own.

"There's nothing wrong with you. The problem is with me."

The thinnest of curtains dropped over her face, but he knew what was happening behind it. She was afraid he'd lost interest in her. Was letting one of her worst fears take root. When her hands, warm in his, flexed to pull away, he held on. "You're more than enough, sweetheart. I've always loved you and always will. I hope you know that."

"Virgil, would you please tell me what you're trying to protect me from?" The fear in her voice broke his heart. *He* was the reason for her pain.

"It's my ex-wife. She's living on Reclamation Island."

Her hands in his relaxed a fraction. "Oh. Wow. Does Jax know?"

"No. I wanted to give it time first."

"You wanted . . . time? Before telling anyone else?" Her forehead creased with concern, then suspicion. Her hands jerked away.

He shook his head. "Allison, don't jump to conclusions."

"How can I not? You drag your feet about proposing, giving me absolutely no logical reason why, and then I find out your ex is back in your life. Why haven't you included me in this? How long has she been around?"

"She contacted me a few weeks ago."

"And you're just now telling me?"

"You know it's always been complicated with my ex. Let me explain."

Stiffening, she stepped back. "I'd love for you to explain. In fact, I think maybe it might have been nice for you to explain a *few weeks ago*, when whatever this is started."

He got on with it. "I don't know how she found us. Due to some protective measures I put in place, she thought we were living on Reclamation. So she got a job there, supposedly, although I haven't been able to confirm what she's doing or who she's working for. And to tell you the truth—"

"Finally, the truth!"

In a flash of annoyance, he threw his hands up in the air. "You want the whole story? Don't interrupt me. And *quit jumping to conclusions!*"

Now that he'd finally worked up the courage to tell her, he needed her to listen. He took a step back and a deep breath.

"Anyway, the truth is I'm concerned she might be in trouble. Always trouble with Crystal! It finds her even when she's not looking for it. I know I'm not responsible for her anymore. I *know* that. But she's Jax's mother. If there's a chance Jax could have a halfway healthy relationship with her, I want that for him, especially now that he's old enough to understand more. I'm sorry you're hearing about it this late in the game. I'm a complete idiot for the way I've handled this—or not handled it, depending on how you think of it."

Her hand was warm on his arm. "Hey. We don't have to figure this out all at once."

He ventured a smile. "We?"

She nodded, her expression still guarded but more open. He patted the hand resting on his arm. Thought about kissing her forehead. Darling Allison! But she didn't look *that* open. Yet.

"What kind of trouble do you think Crystal is in?" Her voice held a compassionate tone.

He shrugged. "Drugs, probably. Or it could be anything. So far, I haven't learned who or what she's involved with. Wallace wasn't able to dig up useful information, which was a disappointment. But next time I'm on Reclamation, I'll try to—"

"Wait a minute." Her hand abandoned his arm. Her eyes narrowed. "Wallace knows?"

"Because he confronted me about all the trips to Reclamation, concerned for you."

Virgil sensed the softness in Allison's expression was for Wallace, not him. "So all those special deliveries were an excuse to go to Reclamation and look for Crystal? A made-up reason? A *lie*?"

The expression on his face must have revealed she was correct, because she stepped back. Then down the curtain came, hiding any more vulnerability. His actions might as well have built a wall between them.

"Virgil, we agreed we would not keep secrets from each other." Tinged with tears, the sound of hurt in her voice caused his insides to ache. "And now you're telling me your ex-wife lives nearby. You've been trying to see her for weeks. Lying about market deliveries that don't exist. Why did you keep this from me? You said yourself this problem is significant. Yet you didn't invite me into it! Didn't *trust* me enough to give me a *chance* to share it with you."

He was past the point where he could have salvaged the wreck, which was now sinking with *Titanic* speed. It would have been far better to be walloped and thrown off the dock by Wallace. He desperately needed to right the ship.

"We're not keeping secrets! I'm telling you now."

"After weeks of *not* telling me!"

"I tried! Several times! Something always interfered."

"Oh, I'm sure something more important came up. Every time." Unable to check the tears any longer, she folded her arms across herself. "Notice I'm not running off, though I really, really want to right now."

What could he do to ease this pain, when he was the cause of it? He reached for her, but she stopped him with a look. Swallowing, he cast about for another way to get them out of this mess.

"Listen—and these aren't excuses but explanations. I'd start to tell you and then your aunts would walk in. A customer would need help. Jax would interrupt. One time I was about to tell you but Louise stared me down. You know that look she gets when she's prepared to shift her entire allegiance to Allison Theodore."

"My *dog* kept you from telling me?"

"Louise can be uncommonly persuasive."

Disbelief crossed her face. Followed by, possibly, a hint of amusement.

Another deep breath, and he got to the root of it. "The thing is, it didn't require much to make me lose my courage. I knew you'd be upset when you found out, and I can't bear to see you unhappy. It feels like my insides are being torn up when I see you feeling anything less than brilliant and safe and completely confident you're loved. I think what it comes down to is I was trying to protect you."

"Sounds more like you were protecting yourself. From seeing me in a way you didn't want to."

He squirmed. The line between protecting her and protecting himself. Was it that thin? "Um, okay. You might be on to a truth there. But I'd also do anything to keep you from being hurt."

She stepped closer—finally!—and put a hand back on his arm. "Would you please forget about trying to protect me? This is supposed to be a partnership."

He could drown in those sparkling eyes. He'd do anything to always make them glimmer. Punch a whack job, wallop a sneaky thief, save a tree, put up with interrupting aunts, label the produce bins with the designated font. *Anything* to affirm she was safe and treasured. "But I like protecting you."

"Fine, if you're doing it because you love me. But don't you dare shield me from something because you think I'm not strong enough to handle it."

So they were back to Allison Theodore being perfectly capable of taking care of herself. If that's how she wanted to view herself, okay. He tugged her close, then closer, until she yielded, moved into his arms, let him wrap her tight.

Snuggling in, she sighed. "So you'll be less protector, more partner?"

He breathed in her lemon-scented hair and shook his head. "Nope. Not going to stop protecting you. It's built into the Virgil Tagaloa package. But one trait doesn't have to cancel out the other. I'll also be the partner you want."

"The partner I need."

Ah! He rested his cheek against her head. No way was he letting fear drive him to hide anything from her ever again. "I'm sorry, darling. I should have told you right away. I'm a complete idiot."

She shifted in his arms, huffing. "You're not a *complete* idiot."

"I feel like I am."

"Well, you're not, so stop saying you are." She looked up at him with a half smile. "I didn't get all brave about loving a man just to find out I'd chosen a complete idiot."

He kissed her. They might have gone on for a while, hard to tell, time stood gloriously still.

Finally, she gazed at him. "No more secrets?"

"Only nice ones."

She snuggled back into his arms, her cheek against his chest. "Okay, now I'll tell *you* a secret." Her teasing tone indicated a secret he would like. "I bought Jax a Jeep for his birthday! I've been waiting for it to be delivered from Hawaii. Tomorrow's the big day!"

His breath caught. Within days of being old enough, Jax had earned his provisional license. Was already a reliably cautious driver, thanks to many lessons with Virgil and Ralph. But a car of his own? A birthday gift Virgil hadn't investigated, let alone okayed?

Allison must have sensed his trepidation, because she left his arms and took a guarded step back. "Why do I get the feeling you're not pleased?"

53

Cool, calm boss lady

Seated on a short stool at the rock wall, Amelia wedged another piece of green plastic into the wet mortar. When her idea of creating a from-scratch mosaic had felt overwhelming, Ed had suggested Amelia follow the low, rambling wall along Tranquility Hill's driveway and add bits of plastic as she felt inclined.

Reaching into one of the wooden buckets Ed installed for islanders to contribute found plastic, Amelia chose a blue piece and lined it up in the mortar. Ed, wearing his hat woven from Hawaiian palm leaves, reinforced crumbling sections of the wall nearby.

The sound of Melissa practicing on her new drum set reached them from the vacant pole barn beyond the main building. Allison's eyes had lit up at one mention of Melissa's secret dream to become drummer of a rock band. Before Allison could order the sparkling red set she and Melissa had decided on, a family on the island's north side offered their teenager's shiny black set. With their son heading off to college, the parents hoped for a more subdued soundtrack during school breaks. Amelia understood how they felt. But Melissa only practiced between noon and five, same hours Wren Islanders permitted chainsaws, jet boat engines, and grinding tractor gears.

Amelia reached for another green plastic piece. Working on the wall mosaic was a nice way to let her thoughts wander and see what popped up. After finding Wallace mentioned in John's letters, she felt like her mind—and heart—needed space to sort everything out.

As John's best friend, Wallace must have known about John's engagement to Amelia. Why didn't Wallace get in touch with her after John's death? They could have shared their memories. And their grief. It would have been nice to hear more about John from Wallace's perspective.

Comparing two pieces of green plastic, Amelia chose the larger and lined it up in the mortar. Pressed the smaller piece in next to it.

Communication went two ways, though. When she chose not to attend the funeral, had she given up her only chance of learning more about the man she'd planned to spend the rest of her life with? It would have been an effort, but not *too* difficult, to locate a Wallace Bernard who'd served in the Peace Corps.

Early on, had she considered looking for Wallace? Much of the time following John's death was a blur, her memory bank of the several years after mostly empty.

Sitting back, Amelia viewed her progress on the mosaic. A random collection of colors and sizes. Would it eventually become a recognizable image? Artwork worth saving?

Sighing, she pulled the bucket close and picked through it, hoping for a piece of sea glass or an exquisite stone.

Tomorrow, the very same Wallace Bernard would land on Wren's beach with Jeeps from Hawaii. She ought to prepare herself. Interacting with Wallace would feel different now, knowing what she knew.

When newly grieving, she'd blamed John's depression and death on anyone nearer to him than herself. If she'd been there, she would have helped. Apparently, no one else had noticed anything amiss.

A sharp edge on a plastic piece pricked her thumb, and the vulnerable emerged in her thoughts. Who else near her might be struggling, right now, and not showing it?

Folks, if that's you, say something. Talk to a friend, a clergy person, a hotline operator. We want you around. That was what she'd say if she were narrating a YouTube video about it.

From what Melissa said, Wallace still honored John by drinking an Irish red ale every month. Wallace downed one on the day of the memorial service for Vanessa and the kids, same day he announced he was leaving with Michael—running from Melissa and the pain they both felt, although no one had said so outright.

Amelia flicked away a thick piece of mortar that had stuck to one knuckle. Had Wallace run from John too? If Wallace had been such a trustworthy friend, why did he allow John to drift off, alone, to a place of no return?

In crept a flip-side thought. She'd been the fiancée absent from John's life except through letters. Would Wallace blame *her* for John's death?

"Jeeps coming tomorrow." Ed's voice startled Amelia, though by now she ought to be used to having people around—both here at the Hill and at Allison's.

Ed was stirring her bucket of mortar, a task she enjoyed doing herself. She shook off her annoyance at his so-called helpfulness. "We'll take time off to watch their arrival. I don't want to miss Virgil's reaction. And Jax's, of course."

"You thinking what I'm thinking?" Ed chuckled.

The old Amelia Theodore would have blurted out her thought that Virgil might not like Allison buying his only son his first car. The new Amelia Theodore was learning to maintain a professional distance from her employees. "Depends. What are you thinking?"

"I'm thinking Virgil's going to be as surprised as Jax that Allison's giving him a Jeep. But maybe not surprised in a grateful way."

Hearing Ed voice the thoughts she'd intentionally kept private felt like an assault on her niece. "Virgil will be thrilled once he sees how excited Jax is."

"Sure. He'll come around. Eventually."

Digging through the bucket, Amelia focused on finding another plastic piece. Chose a jagged orangish bit. Held it into wet mortar longer than necessary, hoping her busy appearance might cause Ed to drop the conversation.

"Virgil's a decent guy." Ed stirred the mortar again.

"Exemplary."

"Amelia?" When Ed's voice cracked, she glanced up. "Speaking of decent guys, I wonder if you'd like to go somewhere with me sometime."

"Go somewhere with you?" They went places all the time. The rehab aviary, grocery market, goat yard, chicken coop.

"Dinner maybe?"

She ate half of her dinners at Tranquility Hill. "We eat together all the time."

"Yes, but with a bunch of other people around. Not just us."

She blinked. Twice. When was the last time Amelia Theodore got asked out on a date? Or was she reading Ed wrong? She went for cool, calm boss lady. "What exactly are you asking, Ed?"

"Hey, you guys!" Melissa's top half appeared on the other side of the wall, her skin damp with perspiration from a robust drum session. "The mosaic is looking terrific!"

Gathering his tools, Ed straightened. "Amelia's got talent for this kind of thing." He tipped his head toward Amelia. "I'll be in the goat barn, preparing for the new arrivals." In case Amelia wanted an answer to her question? Or because Ed wanted an answer to his? He'd have to wait. She was in no hurry.

When Ed had gone, Melissa sat in the grass near Amelia and poked through the bucket of plastic pieces. "Amelia, would you help me with a project?"

"Sure. If I can."

"A friend sent the last of my sister's things—mostly special mementos, clothes, and toys. I think I'm ready to look through the boxes, but I don't want to do it alone. Dad said he'd rather not be involved in the sorting, although he wants to see whatever I decide to save."

Friend Amelia immediately knew she'd help Melissa. Boss Lady Amelia first asked for clarification. "Are you asking me to help you go through Vanessa's things?"

"Yes, please."

Pressing a hand against the wall, Amelia steadied herself. Finding Wallace's name in John's letters. Maybe being asked on a date. Definitely asked to help a grieving sister sort through mementos. So many of life's emotional moments happening, all within a stone's throw of each other.

54

Loving a woman

Seeing Allison scrunch up her face, Virgil grimaced. He didn't feel up to plowing into another argument. The issues they'd just resolved—keep no more secrets, okay for Virgil to sort of protect, no call to question Allison's self-sufficiency—had been plenty intense. Minutes ago, she snuggled in his arms. Now she stood at odds with him, ready to go back to battle.

He sighed. Emotional swings back and forth, hot then cold, plumb wore him out. Life spent loving Allison Theodore was going to be anything but boring, but then he'd known that from the beginning. He'd take a congenial tack.

"Why did you buy Jax a vehicle before talking to me?"

She shrugged. "I didn't know what else to get him, and the Jeep was right in front of me."

That she'd bought Jax a car wasn't the problem. It was what the car symbolized. Driving his own vehicle, Virgil's little boy would suddenly be more grown up. More independent—not at all ironic, because the birthday gift was coming from the most independent woman in Jax's life. But Virgil didn't feel ready to let go. That was the root of it, and the ongoing dilemma of being a dad. When to keep your kid close and protected, when to let him go wherever his heart led.

Same dilemma when loving a woman.

"I wish you had asked me first."

She bristled. "Are there rules about how I spend my own money?"

"Of course not." Virgil ran a hand around the back of his neck. She'd plunked down probably thousands of dollars, for a gift he'd known nothing about. While he'd worried about making minimum payments to the repo man! "It would have been nice to know you were buying a car for my son."

"Your son? How are the three of us supposed to be a family if you keep making rules like that?"

"Rules?"

"He's your son when it's time to buy a car. Our son when we're trying to become a family. Mine whenever he needs help that's less than manly."

Virgil had completely lost track of what they were talking about. "I don't understand. You give him help that's less than manly?"

She threw her hands up in the air. "Whenever Jax needs something halfway motherish, I'm on deck. You hand him off to me like I've got magical powers. As if by being a woman, I automatically have skills. When he's supposed to create an art project for school. When he's sad about a fading friendship. Trying a new hair product. Learning to patch his jeans. Taking care of those kittens he found in the barn. Every time, I'm supposed to help. As if I know how the heck to be a mother!"

He gaped at her.

"I mean, sure, I *had* a mother. An excellent one. But I've never *been* a mother. Suddenly I'm getting a teenager! And now his biological mother might be back in the picture. So what's my role supposed to be? How will I know how to *do* this?"

She burst into tears.

He ought to ease her fears. But blast if he knew how to. Had he ever seen her in this much turmoil? Revealing more insecurity with each increasingly frantic statement?

When he put a hand on her shoulder, she turned away as if embarrassed. Or . . . ashamed?

Understanding filtered into him. She'd offered her raw, unpolished thoughts. Trusted him with her deepest fears. Unloaded more pieces of herself he was bound—and willing—to safeguard.

Still not looking at him, she shuddered out a sigh. "Now I find out I broke a rule by buying him a car, because that's what his father's supposed to do. It's an awful lot of pressure, Virgil, trying to be what everyone needs."

"Hold on, love." Placing a hand on each of her shoulders, he turned her toward him, gently, and made eye contact. "Forget your blasted rules. Forget trying to be everything to everyone. What you said to me, I'm saying to you. You're already everything, and offering everything."

She sniffed.

All those years of single parenting, then suddenly an angel appeared. Maybe he did offload too many responsibilities to Allison. Placed her, unintentionally, in a pressure-filled situation. Now she was feeling overwhelmed, no thanks to her supposed partner—who hadn't seen the warning signs because he'd been too occupied trying to hide something difficult from her. Running around when he should have been with her, listening.

One arm around her shoulders, he wiped the tears from her cheeks. "I'm sorry if I added to the pressure you feel. I'm sorry I've been absent."

She shrugged closer, her way of saying he was forgiven.

Heaving a sigh, he kissed the top of her head. "Feel better now? After throwing all that at me?"

"I'm sorry. Usually I can hold back more. Not let my overwhelm become a burden to others."

Finding her ear, he whispered, "No need to apologize. I like you human."

Whether it was the silence that followed, her fidgeting, or her cautious breaths, something told him she was remembering history with her ex. "What would Tank have done if you let loose like that?"

She shook her head.

Virgil felt a familiar stirring of anger. If ever he was within punch-throwing vicinity of Allison's ex, the entire community would hear about what happened next. He took a calming breath. "Please tell me. So we can build this family *our* way."

She exhaled. "I would never have been that honest with him. He would have turned it around and used it to hurt me."

His arms wrapping her closer, Virgil experienced the odd sensation of two conflicting desires. On the one hand, he envisioned thrashing a man he'd never met. On the other, he was settling the woman he loved. Helping her be strong again. She'd been hopping mad because he hadn't included her in a messy part of his life. When was the last time he felt so cared about?

He patted her back. "You're unexpectedly sensitive."

Pulling away slightly, she arched one eyebrow. "Explain yourself, partner."

He tucked her close again. "Sensitive in an admirable way. I don't think my ex ever insisted I share anything with her. Drugs stole her ability to care, maybe. I tried to protect her. It wasn't enough."

"The Virgil Tagaloa protection package is working well enough for me, now that we're fine-tuning the system."

Laughing, he reached for her left hand, held it to his lips, kissed it. "Everything about you is like a beacon. People naturally look to you for help and leadership. That means you inevitably carry the burden of others' expectations. You're so seemingly capable, people aren't aware when something's bothering you."

She was a conundrum of unlikely combinations. Confidence and vulnerability, connection and independence, flexibility and stubbornness. Of course he wanted to protect her! And if she wanted and needed him to be her life partner, he'd be honored to do that too.

She shifted in his arms. "What about the Jeep? Is it okay to give it to Jax?"

"Oh, are we back to that again? Just when I was getting poetic?"

"I like you poetic." She tapped the watch on her wrist. "I also like being on time, and I'm expecting a scheduled phone call about cargo. Tomorrow is a big delivery day! Goods for Tranquility Hill. And the Jeeps."

"Wait. Jeeps *plural*?"

"One's for me."

"Let me guess. It's high-gloss bright yellow."

She blinked. "Aunt Amelia told you?"

"Nope. No one on this island has breathed a whiff about Jeeps to me, which I find mildly annoying. But not entirely unremarkable, given that the woman I love seems to be extraordinarily skilled at influencing people."

"Are you saying we can give him the Jeep?"

Feeling conflicted, he hedged. "A young man's first car is monumental. A rite of passage. I had my eye on a vintage Intrigue for him."

"An *Oldsmobile*? For a teenage boy?"

He shrugged. "It's a reliable option. I probably wouldn't have chosen a Jeep."

"Jax would. Jeeps are all he's talked about for months."

Virgil tilted his head. Had his son ever mentioned wanting a Jeep? They'd talked about cars, of course. Jax seemed on board with the idea of driving a basic sedan. Or maybe Jax had agreed with the suggestion, knowing it was what Virgil wanted. "You guys talk about cars?"

"All the time. He wants a Jeep because his great-granddad liked them."

"Ah. He never met his great-granddad but has heard stories." Virgil took Allison's hand, ran his fingers across the back of it, tucked it into his own. "Once he gets the keys, we'll probably never see him again."

She shook her head. "His permit still requires supervision. And you set the rules on when and where he can drive." Then she gave a teasing look. "You could ask neighbors to text you if they see questionable activity. Add a tracker to the vehicle. Roll out new features of the Virgil Tagaloa protection package."

Lifting her hand, he kissed it. Pulled her back into his arms. Ran a hand through her hair. Exhaled. "One day Jax will fly from our nest and not come back."

"Maybe he'll meet a nice girl and they'll nest on Wren."

"Now that's a choice I highly recommend."

55

Plexiglass

One advantage to being in a city jail is, once intake simmers down, forty winks are easily had. Winkler and Ralph were probably released after being questioned. Wallace tries not to think about the comfortable hotel rooms they're staying in. He's got his own cell in an outlying ward. Prime digs.

First thing in the morning, he gets shuffled into his half of the visitation area, where Carl Grimwald's on the other side of the plexiglass barrier. Wallace sits across from Grimwald, notes the bruising, and says what needs to be said before anything else. "I'm sorry. I lost myself."

Grimwald nods. "Apology accepted."

"Are you hurt any worse than it looks? You don't have a head injury, do you?"

Grimald shakes his head. "They say you lose muscle strength as you age."

Thinking through the implications of that one, Wallace can't figure out if he feels better or worse.

Grimwald scrapes his chair closer. "They also say what doesn't kill you makes you stronger."

Wallace nods. "Yeah. I've heard that."

"I'm sorry about Vanessa. Nathan. Natalie."

It's been a long, long time since Wallace heard his daughter's name spoken through plexiglass. He's never heard his grandkids' names filter through.

"Everyone at my office is sorry for your loss, Wallace. Everyone I've talked to who knows you, who ever worked with you or for you—everyone is sorry. I know they'd want me to tell you."

Shoot. If Grimwald doesn't stop talking, Wallace won't be able to keep his roiling emotions inside. Wallace nods and, after a minute, says what seems most important now. "My daughter Melissa's talking to her old man again. We're . . . mending."

"Wonderful. Melissa Bernard has always been a powerhouse."

It's nice to hear Melissa's name spoken too. Although it'd be better if it wasn't through plexiglass.

Grimwald stands, smiling. "I'm not pressing charges. Keep me in mind if you ever need a lawyer."

Wallace swallows. He should thank Grimwald. He wants to express his gratitude. But can he trust his voice to come out sounding the way he wants? Stable, robust.

"Well . . ." Grimwald would offer Wallace a handshake, it seems, if there weren't a barrier between them. "Take care."

For once, Wallace is grateful for the plexiglass. If Grimwald, with his bruised eyebrow and scratched cheek, had reached out his hand, trusting Wallace to return the courtesy, Wallace would have lost it. Wept like the wreck he is.

56

Future astronomer

Early morning sunshine filtering through the curtains casts radiating patterns across Vanessa's boxes. Surrounded by kids' clothes and stuffed animals of all shapes and sizes, Amelia and Melissa laughed and cried. After unfolding a small tee shirt with the words *Future Astronomer* across the front, Melissa reached for a plastic telescope. "I gave these things to the kids. I never imagined it'd all come back to me."

"Maybe the kid you adopt will enjoy this stuff." Opening a small suitcase, Amelia pulled out a tiny trench coat and fedora hat, dark sunglasses, and a notepad and pencil. "What's this for?"

Melissa reached for the hat. "Nathan's detective kit. He was pretending he had a job like mine, and this outfit was the best I came up with."

Sitting on Melissa's bed, Amelia pulled a stuffed pink lamb into her lap and fingered its soft ears, worn smooth from smaller hands than hers. "You've mentioned your past work, but you've never said what you did. Or if you miss it."

"I doubt I'll ever do it again. Being a crisis negotiator doesn't jive with being a single mom."

"Whoa! Like freeing hostages? Like I've seen in television shows?"

"Hostage situations are one of many I've negotiated. Though the work's nothing like you see on television. Most negotiations plod along at an excruciatingly slow pace with one goal: guide everyone through the next step with minimal risk of harm. Two degrees in psychology and a lifetime around law enforcement made it a natural fit for me." Melissa held the tiny trench coat in front of her.

Amelia retrieved a toy badge that fell from the coat onto the bed. "Your calm attitude helped, I bet. You're poised and patient. And you come up with ideas quickly."

Melissa smiled. "You're good at that, Amelia. Seeing the best in people."

Amelia squinted. Was she? She'd always tried to look for admirable traits in people. Maybe some of her efforts were finally starting to become habits. After sixty-some years of practice.

Watching Melissa tuck the detective gear back into its case, Amelia felt a wash of new appreciation for Tranquility Hill's assistant director. Melissa's life before Wren must have been so different. "I bet you helped a lot of people."

"Some. That kind of work doesn't always go the way you want it to."

Melissa's voice held the sound of hurt piled on more hurt. How much loss had this girl seen?

"I'm sorry. Cases needing negotiation must be difficult."

"It's all on you if things go south. A lonely place to be. If I become a mom, I want my work to keep me close to my kid. With more predictable hours and less risk."

Straightening, Boss Lady Amelia beamed. "Tranquility Hill to the rescue. Assistant Director Melissa Bernard may show up to work with her adorable kid in tow. I'm officially adding it to my list of nice things to wish for. That you'll be approved soon."

Later, with no updated ETA for the day's deliveries, Amelia hesitated before interrupting Allison in the room she affectionately referred to as her den, waiting until the lovely tune Allison was churning out resolved in a natural pause. "How much longer until the Jeeps arrive, do you think?"

Allison held up her phone screen. "I've been tracking *Lucy Jo* on the app. They laid over in Seattle, so I haven't asked them to pick up the Hill's new residents yet. But it'd be nice to get the goats here sooner rather than later. I'll call Wallace when *Lucy Jo* starts moving."

Not getting the goats until later would be a disappointment. Amelia wandered down to the beach. Collected a few shells. Stashed them in a fabric bag printed with gray goats against a rainbow background, a gift from Macy in honor of the Hill's newest residents, and tried to organize her thoughts.

Sooner rather than later might also be when she should talk with Wallace about their shared connection. Clear any lingering foggy air between them. But Wallace's daughter had become an employee and a friend. Even Wallace's future grandchild might suffer effects if Amelia and Wallace had a falling out. How to approach the subject?

Hey Wallace, remember your friend John who died? He was my fiancé. Thanks ever so much for letting John leave before I knew what was happening.

See? The conversation might derail before it got going. All these years later, Amelia felt resentment toward a man she'd only recently become acquainted with. Same grief, new angle. Like John left all over again. Like someone was standing in front of her who, moments ago, could have stopped John from leaving.

She'd never raised her fist to anyone. But if she and Wallace talked face-to-face about this, she honestly might want to take a swing at him.

Obviously, she needed more time before saying anything.

Pulling out her phone, she added an entry to her audio journal. "What I'm wondering is, why not go on as I always have? For years, the grief has been dreadful. But I'm past the worst of it, aren't I? Talking about it, with someone who was *there*, might make this more painful again." She stopped recording and pondered her own questions. No answers came. Which didn't add to her anguish. But didn't ease it either.

57

Like last time

As *Lucy Jo* gains speed, Wallace sits in the wheelhouse and chows down on the burgers and fries Ralph and Winkler picked up, knowing Wallace would be hungry after a jailhouse's so-called breakfast. Ralph at the helm, they chug north out of Seattle without looking back.

Between fries, Winkler says exactly what Wallace is thinking. "We'd better steer clear of Seattle for a while."

"Yep. Probably best if the girls don't find out we landed in the slammer."

"Agreed, sir."

"On Wren, we can't get into trouble."

"*Much* trouble, you mean." Grinning, Winkler hauls out the boom box and flips it on. Roger Whittaker's voice wafts through the wheelhouse.

Memories roll over Wallace in waves. Being stranded. Drinking too much. Answering Vanessa's phone call. Everything that came after.

When his cell phone rings later, Wallace has been dozing. Or lost in memories. He checks his surroundings. *Lucy Jo*'s running across smooth water under a clear sky. Friends are with him in the wheelhouse. He swipes open the call. "Howdy, Miss Allison Theodore."

"Aunt Amelia and I have a question."

"And it is?"

"We're wondering if you'll pick up goats on your way back."

"Say it again?"

"I bought goats from a farmer on Reclamation Island. They can be picked up anytime."

Wallace squints at *Lucy Jo*'s crowded deck. "I've got your Jeeps on board."

Allison makes a small sound. He pictures her shrugging, unconcerned. Certain Wallace Bernard can handle anything.

"How many goats are we talking about?"

"A few."

"Allison, how many goats?"

"Twenty. Maybe twenty-two by the time you get there? A couple are pregnant."

He swipes off the call and gets Ralph's attention. "Change course. Swing by Reclamation and we'll pick up pregnant goats." While Winkler springs up and down and belts out a woo-hoo—a fan of goats, apparently—a nearby paper tablet with handwritten notes reminds Wallace of another moment from life before. He holds the tablet up to Ralph. "You know this rig? *Pinch Hitter*?"

"Belongs to Lester Locum. Hails from Reclamation."

Winkler comes near, sobering. "I used to see that guy scrounging around Reclamation."

"Since we're headed there, what do you say we do reconnaissance?" Wallace pulls up a vessel tracker app and searches for *Pinch Hitter*. "They're currently traveling west, north of us, no specified destination. If we maintain our current course, we'll come up on them in ten or so minutes."

While Ralph keeps *Lucy Jo*'s speed at fifteen knots and Winkler watches the tracker screen, Wallace peers through binoculars until *Pinch Hitter* appears. The shrimper is sitting high in the water, carrying little or light cargo.

An unexpected wave of grief hits Wallace, like he's pooling into a puddle on the wheelhouse floor. Last time he speculated about *Pinch Hitter*'s cargo weight, Vanessa was alive. She was about to call him, deliver unwelcome news, pack up the kids, head to the airport, start a new life on Wren Island.

He sets aside the binoculars and gazes out the wheelhouse's port-side window. Wipes a hand across the dampness building in his eyes. He could make a comment about how hot it is—unseasonably warm today—but Ralph and Winkler would see through it. Wallace isn't hot. He's sad. The new Wallace Bernard is willing to admit his feelings, unwanted as they may be.

"So what's the plan?" Seated in the captain's chair and steering with his feet, Ralph gazes starboard. Opposite the direction Wallace is looking. Ralph has always been conscientious about offering emotional space in tight quarters. "Or do we have a plan?"

Winkler motions to the tracking screen. "They're turning into Seal Rock's cove."

Wallace picks up the binoculars again. Yep, *Pinch Hitter* has disappeared against the distant backdrop of Seal Rock. "If we get any closer, we'll need a reason to be hanging around when they leave. Last time, I dropped fishing lines."

Last time, Vanessa was alive.

Not liking where his thoughts are going, he reels them in. "Too bad we don't have a crate of mice on board. We could tie up in the cove with freeing mice as our excuse."

"Wonder what your skittery friends are up to these days?" It's a loony-tune question, but Winkler's tone is serious. Since finding out about Operation Relocate, Winkler inquires about the mice several times a week, as if Wallace keeps an open hotline for rodents in trouble.

Ralph is steering with both hands now, turning *Lucy Jo* east of Seal Rock. "Better we stay off shore and unnoticed. If Lester and his crew are moving stolen goods, these flashy Jeeps might be tempting."

"How certain are we they're up to anything?" Winkler's getting wary, as he should.

Ralph checks the wheelhouse's rear window before angling more to starboard. "A while back, Allison was injured and alone on Seal Rock. Lester Locum showed up in *Pinch Hitter* and seemed more concerned about covering his own tracks than getting help for Allison. And Wallace has seen enough to think Locum could be connected to junk being stored there, possibly for resale."

Wallace rubs his chin. "The way I see it, we've got three options. One, head into the cove and tie up at the dock. Confront them with the goods in hand."

Both Ralph and Winkler shake their heads.

"Option two, hang out here and wait for them to leave. If they leave heavy, follow them who knows where until who knows what happens, *if* it happens."

Wallace feels tired thinking about it. When did he lose interest in doing reconnaissance? He used to live for catching any bad guy. Now, what does he care if a dude's dumping junk on a remote island? It's wrong, but it's not directly hurting anyone. And a nice dinner at Allison's house probably waits for *Lucy Jo*'s crew.

Ralph looks as unenthusiastic as Wallace feels. Winkler's distracted by something on the brass edge of the compass. A ladybug, which Winkler lets crawl up his hand.

Wallace sighs. "Third option, give it up. Not our barrel of monkeys."

"Fourth option." Winkler moves to the open window and lets the ladybug fly free. "Hang here, out of sight, watching the tracker. After *Pinch Hitter* leaves, tie up in the cove and poke around. See if we uncover anything useful. Get photos of the shrimper leaving and whatever we find."

Wallace thinks it through. "I guess we could document the stuff I found a few weeks ago."

Ralph navigates *Lucy Jo* to a binocular's distance off Seal Rock's east side, out of sight from the cove entrance and off the path of *Pinch Hitter*'s anticipated return trip to Reclamation Island. They drop fishing lines. Two old geezers and a kid who looks young enough to require a permission slip, supposed to be making deliveries, but they heard the fish were biting.

A lot like last time.

58

Lightweight crime

An hour and a half later, the blip on the tracking screen indicates *Pinch Hitter* is leaving the cove. Heading southwest toward Reclamation Island, as expected. A factor they didn't think of, though, is that from here they can't see how high or low *Pinch Hitter*'s sitting in the water.

The three of them are preparing *Lucy Jo* for the short trip into Seal Rock's cove when the sound of an approaching vessel reaches them, at full tilt, not appearing on the tracking screen.

Glancing at the well-marked patrol craft, Wallace swears. "Fish & Wildlife. Either of you have a fishing license?"

"For traps and pots, yes." Ralph shuts down *Lucy Jo*'s engine and heads for the wheelhouse door. "For pole and line, no."

Moving aside, Winkler shrugs. "I wondered about that. But I assumed you guys knew what you were doing."

"Ha! A valuable lesson learned, Winkler." Wallace moves to descend the wheelhouse stairs and bring in the lines.

Holding an arm out to stop Wallace's progress, Ralph nods toward *Lucy Jo*'s deck. "Leave the lines. Maybe Fish & Wildlife's here for another reason." It's the same clear thinking Wallace has always gotten from his experienced friend. Why act suspicious until you're certain you've been caught?

One of the two officers asks for permission to come aboard—which he's congenially given, of course. While Winkler and the other officer tie the patrol boat to *Lucy Jo*, Wallace scuffs around on deck, going for harmless old geezer. Ralph, owner and operator of the vessel under investigation, handles the formalities.

Turns out it *is* the fishing lines being questioned. A lightweight crime day, apparently. Nothing more compelling to investigate.

They hand over their IDs. Boat operator license for Ralph. Vehicle driver's license for Wallace. State-issued ID card for Winkler—whose lack of a driver's license was conveniently glossed over when Winkler asked to spin Jeeps around the Seattle loading dock.

Officer Drake scans the IDs one at a time. Bringing all kinds of records to light, no doubt. Especially from the last twenty-four hours. He eyes Ralph, Wallace, Winkler. "You boys have been busy."

"Yes, sir." Winkler's response is automatic but genuine. "Got caught up in a scuffle last night while trying to be helpful."

Drake agrees lawful help from concerned citizens is sometimes warranted. He tells them he's been married for two years, is the father of twin boys, and will celebrate five years with the force next November. And he goes easy on them with warnings only. This time.

He gives them back their IDs. "Maybe leave the heavy lifting to the experts, eh?" Wallace's shoulders loosen as the officer makes for his patrol boat.

Just when they could be in the clear, Ralph calls to Drake. "Speaking of heavy lifting, you ever notice anything odd at Seal Rock?"

Drake stops. Turns to face them. "Like?"

"Wallace here thinks someone's storing stolen goods there."

Officer Drake takes his time moving closer to Wallace. "What were you doing on Seal Rock?"

This guy is completely bypassing the main point—stolen goods! His question is legitimate, though, and the mild manner strikes Wallace as pretense. Whatever Wallace says next will set the tone for everything that comes after.

He clears his throat. "You won't believe it."

"Try me."

"I was letting mice go free."

Drake takes that one in. Seems to waffle, but between what? Annoyance and amusement? Maybe Drake's wishing it was quitting time. Wants to head home for dinner with the missus and twin boys.

"My boss had a mouse problem at her house." Winkler's proving a handy defensive teammate. "Wallace trapped them all—"

"Not all." Wallace frowns. "A few rogues still turn up every now and then."

Winkler drapes a skinny arm around Wallace's shoulders. "And Wallace ferries them over to Seal Rock. For a better life."

Glancing around, Drake seems to be grasping for a more routine subject. He jerks a thumb toward the deck cargo. "Who gets the Jeeps?"

Thinking of millionaire Allison purchasing a Jeep for her boyfriend's teenage son, Wallace smiles. "Same girl."

"Girl?"

"Allison Theodore, maybe you've heard of—"

"Allison Theodore is no *girl*." Drake's narrowed eyes are hidden behind his sunglasses, but his scrunching eyebrows reveal displeasure.

"Yes, sir." Winkler again. "We all have the utmost respect for Ms. Theodore. She's our boss, neighbor, and friend."

A slight sense of confusion overshadows Wallace. He has more respect for Allison than almost anyone he's ever known. Melissa is always drilling him on approved terminology, so he realizes an old geezer referring to a woman as a girl is not appropriate in today's world. But he'd meant it in an endearing way.

Like how he'd think of Vanessa and Melissa. Like a daughter.

When he lost one, did another ease, enchantingly, into his aching heart? It feels like he'd do anything for Allison, like he would for Melissa.

Officer Drake has checked Ralph's cargo manifesto and moved to admire the Jeeps. Says his grandfather drove one like the vintage open-top. Same camo paint, if Drake remembers correctly from photos. "Good condition, these Jeeps. The yellow one's so glossy it could have been driven off the lot this morning."

Finally, Drake's back on his own vessel and untying from *Lucy Jo*. Ralph leans over the gunwale, calls out to Drake. "So you'll check out Seal Rock?"

"We'll do what we can." The patrol vessel buzzes off.

Back in the wheelhouse, Winkler raises one hand, fingers spread wide. "Fifth option, turn the suspected problem over to law enforcement."

"Fine by me." Ralph revs up *Lucy Jo* again. "If we don't get going, we'll be delivering goats in the dark."

Once they're underway, Wallace checks the tracker screen. *Pinch Hitter*'s at Reclamation Island's marina, probably tying up at the usual assigned spot.

Fishing in his coat pocket yields two cigars. One with a blue letter *S*, one with a red letter *S*. Always advantageous to know the options ahead of time. He tucks the cigars back into his pocket.

Tapping the tracker screen, he gets Winkler's attention. "As you know from having worked with *Jeannette*'s crew, Reclamation's marina doesn't have a ton of commercial slips. We might find ourselves tying up next to *Pinch Hitter*."

As more of the idea forms in Wallace's mind, Winkler's grin shows he's picking up on it. "I've always wanted to see the interior of a working shrimp boat."

"And why shouldn't you?" Wallace claps him on the shoulder. "Kid like you ought to explore whenever you can. Who knows? You might want to be a shrimper yourself someday."

Closer to Reclamation Island, Ralph calls ahead and requests a temporary slip with both starboard and port-side mooring, giving them a likely chance of being assigned a slip near *Pinch Hitter*.

Bingo! They end up two spots away. With the boats so close, Wallace's modified ultrasonic sensor would power through all that steel and reveal anyone belowdecks. He doesn't have the sensor with him but isn't completely without options.

Pulling out the two cigars, he rolls them between his fingers. Sniffs them. Still potent.

He offers them to Winkler. "If you run into trouble, here's a peace offering that can take the bluster out of someone."

Winkler's eyebrows shoot up. Wallace rethinks and pulls the cigars back. "Smoking a cigar won't make you crave more addictive stuff, will it?"

"Nah, I probably won't smoke it. Cigars make me sick."

Wallace points to the red-letter cigar. "This one will make you real sick. The blue-label one is fantastic. Only offer the red if you want to temporarily incapacitate someone."

"Huh." Winkler rolls the cigars around in his fingers. "You ever smoke them yourself?"

"Old guy like me would be down for a week after smokin' one of those."

"So the red label is the one I smoke."

"The *blue* is the one you smoke."

"What happens if I smoke the red?"

"I told you! You'll get very sick."

"Oh, yeah. You did say—"

"Give me those cigars back."

Waving Wallace off, Winkler scrutinizes the cigars. "Only hand out the red-label cigar to someone I want to get sick. The funny-shaped *S* makes the difference, right?"

"They've *both* got a funny-shaped *S*."

Winkler's peering at it. "This one's slightly more funny-shaped, though."

"And it's *red*."

Winkler's already hopped off *Lucy Jo* and is ambling toward *Pinch Hitter*. When no one answers his inquiry asking permission to come aboard, he skips onto the vessel, looking like an enthralled teenager wanting to be a shrimper when he grows up.

Watching the kid disappear belowdecks, Wallace gets an uneasy feeling. "If he runs into trouble, we'll be too bogged down with goats to help."

Ralph chuckles. "I can't believe you're still using those cigars."

Securing the last line, Wallace shrugs. "It's a matter of supply and demand. I've got smokes. And crackerjack opportunities to share keep turning up."

59

Cigar roulette

After calling out for permission to board *Pinch Hitter*, Frank hopped aboard without it and was accosted by a thin dude with greasy hair. Sketchy-looking. Probably packing.

Behind him stood a man known to Frank. Anyone who'd spent time among Reclamation's lower dredges, even on the periphery not doing anything wrong, could identify Lester Locum.

"Hi, Lester."

"What're you doing on my property, Frankster?"

Frankster. That was a new one. Also a surprise that Lester could identify Frank, although maybe not a shocker on news-travels-fast Reclamation.

If Lester was dealing in stolen goods, he might also be playing with drugs, and the fastest way to get him talking would be to pique his interest. "I'm selling. Wondered if you'd be interested."

"Why would I want your junk?"

Junk. Referring to drugs, stolen goods, or all of the above? Shrugging, Frank glanced from Lester to the thin dude. "Okay then." He turned as if to leave.

"You're not going anywhere yet." Lester motioned for Frank to follow him belowdecks.

Standing in the galley, Frank kept an eye open for signs of illegal activity. When he realized a woman was seated at the table, he was careful not to look directly at her. Guys like Lester liked to give permission for that kind of thing. Frank kept his focus on Lester, with occasional glances at the diversions on the table. A pack of cigarettes. A stack of little papers. A pencil Frank picked up and tapped. Did that make him appear nervous? Might help him appear *more* nervous than he was, which could work in his favor. Tap, tap, tap.

Though he didn't glance in that direction, he knew exactly where the exit was. Blocked by Thin Dude. Thinking of the irony, Frank restrained a nervous laugh. How can a thin dude block an exit? When he's packing.

"What are you selling?" Lester crossed his arms.

Frank came up with a believable story so quickly he impressed himself. Not coincidentally, the story wasn't untrue. It was the reality years ago. And could now be recycled.

He set down the pencil. "Crystal, for one. Can get you all you need."

Both men erupted in laughter. "We've got plenty of that, kid." More guffawing.

Frank took advantage of their distraction to glance at the woman. She looked bored by the galley antics. He hesitated. *Crystal* used to be a way of referring to methamphetamine. Was it possible street language had already changed? This whole shenanigan had seemed like a lark thirty seconds ago. Now he was ready to abandon Wallace's reconnaissance mission. Bolt for the nearest exit and hope it wasn't blocked by a thin dude carrying, with or without a permit.

He shrugged. "Oh, okay. My mistake. I'm trying to get out of the business myself." Again, a line that had been true at one time but wasn't now, because Frank *had* gotten out of the business.

"Good luck with that." Lester scoffed. "You can replace your front teeth, but you'll never escape what's eating at your insides."

Insides. Frank reached into the front pocket of his jacket—an unwise move he should have known not to make. Thin Dude pulled out a handgun and aimed it. Frank raised both hands. "My front coat pocket, two cigars. A peace offering."

Lester nodded. Slightly.

With one hand, Frank pulled the cigars out of his pocket. Ever. So. Slowly.

He offered them. Both men shook their heads. Didn't smoke special cigars, apparently. Only cheap cigarettes—no shocker there. The gun was put away.

The woman held out one hand. "Been years since I smoked a decent cigar."

Frank twisted the cigars in his fingers, trying not to be obvious about scrutinizing the labels. Wallace had said a tainted cigar would knock him down for a week. No telling how one might affect this wisp of a woman.

Red label, blue label. Which one had Wallace said was safe? Frank pulled both cigars closer. "Actually, these cigars might not be any good. A guy pawned them off on me."

"Lemme see." Lester snatched the cigars from Frank. After studying them, Lester looked up. "One label's blue, one's red. What's the difference?"

"One's better than the other?"

He was cuffed up the back of the head by Thin Man, not in a playful way.

"I think, um, the red label's better. Blue? No, red."

With a pocket knife, Lester cut both cigars, then handed one to the woman. "You get the blue label. I can tell it's the better one by the way he's pretending it's not."

Frank nodded. "Yes, I think—"

Lester stuck one end of the other cigar in Frank's mouth. "Smoke it."

Swallowing, Frank waited for Lester to light it. Then Frank drew the smoke into his mouth, swirled it around, exhaled. Didn't taste too bad. He pulled the cigar from his mouth and peered at the label. Definitely red. He took another cautious puff. Extraordinary! Made you feel all tingly and happy inside. His nerves and the roulette must have mixed him up. Red label was the safe cigar.

The woman was puffing away on her own cigar. Maybe she'd be tough enough to not get sick.

Frank smiled around his superbly fine smoke, pulled it theatrically from his mouth. "Full name's Frank Winkler Jr., by the way. Not sure we've formally met."

"Lester Locum." He motioned toward Thin Dude. "This here is Fender."

No surprise when additional identification of Fender Bender wasn't offered.

Lester waved backhanded in the woman's direction. "And Crystal Tagaloa."

"Tagaloa?" Frank nearly dropped his cigar.

Crystal—same name as the drug he'd mentioned!—grinned. "Familiar with the family name?"

"I, uh . . ." The easiest thing to do—not to mention it felt deliciously agreeable, which was surprising since cigars usually made him sick—was to enjoy another puff.

"Tell Virgil I said hi." Crystal's sigh created a cloud of smoke. "I miss him."

"Sure. Yeah, I'll do that." Coughing, Frank tried to not be obvious about angling himself away from Crystal's cigar smoke. How long before she started feeling sick? Jeepers, the galleys in these shrimpers could turn claustrophobic quickly. Somebody remind him never to sign on for a shrimping gig.

"And if your meth supplier is willing to—"

"Can it, Crystal! And gimme that, now we know it's safe." Lester took the cigar from her and popped the end of it in his own mouth. At least now Frank could stop worrying about Crystal getting sick from smoking the tainted cigar. And who would ever care, wiggle-waggle care at all, if Lester lost his bluster? Lester grabbed Frank's shoulders and propelled him up to the deck.

"Well!" Frank took a breath of cleansing marine air, then another puff of his cigar, which was settling his nerves in an altogether satisfactory way. Maybe he *would* take up cigar smoking again! Why not, if Wallace could keep supplying these hunky-dory smokes? He stuck out a hand, got a slippery handshake in return. "No hard feelings? It's been fun."

"Has it?" Puffing away, Lester cocked his head toward the dock. "Git, kid."

60

Hard to miss

It's hard to miss the farmer waiting in the marina parking lot with a trailer full of goats. Looks to Wallace like more than twenty, but maybe because they're moving around, restless. The farmer assures Ralph the two pregnant goats have at least twenty-four hours to go before their own deliveries.

With the farmer's help, Ralph sets up temporary fencing at the bow of *Lucy Jo*'s deck. Not as far from the Jeeps as Wallace would like, but with short interisland runs, it's sometimes okay to crowd the cargo. Pregnant goats should be delivered pronto.

Wallace and Ralph lead two goats at a time from the parking area, down the ramp, along the dock, onto *Lucy Jo*. Once the goats are off their leads and contained within the fencing, enjoying fresh air and abundant sunshine, they can sit right back for a three-hour tour. The fearless crew, including Gilligan, aka Wallace Bernard, is at their service.

With Ralph up in the wheelhouse preparing for departure, Wallace stands on *Lucy Jo*'s deck and hollers. "Hey Winkler! Where are you?"

Winkler appears from belowdecks on *Pinch Hitter*, followed by a second man. Smoking cigars, Winkler and the man exchange a new-best-friends handshake. Then Winkler hops off *Pinch Hitter*, strides onto *Lucy Jo*, and sits on the deck with his back against the gunwale. In no hurry to report his findings, he fondles the ears of a curious goat poking through the fenced area. Waves his cigar in the air and squints up at Wallace. "About time we shoved off, isn't it?"

Wallace grumbles through casting off, then joins Ralph in the wheelhouse. "When's he going to tell us what he found, do you think?"

Ralph mutters a response.

They're two nautical miles from Wren when Winkler stands, leans over the gunwale, and retches. Not coincidentally, the four goats nearest Winkler sway, retch, lie down.

Swearing, Wallace powers down the wheelhouse stairs and crosses the deck in seconds. He strips the smoldering cigar from Winkler's hand. "You're smokin' the wrong one!"

"I am?" Winkler's too woozy to focus.

More goats, breathing more cigar smoke, are retching and lying down. Wallace tosses the cigar overboard. Remembers to hope no fishies get to it.

Winkler will be all right. But the goats? Their body weight's much less than a human's.

Leaving Winkler to retch, Wallace opens the fence and steps in to investigate. The goats that showed the first signs of being sick are already starting to look okay. Holding a hand lightly against a goat's front, Wallace tries to feel for its heart rate, but it's hard to know where to find that or what's normal for goats. These don't seem distressed or anything.

They get curious. One chews Wallace's shoelace. Another bumps Wallace, and goat and man enter a whiskered face-off, a battle of bad breaths.

Shooing the buggers off, Wallace steams back to Winkler, a dozen reprimands passing through his mind. *Didn't you listen? Didn't you check the label?* But he can't beat up on Winkler, not when the kid's feeling so awful.

"Wallace!" Ralph hollers from the wheelhouse.

Reaching Winkler, who's curled in a fetal position, Wallace leans over him. "What'd you find on the shrimper?"

"Tell ya later." Winkler's eyes are squinted shut.

"Why'd you give away the good cigar?"

"Later."

"You can give a *full* report later. Right now tell me *something* worth knowing."

Winkler responds with a groan, followed by another heave.

"Wallace!" Ralph again.

Fed up with the whole project, Wallace straightens and turns to see what Ralph needs, mouth dropping open as he realizes he marched out of the goat fence without closing it up behind him.

The math is disappointing. Three goats, including the two pregnant ones, are still in the fencing. So the loose goats total at least seventeen.

And they're everywhere! Climbing the wheelhouse stairs. Standing on the roof of the yellow Jeep, which isn't so shiny anymore. Hopping between Jeep hoods and chewing on antennas. Poking a head into a backseat window. Climbing a back bumper.

With Winkler still retching and Ralph powering *Lucy Jo* toward Wren on a timeline, Wallace does what he can to corral the goats. He's never herded cats, but it must be about the same. And goats *talk* so much! Every bleat is a reprimand of Wallace Bernard.

Slipping on fresh droppings, Wallace gives up trying to return the loose goats to the pen. Instead, he watches their movements like a hawk, swooping in wherever he can potentially prevent the most damage. A couple of goats seem to be turning especially mutinous. Sitting in the driver's seat of the vintage open-top. Butting a head into the now-closed door of the wheelhouse. It's hard to tell if Ralph is shaking his fist at the goat or at Wallace.

When Wren Island comes into view, the sun's setting, passing behind clouds near the horizon, dimming the day. Wallace stops sort of wrangling. With any luck, they can pull *Lucy Jo* onto the beach unnoticed. Knowing Allison, though, she's been tracking their progress. Probably got binoculars trained on her precious Jeeps and goats at this very moment.

They're about four hundred yards out from Wren when the hydrophone gong sounds. A pod of orcas is traveling west to east, close to shore, directly across *Lucy Jo*'s path. Ralph drops the engine into idle, which ought to settle the goats but only serves to punctuate the continuing show. Only difference is the moving stage has come to a halt.

The gonging draws everyone's attention to the water. Islanders on the beach looking for orcas notice the goat circus has come to town too. No admission fee required.

In the audience are two women wearing matching lavender hats. Amelia scrambles to hold binoculars up to her eyes. She and Melissa point at each goat's new antic. Shriek with delight. Double over in laughter.

Wallace can't hear what Allison's muttering, but her body's as tight as a violin string, indicating she's reverted to one of her standbys. *Are you kidding me?* Near Allison, his mouth catching flies, Virgil is probably wondering which idiot agreed to transport twenty goats and two Jeeps on the same cargo deck. Jax is hooting and hollering. Macy's shaking her head, hands on her hips. Shasta's blowing rowdy kisses to Ralph, who isn't returning them.

That's when the setting sun breaks through a gap between the clouds and the horizon, like a spotlight illuminating a stage. For the next few minutes, Wren Islanders are treated to a brilliant show in vivid technicolor. Breaching orcas in the foreground, bleating goats in the background.

Surrendering to the humbling absurdity, Wallace picks up one of the smaller goats and raises it high. Waves one front hoof like the goat is saying hello. Is rewarded with a chorus of cheers from the beach.

61

Supercouple

Standing on the beach, Amelia held tight to the lead line Frank handed her. Thanks to Louise's exuberant barking, five goats had already leaped off *Lucy Jo* and scampered into the forest. Unless they got rounded up, Wren Island would become home to a feral goatherd.

The rounding up would have to wait, though, until after Jax was presented with the vintage open-top Jeep as his belated birthday gift. Under *Lucy Jo*'s spotlights, Jax and Allison and Virgil rhapsodized over the vehicle's features. Watching the warmth emanate from the three of them, Amelia smiled. She must have been wrong about Virgil being upset by Allison's choice of birthday gift for his son.

"I can take that goat now if you like." Frank's voice wobbled, but Amelia handed the goat over with relief, not wanting to be known as the dowdy aunt who lost a goat.

"You look green." Melissa swept an appraising look over Frank. "Kind of wrecked."

Face reddening, Frank shrugged as he and Melissa headed toward Tranquility Hill, a string of goats in tow. "Your dad got me and the goats sick."

"Sick? Something contagious?" Melissa dropped back an even safer distance. "My dad looks healthy. How'd he cause it?"

The two young people advanced out of earshot, leaving Amelia to imagine what Wallace had done. She drew a blank but observed that Frank wasn't the only person annoyed with Wallace. After landing *Lucy Jo* on the beach with the routine shouting and swearing, Ralph hadn't spoken to or looked at his old friend. Allison was delighted with the success of her gift but equally annoyed at the condition of her cargo. Macy rattled off instructions about how the delivery *should* have gone. Shasta mumbled something about goat perfume, then pinched her nose and walked off, not flirting with Ralph *or* Wallace.

Amelia watched Wallace working by himself, head down. He folded the fencing that had proven insufficient for the goats. Hosed off *Lucy Jo*'s deck. Stowed equipment. He seemed . . . disappointed. With the way the delivery had gone? With himself?

A funny feeling stirred inside Amelia. Sympathy? Sorrow? If Wallace felt so dejected about not getting Allison's special delivery right, how did he feel when John left?

Without a word, Amelia climbed aboard *Lucy Jo*, found a broom, and started sweeping. She was standing outside the wheelhouse, at the top of the stairs, when Jax helped Macy—first to ride in Jax's new car!—into the passenger side of the Jeep, as politely as a professional chauffeur. Virgil gave the Jeep a quick tap on the hood, then waved as Jax spun off from the beach, Macy whooping next to him. Nearby, Allison stood alone, looking fragile.

Virgil adjusted his Wren Island ball cap, strode toward Allison, pulled her into his arms. Kissed her as if they were the only people in the world. For a few glorious seconds, they were. Allison and Virgil, supercouple. *And that's all one word, folks.*

"Ah. True love." Wallace's voice reached Amelia from the bottom of the wheelhouse stairs. Looking up at her, he didn't try to hide his tears. Then he turned back to gaze at the couple on the beach. "Most valuable commodity in the world. Best gift you could hope for."

That simple sentiment changed Amelia's mind. She would tell Wallace about their connection. Not tonight, but soon.

"Now, missy." Wallace made his way up the stairs and offered his arm. "Hand me that broom and let's get you back to earth. Don't want to add one more mishap to the list of things I did wrong today."

She matched his smile with one of her own. Maybe she'd tell Wallace over an Irish red ale at a beach bonfire. Maybe she'd tell him while enjoying a buzzy brownie. Or a walk along the beach.

Too much time had already been lost. They'd lived entire lives. Loved others, lost others. Grief had shaped both of them and would continue to. Talking about losing John would be difficult. But wasn't it worth finding out if grief shared felt any less wearying than grief endured alone?

62

Warning signs

Early on the morning after the fiasco of the Jeeps and goats, Wallace traipses all around Wren. Tracks and scat indicate the stray goats have crisscrossed Wren three times already.

Melissa thinks they'll eventually rejoin the Tranquility Hill herd. Seems like a pipe dream, though. Once a goat's caught a whiff of freedom, why would it let itself be penned up again? Wren Island's craggy outcroppings, protected meadows, and mild climate add up to a goat paradise.

He'll leave food out for a few weeks until the strays figure things out for themselves. Probably Wren Island will end up with wild baby goats. Kids, they're called.

Walking under the walnut tree at the end of Allison's driveway, he pauses to listen. Virgil said the birds nesting in the branches above are wrens. By the sound of it, the entire peeping lot is hungry for breakfast.

At the market, Wallace orders a cinnamon pecan muffin.

"With scrambled eggs and three sausage links?" Jax is already dripping oil into a frying pan. Wallace has become predictable.

He nods. "Butter for the muffins, ketchup for the eggs, mustard for the sausages. Coffee, black. How do you like your new ride?"

Preparing Wallace's breakfast, Jax launches into an enthusiastic description of the vehicle's features. No mention of damage caused by the goats. It will be a different story if Wallace asks Allison how she likes her new ride, so he's not planning to. He ought to insist Winkler scrub both Jeeps clean, fill in the dents, wax the wheels. But Winkler has conveniently disappeared this morning. Probably sleeping off lingering effects from the cigar.

Wallace is plowing through breakfast, sitting outside on the market's covered porch, when Ralph lands on the beach with an early delivery. More tourists. They clank their gray Toyota sedan off *Lucy Jo*'s ramp and tear off up the road, in a hurry to get wherever they're going, which can't be far. As soon as you've built up any speed on Wren Island, you're already coming to another edge.

Tourists like those whiz around the island recklessly. Didn't anyone think of that before Allison poured gazillions into paving the roads? Seems like bossy Macy Johansson would have had it on her radar.

Complicating matters, Wren Island is home to wandering goats now. What if one steps onto the road at the wrong time? After Ralph grudgingly returns Wallace's wave—it'll require more than a botched delivery to unravel their friendship—Wallace pulls out his phone.

It's not hard to find an online resource for ordering yellow, diamond-shaped warning signs with the outline of a goat. He orders enough signs to install around every blind corner and along the island's one straightaway, the road leaving the beach.

Wallace Bernard, taking care of things. Feels good after the misfires of the last forty-eight hours. Also, he likes the idea of living on an island with warning signs about protecting goats. That's something he's never experienced before.

Greatest of All Time. That's what Melissa said GOAT is an acronym for, one time when they were working together in Allison's boathouse. Melissa didn't go any further into the thought, like to say her dad was a GOAT. Vanessa would have. Maybe Melissa was about to but the conversation got interrupted.

After breakfast, he follows rambling tracks again. Goats don't seem to have any concept of efficient travel, and Wallace ends up where he and Amelia Theodore stack rocks.

What do you know? Amelia's there too. First time they've been there at the same time.

"How did Frank and the goats get sick?" Amelia presents the question as if she and Wallace are in the middle of a conversation instead of having just noticed each other. Women do the most unexpected stuff.

"Smoked a bum cigar."

It's perilously gratifying to hear Amelia giggle. She lights up like Sirius on a moonless night when she's delighted. No wonder he hams it up when he's around her. For a man in love with Amelia Theodore, keeping a distance would require a galaxy shift.

A memory, long forgotten, floats into his mind. John's words. *Heaven and earth would have to trade places to keep me from my girl.* How could heaven and earth have traded places without Wallace knowing?

A whisper of wind rustles past him. More like rustles through him, because nothing else around him stirs. Not a leaf or tree branch. He felt the air, though. Didn't he? Maybe he's going cuckoo from living on this island. Ordering road signs to protect goats might be the latest indicator.

Amelia's studying him. Her eyes are squinted, her lips working like she's debating what to say. He knows the feeling, and it's excruciating to see it reflected on her face. *Say it now*, he wants to tell her. *Before it's too late.*

Instead, he waits. A helpless old geezer, and it's not an act.

Finally, she finds her voice. "Can we talk?"

His first reaction is to raise a defensive wall. Rarely has anything pleasant happened when a woman insisted on a conversation. Obviously, this first question is not the difficult part Amelia's struggling with. Of course they can talk. They are talking, aren't they? He could bring up the weather report next. Or ask about the goats. But from the look in her eyes, something troubling is coming.

Question is, what hard thing could Amelia Theodore have to say to Wallace Bernard?

63

Choices

They take turns stacking rocks while Amelia works up to whatever she's trying to say. Wallace tries to lighten the air by cracking a joke about a cigar-smoking goat—which falls as flat as most of his jokes do. Melissa calls them dad jokes. What other kind of joke would a dad tell his girls?

Whatever Amelia's working up to, whatever she's hoping for from him, he's probably going to give it to her. At any cost. Maybe he's gone soft. One too many losses. An old man grieving the dead, still celebrating the living. If it's within his power, why not give Amelia what she wants? Assuming he doesn't monumentally mess things up trying.

After positioning another rock, Amelia looks at him. "You and Ralph go way back, don't you?"

"Yep. Cellmates at Rikers Island. Late sixties, early seventies."

"Rikers Island. That's prison, right?"

He nods, bracing himself to answer the question most people ask next. *What'd you do?*

Not Amelia. She lets it go. Hands him a flat rock.

Stacking it, he thinks more about her question. "Ralph's been a loyal friend to me."

"To us too. Especially Allison."

When telling Wallace about Allison's brush with one of the FBI's most wanted, Ralph downplayed his role. But it wasn't hard to read between the lines. Ralph saved the day. With help from good ol' Virgil. Wallace considers saying what he knows but leaves that story for another time, certain Amelia is venturing toward the more troublesome topic.

Another rock balanced, she folds her hands into each other. "What were you doing in July 1975?" It's the most random yet oddly pinpointed question anyone's ever asked him.

"Say it again?"

"July. 1975."

He gets the distinct impression she knows exactly what he was doing. For that reason and others, he tells the truth. "Peace Corps. Montserrat. Nice island in the Caribbean."

"Swapping chili powder for paprika?"

Everything inside suddenly feels jumbled. How could Amelia know about the joke he and John played on a disliked food vendor to help their favorite vendor gain business? A jar of chili powder swapped for a jar of paprika to ruin a batch of seasoned mountain chicken—which wasn't chicken at all but frog legs.

The past connects to the present as he recalls razzing John for detailing every second of his life by writing a boatload of letters to his fiancée. Her name—the one he couldn't remember for decades—flutters into his mind. Amelia!

His recognition of her is mirrored in her eyes. Here with him is the woman he should have contacted decades ago. The woman whose heartbreak he might have tried, somehow, to ease.

"I thought it was true love." She's dropped her voice. In it, none of the anger he would expect for the way he left her to grieve alone.

"It *was* true love. John loved you more than anything."

"Then why did he *leave*?"

She turns away with her tears. Wallace is about to reach for her hand when she cries out her next question. "And why did you *let* him leave?"

The accusation stops all forward movement. The universe slows to a crawl, stops for half a heartbeat. The question that circled in his head a million times has now been voiced, echoing as it travels across dune grass, sand, and ocean. Headed where, though? To a final resting place?

Or will it become another of the world's wandering aches that never find peace?

While she retrieves a tissue from her bag, he thinks of all he wants to say.

I wouldn't have let him leave, if I'd known.

I would have said something, if I'd known.

You're right. I should have done more.

None of those truths will make a difference now. He says the only thing he can. "I'm sorry."

"We had plans." She's crying.

"I can imagine." He nods.

"We were going to make a life together."

He nods again.

She wipes her eyes with the tissue. "If I'd been there, I would have stopped it from happening."

He doesn't have an answer for that. Maybe she *could* have stopped it from happening. Taken care of what he failed at.

Halfway smiling, she shrugs. "But I suppose if Wallace Bernard was there and *he* wasn't able to stop it from happening, I might not have been able to do much either."

A fissure opens inside him. Fresh, rejuvenating air rushes in. Does she see him that way? Have that much faith in him? Believe if anyone could do what needs doing, he could?

Every part of him aches with sorrow—his and hers and John's. "I'm so sorry."

After wiping her eyes again and then her nose, Amelia tucks the tissue into her bag. "Thank you for your condolences."

"I didn't know how desperate John felt. If I'd known . . ."

"I didn't know either. Maybe we're both to blame."

Her hand touches his, warm and soft. He holds it and her gaze. "Maybe neither of us is to blame. We each make our own choices. John made his. You and I made choices that somehow brought us to this time and place."

Releasing his hand, she chooses another rock and stacks it on a pile. "It's amazing you ended up here on Wren."

"Yep. What are the odds?" As amazed by her resilience, he takes his turn stacking a rock.

"It's as if you were meant to be here. Like the universe made it happen."

While Amelia's looking for her next rock, Wallace sees a fox appear at the edge of the brush. A twitching nose, bright eyes, perked ears.

Once Amelia has set her rock in place, Wallace points to silently signal her. *Look over there.*

Peering into the brush, Amelia's confused. "What am I looking for?"

"A fox."

"Where?"

The fox is unmoving but in plain sight. Amelia's still squinting, maybe wondering if Wallace is playing a joke on her. That darn macular degeneration had better be prepared for battle. Wallace Bernard isn't going to let Amelia Theodore, galaxy girl, get taken down by an inconsequential setback like failing eyesight.

"The fox is gone now." White lies are sometimes appropriate.

"I saw Miss Fox here once before. So maybe you did see her."

There's no *maybe* about it. But from now on, he's referring to Miss Fox by her proper, Amelia-given name.

Amelia's still talking. "Seeing her again is on my list of nice things to wish for."

"Your what now?"

Amelia is all lit up again, talking about stuff she hopes will happen. Miss Fox having pups. Melissa adopting a kid—pure whimsy, since Melissa would never tolerate the dirt from a goat. Allison and Virgil getting married. Tranquility Hill rehabilitating a quail named Muffin Top.

With supernatural flexibility, Amelia is springing back from the tears. Has she always been this remarkably resilient? Think of all John missed out on!

Clearing his throat, Wallace reaches for her hand again, as if they're meeting for the first time. "Hi. I'm John's friend, Wallace Bernard. I hope you'll consider me your friend too."

He figured she'd giggle at that. Holding his breath, he waits to see what she'll say next.

"We've always been friends, Wallace."

Not what he expected. So much better.

She squeezes his hand. "We just never knew we were friends before. Now, we'll know for the rest of our lives."

64

On the Hill

A few days later, working alone at Tranquility Hill, Wallace hauls a wooden chest of drawers out of storage and into the sunshine. Wipes the dust off, flips on the electric sander, goes to work refinishing the surfaces. Sweats from the effort and the warm sun on his back.

Rotating the sander in light circles across the rich-toned wood, he mentally ticks through projects that still need to be completed before the Hill opens as a retreat center. He's in charge of repairs in the living spaces for himself, Melissa, Amelia, and Winkler—though not much fuss will be made about Wallace's corner room at the end of the main building, among the common folk.

"Don't say *common folk*." Assistant Manager Melissa was quick to correct when Wallace mentioned it. "They're guests, Dad."

"As long as they understand they're not royalty. Nowhere near the same league as you girls."

Officially the groundskeeper, Wallace will also cover miscellaneous tasks as needed. Head honcho Amelia said it'd be a tragedy to not tap into his hawkeyed surveillance skills. He'll definitely keep tabs on her cottage on the Hill's south border, close to Allison's house. Bossy Macy, unhappy about losing full-time charge of her youngest sister, will want regular reports.

Flipping off the electric sander, Wallace checks the dresser's surface with his hand. Still uneven, but almost there. He wipes sweat from his brow, then swaps in a lighter grit and starts up again.

Other than the dresser, Melissa has taken over renovating her two connecting rooms in a private area of the main building. She keeps talking about adopting a kid, but Wallace has never seen squeaky-clean Melissa interact with the goats, so it will never happen. Why adopt one baby goat? They're happier living in a herd. People can be too.

Once anyone figures out what Twinkle Toes Winkler is good for in the herd at the Hill, he'll get an official job title too. Currently, he spends too much time dancing around Wallace's inquiries about Lester Locum and flunking at stunts designed to impress Melissa. At least Winkler's low maintenance. Said he doesn't mind the leaky roof of the yurt on the north border because it allows fresh air and a view of the sky.

Actually, Winkler said he likes admiring the *starry* sky—another failed attempt to interest Melissa. The poor kid has no idea what he's up against. If Melissa doesn't set Winkler straight soon, Wallace will say something. For now, he's having too much fun watching the kid spin his wheels.

Ed Piper's spinning too. Not in a direction Wallace likes, and Wallace doesn't feel a whit of remorse for being critical. It's one thing to finagle circumstances out in the open. It's another to use shifty tactics trying to secure something—or *someone*. For instance, Ed recently made an under-the-radar switcheroo so his scheduled work hours coincide with Amelia's. Next, the pip-squeak wowed Amelia with suggestions for improving the rehab aviary—even though she herself came up with the same ideas weeks ago. Ed sits next to Amelia at nearly every meal and "helps" her—though she doesn't need help and often tells him so. And what about all the times Ed drops by Allison's house unnecessarily? Relaying banal bits that could wait to be communicated at the Hill during all those coinciding work hours.

Amelia's giggling a lot these days, which of course is nice to hear anytime—but at stuff *Ed* said. If John were here, he'd make a move toward securing his girl.

Wallace will keep an eye on the situation. Monitoring activity on the Hill is in his job description.

He turns off the sander, runs his hand over the wood surface. Real smooth. Ready to be wiped clean again, then stained. Back in the dimly lit storage shed, he cools off a bit. Digs out another piece in need of sprucing up, a wooden rocker. Outside, he squints at the bright sunshine and Amelia, who's approaching with a clipboard and pencil, looking all official. Wearing a bucket-style Wren Island hat on her head and binoculars around her neck, she's the cutest property manager he's ever seen.

"Thanks so much for fixing up the old furniture." When she smiles, the sunny day gets brighter.

Unable to think of what else to do, he just grins. Ever since Amelia told him about their past connection, he's felt unexpectedly in awe of her. And Amelia seems easily pleased with everything Wallace does too, which is unnerving. His grin fades a bit. It's only a matter of time before he makes a colossal mistake and topples down from his current position in her high esteem.

She cocks her head to one side. "Allison has invited us to lunch at her house. Grilled bratwurst and baked macaroni and cheese. Noon. Will you be there?"

"Sounds good."

"Melissa has news she wants to tell all of us at once."

"That so?"

Wallace knows better than to try to figure out the news himself. Melissa has always found it thrilling to throw the unexpected at her old man. At least now she's beyond the heart-stopping stuff she used to fling around during her teen years.

Leaning against the storage shed, Wallace wipes more sweat and makes a mental note to change into a fresh shirt before lunch. Maybe put that sail iron to use first and press the collar. He watches Amelia make notes on her clipboard. "You adding an item to your list of nice things to wish for?"

Still scribbling, she giggles. Holy smokes, look at her come alive. No wonder Ed Piper does dippy stuff around her.

Looking up from her clipboard, she cocks her head again but doesn't say anything. Wallace gets the uncanny feeling she's looking inside him, seeing what he'd rather not be revealed. Might be risky to study Wallace Bernard so carefully.

"Guess the most recent wish to come true."

Relieved at the direction of her thoughts, he says the first idea that comes to mind. "You wanted Allison and Virgil to find true love?"

Her gasp of surprise tells him he's hit the nail on the head. Wallace Bernard pulled out something nice Amelia Theodore wasn't expecting. Feels more than a little heartening.

Straightening, he steps closer. Within touching distance. He could reach for her hands, if he wanted. Who's he kidding? He wants to. But he'll resist. For lots of reasons. Though he can't come up with a sensible one at the moment.

Sighing, she holds his gaze. "Guess what's at the top of my list of nice things to wish for now? I'm waiting for Virgil to propose. Maybe it's old-fashioned of me, but I want Allison to experience the loving marriage I missed out on."

Seemingly of their own accord, his hands reach for Amelia's. Her quick step back reveals initial uncertainty. Then she relaxes, okay with holding hands for the moment.

"Amelia, you are one of the most remarkable women I've ever met." His voice sounds a bit odd. Husky. Deeper. Kind of scratchy. The older he gets, the more often these unexplainable quirks happen. "If I had a list of nice things to wish for, it would consist of one line item. I want Amelia Theodore to get everything on *her* list."

He's said too much. He can tell by the strange look crossing her face. Wallace Bernard has said too much? Unfathomable.

She releases his hands. He takes a deep breath. For too many years, he held off on speaking the truth. He doesn't regret doing so now. But will he regret how speaking the truth changes their relationship?

"Wallace, I want to be upfront about my situation."

"Go for it."

"I'm very much looking forward to living independently. For the first time in my life."

He bobs his head. "This is an exciting time for you."

"Since you know about my relationship with John, I want to release you from any obligation you might feel. No need to take care of John's girl. That would be complete nonsense. I've worked really hard to get to where I don't need taking care of."

"No obligation. Would be complete nonsense. Don't need taking care of. Got it."

Though he isn't at all sure he's understood. What exactly is she telling him? Back off of everything that concerns her?

"I've got lots of responsibilities now and will need help when we're both living and working at Tranquility Hill."

Squinting, he studies her. "You'll need my help?"

She nods. "And since neither of us is interested in a romantic relationship . . ."

Despite the sinking feeling, his head bobs again. "Not interested at all. It's as simple as Boss Lady Amelia Theodore needs help from Wallace Bernard, employee."

Then his left eye kicks in with a big-time tick. A dratted giveaway he's not telling the truth—as much a surprise to him as it would be to anyone, not that anyone's going to find out. Certainly not Amelia, with her glossy pink lips forming words that come admirably easily. Look how confidently she communicates! Pressed collar or no, he'll be lucky to halfway keep up with her in this amazing new direction. She's independent, resourceful, optimistic, shiny, eager, interested, open—

"So you're willing to be that person for me?" Her question interrupts his thoughts.

He definitely missed part of the conversation. Swallowing, he employs a trick Melissa the psychology major taught him years ago. Repeating the last words as a question almost always prompts clarification.

"Be that person for you?" On a whim—Wallace Bernard speaking freely!—he adds a second question. "Is it on your list of nice things to wish for?"

"Nope. Not on the list. I already feel I can share every hope and fear with you. So finding that person skipped right over to my list of nice things that happened unexpectedly."

He gapes at her. "You've got a list for that too?"

Smiling, she turns to leave. "Remember, lunch at noon at Allison's house."

Watching her walk off, he inhales sharply when he sees her yet again lose her footing and stumble. But she doesn't fall. Just carries on in that determined way of hers.

Rubbing his chin, he wonders. Can he be the person Amelia Theodore shares every hope and fear with? While not hedging toward a romantic relationship? A challenging endeavor. But from whatever angle he looks at it, he figures Amelia Theodore has, in one way or another, always kept him on his toes.

65

Show-and-tell

Walking to Allison's house, fresh-pressed collar laying nicely against his neck, Wallace practices using the new accessories he's picked up, not because he needs them, but because he hopes they'll interest Amelia. He stashes them outside the service entrance, where they'll be handy for show-and-tell later.

In the kitchen, the table's set, Macy's lining up dishes on the counter, and the girls—Melissa, Amelia, and Allison—are bouncing around in their own world. With nothing for Wallace to help with, he's mostly in the way, so he scuffs out to the back patio.

Virgil's escaped the Henhouse by taking responsibility for grilling the bratwurst. Wallace joins him, wishing he'd thought to bring a couple of blue-label cigars. His nerves are raw from giving up alcohol, which he'd considered doing after losing Vanessa, then decided definitely to do after learning Amelia was John's fiancée. Drinking has already cost him too much. And why bother with an Irish red now that he can remember John in a more fulfilling way, in the company of Amelia? Wallace pictures John giving him a thumbs-up on the decision. And offering him a cigar to help him get through the jitters.

An even more welcome diversion right now would be learning what happened with Winkler aboard *Pinch Hitter*. It's high time to pin down Winkler on how the cigars got mixed up—when the kid returns from making the deliveries Wallace assigned him, a humanitarian effort to help Winkler cool his jets about Melissa.

Rotating items on the grill, Virgil nods toward Wallace, who nods back, fielding the impression Virgil might still be a tiny bit peeved over Wallace's accidental dislocation of Allison's shoulder the night Vanessa and the kids died. What man wouldn't be annoyed with another for hurting the woman he loves?

"I don't think I ever told you how sorry I am about dislocating Allison's shoulder." Lots of apologizing lately.

Virgil chuckles. "Water under the bridge."

"Speaking of apologies, looks like you reconciled things with your golden girl. How come you haven't put a ring on her finger yet?"

"I'm working on it."

"Might want to move faster, Romeo. Life is short."

A clanging interrupts them. Shasta's whacking a bronze cowbell, new since the last time Wallace came for a meal. And she's all dolled up in flashy clothes sporting buttons, fringes, and other doodads. When she waves, the bracelets circling her wrist jingle. "Hey you two heartthrobs! We girls are ready for weenies!"

"Holy—"

"Careful, Wallace. Louise is right next to you." Shasta motions toward the vicinity. "Eyeing the weenies."

The ground could swallow him up right now, he wouldn't mind at all. He fumbles with a platter until Virgil gives the okay, then helps pile on the cooked bratwurst. Before he and Virgil head inside, Wallace shakes his head at Shasta's retreating figure. "Think she'll ever stop fishing?"

Virgil rolls his eyes. "I wouldn't bank on it."

Sneezing at the fading trail of perfume, Wallace snorts. "Allison should put stricter limits on how Shasta spends her money."

"Try telling that to Allison." Virgil chuckles. "She's added limits, and she's teaching Shasta how to stick to a budget. They're making progress, I think."

"Well, any progress is worth celebrating." Wallace thumps Virgil on the back—careful to not get his hand caught in hair. "Let's go eat."

When they return to the kitchen, Ed Piper is kissing Amelia's hand, complimenting her about one thing or another. Amelia pulls her hand away and glances around the room with an unsettled expression.

Fox in the henhouse! Instead of yelling the words like he wants to, Wallace snags a seat next to Amelia at the table, finagling Allison into the chair on Amelia's other side. He's rewarded with a pleased sigh from Amelia.

How do you outsmart a fox? Be more foxtastic.

Once they're all settled at the table, Melissa's news bounces out of her. "I've been approved to adopt a kid! It could happen really quickly now!"

While everyone offers their congratulations, Wallace shakes his head. "Didn't realize you were waiting for approval, honey. I say if you're set on having your own baby goat, you're welcome to pick one out from the herd."

The room erupts. It's disturbing, hearing everyone laughing at him, not with him. He's tempted to knock Pip-Squeak Piper's guffawing head right off its wobbly socket. Amelia isn't laughing, though. She's giving Wallace an adoring smile that is far more unnerving than a roomful of people laughing at him. What has he said that would bring out such tenderness?

"Dad?" Melissa's voice, breathless from laughing, sounds like Vanessa's. With a catch of his own breath, he turns to gaze at his stunning daughter. "I'm adopting a *child*. Now I see why you haven't seemed concerned."

"A *child*? That's not what I . . ." That all this time he thought Melissa was talking about a baby goat is painfully obvious, and his swelling heart prevents him from saying more. Nathan and Natalie didn't make it to Wren. But Melissa, with her exceptional way of seeing the world, has found a way to give Wallace the honor of again being someone's grampy.

"I think it's a wonderful idea, honey. Are you getting a baby? Or an older kid?" A passel of additional concerns surfaces as he pictures his daughter raising a youngster burdened by years of untold issues.

"I'm asking for a toddler. Two or three years old."

"Oh boy, that'll be fun." With Amelia's optimism, the conversation mercifully sidesteps away from Wallace.

"Through the diaper stage, hopefully." Macy nods knowingly.

Allison raises her hand as if she's a student in a classroom. "I claim the role of favorite aunt. Since I have three favorite aunts, I've had plenty of examples."

Virgil's the only one with reservations about Melissa adopting a child. As a single parent, he's familiar with the daily struggles.

"But you're not on your own." Amelia beams. "You've got all of us."

The conversation continues to roll. Ed's the only one without an opinion. He eats bite after bite of macaroni and cheese as if this were any old conversation, not one that's changing *everything*. Wallace squashes his annoyance. Focuses instead on the joy of watching Melissa light up about her dreams.

When they've finished eating, the Henhouse kitchen is cackling with help, so Wallace nudges Amelia toward the service entrance door. "Come see."

He retrieves the two pairs of trekking poles, hands Amelia her set, and demonstrates with his own. The foot on one side steps forward, the hand on the same side goes back. Other foot goes forward, other hand goes back. "These will provide stability whenever my boss sends me traipsing all around the Hill. Thought you might like a pair too."

She tries them. "They feel clunky."

"Clucky?"

"Clunky."

He shrugs as if her approval makes no difference to him. He knows enough about women to recognize when to back off, let her come around to the idea on her own time. "It's your decision. Thirty-day return policy if you decide you don't like them."

"Thanks, Wallace. I'll try them."

"We can practice together if you want." As soon as he's said it, he realizes it sounded as if he thinks she won't be able to figure it out on her own. "Not that you need—"

"Wallace, it's starting to feel like you're hovering."

He steps back, nodding. "No hovering. Got it."

"I appreciate you thinking of me with these nifty poles. Thank you."

"My pleasure."

Collecting his own set, he takes off down Allison's driveway, getting the hang of it as he goes. After a few strides, he exaggerates his movements as if he's having a terrible time with it. Legs and arms akimbo as if he's slipping on ice or he's a baby giraffe learning to walk. He's starting to think the effort might not be worthwhile, that Amelia might not be watching him, might have even gone back inside the house—and what if he throws out a hip flailing like this?—when he hears what he hoped to.

Amelia Theodore, giggling. At foxtastic Wallace Bernard.

66

His job description

Later that afternoon, Wallace walks the Hill's perimeter to check the fencing. Before they open as a retreat center, they ought to clearly mark the boundaries. Stave off any yahoos from wandering close to Allison's house.

At Nathan and Natalie's Playground, Wallace sits on the wooden bench he designed, assembled with stainless steel hardware to endure the elements, triple-checked for sturdiness and safety.

Not long ago, he pictured Wren as a castle with a moat around it. Vanessa, Nathan, and Natalie never reached the refuge. But Melissa did, though, and is adding another person to their family. What joys and sorrows still lay ahead?

He wanders over to the playground equipment, pulls a screwdriver and wrench from his tool bag, confirms everything's shipshape.

When he's finished, the sun's already touching the tips of a stand of leafless birch trees. These are short days, early in winter. He makes his way back up to the main building, using his new trekking poles for balance. Has Amelia gotten comfortable with hers yet? He won't ask, in case she thinks he's hovering.

Approaching the courtyard of the main building, he sees it. Not the very last thing he'd want to find at Tranquility Hill, but definitely in the last one hundred.

Pip-Squeak Piper. Cutting wires to the outdoor sound system.

The 24-7 monitoring of a hydrophone located off Wren is Amelia's pride and joy. Anyone in the courtyard can listen when orcas sing.

Why would Ed destroy one of Tranquility Hill's iconic features?

Probably so he can swoop in once the problem's discovered, immediately know how to fix it, and further ingratiate himself with Amelia. Wallace can hear the accolades now. *Look how great Ed is, everyone. He saved the day, saved the retreat center, saved the whales.*

Maybe Amelia Theodore is trusting enough for the wool to be pulled over her precious, hardworking eyes. But Wallace Bernard has been around enough hoodlums to recognize one even from a distance. It's in his job description to watch for suspicious activity.

Propelled by his poles, he barrels the remaining distance up the hill and plows into the courtyard. It's against his principles to accost a man if both his feet aren't on solid ground, so he waits until Ed has descended the ladder's last rung.

Ed has the nerve to offer a benign greeting. "Hi, Wallace."

"What do you think you're doing?"

Ed glances at the wire cutters in his hands, then back at Wallace, casual. As if he hasn't just been caught red-handed! "I'm replacing the—"

"Replacing? More like ruining!"

"Ruining?" Ed squints. "I'm fixing the sound system."

"Bah! I saw you snipping wires! That's not *fixing*. That's breaking. Now you'll need to fix it, and you'll be able to easily, which is what you want. Isn't it?"

"You've lost me, Wallace."

Out of the corner of his eye, Wallace notices Amelia has stepped out to the courtyard. "What's going on out here?"

Working up steam, Wallace huffs the answer. "He's destroying things so he can fix them."

"Ridiculous!" Ed's finally starting to get peeved. "You're seeing things that haven't—"

"Don't tell me what I have or have not seen!"

"Wallace?" Amelia again.

Ignoring her, Wallace hones in on the crux of the problem. As soon as this is out in the open, Amelia will understand why it's paramount he get to the bottom of it. "It's a pattern, Ed Piper. And I don't like it. Not one bit. You won't keep getting away with this kind of thing. If I ever again see you—"

"*Mister* Bernard!"

The use of his full name would have stopped him cold, even without the sizzling tone. Swallowing, he turns. Amelia's fuming, and all the steam's being fired his way.

She jerks her thumb toward the building's interior. "In my office. *Now.*"

He hesitates. Will Amelia also hightail it to her office? It's always been *Ladies first* in his world. His boss has told him to go to her office but hasn't yet made tracks there herself. Should he wait for her?

When she holds her ground, he huffs past Ed and down the hallway. Waits outside her office door. Doesn't seem right to barge in without the boss present.

A minute or two later, she comes down the hallway, wordlessly passes him, sinks into her desk chair, and motions for him to sit across from her. He perches on a wooden chair he refinished a week ago.

Conflicting emotions race through him. On the one hand, he's in a whopper of a sticky wicket, and the gavel's about to come down. He's got a new suspicion Ed was carrying out a job Amelia was aware of. She might have even assigned it.

On the other hand—and it'd probably be best if he didn't dwell on it much, though it's difficult to ignore—an astonishingly appealing woman sits across the table, intensely angry yet pulling herself together in a most admirable way. When she closes her eyes, takes a deep breath, and releases it, he tries to think about *anything* other than how much he'd like to—

Reopening her eyes, she pins a look on him. "What just happened?"

He clears his throat. "I caught Ed cutting wires to the hydrophone sound system."

"You *caught* him?"

The emphasis knocks him off-kilter. He rubs one hand along the edge of the wooden seat. Got a silky smooth finish on this one. "Cutting wires didn't seem like a task Ed should be doing."

"In your never-ending pursuit of watching for suspicious activity around Tranquility Hill, did you ask Ed what he was doing?"

Wallace shifts his jaw from one side to the other. *Did* he ask Ed? If so, did he listen to the answer? Unsure, he sort of shakes his head.

Leaning forward, Amelia crosses her arms in front of her on the desk. "Let me tell you what I think happened."

He leans forward too. No telling where this might go.

"For whatever reason, you've decided Ed needs to be monitored. You've developed seemingly unfounded suspicions about him. Meanwhile, Ed's belonged on this property for years. He's always been helpful and never asked for more than he was due."

Wallace scowls. That last misperception can't go unchecked. "Ed often takes credit for things he shouldn't."

When Amelia frowns, Wallace keeps putting words together. "How about when he took credit for the new sanitizing routine in the aviary? For the brighter overheads, warmer nest lights, slip-proof rugs on the floor. Those were your ideas, not Ed's. Yet he waltzed around like the sliced bread everyone needed."

"What are you talking about?"

"You told me yourself, weeks ago, about your ideas for those improvements. Now Ed's getting applauded for projects *you* deserve credit for. It's not right, Amelia."

A look of astonishment—or disbelief?—crosses her face. "You're upset because you don't think I'm getting credit I deserve?"

"Darn right I'm upset. Excuse my French." He glances around. "Wouldn't want the dogs to hear taboo language."

She blinks. A couple of times. It was hardly swearing, though. Not like language he used long ago, during the worst years. *Welcome to Wren Island, where you willingly give up drinking and swearing.*

To his complete and utter surprise, Amelia starts laughing. Not at him. More like *because* of him. He ventures a half smile, which makes her giggle more.

"Oh Wallace." Standing, she comes around to his side of the desk, reaches for both his hands, brings him to his feet. "I think we've determined that Wren Island with Wallace around will always be far from unremarkable."

He lets that statement sink in. Should he be flattered? "Who said it would be anything else?"

"That's a story for another time."

Her hands in his are warm. Maybe this hand-holding is going on longer than it should—boss-employee relationship and all that. But how could anyone let go of Amelia Theodore, galaxy girl? His hands feel cold and empty when she releases them.

She's speaking, all business. "Please go have a conversation with Ed about what he's working on. Ask questions, Wallace. And *listen*. Try to resolve whatever's not right between you two."

He finds Ed still on the patio, working, and apologizes. Asks questions. Listens. Learns the wiring all needs to be replaced. Yes, Ed would appreciate help, assuming Wallace doesn't blow up at him again. Ed believes his mild manner has so far kept him from being beaten up in life. He'd like to keep his record unblemished.

Never been walloped? Has the pip-squeak been hiding in a hole his entire life?

While still marveling over Ed's passivism, Wallace sees Winkler amble out of the forest and up the path toward his yurt. Joining Winkler, Wallace claps him on the back. "Welcome home, kid! Time's up. Tell what you found on *Pinch Hitter*. Any sign of trafficking stolen goods? Drugs?"

Winkler brings his hands together prayer-style and taps his fingers. "Wallace? Is that you? Can't be sure, after receiving such a congenial welcome."

Wallace chuckles. Another opportunity to make amends. "Sorry if I've been hard on you, kid. At first I wanted to see what you're made of. Now the habit's so ingrained it's hard to break."

"Apology not necessary, but accepted."

"That's awfully sophisticated of you."

"I'm not a complete write-off. I've picked up a few manners here and there."

"Okay, sure. So? What'd you find on *Pinch Hitter*?"

Winkler shakes his head. "Not until I talk to Virgil."

"Virgil? What's he got to do with Locum?"

"It's a family matter."

Wallace frowns. As far as he knows, Virgil's ex is his only so-called family on Reclamation, and Wallace dropped the ball on finding out more about her. Whatever Winkler discovered on *Pinch Hitter* must relate to Crystal Tagaloa. "Why have you waited so long to say something?"

"You had me running cargo all week! Even though I still felt green from that crummy cigar!"

"But you're better now, right? And there's no time like the present. Let's go find Virgil."

67

Something better

Sitting at a table in the market café with Virgil and Wallace, Frank played with the salt and pepper shakers. Lined them up, one plus one equals two. Separated them, one and one. Slid them back together, waiting for Virgil to process the news about Crystal.

Outside, Melissa pulled up on an ATV and crossed the porch to meet Jax, who was tidying tables. Watching Melissa load potted blueberry bushes, Frank sat up tall. Noticed Wallace maybe frowning at him. But Melissa kept working without a look their way.

Hazarding a glance at Virgil, Frank felt awful—and not from lingering effects of Wallace's crummy cigar. From seeing a man as strong as Virgil process a boatload of grief.

He didn't seem emotionally attached to Crystal. More like the recent news had deepened old regrets in fresh ways. Virgil was just being his usual, caring self. When people hurt, Virgil hurt. Frank made a mental note of a trait he'd like to develop himself. Or maybe not, if it led to so much pain.

Virgil looked up. "Thanks for telling me, Frank. How'd she look?"

Frank recognized the unspoken concern behind the question. "I didn't see any bruises or injuries. She didn't seem high or drunk. Just kind of . . . past caring. Though she did light up when we talked about you. Literally, because that's when we started smoking Wallace's lousy cigars."

Virgil shook his head. "I don't like the idea of her working with Lester Locum."

Frank snorted. "Who would?"

"It's not my responsibility anymore though."

"True."

Next to Frank, Wallace shifted in his chair, making it creak. "Winkler and I could go back over there and scout around."

Oh great. More reconnaissance, in Wallace Bernard style. Frank didn't think he'd ever be up for that again. Although he'd be willing if it meant helping Virgil.

Exhaling, Virgil smiled at them. "Thanks, but I think we'll be okay for now. I'll try to get her on the phone again, mention Frank relayed her message, ask if she still wants to meet."

Wallace shifted in his chair again, a couple of times. Creak, creak. "You're not barging ahead with this, right? First you're talking to Allison?"

Standing, Virgil laughed. "You kidding? Before I do *anything* from now on, I'm talking to Allison."

Frank stood, and Virgil clapped him on the back. Wallace stood, and Virgil shook his hand. "Thanks, guys."

"No problem."

"Anytime."

As Frank and Wallace walked back to Tranquility Hill, Melissa drove past on the ATV, carting the potted plants. "Sorry I don't have room to give you guys a lift."

They waved her off and kept ambling.

"You're making cow eyes at my daughter again."

Frank watched the figure buzzing up the hill. "Well, she's . . ." How would he describe Melissa? Attractive. Comfortable. Friendly. A girl he admired and enjoyed being with. "She's intriguing."

"Yes she is. But in case you haven't figured it out, you're not her type."

Frank huffed. Wallace held a lot of sway, but even he couldn't interfere with fate. "You can't stop a romance once it's underway."

Wallace got a big laugh out of that. "This isn't a romance, and you know it."

Sighing, Frank admitted Wallace was right. Melissa had become a reliable friend. He'd wondered if love at first sight was a real thing. Maybe intrigue at first sight was real.

Wallace elbowed him. "Cool your jets, son. The right girl will come along in time."

Three points to think about. One, why should *he* cool down when Wallace and Amelia were kindling a beach bonfire? Or at least a warm glow in a firepit.

Two, would there ever be a girl right for Frank Winkler Jr.?

Three . . . "You called me *son*."

"That a problem? I've been doing lots of apologizing lately. Might be able to muster up an apology for that too."

Frank shook his head. "Apology not necessary."

"Where's your real dad?"

A familiar ache worked its way through Frank's insides. "At home, where my mom would welcome me if my dad would allow it. But he doesn't want me in his family anymore. The last words he said to me were *You're a disgrace*."

They walked on for a bit, neither saying anything. Finally, Wallace spoke.

"I have no right to, but I'm offering a stand-in apology from your dad. Because I think someday he'll realize he's missed out on the irreplaceable. Once your time together is gone, that's it."

Frank watched his feet take one step at a time. "Unless you believe in heaven."

Wallace didn't reply.

"Michael Grant says everything we long for in this world will be what heaven is. We just have to trust Jesus to get us there."

"Does your dad trust Jesus?"

They'd reached the turnoff to Tranquility Hill. Pausing, Frank took in the view. The road he'd just walked, the market where he'd met with friends, the beach and dock he'd driven boats to and from—first as an outsider, then as

someone who belonged. And, beyond, a sapphire ocean pulsing under a lim-
itless supply of cleansing air.

"I don't know about Dad. But I do." Frank squinted. "What about you?"

Wallace started walking again. "What about me what?"

"Do you trust Jesus?"

"Bah." Wallace threw Frank a look indicating he should know better. "A coot
like me can't go in for that stuff. I'm too far gone."

Frank held out one arm to stop Wallace's progress. "Isn't that the point?"

"Say it again?" Wallace peered at him.

"The worse off we are, the more we understand our need to be rescued. Admitting we're a wreck fuels our craving to hope for, to *reach* for, the something
better we know is out there."

68

Awareness

The same dream visits Wallace that night. He's going along thinking every-thing's fine. Someone's with him. He doesn't know who. Might be anyone. Then the person starts disappearing. But it's someone Wallace wants with him, wants to not let go of, absolutely cannot let go of. If he can say something, *anything*, he can stop the disappearing.

"Help me!"

His own voice wakes him up. In a flood of awareness, he identifies the person in this recurrence of the dream.

Amelia Theodore.

She's specific and real, bright and glowing, lavender and sparkles. Radiant with hope she offers others. Living proof a tiny bit of redemption might spill into an old coot who'd given up on finding it.

He lies there, staring at the ceiling, and makes the decision he was already headed for.

From now on, his full-time, permanent mission is to give Amelia Theodore everything she longs for and more. Because the honest truth is—and he'd swear it even in front of the prison minister's god—Wallace Bernard loves Amelia

Theodore. With everything in him, though not everything in him is worth having.

Certainly not everything in him is worth *saving*. But the more rubble, the more gaps among the wreckage. Ever-expanding fissures where hope might trickle in. Amelia can't be his salvation—no woman can—but maybe by loving her, by pouring all he has into helping Amelia create the life she longs for, he can finally find the peace that's always seemed beyond his reach.

Even better, maybe he and Amelia will find that peace together.

69

This is new

"So now I need to think about what to do next." Virgil studied Allison's face, trying to discern what thoughts Frank's report on Crystal had generated.

"*We* need to think about what to do next." Allison's correction came with a smile.

"Have I told you I love you today?"

"Love you too, partner."

Their tentative plan included options that would empower Jax in the situation yet keep all of them within the healthy boundaries Virgil had already established. Virgil called a family meeting for Tuesday, after the lunch run. He built up the café's fire and switched the *Open* sign to *Closed*. Made three deluxe hot cocoas by combining melted chocolate ice cream with milk and cocoa. Extra marshmallows for Jax, cinnamon and a shot of espresso for Allison, plain for himself.

After delivering the drinks, he sat in a chair at the table where Jax and Allison were piecing together a 3D jigsaw puzzle of a Jeep. Exchanged a quick look with his partner. Cleared his throat and reached for his son's hand.

Jax looked up at him. Virgil smiled. Then Jax looked at Allison and lit up. "Oh! *Finally* you guys are getting married!"

Virgil's jaw dropped open. "Appreciate the enthusiasm! But that's not what this family meeting is about."

Holding up her left hand, Allison shrugged. "No ring yet, Jax. I'm still waiting too."

When they both sent Virgil amused but chiding looks, Virgil rolled his eyes. "Can we please get on with what we *are* here to talk about?"

"Sure, Dad." Jax wiggled his eyebrows. "But you do know this is like the longest pre-engagement ever."

"Okay, okay. We have another important topic to talk about first." Virgil took a deep breath, waited for Jax to settle. "I spoke to your mom on the phone recently. She's living on Reclamation."

Curiosity seemed to be his son's primary emotion. "She lives that close?"

Virgil nodded. "Been there for a couple of months. Said she'd like to see you. If you want, we can go to Reclamation together. Though you should know that, so far, she hasn't shown up when she said she would. If you don't want to see her or if you want to think about it for a while, either of those options is okay too."

Jax got a perplexed look on his face. "This is new, isn't it? She never lived near us before."

"If she did, I didn't know."

"Wonder if it's also new that she wants to see me?" Jax's question seemed mostly spoken to himself, and Virgil had no answer.

He shot a glance at Allison. Her peaceful composure seemed to be holding all of them together. When Jax looked at her, he would find a calm confidence indicating any mother in her right mind would be proud to know Jax. How did she communicate all that without words?

"What do you think I should do, Allison?"

She leaned forward, arms on the table, and held Jax's eyes.

"If I were a mom, I'd want to spend every possible moment with my kid. Crystal has missed out on a lot. But today you're in the driver's seat, and there's no right or wrong answer. I think you should choose whatever path feels right to you."

Virgil ought to be accustomed to the experience by now, but holy moly, the bottom dropped out from under him. How did she do that? Suddenly become more beautiful, even though a minute ago he couldn't have imagined her more brilliant than she already was.

Jax nodded. "I'd like to meet her. Can we all three go?"

Tapping a puzzle piece into position, Virgil smiled. "One family outing to Reclamation, coming up. Remember, son, so far, your mom hasn't shown when she said she would. I'll do what I can to arrange a meeting."

"Yeah, we might be in for another letdown. But at least we'll get good ice cream on Reclamation." Jax slurped his hot cocoa. "Bring cash, Dad. You can save the credit card fee."

70

Family outing

Driving *Incremental* into Reclamation's marina, Virgil slowed his speed and gave the departing Washington State Ferry plenty of space. Even so, the two vessels passed each other close enough for the handful of passengers on the ferry's deck to call out greetings. Virgil raised his hand in acknowledgement, then glanced at his crew. Allison was saying something to Jax, who burst out laughing, sending the sound of a teenage boy's glee echoing across the water. Smiling, Virgil returned his attention to navigating the channel. Caught Allison's eye as she repackaged the cheese they'd snacked on during the trip over, placed it in the refrigerator, and secured the latches, nice and easy.

Jax resumed monitoring the depth finder, reporting changes, though there weren't many in the channel. A slight tremor in Jax's voice indicated that despite the earlier moment of hilarity, he was feeling nervous about meeting Crystal. A sentiment Virgil and probably Allison shared.

Virgil pulled into a temporary slip. The three of them had tied up together so many times before, they now did it without speaking, as if on any other family outing. Virgil nodded toward town. "Shall we?"

Walking up the dock toward land, he checked the time. Moments from now, Jax would meet his mother for the first time in his memory. Virgil would face an embodiment of a painful past. Allison would be introduced to the ex-wife of the man she wanted to marry. All that was about to happen, if Crystal showed up.

On the boardwalk in town, Virgil recognized the jeweler who'd designed Allison's engagement and wedding rings. Walking toward them, Thomas Barnes beamed at Allison.

"There's the lovely lady! Let's see how that ring fits!"

While Allison glanced around confused, Virgil widened his eyes, signaling for the jeweler's discretion. "Sorry. You must be confusing us with someone else."

Thomas shook his head. "Hard to forget a ring like that. I don't often get to—"

"Jax!" Virgil pulled the boy close. "Why don't you take Mr. Barnes down to *Incremental* and show him the new *lifesaving ring* we added."

"Huh?"

The expression on Virgil's face must have shown his desperation, because Jax kicked into action. "Oh! *That* ring! Please come with me, Mr. Barnes."

Taking Allison's elbow, Virgil steered her down the boardwalk and called over his shoulder. "Catch up with you later, Thomas! We're late for an appointment." A few steps later, he saw Jax setting things straight with the jeweler.

"Virgil?" Allison stopped walking and pinned a look on him. "We're not so late we can be rude to people. And leave Jax behind? What if Crystal finds him alone? What if Jax changes his mind at the last minute? He needs us near him today."

"Said the woman who didn't think she knew how to be a mother."

Thrilling, to come up with a line to make her flash one of her soft smiles. And kiss him! He took her in his arms, right there on the boardwalk, and made the most of it.

"Earthling to the intergalactic palooza." Jax, interrupting.

Virgil released Allison, who cocked her head at Jax. "That was quick."

The boy shrugged. "Once you've seen one lifesaving ring . . ."

"Hmm." Allison nodded, slowly.

Sometimes when she was piecing things together, she'd stop talking in the hopes one of them would cave and drop a clue. But Jax remained splendidly silent. Virgil too. Mostly by avoiding eye contact. Appreciating the winter-themed decor on Main Street—evergreen boughs tied with ribbon, paper snowflakes in shop windows, white lights strung high. Plenty of eye-catching boats in the marina too.

Lifting one ringless hand, Allison fingered the row of diamond studs along one ear. "Funny that a jeweler would be excited to see a boat's new lifesaving ring."

Virgil balked. Of course millionaire Allison Theodore was familiar with the jeweler nearest to Wren.

"Yeah, people are unpredictable here on Reclamation." Jax to the rescue again.

Grinning at his son, Virgil reached for Allison's hand and headed for the pub. "Everyone ready to see what happens next?"

When they entered The Turkey & Hambone, the smells of marinara sauce, sizzling steak, and clam chowder greeted them. Zane Goodnight guided them to a private corner near the massive stone fireplace. Shook his head.

"I'm sorry. I don't think Crystal is coming."

Virgil pivoted to see his son's initial reaction. Disappointment. And . . . relief? He turned back to Zane. "Any idea why?"

"Lester Locum got picked up for petty crimes last night. Ferry attendant said he saw a woman who looked like Crystal board the ferry that left a bit ago. One of my employees found this envelope on the coffee bar."

While Zane moved to retrieve it, Virgil put a hand on his son's shoulder.

"I'm okay, Dad." Jax smiled up at him. Virgil kept one arm around him as Jax accepted the envelope Zane offered.

"Thanks." Jax nodded at Zane before handing the envelope to Virgil. "I don't want to open it yet."

Tucking the envelope into his jacket pocket, Virgil exchanged a look with Allison. She was standing tall, confident, capable. Ready to be whatever Jax or

Virgil needed next. Doing that thing where she was being strong for everyone else, regardless of any hurt she felt on the inside.

"I really am okay." Jax nodded again.

"You don't have to be. You can feel however you want about this." Virgil gave his boy's shoulders a squeeze.

"It has never felt like she was part of us. So it feels the same now." Jax shrugged, but his shaky voice revealed deeper emotion. "She's always been a person remotely connected to me. I'm glad to have always had you, Dad. And now Allison."

Watching Jax send a heartfelt smile toward Allison, Virgil was both sorry and grateful he now had a partner in witnessing the uncrossable gap between a negligent mother and her child.

Turning to gaze at the pub's wall menu, Jax moved right back into the ordinary. "Anyone else hungry?"

They found a booth by a window facing the street, where Jax could sit opposite Virgil, how they'd always arranged themselves. Allison slid into the booth ahead of Virgil and tucked into the corner, right where Virgil wanted her in a crowded restaurant. Maybe he couldn't shield her from every danger in the world, but for at least the next hour, a physical threat would have to get through him before reaching her. If he told her he was thinking that way, she'd ask if he'd added a new feature to the Virgil Tagaloa protection package.

He smiled at her. She winked back.

They placed their lunch orders. Loaded nachos and iced tea for Allison. Burgers for him and Jax, one coffee, one Pepsi. Their favorite appetizer, because Virgil felt like splurging. When the drinks and mozzarella sticks arrived, Virgil said a quick prayer of thanks out loud. They raised their glasses and toasted Reclamation Island, family old and new, good deals on ice cream.

After inhaling half of the mozzarella sticks, Jax nodded. "I'm ready to look at what she left for me."

Virgil handed over the envelope.

The restaurant bustled with activity, but quiet descended over their booth. Jax pulled out a piece of paper with a short note in Crystal's handwriting. A folded bill fluttered to the table. He glanced at it, then read the note aloud.

"*Dear Jax, sorry I wasn't here for you. I still love you. Have fun. Crystal.* And she added *your mom* in parentheses."

He picked up the bill and unfolded it. "Ten dollars?"

Virgil threw a glance at Allison. Her closed lips signaled Virgil was on deck for this one.

"It's the thought that counts, son."

"Great. A whole ten dollars of thought."

"It's a nice note."

"Except she had to explain who she was."

Silence fell across the table. Jax rereading the short note to himself. Virgil trying to come up with something helpful to say.

"She said she loves you." When Allison spoke, they both looked up. "She said she *still* loves you."

Jax acknowledged this with a nod.

Virgil got his son's attention. "We don't always know how much it costs when someone gives of themselves. Ten dollars might have been a significant sacrifice."

Allison wiggled on the bench. "It must have cost Crystal to write that note, knowing she wouldn't be here in person. She missed seeing how grown-up you are. Your warmhearted smile, your favorite shirt, the way your hair styled so slick today, and—"

"Okay, okay!" Back in form, Jax rolled his eyes.

With parental sternness to rival any, Allison pointed to the cash on the table. "Gas money. Just because we gave you a car doesn't mean we're paying for all the fuel you burn up."

Jax stuffed the money into his pocket. "Ten dollars won't get me around Wren once. You'll have to come get me in *your* Jeep."

"I always have time for a good-looking man, last name Tagaloa." Allison swirled a mozzarella stick in mustard. "But don't get any ideas about *driving* my Jeep. I've seen how you run yours up against the brush. I'm trying to not get scratches on mine—not counting the damage from the goats, obviously."

"I'll *never* get to drive the yellow Jeep?"

"Not for a long while, I'm afraid."

When Jax threw him an exasperated look, Virgil grinned back.

71

Like us

Virgil spent the following morning looking over his shoulder. He'd reiterated to Allison half a dozen times they would not need her help taking inventory. That it would be quite disruptive if she stopped by the market. No, they wouldn't dream of labeling anything without her. Just don't be surprised if the door was locked right up until dinnertime. They'd be that preoccupied.

Digging through another box in the attic, he found what he was looking for, solar-powered outdoor lights. He handed them down the ladder to Jax, who added the lights to the growing collection, then wandered over to the window.

"Any sign of her?" Virgil made his way down the ladder.

"No. But gee, Dad, we still have so much to do. I almost wish she'd drop off an organizational chart."

"For her own proposal?"

"It'd be better than the mess we're making."

Joining his son at the window, Virgil pulled out his phone. He should've asked someone to keep Allison occupied this morning. Not one of the aunts. Any of them would be curious and jump to a conclusion, probably an accurate one. He texted Wallace.

Can you keep Allison away from the market today? And off the trails between her house and Tranquility Hill? Sorry to ask last minute. Jax and I are working on a project we don't want her to know about.

Wallace's reply came a minute later. *No problem, Romeo.* With a grunt, Virgil tucked his phone away.

Jax elbowed him. "Can I see the rings?"

Virgil ushered Jax into the office, opened the safe, drew out the velvet box.

"Wow." Jax whistled. "And that guy on Reclamation made them?"

"Yep."

"This is really happening!"

Virgil closed the rings into the safe and locked it. "We still need to assemble the picnic table. Load the wood chips. Find the hammock. Will you go look for it in the shed?"

When Jax took off, Virgil ticked through mental notes, no organizational chart required. Picnic table, hammock, solar lights. Cedar chips for the trail. Stainless-steel water bowl for the dogs. He looped through a string of solar lights, calculating how far they'd go.

Jax came running back in. "Guess what I found!"

Virgil didn't bother looking up. "The hammock, I hope?"

"A box of fireworks!"

Skeptical, Virgil followed Jax out to the shed. Sure enough, an old box of pyrotechnics had been forgotten under a pile of other stuff. Virgil opened it, carefully. Held up the contents.

"*One* firework?" Jax was disappointed, moving toward disgusted.

Virgil checked the manufacture date. Still good, but not for long. They could set it off next Fourth of July. He'd need to post lookouts, people to watch where sparks landed. One could never be too careful about fire danger on an island. And the noise from even a single firework might startle the wildlife. Seemed like a lot of trouble for a few seconds of glitter.

He packed the explosive away again. "Well, now we know it's here. Ah! The hammock."

They loaded everything onto the truck and drove to the trailhead. From there, they could cart everything in using wheelbarrows. On the short spur from the main trail, they cleared the encroaching brush, widened the path, spread cedar chips. Then they went to work improving the neglected orchard Virgil had found while birding. They dragged fallen branches from under the apple trees into the forest brush. Hauled in the picnic table, assembled it, set it in a mossy area, covered it with a tablecloth. Strung the hammock between two sturdy pines. Dug out a firepit and set stones around it. Set the water bowl for the dogs near the underground spring.

Installation of the solar-powered lights got complicated until they worked out a system. Virgil hung strands around the highest branches he could reach, while Jax fed him a seemingly unending supply of lights.

"So the rule is you can't spend any money at all?" Jax unrolled more lights.

Virgil threw a strand around a handsomely gnarled, leafless branch. "Nope. Got to propose on a budget of zero. Dollars, that is."

"Because she wants you to know she loves you with or without money."

Throwing another strand around an exceptionally sturdy tree, Virgil smiled. His son was growing up right before his eyes.

"How will you ask her?"

"I'll say, *Allison, will you marry me?*"

"You'll have to be more flowery than that, Dad."

He adjusted a strand to wrap around a thick, weathered trunk. These were details he didn't want to talk about with his son. Maybe later. Not right now, when he was feeling more nervous with every passing hour. "Don't worry. I'll be flowery."

"And you haven't spent any money?"

"Just the rings."

"What about the lights? Will they work if they've been in storage? And is this orchard definitely on Allison's property? It'd be awful if we had to remove all this stuff because the owner didn't like it."

"We're on Tranquility Hill property, though no one from the Hill seems to know about this grove."

"But somebody planted it sometime, right?"

"A homesteader probably. Maybe fifty, sixty years ago."

"Does it matter no one's been taking care of it?"

Coming to the end of a strand of lights, Virgil motioned across the orchard. "Look around, son. How would you answer your own question?"

Jax studied the overgrown trees, their winter-bare branches touching each other in a dense, tangled canopy. His gaze lingered on the abandoned birds' nests. He stepped around a branch bent low to the ground, where last fall's soft, squashed fruit was returning to the earth. Turned back to Virgil. "I think this orchard will do better with us taking care of it. But I think it was doing okay on its own too."

Virgil agreed. "The trees in this orchard have grown wild and strong. They've become exceptionally resilient. With care and attention, they'll thrive even more."

"I get it. The trees are like us." Jax handed Virgil another strand of lights. "Are you *sure* this orchard is part of Tranquility Hill? You might want to do more research. We've both got a lot riding on this."

Gritting his teeth, Virgil focused on arranging a light strand. He was antsy enough without his teenage son mentioning additional concerns. Curb the spending. Check the lights. Research the location. Talk flowery enough.

He tossed his phone to Jax. "*You* check the location. If we're not on Tranquility Hill property, pretend we are and don't tell me until tomorrow."

The lights were all up, finally. They sat at the picnic table and ate their sandwiches. Jax returned Virgil's phone. "You're in the clear."

Virgil acknowledged this with a relieved nod.

The grove filled with birdsong. The spring bubbled placidly. A hint of a breeze whispered through the tips of the tallest surrounding evergreens, then swept down to stir the dry grasses and ferns at the forest's edge.

"There's just one other thing I'm worried about."

Closing his eyes, Virgil took a calming breath. "Jax, if it's another potential problem, I don't want to hear it."

"I'm wondering how I'll know if Allison says yes."

"Oh." Virgil opened his eyes. "I'll text you. Or call."

"Get on your phone right after she says yes? Not cool, Dad."

Virgil packed up the trash from their lunch. "We'll come tell you. It won't be all that late."

Jax shook his head. "No way. I don't want you guys showing up while you're still smoochy and smooshy."

He chuckled. Tonight he would bring the woman he loved to this place. Tell her he loved her. Ask her to marry him. And if—when—she said yes, then yeah, they'd probably . . . He spent a few moments imagining how promising it was going to feel to put a ring on her finger. Hold her in his arms, feel her cling to him. Head into a brilliant future together, both of them lit up like the Fourth of July.

Jax sighed. "I guess I can wait until tomorrow morning to find out."

Standing, Virgil motioned it was time to get going. "Tell you what. If you'll round up a couple of people to act as lookouts, I'll send a signal you can't miss."

72

Entangling

After double-checking Allison's engagement ring was stowed securely in his pocket, Virgil held Allison's hand in his and guided her along the trail between her house and Tranquility Hill. The sun had set, the cloudless sky was fading deep blue to light blue to orange. There'd be little to no moon tonight, only a broad canvas of twinkling stars.

They took their time walking, comfortably quiet. Virgil rehearsing what he was going to say. Sensitive Allison probably anticipating something was up but letting him roll. A small animal skittered off the trail and into the brush. An owl hooted. Deeper in the forest, its mate answered.

At the turnoff toward the grove, Allison commented about the first change. "Someone's put down new cedar chips! I never realized this was a trail."

"Hmm."

Thankfully, she didn't say more, though she was doing the square breathing she did when trying to calm herself. He gave her hand a gentle squeeze. She intertwined her fingers in his as they followed the trail around a bend. When they stepped into the grove, she gasped, the effect every bit as satisfying as he'd hoped.

The solar-powered lights strung around magnificently unruly trees gave off a soft glow. The hammock swayed in a slight breeze, stirring the dripping scent of pine. The picnic table was set with sandwiches, drinks, and battery-powered candles. A warm fire burned in the pit.

She finally exhaled. "What *is* this place?"

Touching her shoulders, he turned her toward him. Gazed into gorgeous brown eyes he could never see enough of.

"*Our* place. A sanctuary for peace, healing, celebrating, grieving. A place for our family to just *be*. Alone or together. You. Me. Jax. The dogs."

She was speechless. He went with the momentum. Moving into the moment he had hoped for, prayed for, planned for.

"Trees can become stronger when planted near each other. They lean on each other, share nutrients through their roots, support each other during storms. A tree that's fallen can provide everything a young tree needs to grow. Sometimes trees get tangled up in each other. In an infinite cycle, trees uphold each other."

Still holding her hands, he dropped to one knee. Gazing up at her, he thrilled to see she recognized what was happening and was holding her breath in anticipation. Spring-loaded and ready to fly.

"True love is entangling, in a gloriously extravagant way. If you'll let me, I'll spend the rest of my life proving it's the best kind of love."

He paused, not wanting to miss a fraction of how she'd respond to what came next.

"Allison Theodore, will you marry me?"

73

Whoop! Whoop!

Lighting her way with a flashlight, Amelia lugged her load down to the beach. Fabric bag with binoculars and mittens slung over one shoulder, foldable camp chair in one arm, trekking pole in the other hand. Macular degeneration made it difficult to see in dimming daylight, let alone once it became completely dark. Hopefully someone would help her back to the house later.

Wallace had insisted on throwing a stargazing party tonight—though Amelia couldn't imagine why they had to set up all the way at the end of Allison's dock. It would have been less hassle and much warmer to stargaze from near the house like usual. Not a complaint, just an observation.

Where the dock met the beach, Melissa greeted Amelia, relieved her of the chair, and walked with her the dock's length. Out to the very end! Macy was already bundled under blankets in her own chair.

"Ah!" Wallace pointed to Amelia's trekking pole, then to his own propped near his chair. "Great minds think alike."

She waited while he unfolded her chair, which she could have done herself. But Wallace liked being helpful, and she liked it when he felt pleased about being helpful. Besides, the wait gave her a chance to catch her breath after the walk from the house.

"Much appreciated, kind sir." She sank into the chair, smoothed her flannel plaid skirt, pulled out her binoculars, and scanned the sky. Not a wisp of marine haze.

After snugging one end of a blanket under her booted feet and the other up under her chin, Amelia turned to Wren Island's star expert. "What are we observing tonight?"

Melissa rattled off the usual highlights. It wasn't as if galaxies could move around.

When Jax and Frank arrived with lanterns, spiced apple cider, and roasted peanuts, the dockside gathering began to feel more like a party. Everyone eager to look at heavens that rarely changed! Peering through her binoculars, Amelia picked out what looked like a star traveling across the sky. "Satellite!" She pointed it out for the others.

Next to Amelia, Macy leaned forward, studying the water. Amelia aimed her binoculars and found a boat bobbing a few hundred yards off Virgil's dock. When Macy spoke, her tone was in full managerial mode. "Jax, who on earth has borrowed your fishing pontoon?"

Jax's answer came easily. "Ralph and Shasta volunteered to be lookouts from the water."

"Lookouts? For *what*?"

Jax glanced at Wallace, who shrugged an answer. "Fire danger?"

"In January? Those two come up with the strangest ideas." Macy huffed her way around the ridiculousness of it.

Giggling at her sisters—both Macy and Shasta—Amelia glanced back at Wallace.

He was smiling at her in a knowing way. "A January day like no other."

Amelia drew in a quiet breath. *A January day.* She pulled her phone from her bag. Fumbled to wake up the start screen and check the date. Yep. Fifty years to the day since John died.

Wallace hadn't mentioned the rememberversary to Amelia before now. Come to think of it, she hadn't seen him drink an Irish red ale in a while. Was he forgetting John? Not caring as much anymore?

Was *she* not caring as much? Forgetting to miss John?

Glancing around, Amelia registered who else was missing. "Hey! Did anyone tell Allison and Virgil about this stargazing party?"

No one seemed to have remembered. She and her sisters were getting better at knowing when to give the lovebirds space, but they should have at least thought to invite them.

How could so many important people be not thought of all at once?

Stricken, Amelia looked at Wallace again. The expression on his face nearly knocked her knees out from under her—or might have if she hadn't already been sitting down. Delight. Reverence. Comradery. Like he was about to give her an out of this world gift.

Mixed into it all, a hint of . . . mischief? Good thing she'd straightened out his misplaced notions of romance. She settled back under her blanket, sipped her spiced cider.

When an airplane went over at high altitude, a blinking blip traveling across a darkening sky, everyone got quiet. Would Vanessa and her kids have enjoyed stargazing on Wren? The tragedy of their deaths was, in a roundabout way, the reason both Melissa and Frank had come to Wren. In a similar way, Amelia had come to Wren because her sister Anne had died and left an inheritance to Allison. Grief and gratitude, pain and promise, inextricably tied up together.

When the plane disappeared from sight, Melissa sighed. "Hope those travelers end up somewhere nice." Murmurs of agreement worked their way around the dock.

The clear night sky brightened with constellations. The sea died down under a blanket of crisp, clean air. Pointing to a shooting star, Amelia made a few unspoken wishes, each already on her list of nice things to wish for.

Later, the stargazing party lost its shine. Jax became unaccountably sullen. Wallace paced the dock, though Amelia couldn't imagine why he felt impatient. They'd already observed tons of neat stuff against the magnificent backdrop of Wren Island's night sky.

Standing, she packed away her binoculars and folded her lap blanket. "It's been fun, everyone. But I think I'll turn in. It's late, I'm cold, and—"

A shrieking streak of fire shot upward from Wren's center, piercing the night sky with an explosion of red and gold. At the same time, Jax jumped up. "Whoop! Whoop!"

It was all so unexpected, Amelia lost her balance. Would have toppled over, maybe off the dock and into the water, if Wallace hadn't put an arm around her waist. Her first thought was one of embarrassment. He'd feel her chunky middle section! Her second thought was one of surprise. How had Wallace gotten to her side so quickly? His whiskered face was framed by a blur of sparks falling to the water.

"Fireworks!" She'd expected to sound pleasant and happy. Instead, she sounded breathy, overeager, and . . . *Sensual*?

One arm still around her, Wallace looked pleased as punch. Was he going to renege on their nonromantic relationship and kiss her?

Would it be so terrible if he did?

Jax's voice broke in. "*One* firework. Dad's signal. Allison said *yes!*"

Pandemonium broke loose. Macy was immediately offended about not having been alerted to Virgil's plans for the proposal, but only long enough to say so before switching to planning the wedding. "Our Allison will get the wedding of her dreams. She'll need help managing the details, of course."

Jax bobbed among each of them and shook hands, receiving and—paradoxically—offering congratulations. Melissa and Frank giggled together. And Wallace . . .

With one arm still supporting her, he looked as if Amelia had given him a gift he'd been hoping for. Yet she was the one who had just received a gift! Allison and Virgil finding true love, creating a life together in a committed marriage, had topped her list of nice things to wish for. One breathtaking firework signaled her wish was coming true.

Tearful laughter bubbled up. Amelia let it out—and felt Wallace's hold on her strengthen.

"Fifty years today." Her voice came out in a whisper.

He nodded. Hadn't forgotten. Had let their changing lives embrace a new way of remembering.

She sniffed. "Virgil finally asked Allison to marry him."

A hint of mischief crept back into Wallace's features. "Put another way, Allison and Virgil found something worth hoping for together."

74

Her own ideas

The morning after a single firework marked a special day on Wren, Amelia made her way downstairs to the kitchen at Allison's house and prepared her own breakfast. Fruity loops cereal with milk. Soon she'd be eating breakfast at Tranquility Hill every morning, instead of sitting at the table when Macy bustled in, clunked glass bowls from the fridge to the counter, threw vegetables into the blender, and let it whirl.

"Mark my words, Melia. It will be the wedding of the century."

Amelia finished a bite of cereal. "I'm sure Allison has her own ideas about what she wants. We'll offer to help, of course."

"Help? As in, we'll make it happen! Managing caterers, cake, musicians, ice sculptures, custom monogramming, hand-painted signs. We'll need to find a venue. And where will everyone stay? We'll scrunch guests into that retreat center of yours. You'll need to get it up and running straightaway, Melia."

Amelia peered at her sister. "Who are these masses of people you expect? Seems like Allison might want a simple ceremony."

At Macy's horrified expression, Amelia laughed out loud. But Macy shook her head, serious. "Why keep the event of the century simple? That girl deserves to have it all, and I'm going to ensure she gets it."

After rinsing her dirty dishes and putting them in the dishwasher, Amelia dried her hands and hugged her sister—the one who liked being large and in charge. "Allison already has it all. She's got Virgil."

Even from the service entrance door, Amelia could hear Macy's continued muttering. "*And* she's got millions. And she's got *us*."

Amelia collected her trekking poles from the patio. Took the path through the dunes to the beach, worked her way around clumps of seaweed and debris. Picked up shell bits and dropped them into the fabric bag printed with goats hanging from her shoulder. She hoped the wedding of the century turned into the wedding Allison and Virgil wanted. Each of them had come so far to find true love.

And what about Amelia Theodore? Here she was, sixty-eight-years old, and a hint of romance had briefly been resurrected. First Ed, with his interest in dating her—even though sometimes his compliments also drew attention to her faults. Decades of nothing, then all that? No wonder her head had been turned. Slightly. But Ed Piper would always be the man who hadn't been noteworthy enough to get a postcard from Hawaii with cool surfer dudes on it.

Back when she was choosing those postcards, she hadn't known Wallace—had only known *about* him. Had she *known* him, would she have sent him the postcard with cool surfer dudes? If she ever returned to Hawaii, she'd look for something special to send Wallace.

And what about last night? She'd wondered if he might kiss her! All he'd been doing was helping her find her balance. Though he did hold on a bit longer than necessary.

Of *course* he'd kept his arm around her. The dock at night was risky! Of *course* they'd shared a special moment. The fiftieth anniversary of losing someone they both loved. That wasn't romance. That was friendship.

Plus they were both carting too much baggage to get romantically involved. For one thing, Wallace had lived as a bachelor for years. He'd be reluctant to give that up, though living at Tranquility Hill wasn't exactly living alone. For another thing, she was about to live independently for the first time in her life. Starting an entirely new chapter!

Not that she didn't need help. Also, she *wanted* help. And that thought on its own was enough to make her prop her trekking poles against a driftwood log, sit, and add an entry to her audio journal.

"At first I was offended when people assumed I needed help. Maybe because I didn't want to admit it. And sometimes people—Ed's a prime example—ask in a way that comes across as condescending. But the way Wallace offers support comes across different. He starts looking disappointed when I haven't asked for help in a while. He's certainly devoted to those he loves."

Switching off the recorder, she took a breath. *Devoted to those he loves.* That seemed about right. Wallace Bernard, loving others in his own way.

She tucked away her phone. It was handy to be able to record a voice journal. But it also felt empty when her own voice was followed by silence.

What would Wallace say about all she'd just shared? Maybe someday she'd ask.

Just then, Amelia heard a horn honking, over and over in a rhythmic pattern, from up near Tranquility Hill. Then she saw a dozen seagulls swoop toward the sound and follow what sounded like the retreat center's pickup truck lumbering down the hill. A flock of seagulls flying down the road!

Standing, Amelia collected her trekking poles and other accessories and headed for the market. When she arrived, she saw seagulls perched on and around the Hill's pickup.

Recognizing the driver, Amelia took another few steps forward. "Wallace? Why are all those—"

She tripped—but recovered her balance, thanks to her trekking poles.

Leaning his head out the driver's window, Wallace cocked his head. "You wondering why these birds are following me?"

With a chuckle, he clunked open the truck door and stepped out to meet Amelia, white seagulls scattering around them.

75

Known

The next morning, Wallace rises early. He's not at all certain the seagulls that followed him yesterday will show up again today like he told Amelia they would. A perk to having wings is the ability to fly off with no advance notice. He pulls up to the house—Allison's house, predictably dark in the early morning light—and eyeballs the service door.

Shifting his position, he weighs the options. He could exit the truck, meet Amelia at the door, guide her down the stone steps and across the gravel path, help her into the passenger side. If he does, will she think he's hovering?

He stays where he's at, behind the wheel. Unwraps a piece of spearmint gum, sticks it in his mouth, chews. Doesn't unfasten his seatbelt, but he's ready to if signs point toward his assistance being required outside the vehicle. Then he'll hop out. Though *hop out* is referring to his movement optimistically.

In the morning stillness, he waits. Allison might look out her bedroom window. Her view is over the driveway. If he sees the curtains move, he'll wave. She'll recognize the truck.

Leaning forward, he winces when he bumps the steering wheel with his bum knee. He rubs it, then sits back from peering through the windshield. There's no hurrying a woman. Amelia will appear when she appears.

He's about to roll his eyes—ten minutes late already!—when the service entrance light clicks on and the door creaks open. A soft glow backlights the woman he's been waiting for. She's dressed for the cold, wearing a puffer jacket and her infamous lavender-colored hat.

She climbs in the truck, and when she's closed the passenger door, the two of them are alone in a sanctuary, their distance across the truck's bench seat bridged by a touch of hands.

"Good morning." Her smile, soaring through him first thing in the day, is the best gift he could hope for. Man alive, it feels reassuring to be known.

"Morning." He gives her hand a quick squeeze—lightly, to accommodate arthritic fingers—then releases a sigh, so unrecognizably contented that, for a second, he wonders if it came from him.

He starts the truck engine, confirms she's belted in, and heads toward the road. The sky is becoming less black, more sapphire. A new day coming on. At the market, he pulls into a parking spot, gets out of the truck, and is coming around to her side when Ralph lands *Lucy Jo* on the beach and helps a passenger disembark. With a wave at Wallace and Amelia, Ralph reboards *Lucy Jo*.

Lugging duffle bags, a backpack, and a crossbody messenger bag, the newest arrival on Wren also seems buried under layers of clothes, topped by at least one oversized coat. The visitor begins trudging up the road off the beach.

"Wonder who that is." Amelia voices Wallace's own thought.

He's trying to be more congenial these days, mostly because whenever he makes an obvious effort in that direction, Amelia sports a pleased, proud expression. The visitor within calling distance, Wallace gives it a go.

"Good morning!" He adds a friendly wave, then peeks at Amelia. She's waving too—also wearing the smile he banked on.

One thing he's never established is a foolproof way of determining whether an unfamiliar person is naturally shy or intentionally avoiding conversation. This person—maybe a guy, maybe a gal—finally hauls their eyes up from watching their own feet make routine progress, registers Wallace and Amelia on the market porch, then shifts their gaze back to the road. A potentially concerning amount of time passes before any verbal reply reaches Wallace and Amelia.

"I'm saying hello."

It's the first phrase Wallace has heard this person say, so he can't confirm whether the high and tight tone is normal or, as is common among the guilty, a result of nerves. And is it a man or a woman under all that bulky clothing?

The visitor looks their way again. "Taxi?"

Next to him, Amelia whispers through a giggle. "A *taxi*? On Wren?"

Wallace frowns. Best to clear things up right away for this tourist. "No taxi on Wren." The person continues lumbering up the hill.

It'd be nearly impossible for someone to arrive on Wren via *Lucy Jo* and expect taxi service. Ralph tends to be upfront with passengers about Wren's amenities. Keeps him from being roped into additional jobs. Was the visitor's question about a taxi a distraction technique?

"Could be anything going on under that oversized coat." Rubbing his chin, Wallace glances at Amelia.

She cocks her head at him. Same way she does when she's thinking up a project, often one that involves him learning skills he's never considered before, so he braces himself to hear her next whiz-bang idea.

"You know, Wallace, you could start your own detective agency."

He starts into a guffaw, then realizes she's serious, ticking off reasons on fingers with nails painted pearly pink. "You're naturally suspicious—in mostly helpful ways. Not afraid to ask questions. Street-smart, having been around the block a few times. And you know how to fade into the background when you want to."

He's not establishing a detective agency. Not that he isn't above *unofficial* sleuthing. He'll maintain low-profile surveillance while giving Wren's newest visitor time to settle in. And let down their guard.

Turning to Amelia, he shrugs. "I've missed obvious clues before. I wasn't in tip-top form when I assumed Ed was doing something he shouldn't."

She puts a hand on his arm. "You weren't entirely wrong, either. We'd best continue being mindful."

"And I was off my game when I thought Melissa wanted to adopt a goat."

Withdrawing her hand, Amelia elbows him. "Why would Melissa want a GOAT? She's already got the greatest of all time for a dad."

76

Another first day

He and Amelia are arguing about which one of them is the GOAT—acting like a couple of kids on a playground—when Virgil opens the market doors, raises his eyebrows, and welcomes them inside. Amelia heads for the glass muffin case. Wallace wanders over to the bulletin board and studies the list of visiting vessels. Nothing out of the ordinary.

Joining Amelia near the baked goods, Wallace gets Virgil's attention. "You know anything about the tourist Ralph just dropped off?"

"Ed Piper mentioned a friend might visit."

"A friend of Ed's. Corking news." Wallace shoots a conspiratorial look toward Amelia, but she's studying the muffin options.

"Is Ed's friend staying at Tranquility Hill?" Amelia is so close to the glass case, her voice gets amplified off it.

Pulling a pencil from behind one ear, Virgil leans against a cabinet and makes notes on a paper tablet. "You'd know better than me." Virgil Tagaloa is the picture of contentment. Unconcerned about much except getting on with marrying the woman he loves.

The issue that just surfaced bothers Wallace, though. Didn't Amelia or Melissa or Winkler or *anyone* keep track of who was coming and going at the

Hill? The groundskeeper's job would be less complicated if background checks were a prerequisite before an overnight stay. Wonder how he might suggest that policy to his boss.

He glances at her again. She's taking an awfully long time deciding on a muffin flavor. Now she's talking through her options, which she's been doing more often lately. Better than not saying enough.

"The rhubarb bran would be nice with a soy latte. And strawberry jam."

"Strawberry mint jam." Having corrected Amelia, Virgil makes a note on his tablet.

"Oh, I see now." Amelia scans the case. "Or I could choose peach almond, or espresso vanilla, or—"

"Espresso with cream cheese spread." Virgil makes another note, calm and matter of fact, as if people get muffin flavors wrong all the time.

Wallace is about to scowl at Virgil—is it necessary to immediately correct Amelia's every mistake?—when he realizes what's happening. Uncertain she's seeing the options accurately, Amelia's talking out loud, *hoping* she'll be corrected if wrong.

And she's only going for the low-hanging fruit in front of her. She hasn't looked at the giant menu board above the counter. *Because it's too far away for her to see clearly.*

Wallace takes a few steps back—he doesn't want to appear as if he's hovering—and joins the conversation. "That other menu board says today's special is apple streusel muffins. You got any of those, Virgil?"

"Yep."

"Ooh! Apple streusel is an option?" Amelia has perked up, and the unobtrusive, under-the-radar game of helping begins.

"And you've got pumpkin chocolate chip? And lemon blueberry? Good golly, that's tiny print, Virgil. You hoping nobody will notice that option?"

"Yes to all of the above. The lemon blueberry muffins will take a few minutes to thaw."

"So many choices today!" Amelia puts a hand on Wallace's arm. "I'd like a peach almond muffin. With a mocha, please. If we come back tomorrow, I'll get a different flavor."

"Your wish is my command."

Wallace requests a ham-and-cheese croissant—different breakfast item than any he's chosen before—and a mocha. Plus a bag of day-old bread. He and Amelia settle their bills and head back out to the truck. The sky is brightening more, melding deep blue into pale blue, though the sun won't be up for a bit. Takes time for a new day to get going.

When they're both buckled in, Wallace turns to Amelia. "Ready?"

"If you are."

Seeing her happy floods him with joy. Like everything he ever wanted is coming true. Maybe keeping a list of nice things to wish for is a bit like praying, though with his checkered past he won't be allowed much airtime. So he'll limit his list to one line item. Do all he can to make Amelia's wishes come true.

Before he turns the ignition key, he gets her attention. "There's something about the upcoming escapade I've waited to tell you. This birdbrained idea came from John."

She nods. "I think John would like knowing old memories are being resurrected and made new. Here on an island he didn't know existed."

"Yep, John would get a kick out of this."

Shifting the truck into gear, Wallace pulls away from the market. Once they are moving up the hill, he begins honking the horn rhythmically.

"When do I start?" Amelia shouts over the din.

"As soon as they notice. Here they come! Roll down your window and toss a quarter slice at a time as high in the air as you can."

The truck toodles all around Wren, Amelia laughing, raucous seagulls following. Every time Amelia tosses a piece of bread, a bird swoops to grab it. When the bread's gone, Wallace quits honking the horn and drives back to Tranquility Hill.

After parking the truck, he creaks out and comes around to the passenger side. Stands near in case she wants help, which she doesn't. She hands him the bag of breakfast items from the market. He balances it and one of the mochas while she holds the other mocha and slams the truck door closed.

He's heading off to their favorite picnic bench at the edge of Vanessa's Butterfly Garden, leading the way so it won't look like he's hovering to help, when her voice reaches him.

"Mister Bernard?"

He halts. Straightens. Turns.

Surrounded by golden light reflecting through millions of dew drops across the meadow, she's grinning like another galaxy-shifting idea is forming. "Look! The sun's come up. Makes the world seem new again, doesn't it?"

He sets their breakfast on the bench. Retraces his steps. Stands before her.

"Only people I'm in trouble with call me Mister Bernard." His wavering voice nearly gives out on him. He pushes through. "Am I in trouble?"

"You're trouble. But not *in* trouble. At the moment." More of the giggling that might forever be his undoing.

He closes his eyes.

I love you.

Can he speak this truth? Offer everything in him, though not everything in him is worth having. Opening his eyes, he clears his throat. She's turned away from him, squinting at the glittering meadow.

"All that humming." Her voice is full of wonder. "Bumblebees? Starting their work again today? Busy, busy. And buzzy, buzzy. Isn't this meadow special?"

"Yes, it's a nice place to—"

"Welcome to another first day of the rest of our lives, Wallace!"

Another first day. And a nice place to tell you I love you. He maneuvers the words around in his heart, willing them to become a spoken message.

Facing him again, she's smiling broadly, in full boss lady mode. "Lots of projects happening here on the Hill today, and I'm going to need help. From the person I'm happy to share every hope and fear with! Thank you for being that friend for me."

"Pleased to. And I hope you know . . . " He swallows. "That is, I'd like you to know . . . "

She tilts her head in the way that makes him feel like she sees every part of him, the ruined pieces too, and, determined to find something to save, isn't afraid to pick through the rubble. Her smile softens. "I think I understand, Wallace. Our friendship means the world to me too."

I love you in a way I've never loved anyone before. The words get stuck inside him.

She glances around the vibrant meadow. "This is a hopeful place, isn't it?"

He bobs his head. "We're very much in a hopeful place here."

"How about we start by eating our breakfast? Then tackle our to-do list. From there, we'll hope for nice things to happen unexpectedly."

Drawing a steadying breath, he offers his arm. "As you wish."

A Note from the Author

Dear Reader,

Writing a story about grieving characters wasn't my plan. But like the stories that make up our lives, fictional stories sometimes take unexpected turns. The beauty of writing interactive serialized fiction is that the process allows a story to develop in directions readers want. Imagine my surprise when readers of early drafts of this Wren Island story indicated they wanted to see *more* grief on the page. Wanted to linger in the darker moments. To go deeper, get more raw.

Maybe, like Amelia, you've been grieving privately. That is so okay! If, like Amelia, you wonder at some point whether grief shared might feel different, perhaps less wearying than grief endured alone, I hope you'll reach out to a friend, trusted neighbor, or clergy person. If reading this story has been a balm, my heart celebrates with yours.

Laughter can be a balm too! Some of the funniest moments in this story—like Beano as a prerequisite, tainted cigars in a roulette, inquisitive goats on a boat ride—were inspired by readers. And who knows what might happen next?

Remember the mysterious visitor Wallace and Amelia encountered in chapter 75? That character will be the star of the *next* Wren Island story. As I write this note, I don't know any more than you do about the character. Who are they? Why did they come to Wren? How might Wren change with their presence? Wren Islanders everywhere (people like you who subscribe to receive my emails) will help shape the next story as I write it.

Subscribe today to receive email updates and your free copy of *A Wren Island Companion*, packed with interesting tidbits, behind-the-scenes peeks, and recipes. Then watch your inbox for opportunities to influence what happens next on Wren Island. Created with you in mind, Wren becomes even more marvelous when you're here.

Gratefully,

Laura

Share the Wren Island Spirit

"You won't find Wren Island on any world map, but it does exist. We find it whenever we imagine what could be. Whenever we reach for courage, anticipate joy, trust in love, hope for something better." —Laura Joy Lloyd

Here are a few easy-peasy ways to share the Wren Island spirit:

- Invite a friend for a walk and look for interesting treasures.

- Be honest when talking about life's disappointments.

- Celebrate someone else's achievement, big or small.

- Ask a friend to help you try something new.

- Write an encouraging note on social media.

- Review Wren Island books on Amazon, Goodreads, and elsewhere.

- Tell your book club about Wren Island.

- Bring Allison's buzzy brownies to a potluck.

- Listen to Laura's podcast and the Wren Island music playlist.

- Tell someone about your list of nice things to wish for.

- Look for ways to be extra kind, in your own unique style.

- Whenever and wherever you can, give life your best.

Find more ideas on the author's website. Thanks for sharing Wren Island! laurajoylloyd.com

Whether you're pondering quietly in your own head, chatting with a friend, or engaging in lively discussion with a book club, may these questions about the stories and characters you encountered in *Far from Unremarkable* be launching points for endless inspiration.

1. Wallace cares deeply about his daughters but has difficulty communicating his feelings in words. In what ways does Wallace express his affection and concern?

2. Wallace considers the situations of critters other people may not notice or think about. Why do you think Wallace cares so much about critters? Have you ever known someone like this?

3. In a dream, Wallace panics about losing someone. Describe a dream you experienced that seemed to hold special meaning for you.

4. Amelia indicates she's felt mostly invisible for most of her life. In what ways do you identify with that feeling?

5. Have you ever wished, like Amelia, you could wave a magic wand and watch a team of people do everything you asked? In what ways might imagining this be helpful? In what ways might it not be?

6. Wallace tells Amelia, "When you stop feeling sorry for yourself, the rest of the world will too." Do you agree? Why or why not?

7. Frank remembers people suggesting he turned to drugs in the past because he was "trying to fill the emptiness inside." In recovery, he waffles between giving attention to that emptiness and ignoring it. In what way can you identify with his experience?

8. An unexpected conversation in a convenience store leads to Frank receiving a gift that can significantly alter his future prospects. Describe a time when someone's generosity changed your life, even in a small way.

9. The relationship between Virgil and Allison gets bumpy, partly because neither of them is entirely forthcoming with the other. When is it appropriate to keep a secret from someone you love?

10. Amelia doesn't think tourists will understand that Wren is "a grieving island." She also says she's "missing memories that would never be made." In what way can you identify with her thought or feeling?

11. When alone, Amelia sometimes realizes new ways of thinking about the world. Do you think she could experience the same revelations while in conversation with other people? Why or why not?

12. Amelia discovers something new in a letter she received from her fiancé decades earlier. Have you experienced discovering something significant you did not know about a past event or circumstance? How did the discovery change or impact your life?

13. Amelia confronts Wallace about their shared past while still processing her own emotions. In what ways does her talk with Wallace prove helpful? Do you think she would have benefited from waiting longer to talk with him? Or from saying something to him sooner? Why or why not?

14. According to Wallace, a man with his background "will never experience peace." What does this say about how Wallace sees himself? What would you say to Wallace in response?

15. Both Wallace and Amelia are hit with grief at unexpected times and in unexpected ways. Have you experienced unexpected bouts of grief? If so, what advice would you offer for dealing with them?

16. While walking on the beach, Amelia finds pieces of plastic and repurposes them into a mosaic. What ideas do you have for turning trash into treasure?

17. Boss lady Amelia attempts to establish boundaries regarding relationships with friends who are also employees. In what ways are her efforts helpful? In what ways do her efforts cause difficulty?

18. Virgil and Allison decide to create a family in their own way, yet their experiences from past relationships continue to influence their expectations of each other. What advice would you give them?

19. Where do you think the relationship between Amelia and Wallace will go from here? What do you *want* to see happen in their relationship?

20. If you were keeping a list, like Amelia's, of nice things that happened unexpectedly, what is one thing that would be on your list?

Acknowledgments

Thank you, first, to my marvelous email subscribers! Your contributions of ideas and dreams for this story helped Wren Island become even more glorious. What a joy to share this journey with you!

Deepest thanks also to the individuals and families who graciously unveiled their experiences with profound grief. Their honesty and bravery contributed to the resonance of this novel.

I will inevitably miss naming someone here. Please know you, too, have made or are making a difference.

A far from unremarkable editor, J. B. Wilson, is the secret sauce behind this story. Jill saw the bigger picture before I did. Offered ideas for messy points. Helped me get back on track when I wondered if I ought to scrap the entire manuscript. Fixed ticky-tacky details I probably never noticed. (All errors in the final version I claim entirely as my own.) She is absolutely amazing. Thank you for being you, Jill.

After reading the first draft of the first scene, Ginny L. Yttrup, extraordinary novelist and editor, was the first to suggest we keep Wallace around. She continued offering helpful critique, even when doing so became unexpectedly sacrificial. Then, just when the finish line for this book was in sight, she helped me up my game yet again. You are a dear, Ginny.

Steve Kuhn of Kuhn Design Group accepted the challenge to create a second book cover as perfectly Wrenish as the first. And nailed it!

Matt Jones and the team at Jones House Creative refreshed Wren's home on the web so readers everywhere can experience an oasis of inspiration.

In a house up the hill from mine, Suzanne Dawson generously used her artistic skills to create Wren swag we can be proud of. She thoughtfully timed her design and production check-ins around my deadlines, regularly offered me tea, and even gave me an owl feather.

Tessa Burns offered helpful feedback on many, many drafts. She also created the enchanting Wren Island map. In truth, much of the island vibe has been inspired by Tessa simply being herself—honest, whimsical, thoughtful, passionate.

Julie Little read endless early drafts and added suggestions from her uniquely thoughtful perspective. Then she read the nearly finished manuscript and *again* offered pertinent feedback, somehow with more enthusiasm than ever.

Linda Avellar and Lori Singaraju critiqued draft after draft after draft. Plus, they inspired me by writing their own delightful novels!

Jeremiah Friedli, Bart Jeffress, and Tim Riter painstakingly offered gritty (and often entertaining) suggestions for how Wren men might be presented on the page. Their insight, especially about how relationships on earth might influence and reflect our relationships with our Savior, added depth to this story.

Andrew Culbertson of Culbertson Marine Construction answered lots and lots of questions—so many, across such a lengthy time span, it would have been understandable if Andy had started ducking out of sight whenever he saw me around town. Instead, he continued to enthusiastically share his knowledge.

Jonathan and Melanie Ross helped refine boating-related details and took photos of Wren swag being sported up and down the west coasts of the United States and Canada. They encouraged people to *believe* in Wren Island.

Shelley Cramm and Janine Wentworth connected the metaphorical dots linking a neglected apple orchard with a desirably entangled relationship. Plus, they assured me it was normal, in some circles at least, to give verbal instructions to houseplants.

Around my kitchen table one morning, while beachcombing that afternoon, then throughout dinner, sisters Emma, Abigail, and Grace fluttered with ideas for giving Frank attractive traits. I've done my best for now, girls. I'm sorry he's still a bit old for you. I pray each of you will one day find your own Frank, fall deeply in true love, and live happily ever after.

Thank you to friends who regularly encouraged me along the way! Marlene Anderson, Inna Chon, Sheri Gates, Cheri Gregory, Joan Husby, Ginger Kauffman, Wendy Miller, Curtis and Nicoline Payne, Mary Pero, Barb Robinette, Raoul and Lynda Robles, Kolleen Smith, Lauraine Snelling, Aleta Stover, Holly Varni, Essea White, and more!

Galaxy girl Sarah Marie Sonoda helped polish all things starry on Wren, then went on to see the heavens up close. I still hear her voice in my head. *Big hugs. You are not alone, Lala.* Thank God we have the hope of eternal life together.

Clair de Lune, devoted canine companion, proved herself the world's most reliable foot warmer hour after hour, day after day. And she came with built-in reminders to take stretching breaks.

My steadfast family—Dad, Mom, Linda, Roy—always propped me up, helping me be strong enough for whatever happens next.

Is this the best part of writing a novel? Looking back and noting the community that helped bring it into existence?

Thank you to my Lord and Savior. For this life. For everything.

About the Author

Laura Joy Lloyd writes uplifting contemporary stories set on Pacific Northwest islands. Through an innovative style she calls *interactive serialized fiction*, Laura invites readers to influence many of her projects in real time as she writes. Laura also enjoys swimming, knitting, keeping company with creatives, and organizing whatever feels messy.

Connect with Laura!

Website: laurajoylloyd.com

Facebook: facebook.com/laurajoylloyd

Instagram: @laurajoylloyd

Coming Soon

Book 3 in the Make It Home series by Laura Joy Lloyd

laurajoylloyd.com